MICHAEL CASEY

IN NOMINE PATRIS

Michael V. Casey
mvcaseyauthor@gmail.com

Ordering Information:
For details, contact mvcaseyauthor@gmail.com.

Print ISBN: 978-1-09835-623-1
eBook ISBN: 978-1-09835-624-8

Printed in the United States of America on SFI Certified paper.
First Edition

To Lipi, Tim, Jack, and Tommy,
The Most

CHAPTER ONE

The Meeting

Okay, you might want to listen up; I don't have much time.

I've been at this game a long time now. Nobody knows it better. Which is why I can't stand it anymore. In my racket, I've climbed the mountaintop, but what I see from the summit, across the span of my life, is disappointment. Don't get me wrong; I've had plenty of success. But it began to dawn on me toward the end of my career, and then hit me head on, gestalt, in a turn of life's sweet knife, that I could have accomplished so much, had the power and opportunity, yet did so little.

Don't take out your violins.

I walked into court one day last month, which is remarkable, because I don't go to court; those guys come to me. But this time an old neighbor, long-time supporter, was getting a hard time from a judge whose black robe he wouldn't be wearing if not for me. The judge with the short memory, who now thinks God put him there, must not have heard the name of the law firm that bore my name, when he told one of my associates that my guy had until August 1, the date of the next status, over our objection, to fix his building. So I show up with my guy at the August 1 status, first time in years, because I'm pissed, and see Judge Petty Tyranny do a little convulsion when I approach the bench, and the judge asks whether the work has been done, and I say no, because it can't be done, and the judge says well I ordered it to be done, and I say then we'll have to enter another order, and the judge, out over his skis, says in a bloated voice, okay I'll give you one month from now, when I expect to see you and your client in my courtroom to tell me the work has been done, so I bore into him and say, I'm sorry Your Honor, I have a funeral to go to that day, paused, let him chew on that a bit, but, I say, we could probably get this done, one way or the other, I emphasize, by November 6, Election Day, when the judge is up for retention. Although not the sharpest knife, the judge has a keen, visceral sense of when his livelihood is at stake, and, leaning forward, in a voice only I and the court reporter can hear, mutters, "Next Case."

It's like that. All over town. Each December I hold a fundraiser, and they line up in their finest out the grand ballroom door to kiss my ring and throw big checks in my campaign chest. It's pretty pathetic really, and not because they like me. It's because of what I can do next time they want a bond deal, airport terminal, high-rise, change in the law, Streets and San job, black robe, or virtually any state political office. The three branches, attached to strings, that I control.

I sound like an ass, I know, but I'm not bragging; it just happens to be true, and I realize as I say all of this that I'm not proud of it. Anything but.

To sum me up, I'm sixty-eight years old, I have power at my disposal, I have wasted my life, my dear wife is dead three years now, my only child is a royal pain in my ass, I'm a hypocrite, going through motions, I'm feared more than liked, my best friend just died, and now you can get out the violins.

But not for long. I've decided it's not too late. I'm going to enter a new chapter, throw a grenade into the works. Perhaps given time I can reform myself and what I control. And I've got some ideas about how to go about doing it.

So I'm in my chair, front and center, ringmaster in the Council chambers, the mayor presides, his minions atwitter, my aldermanic brethren lounge around and about me, in cushy red chairs with the city seal, cameras, red lights on, along the wall. The meeting's been going on for two hours now, committee reports, Finance, then my Budget Committee, Police, and Zoning. Zoning—curb cuts, side yards, alleys, nonconforming uses—godawful boring, and valuable. No one pays attention. Thirty-eight items on the report. No controversies, because a zoning item is not reported out unless it received the alderman's approval, and if an alderman approves a zoning matter in his or her ward, it's golden. So all the zoning matters get reported out, and then thrown into an omnibus, and as long as anyone can remember, get voted on and passed together. Except this time.

Item 31, 32, 33. Item No. 34; I rise to my feet. No one notices. I look back at Alderman Marino. Item No. 34: zoning variance for the property located at 2620 W. Jackson Boulevard. (Not my ward.). "Mr. President," I say, the chamber stirs; I don't wait to get recognized. "Mr. President, Alderman Marino and I wish to defer and publish Item No. 34 on the Zoning Committee Report." A tremor ripples across the floor. My brethren look at me and then back at Alderman Marino, slumped and asleep in his chair.

I sit down. The Zoning chair is speechless. The mayor beckons an aide, who hurries over to the guest box, where the commissioners sit, Buildings, Zoning, whispering; Alderman Gusman, Finance chairman, rises from his chair, all staring bullets. They all know about Item No. 34.

Defer and publish. Nice little maneuver, Council Rule 16, rarely used, allowing any two aldermen, preferably awake, to postpone any matter on the meeting agenda until the next meeting, ostensibly, for further consideration.

I smile at the committee chairs, the commissioners, the mayor, Alderman Gusman. They can't do anything about it. The mayor shrugs. The Zoning chair, begrudgingly, continues with his report. And now they know that I know.

I didn't stick around long. Went to my office, grabbed my briefcase. Dorothy tells me the mayor wants to see me. I tell her he can go to hell, knowing she'll tell him, with great tact, that I'm indisposed. The zoning map for 2620 W. Jackson is open on my desk. I head to the basement garage, jockeys racing to get my Eldorado, which I roll up into the bright bustle of Clark Street, take a right on Madison, duck under the El tracks, then north on Franklin to Oak Street, to my condo on the Inner Drive. Take a long walk through the Gold Coast, up past the cardinal's mansion, over to the lake, along Oak Street Beach, under Michigan Avenue to home, Manhattans for dinner, early to bed, can't wait, to get ready, to go. Early to rise, sleeping bag, pillows, Hudson Bay blanket, duffel bag, cooler, baguette, pâté, Boursin cheese, water, yogurt, granola, sundries, packed in the trunk, and the Eldorado, bursting from the underground garage in the morning sun, off and away, headed for the interstate, and up and out of town.

And what a town. Gleaming towers of steel and glass reflect the sky in my rearview mirror. Not proud of much these days, but I am proud of this town. Frank used to crow it was his kind of town, but for me it's been home since the day they cut my mother open just a couple of blocks off Olive Park Beach. Ripped open, thrust into the omphalos, of Algren's grit, Sinclair's blood, Bellow's mind, Sandberg's shoulders, and Hemingway's wide lawns. Bungalows and gangways of regular guys and strong women, first generations, strivers, hucksters, old world hordes in one bedrooms on the West Side, alley mechanics, stowaways, and refugees, Black exodus, promised land, red brick, concrete, steel girder and beam, gunshots, broken bottles, fire escapes, losers, a busted nose, forest preserve corpses, and smarts and talent over generations since the beginning of time never before released into the world for lack of the right time, the chance, a break, opportunity, rising up, from each vaulted sidewalk, littered lot, safe house, and school room, with nerve, guile, hustle, and freezing winds off the lake. Fops and phonies don't survive here. Boys' Town is tough deep down. But if you're looking for the new world, a place you can set deep roots in shallow soil, plant your feet, and scrape and claw, and shake hands, and build, and start a business, and raise a generation, where it doesn't matter where you came from, or who your parents were, if you're willing to work your ass off, then you just might make it here, because we're all on the make here, which is why it rises now in my rearview mirror, from Sullivan, Wright, and Le Baron Jenney, Burnham and Root, and Holabird and Roche, Van Der Rohe, Skidmore, Goldberg, and Jahn, a *cheveaux de frise* of Monadnocks, Rookeries, Prudentials, and Hancocks, each rising into cloud, red-black, green-gold, silver-blue, shining in the sun and twinkling in the dark.

In my rearview now, heading out of town, to my other life, my great escape, exhilaration, leave it all behind, for a few days, long trek, short while, dash into phone booth, change clothes, voilâ, more powerful than a steaming locomotive, wing tips to cowboy boots, heading northwest, from the shore of the Great Lake to God's country: Southwest Wisconsin, foreign land, to the Property of ours, home away from home, little matter to attend to, for old Ray, breathed his last, best of friends, last one really, Ray's rundown resort, Wisconsin River, canoes, cabins, RVs, that sort of thing, near Spring Green, uplands, deep ravines, tall hills, open fields, where the river bottoms and runs hard to the west, dreaming, hours, millions of miles away, thank God, as I head down the interstate, faster than a speeding bullet, ten lanes, bumper to bumper, semi-trailers, brake lights, car horns, all inching toward the north side of town.

North Side, my side of town, Queen of Angels Parish, 47th Ward, all that mattered. The church, for divine guidance, the ward, for everything else. Never knew my dad. Died of TB when I was three. Tell me he was tough, and loyal, thick on feint praise. Suspect the bottle an issue. My mother, may she rest in peace, plush for comfort, thick red hair, Red Delicious cheeks, always kind, always working, always sad, died of heartache, with a rosary in her pocket, when I was ten.

For me, as a kid, Uncle Terry, mom's brother, was the guy. Terry had the knack, knew what people wanted, needed. Good for a story, laugh, pat on the back. Precinct captain extraordinaire, hustling votes in rain or snow, from the living and the dead, every house, duplex, three-flat, and tavern in the ward. Terry climbed each step, knew each alley, kitchen table, mostly Irish and German, for years learning the trade, how to get things done, who to talk to, back passages, gatekeepers, where the bodies are buried, skeletons in closets, tumultuous, Byzantine whisperings and conspiracies of clout and weakness, getting ahead or leaving behind, from neighborhood to City Hall, precinct captain to alderman, and the pinnacle: committeeman, king of his limited domain.

Could have done better, but the ward was good enough for Terry. Content to control what he knew, stick to his knitting. No dreams beyond the border, not for lack of ambition, but a nose for what was at stake, eyeing from a safe distance the shifting sands of big fish downtown, no getting around that, best be comfortable with what you had, which, if you played your cards right, was quite a lot.

Nothing happened in the ward without Terry knowing about it. Everything needed his approval: business license, pothole, street lamp, garbage bin, driveway, building permit, nothing too big, nothing too small, nothing without a price, and everything mattered, except it didn't, unless you kept track, which, as busy as he was, might slip from time to time, but that was where Aunt Audrey, his wife, filled the void, religiously, her mission: no one got anything without paying for it, one way or the other, now or later, all stored away for use at the right time, and if Terry was the get along, smiling face of the ward, Audrey was the enforcer.

Her weapon: the Look. She preferred saving it for Sunday Mass, lurking in the weeds of pews, until her vulnerable prey—whose son-in-law got the job he wanted in the Clerk's office but never ponied up at Terry's chicken dinner fundraiser—walked back from Communion down the main aisle, and Audrey, ignoring the husband, with a slow turn of her pinched face sized up the timorous wife, who, knowing Audrey, lived in fear of just such a moment, when Audrey, with the body of Christ still on her tongue, impaled the wife with the Look full of nothing less than a slow, tortuous death, and the wife, weak-kneed, cursing the husband all the way home, and a check arriving at the door the next day.

But that's how it worked. And it was only fair. Short memories were not an option. *Quid pro quo*. Nothing's for nothing, nothing's in writing, and nothing needed to be, when you had Audrey keeping score, and fixing the game.

Fixing, of course, is the wrong word. After all, since when was getting things done for people a bad thing. Today, facilitators, honorees at banquets for public service. Fixers get indicted. So there's always that. Another reason to stay small.

There were always those in the business who got picked off from time to time, the small timers who misunderstood the payoff, that public service was not commensurate with a living wage, the entitled, underpaid, under-appreciated, the not-so-very-smart ones, who needed additions on their homes or overpriced tuition they couldn't afford for undeserving kids.

You can see them from time to time on the six o'clock news, the dreaded Dirksen Building walk, camera glare, trial, testimony, plea deal, jail time. But the worst was the press conference, with the US Attorney in his high hat, taking credit for the verdict he didn't win, suppressing glee under a public safety face, barely disguising his own ambition, his role in the game. But that's how it's played, losing is the fate of the greedy.

Terry and Audrey were too smart for that. Big fish posers get hooked. You can make a good living in a small pond, so Terry and Audrey sat on their lily pads and ruled their swamp, with me, the tadpole, at their beck and call.

So it was pre-ordained that I got involved in the family business. Terry and Audrey owned a three-flat; they had the top two floors; Mom and I the first, until she passed, when I moved on up, and became Terry's ward, so to speak.

Rang doorbells for mediocre judicial candidates in third grade. Precinct captain in eighth. Wide-eyed, blank slate, impressionable, and eager, with Uncle Terry and Aunt Audrey teaching me the ropes, classroom of life.

Once a month, year after year, at Terry's side, on Ward Night in the storefront on Lincoln Avenue, masses in overcoats huddled on metal chairs under fluorescent lights, seeking a path through the machinery, cranking gears, waiting their turn to be called into the backroom, where Terry and I sat behind the gray metal desk, Ward Map and the Old Man's picture on the wall, and we would listen, carefully, to the dreams, ambitions, and delusions, the travails, woes, lives laid bare, the greed, love, angles, tears, con games, the modest favor, the grand schemes, but mostly the ancient *a priori* yearning for something just a little better than now, from the beginning of time, some leg up, blanket, bauble, or trinket, a better road, a good job, a bad neighbor, sick child, aging parent, the humble, small, tearful beseechings that peel away the skin, until each sinuous, bloody, beating heart of self-interest is plopped down in the middle of Terry's metal desk for the two of us to pore over, pull apart, analyze, what's been said, what left out, who's lying, who can help, where to go, the possibilities, back channels, what we can do, what we can't, and do we want to, are they worthy, lifting or dashing dreams, the deserving leave with hope, the rest with rejection, another in a long line of resentments and grudges, and from it all, for me, in my youth, the raw uplifting desire to help, the satisfaction of being able to do so, whether for me or them irrelevant then, not even considered, my education, my driving force, rising above the fray, to one by one enrich our little community on the North Side, our red brick network of bungalows and three-flats, and make it just a little better place to raise a family and live a life. I actually believed all of that then, thanks to Uncle Terry, and, like a first love, it has always stayed with me, a *raison d'être* deep down, no matter how often forgotten or betrayed over the years, but maybe time to be rekindled.

Miles from the Loop now, but hardly moving, as I approach the parting of the interstate sea, north to North Shore, or northwest to O'Hare, thousands of vehicles, single file lanes, converging together, bending curves, from all directions, stopping, lurching, always, here, concrete crossroad, intersection of future and now, sluggish metal current, fume spewing, clogged artery, gargantuan gridlock, from here, my destination: our Property, the country, Shangri-La, a distant dream, inconceivable that in one direction, this road leads to there, but in another, so close now, my home, my whole life, everything, a few miles to the east, tucked away in block after block, street after street, gangway and alley, one neighborhood after another, indistinguishable, until the first glimpse, of knowing, innate, familiar appears, my little corner of the spinning globe, a back forty of bungalows, churches, dry cleaners, coffee shops, pizzerias, storefronts, a boy, a man, a family, none, tragedy, comedy, memories, coming of age.

Worked summers for the Park District, class president my senior year at Loyola Academy, scholarship (through Uncle Terry) to U of I, and out of school to work for the Mayor, Ed O'Brien, the Old Man, known since a boy. First in the mayor's Office, then IGA, Intergovernmental Affairs, mayor's arm-twisting legislative branch, where I learned the game, the process, the players, and from the Old Man, how to play everybody off each other. Law school at nights, transferred, with the Old Man's blessing, to the Budget Committee, poring over bleary-eyed line items, one by one, each department, each salary, each obscure rainy-day fund, budget hieroglyphics, where everything is buried, and paid for, and hidden behind secret doors and locked vaults, keys to City Hall secrets. And I loved it, details that no one cared to know, dots no one could connect, the power in knowledge of the arcane, how they would have to come to me, who had taken the time, put in the work, because they had not, but most importantly, how to get what you want, or back then, what the Old Man wanted, and prevent what he didn't. But that wasn't always easy to tell.

He spoke in grunts and stabs, in scowls, and smirks. Those who could read him rose in the ranks; those who could not died slow deaths in Water Department cubicles. Cross him and you were done. Look pretty, like a candidate, with an agenda, and you were done. If you couldn't deliver votes, dressed too well, spoke a little too elegantly, or to the press, were ambitious, egotistical, presumptuous, ungrateful, disloyal, needy, forget about it, done. But if you were smart, loyal, God fearing, kept your head down, and always understood who was number one, you could go far.

I learned my lesson early on. At the time, I was the Budget Committee's guy at the pre-Council prep table. Least senior person there. Speak only if spoken to. Any project needing public financing had to go through City Council, and nothing happened at City Council without the Old Man's approval. He had the votes. If you wanted development in your ward, you had to go to him, hat in hand, tail between legs, with something in return. Aldermen and alderwomen were among the faithful, the heretics, or in purgatory. Most of the time you could tell who were among the faithful, and always the heretics, but you could never be sure who, by some small indiscretion or good deed, may have snuck into purgatory through the Old Man's back door, and the only one who truly knew who fell where was the Old Man, which, when it came time to work on Council meeting agendas, complicated matters, because the answer to whether a project was approved or not came in a grunt or a nod or smirk that even his closest aides had difficulty deciphering, and little courage, if not outright fear, to seek clarification.

So we're at a final pre-Council meeting, the Old Man at the head of the table, scowling. A mixed-use development in the Third Ward (majority Black) comes up, the Old Man says nothing, we go to the next item. Third Ward alderman has been on the outs for most of her short career, delighting in taunting the Old Man for the newspapers, but over time sees that ranting at the Old Man doesn't get her streets plowed, potholes filled, street lights changed, or garbage picked up, and may well lead to the loss of a job, so she's whistling a different tune these days, and the Old Man has relented somewhat of late, which is why this particular item got on the agenda at all. His silence is never resolved, but it's on the agenda, and he didn't say no, so now we're at the actual Council meeting, my Budget chairman, South Side Black alderman, survivor, playing all sides, especially the Old Man's, is handling the Finance Committee report, because its chairman is under indictment, and the Third Ward development ordinance comes up, next on the agenda, and he reads it, stops mid-report, and motions to me across the Council floor. I go see him, everyone watching, the Old Man presiding, glaring at me now, grimacing, my guy whispers to me, you sure this is okay, and I think, well you were there, you saw what happened, and I say, I'm pretty sure, which he takes as full steam ahead, because he has his own deals with the Third Ward alderman, and reports the ordinance, which is now out of the bag for all to see, as opposed to forever banished to oblivion, and the Old Man visibly squirms in his high-backed chair as if he were passing a kidney stone, and the vote is taken, ordinance passed, the Third Ward alderman smiling like a Cheshire Cat, and the Old Man turning a shade of purple.

We get back to our office after the meeting to a message that the Old Man wants to see my boss, the Budget chair, and me. Not good. We take the elevator up to the fifth floor in silence. As soon as we get to the mayor's office we're rushed into the anteroom, unprecedented, and just as quickly ushered into the inner palatial sanctum, where the Old Man is sitting at the far end of the large room behind his huge desk, and we take a seat in the two small wooden chairs facing him. The Old Man turns to my boss, "who the hell told you to let that go through?," and my boss, extending his arm in my direction, says he was told it was good to go, and so they both look at me. Was I scared? Goddam right, never as much before or since. The Old Man, the single most powerful man to ever sit behind that desk, ruler of the second largest city in the greatest country in the world, maker of Presidents, controller of fates, bores into me, and roars in a truly venomous voice: "*Are you just stupid or are you trying to fuck me?*"

I figured it was a rhetorical question. There was nothing to say, then, after he told us to get the hell out of his office, or after, to anyone, my boss included. Of course, I replayed all events leading to that dressing down, sycophant inner circle, imperious weakness, cowardice and boorishness, but above all, the overriding goal of self-preservation in the blame game of sharp knives. Okay fine, lesson learned, no one's fault but mine, no one mourns the fall guy, and under no circumstances was I ever to wear the Jacket again, yeah right.

The Old Man let it pass, knew I was young, with much to learn, and after a while approved my transfer to the Finance Committee, where the real action was, is, under the tutelage of crafty old Tom McClean, fresh off a not guilty verdict in federal court. Too smart for them, jury loved him. My mentor. Prince of Finance, and the Council, Old Man's right hand, and seer. Ruled the unruly, controlled the purse, marshaled the votes, granted favors, killed deals, buried the ambitious, assessed faults, exploited weakness, rewarded loyalty, greased the gears, and conducted the show. No one did it better, then or since, though I've tried.

Idolized the guy. Short and wiry, tough and shrewd, somehow grand in stature, hurting only those who had it coming, mostly the disloyal. Inscrutable, stoic, measured and terse, regal and crusty, driven not by a dollar or fame but the sheer thrill of the chase, the game, to be perfected and controlled, and won. Those who feared him thought he was in it for himself, because that's how they played the game, but he wasn't like them, so they never could see, through their sullen suspicions, that he bore the mark of those who deep down may actually care about something other than themselves, his faith, family, the perfectibility of humankind, nobility, and a goodness and kindness, which, kept concealed by demands of realpolitik, might surface from time to time, in the company of those he saw as like-minded, in hushed, grave tones, to signal a break from the game and the coming of truth from the master, when he took me aside after a fractious battle over a new stadium deal, which left everyone a little bloody, to confide in me one on one, which made it stand out, to admit to me, as if revealing the dark mystery behind his life's work, to tell me in a serious, hushed tone, as if revealing a universal truth that only experience and a wizened mentor could impart, to explain the irrational and unexplainable, almost ashamed to confess to one so young, a reflection of a younger self, who needed to know if I hoped to succeed, that if I were to make this living my life's work, I had to understand, that "Nothing," he whispered, "nothing, is on the level."

Which, even though it came from him, I didn't really believe at the time, but over the years that too has been proven, again and again, because all but a few, and hardly anyone in this business, care about anything but more. And so, over time, unwittingly, but intentionally, the councils, boards, and committees we write into our laws, reflect and serve to protect our abiding carnal desire for more. Sharing may be a necessary evil, but only on the little things, only as a deception, for good press, to keep the lid on. Put the right way they'll believe in anything, the truth is unimportant, it's how you say it, how good it will be for everyone, but especially for you, enough to get reelected or the gig is up, while the real work gets done behind the scenes, to line pockets, fatten cats, and grease wheels, the ultimate ulterior motive, and man have I perfected that art.

Traffic still tight, passing O'Hare, sub-speed, but moving, under the shadow roar of flying fortresses in formation, one after another, lined up, always, over, across the Great Lake, waiting their turn, silver bellies, fragile wings, floating to the tarmac, to reload and rise again, sharp, climbing, angular, wheeling, steep banks overhead toward other towns, destinations, far above an Eldorado now passing runways and warehouses, industrial parks and rail lines, into and out of one suburb after another, over wide highways lined with green glass boxes, and their antiseptic lobbies, Muzak elevators, young receptionists, cheap carpets, cubicles, paper thin walls, architects who've sold their souls, no sidewalks, streets with names of developers' children, empty parking lots, plastic air, fast food, perfectly pleasant, expedient and bottom line, brand new and past their prime, towns named after forests, and trees, and hills that no longer exist, slouching into one another, until the spaces between begin to stretch, beyond electrical substations, into expanses, with signs, for sale, zoned commercial, and then a field of corn, under siege from all sides, and then another, and then ahead a bridge, over a river, the mighty Fox, flowing border of exurbia's last reach, and beyond, traffic clears, picking up speed now, the sky opens, farms fight back, where the world was once what it was, upright, grand, redeeming, old school, the days.

Worked for Tom McLean in Finance for two years, and graduated from law school, when Hitler and the Japanese intervened, Army JAG officer during the war, no hero, but I served. Went back to work for McLean for a couple of years after the war, then took a job in the City's Law Department writing ordinances, power of the pen, Clarence Darrow's old job. The Old Man, taking heat at the time for a couple bribery scandals in Building's inspection bureau, went on a reform kick, of all things, so we went scrounging around for some toothless feel-good reforms to push the scandals to the back page, and one of the Old Man's policy hacks comes up with the idea of writing an ordinance which says you can't work for or do business with the city if you or any of your employees owe the city money. No brainer, right? The Old Man signed off on it, we wrote it up, introduced to Council, no discussion, no debate, passed in record time, and the Old Man's picture appears on the front page taking credit for cleaning up City Hall.

And then it came to enforcement. Turns out, unbeknownst to us, almost everybody in town owes the city money, including just about every business in Ernie Janssen's ward, on which Ernie relies for campaign funds. So now everybody is up in arms, the Old Man is pissed because Ernie's pissed, and Ernie calls for a meeting with the affected department heads, several aldermen, the policy hack, who, regrettably, could not attend, and me, again, holding the bag. Ernie looks at me and wants to know what idiot came up with such a bonehead idea without bothering to figure out its impact, and, more importantly, without clearing it with him first. Ernie is six feet tall, two hundred and eighty pounds, large wrists, bear paws, ruby pinky ring, fake Rolex watch, round bald head. When he grabs his wrists and leans across the table with steam from his ears you think he may strangle and eat you. He puts on his show with great bluster, which will be retold many times back in his ward, and says that I must be trying to undermine and embarrass him, which, he sputters, he doesn't take from anybody, and that if I, (the perfect foil), don't fix this harebrained law by the next meeting he will have my hide, and concludes, in a flourish, jabbing a fat finger at me across the table, that I needed to know that he will never forget this, rising to his feet, towering over me, pointing between my eyes, that in this town what goes around comes around, or, as he most succinctly and effectively bellowed in his gruff, threatening voice, "*Fuck me? Fuck you!*" and walked out of the room. We gutted the reform the next meeting, without any mention in the press. The Old Man was amused.

So the question I wrestled with then, in my youth, other than the issue of the Jacket I was forced to wear, again, was whether, as a matter of public policy, what motivates a reform measure matters at all, so long as the idea ultimately is a good one, and furthers some legitimate public interest. Did it matter if the Old Man didn't give a shit about doing the right thing so long as he did the right thing even if solely because it served his own all abiding interest in getting reelected? End and means and all that rot. And I concluded back then that it didn't, because that's just the way the process worked. If you couldn't get good press out of something what was the point, and if coming up with a meaningful reform could get you on the front page, well then, that was the whole idea, and everybody, but especially the sponsor, benefitted. Except everyone didn't benefit, because no one really cared about whether the reform worked or not, only about the attention it got, so if it got the press you wanted, and then got deep-sixed in committee, or gutted in a rewrite, it didn't really matter, because the point all along was not the public interest, but your own, and there's the slippery slope, because over time nothing else became important, what mattered was whether it made you look good, so that if a scandal broke about cops beating Black kids in the back of paddy wagons, the goal was not to stop the beatings, but to take whatever half measures were necessary to weather the storm, let the issue die a slow death, and get on with the business of City Hall. So you buy some time until the next uproar happens, and of course it will because you never addressed the problem in the first place, but by then it might be someone else's problem, and even if it's still yours, well, you know what to do. The end is self-preservation, the means irrelevant, reform forgotten.

So, you might ask, as my idiot son would, does, where are the idealists, the Young Turks, the untainted, willing to rock the boat, buck the system, and elevate the public interest over their own? Well, we eat them for breakfast. No organization, no money. If they run, we'll challenge their petitions so they don't get on the ballot, and if they do, we'll get some schmuck with the same name on the ballot to split the protest vote, and teach them that, in this town, if they want to get anywhere they have to play by our rules, and the smart ones, those who have a shot, begin to understand, slowly at first, but instinctively over time, that compromise for the greater good, and your own, might do the trick, no harm in meeting people half way, a little here, a little there. You can see them in slow motion, sliding as they start to rise, in better suits and bigger cars, without even knowing what's eating out their insides, or how they resemble the hacks they once scorned, until there's no such thing as the greater good, there's just me and us and then everyone else, and it becomes such a way of life that over time it doesn't even occur to you that you've sold out, let alone when or how it might have happened. Lies and rationalizations become truths, you spin life stories, not even bothered by the possibility you might have been that way all along, even when you were wearing your white hat, you look out for number one, no need to confess now, so long as you got reelected, and even if you were honest about it and knew how it all happened, you just didn't care anymore, it didn't matter, it would always be that way, no use butting your head against brick walls, until by some strange twist of fate you got to my age, alone, with regrets, and memories of my wife and idiot son.

So the Old Man asked that I serve as his election lawyer. Sounded good, but no big deal, the result never in doubt, but I get all the papers together in case I need to run to court, which I don't, recruit poll watchers, and sit around all day fielding calls about fistfights in precincts, signs too close to polling places, machines down, that sort of thing. By midnight, the Old Man is in bed with a smile on his face, but I'm still in the Hall, because some of the aldermanic races are tighter than we thought, and one of the Old Man's favorites, Polish guy on the Northwest Side, is sweating it out. So I get a call to go up to the Election Board, and here's what to say, and all you say, so I go up to the eighth floor, no one around, door unlocked. I wander through cubicles toward low voices in the back office, where the chairman of the Election Board and his young assistant are sitting around a table with, to my surprise, the alderman. Now it's the chairman and his assistant who are surprised, they know I'm there for the Old Man, his picture on the wall looking down on them, it's called gravitas. There's an issue with absentee ballots, apparently, which is inconvenient, because the alderman, fidgeting nervously, is holding on to a very slim lead. The box of absentee ballots sits ominously at the end of the table, making the alderman nauseous. You can't trust those who care enough to vote absentee, most unlikely to be on board. While he looks at the box, the alderman is wondering what he's going to do if the impossible should happen, he's been on the dole, as a public official, for twenty years, he doesn't know anything else, no skills, no prospects, two kids in college, and a wife whose hobby is cutting him to size. It's all or nothing for him he's telling the chairman of the board and his young assistant, not comfortable that the whimpering alderman had paid them a visit at this late hour, and giving him the cold shoulder, until I walked into the room, and by my presence indicating that the Old Man, without whom the chairman and his assistant would have to work for a living, cared about this one. As instructed, I asked, "Is there a problem here?" The alderman, emboldened, looked accusingly at the chairman and his young assistant. A tense silence ensued. I wasn't about to say anything, I'd learned that much. The chairman, thinking about his own prospects, looked at the assistant and gave a reluctant nod, the young assistant rose from his seat, grabbed the box, and took it out of the room, God only knows where. The chairman extended his hand to the alderman over the table, offered his congratulations, and said that it had been a long night and that it was time we all went home. Which we did. The alderman relieved, the Old Man pleased, it's bothered me ever since.

But I did my job and kept my head down, wrote ordinances, testified at committees, in support of their favor, saw they made their way to a vote, twisted arms when necessary, and worked with the Old Man to ensure that Council meetings went without a hitch, all egos and agendas aside. From time to time we'd write an ordinance and feed it to an alderman who needed a little nudge in his ward, like Alderman Wilson from the South Side, to whom we gave an ordinance that would bar the city from doing business with South African apartheid companies, even though the city didn't do business with South African apartheid companies, but then, nobody else knew that. So Wilson, author of the bill when it gets introduced, gets front page coverage, with his picture alongside no less, it gets to committee, where someone has to explain it, and since Wilson doesn't know anything about it, because I wrote it, I'm the sacrificial lamb, but I have no problem with that, I enjoy it, I understand these aldermen, or so I thought, and I take my place next to the committee chairman and I methodically explain the purpose of the bill and how its provisions achieve its goals, and then the chairman opens it up to questions, and one by one, but only because reporters are there, otherwise no one would give a shit, the aldermen assigned to the committee, (they were all men), ask one off the wall question after another until one guy asks if a slight change could be made to a meaningless provision, unusual but not unheard of, and I pause, as the committee chair and Alderman Wilson wait for my answer, thinking over whether such a change might work, and, not seeing a problem, confidently testify that such a change would indeed be possible and would not affect the purpose of the bill, which causes a minor commotion in the committee room over where Alderman Wilson is sitting, as he rises from his chair, grousing and sputtering, all six feet five of him, deep voice, former cop, no messing with him on the street, and he says, "Point of Order Mr. Chairman," (which it really isn't), "nobody's gonna tell me or anyone else here what to do with *my* ordinance, and it sure as hell's not up to *him*," he says in my direction with the disdain of one addressing a worm, (if we were in an alley on his old beat at this point he'd be grinding my face into a brick wall), "it's *my* bill, got *my* name on it, and nothin' happens less it goes through *me*, got it? So if anybody wants to dot an i or cross a t on *my* bill you gotta see *me*, not *this* turkey," he says, pointing at me. Of course, if anyone, including Alderman Wilson, ever wanted to change anything in the bill I wrote, they would have to come to me, but look, I get it, and he was right, the ordinance did have his name on it, it was his bill, and I was making him look bad, and I had worked with these guys long enough to know, that as crazy as it seemed, I was the one who was out of line, that was the world I chose to live in, and the unwritten rules I needed to learn to get ahead, so I probably should have been grateful to Alderman Wilson, for just another in a long line of lessons which prepared me for what happened next.

But anyway, you see the progression. By the time I was thirty-five years old I had served in the trenches of the most significant functions in City Hall, and had learned from masters of their craft, so that even back then there were very few around who knew the ins and outs as well as me. And it wasn't as if I had it all planned. Maybe Terry did, and the Old Man sure as hell knew what he was doing. I mean, I was good to have around, talk my way out of an alley, into a penthouse, but kept my mouth shut, smart, respectful, I could be trusted, and most importantly, I was too young to be a threat, so it made sense for them to make sure I learned what I needed to know to do their bidding, more a private than public servant. But that was fine by me. Heady stuff, I was at the table, and I loved it, probably even thought at the time they were my choices, but I didn't really care how it happened, because it did, and when I walked into a room, like that night at the Election Board, they all knew, unless you were higher on the pecking order, and there weren't many, that it probably was best not to fuck with me.

Through all these various jobs, training grounds if you will, I was helping Uncle Terry and Aunt Audrey with the ward, going to Ward Night each month like a holy day of obligation, handling zoning requests, keeping track of contributions, fielding judicial candidates, that sort of thing, ringing fewer doorbells, more big picture, so that when Uncle Terry died of a stroke on Lincoln Avenue one night, Aunt Audrey, in her grief, may have had more than a fleeting thought of taking his place, but for the Old Man, there was no question that I would be the appointed successor, no one more qualified to take over, and seamlessly take Terry's place in the history of our family and the ward. And seamless it was. I was appointed alderman, and with Audrey at my side, we were off and running, literally, a year and a half later I ran unopposed, all sewn up, the Old Man put me on the Budget and Finance Committees, unheard of for one so young, elected as the ward committeeman a year after that, and man I was on my way.

For the first several years in the Council I took a backseat, did my homework, watched McLean and the Old Man run the show, and took care of my ward, but the aldermen would come and ask for help, because they knew I knew what was up, and I'd help anyone who'd ask, for nothing in return, racking up chits, and keeping track, what does this budget item mean, how do I get my son-in-law on the bond counsel list, how do I write this ordinance, can you talk to McLean for me, what does the Old Man think, about anything. Silk stocking law firms, Forbes clients, would call, navigate Finance, Law, posture the bond deal, what were its chances, how to get a zoning variance, can you talk to him for me, how to eke out a few more floors in their building development, a new runway for the airport, concessions, this building inspector's on my ass, we're getting the run around, avoiding landmark designation, like an ongoing ward night for the whole damn city, and soon I became the go-to guy for the inside scoop, the guy who could talk the fat cats' language, skyscrapers to three-flats to single families, skyways and alleys, in a sharp suit and tie, who understood the business, how important the money men were, how they needed to get things done, and why, and sooner rather than later.

I'd attend every fundraiser, still single at the time, invited to all of them, all over town, and then, by the time I was thirty-eight, I started to call in some chits myself, holiday party, generous mood, upscale, no more chicken dinners, just a big ass room in a Michigan Avenue hotel, with open bar and top-shelf booze, and all those folks I'd helped over the years, aldermen, and state reps and senators, lawyers and venture capitalists, moms and pops, condo developers, City Hall denizens, and entrepreneurs, gray hairs, and up and comers, like me, would gather, get happy, flirt in their finest, spread holiday cheer, and make modest, at first, donations to my campaign fund, year after year, even though I never had to run a campaign, because I made sure I never had any opposition, it would just be a waste of anyone's time and money, or so we made sure they thought. Year after year, bigger parties, bigger donations, CEOs who couldn't be bothered began to show, even the Old Man and McLean showed up a couple of years, knowing that as word got around, attendance would swell for years after, and over time it became the politico party of the year, see and be seen, swirling glitter in golds, reds, and greens, with tinsel and cleavage, and checks, and chandeliers, and amidst the maelstrom, I worked the room, all humble, low profile, no long lines back then to shake my hand, still young, self-effacing, aw shucks, public servant, so nice you could make it, we'll have another good year, you're the best, can I call you, glad to help, thanks for your support.

And over time, as the coffers began to swell with big money, at least for back then, we began to spread the wealth around, Audrey and me, for anyone running desperate for cash, our investments, but shrewd, betting on winners, portfolio in human capital, those with a chance, or a tough race, those you could count on to remember, those you could turn, a grand here, five there, ten to get over the top, at just the right moments, in the right races, for greatest effect, at first in the city, then the county, then statewide, back no losers, and if you did, they would run again, and they'd win, and they'd never forget, and if they did, Audrey made sure they didn't. With the investments came dividends, they couldn't say no whenever I asked, which was seldom, but when I did, my judicial candidates won, my precinct workers got jobs, either in the Hall or outside, one by one building the ward, organization, Ward Nights became more crowded, more left happy, more to count on election day, in our ward, and any other, get out the vote, need some bodies, give me a call, they'll never know where it came from, tsunami, we'll overwhelm them with mercenaries, foreign legion from my ward, for any duty, each with his or her own good job, each supporting a family, because of what I made possible for them, and each with an extended family to spread the word, from ward to ward, all across the city.

It got to the point that by the time I was forty I had a hand in everything. When the committeemen met for annual slating, to choose party candidates for local and state office, nothing happened, no one got anything, without my knowing about it, respectfully of course, always deferring to the Old Man, deftly, quietly, weighing in without showing my hand on the scale, Assessor, Appellate Court, County Commissioner, Board of Tax Appeals, General Assembly, Sanitary District, every political office in town and county, controlled, because if we chose them, they won, one party town, thanks to the Old Man, so if you wanted to get ahead, if you wanted to win, you had to come to us, and once you had our blessing, you were hooked, forever indebted, which is how we wanted it, so that whenever we wanted anything, we got what we wanted. I wasn't the only one who'd perfected the game, I wasn't a kingpin yet, there was always the Old Man, and McLean, and a couple of other players, like Gusman on the West Side, but few who had mastered the art of spreading wealth and collecting chits, and no one knew the extent of our tentacles, not the Old Man, McLean, or anyone, just Audrey and me.

Passing Rockford now, I-90, hypotenuse northwest, speeding in and out of traffic, construction, changing lanes, each car one driver, somewhere to go, fast, toward the border, Agriculture, Industry, Recreation, gateway to the promised land, jump off the speedway, leave the interstate behind, banking ramp onto country roads, still not close, long way off, but now away, away from angst, pinched shoulders, the grind, onto smooth two-lanes, thrilling rise and fall, curve of meadow and woods, windows down, deep breaths, open-air clouds marching over quilts of green, rolling, far as the eye, soft, soothing memories blowing across the fields, comfort, peace, together, my love.

In the midst of all the ruckus back then, at one of the five or so funerals I attended a month (what I told the judge wasn't off the mark), I was introduced to a shy, blue-eyed, auburn haired, South Side girl, Nativity of Our Lord Parish, Visitation High School, twenty-seven, mantilla, delicate, porcelain, plain beauty, impaled me then and there. Took me a while to get my act together, always a bit uncomfortable that way, never really that interested really, other than the obvious, which carried baggage, to avoid at all costs, wary, of dark eyes and ulterior motives, climbers, one too many and a wild night could end a career. I was an easy mark, suspicious, cautious, and too busy. Asked around a bit, her name was McCauley, Ellen McCauley, they called her Nell. Her dad had his own insurance agency on the South Side, and did all right. Daughter like her mom, behind the scenes, respectful, woman of faith, supportive, grounded, non-confrontational, inner strength and elegance in her own understated way, and generally shy. Nell worked in the family business, admin stuff, books, receivables, precise and thorough, lived at home, church choir, never in a tavern, one fling to speak of, after high school, ended in disgust, resulting in certain conclusions about men in general, spinster apprentice, until I came along. Don't know why exactly, but the arrow struck hard, no pretense I guess, rare from my world, innocence, certainty, and kindness. I truly loved everything about her, then and every day since.

Took a while, easy at first, but eventually, got on my knee and got married in her church, I was forty-two, Nell twenty-nine, small ceremony, her dad's dime, fine with me and suited her, with the Old Man and Tom McLean in attendance, and everyone impressed. But she was the star, my star, that day and forever after, no one ever came close. My conscience, my compass, tough on principle, accepting of weakness, well-read, prescient, soft spoken but tough-minded, saw my work as spectator sport, reveled in the angles, who was playing whom, who was on the rise, who to be indicted, warning about him, careful about her, always my back, at my side, at her side, protecting family interests, adviser at breakfast, before turning out the lights, gently suggesting, never insisting, always vigilant, my rock when I wavered, my guide when lost.

Lived on the first floor below Aunt Audrey for a short while, until Nell got pregnant, then bought a sturdy little bungalow on Wilson Avenue near the river, Queen of Angels Parish, near the Ravenswood line, Rockwell stop. Tough pregnancy, just not built for it, never admit it, tried to hide it, tough to see, suffering, little bugger never gave her a moment's rest, then or after, but eventually, on his own terms, he came into the world, and changed us forever. She deserved better.

Lived in the bungalow a couple years until a large brick Georgian became available a half block away, backed up right on the river, grand house, fit for a committeeman, and we moved in, and the streets were cleaned, alleys plowed, trees trimmed, and the tidy little neighborhood rose on a cloud of pride and privilege.

Single all those years, I'd saved enough to buy the house, but barely, little stretched, campaign funds were tempting, but out of the question, so the time had come to start providing for my wife and son. Been thinking about it for a while, pull the trigger when the time was right, seen these guys working the real estate tax game, pretty good gig, lawyers who don't practice, that would be me, so hung out my shingle for the first time, got into the real estate tax business, and started making some real money, not at first, took several years for the cash to start rolling in, but once it did, man, it flowed, and what a scam.

And this is how it works: it starts with the Assessor, an elected position, it's his office that comes up with an assessed value for your house, and the tax you pay is based on that assessment, the higher the assessment, the more the tax, on everything, single-families, two-flats, condos, office buildings, everything. The current Assessor has held the job now for ten years, one of those guys who, when he first ran, lost, got depressed, would never run again. But I saw something in him, the weakness maybe, pushed and backed him next time around, for Assessor, when he ran, won, and, let's just say, he's been grateful ever since. So it starts with my friend, the Assessor, who sends his troops out to assess all the real estate in town, whose job, you might expect, would be to accurately assess the value of each building, but that's where you'd be wrong, because the assessments never approximate fair market value, sometimes high, sometimes low, just enough to keep you guessing, just enough to make sure that no one can figure it out, just enough for a little ambiguity, a little room to move, just enough to make building owners hire a politically connected lawyer to file an objection to the assessment, especially the commercial buildings, high-rises, with millions on the line. And that's where we come in, cuz the process isn't straightforward, that would defeat the purpose, just a little complicated, Kafkaesque, just enough, so you need our help. We file an appeal of the assessment, reviewed by staff the Assessor hires, from his ward, and they make a decision, which then goes to the Assessor, my guy. His decision can be appealed to the Board of Tax Appeals, five elected positions, all slated, all owe me, two from my ward, just a call away. I specialize in high-rise real estate taxes of course, that's where the money is, and the owners know how it works, they've been around, and they don't really care, so long as they get the same deal as everybody else, so they hire my capable office, and never complain about it, cuz they know how to fix it, without paying a dime. I own the Assessor, the Board, they know that, so they give me a call, top guys in town, I turn it over to my staff, all the work I do, my work already done, years ago, and my staff gets to work, comps, forms, filings, cookie cutter stuff really, Learned Hands aren't required, and we file our objections with my friend the Assessor, and file appeals with my friends on the Board, and always win, and the assessments are reduced, our clients save a ton, we get paid a percentage, the Assessor has lavish fundraisers, and everybody's happy, no one's the wiser, and the system just keeps chugging along, year after year, it's a gold mine, and it's all legal, though it stinks to high heaven.

And once that whole gig was up and running and the money started rolling in we were on our way: Nell, little Billy, and me, and we were happy, and comfortable, and I loved my job, loved playing the game, one of the best at it, especially after Tom McLean passed on, at which point the Old Man appointed me Finance chair, and I never looked back. Never let it get to us though, sure fire way to lose respect, and support, so kept it low key, but for the Eldorado, and then the Property outside Spring Green, and then the condo off Oak Street with the lake view, kept on the low down, our *pied*-à-*terre*, indulgence, Nell embarrassed by the doorman, but loving the view, the fur coat she never wore outside, playing her piano in the clouds.

So the three of us and Audrey carried on, comfortably, for years, doing the Old Man's bidding, floor leader, arm twister, and, over time, as his peers passed on, one of the few he could trust. My own bidding not far behind, everything bigger, everything better, Nell at my side, fundraisers overflowing, banquets, awards, for this, for that, my Rolodex, posh hotels, penthouse suites, old money clubs, power lunches with silk suits, bond counsel, and Hermès ties, Ward Nights with blue collars, more at home, filling jobs, making deals, Billy in the Latin School, backing winners, black robes, no losers, no waves, largesse for the needy, armies of debtors, the beholden, fearful, ask not, demand seldom, discipline wrongs, severely (Audrey), exponential force, tentacle control, collecting chits by the fistful, and raking in fees for tax work I never had to do myself. The best of years, a golden decade, while Billy was still young.

And then, one morning, the world turned upside down, when, after a large breakfast, the Old Man slumped over in his chair behind his desk and never again saw the light of day. City Hall footings and granite blocks groaned and shuddered, with wheels turning, gears cranking, what's in it for me, from the deputy mayor to the bootblack, for some, trepidation, the security blanket stripped away, for others, opportunity, walls torn asunder, for me, nothing to fear, genuine loss, one of the few, I'd miss the Old Man, patron, benefactor, but a force no longer, and in his wake a palpable void, a vacuum itching to be filled, and a torch passed, with no ring left to kiss, the dawn of independence. You would have thought his passing would have thrown the whole apparatus up for grabs, but the Old Man, as with every-thing, had a plan, a plan of succession, which involved the deputy mayor, the alderman of the Old Man's ward, subservient, ass kiss, full of himself, a South Side Serb married into the Gold Coast and thought he belonged there, rode the Old Man's tails to heights he could never have accomplished himself, and everyone but him knew it. Tough to tell what the Old Man was thinking, best guess, give everyone a breather, continuity, for a short time, until everyone and everything got sorted out, and then throw it up for grabs, and by then what the hell would he care, he'd be six feet under, he'd done his part, time for others to step up, he probably thought about me.

But I just wasn't the front and center guy, I preferred behind the scenes, behind the headlines, where the money was. I never needed to be stroked, the trappings, more like Tom McLean than the Old Man, conditioned to serve, the more you got the less you controlled, and what I had, which was a lot, I controlled, best not risk throwing it all away, besides, it wouldn't be good for Nell, just wasn't cut out for that type of thing, God bless her, just another reason I loved her so, so I did the good soldier thing, served the new mayor, sort of, as Finance chair, floor leader, but pathetic really, watching him maneuver for support among flesh-eating sharks, smiling knives plotting against him, mutinous, biding their time. Two years later, he got his chance, up for election, prove he was his own man, the Old Man reincarnate, except that he wasn't, just the legatee of a broken machine. He appeared before the committeemen, polite applause, disaster, never saw it coming, and when the time came for the city to let him know what it really thought of him, he got trounced, in a strange twist, orchestrated by Gusman, brilliant really, and a band of rebels, outsiders, who never saw the light of day under the Old Man, who rallied behind Alderman Earl Williams, former cop, who swept the Black vote, the lakefront, his fellow coppers, while the South Side Serb split the White vote with an Irish crackpot from the Northwest Side, and Gusman and Williams licked their chops as they eked out a victory, just enough to turn the city on its head, bury the broken machine, and make the Old Man turn in his grave.

But when the time came to govern, they had to deal with me. Not that I wanted the role, but having been the Old Man's floor leader all those years, there really wasn't much of a choice. I knew where the votes were, hustled to keep them together, cashed in some major chits in the process, but in the end, I safely had twenty-nine out of fifty, and for the first time in a long time, the city discovered what type of government it had. Everybody was so used to the Old Man having his way, that few knew, when push came to shove, that even the mayor needed twenty-six votes to get anything done. No budget, no appointments, no bond deals, no ordinances, not much of anything any self-respecting power monger would care about, and Williams and Gusman and their band of discontents couldn't do anything about it, because they hadn't spread the wealth around like I had. And it wasn't the past, it was the future everybody looked to. If they thought I was done without the Old Man, they would have run to Williams, but they didn't, they thought I was the better bet, the one who'd protect their interests, and they were right, and so we stuck together, our group of twenty-nine, blocked everything Williams wanted, passed our own budget, passed our ordinances, and man were they pissed, having thought they finally scaled the mountain, only to find they didn't control anything. I confess, for a government geek like me, it was great fun, entirely new political terrain, and plenty of legal challenges, but I knew the statutes, the regs, the rules of order, the budget, I knew I had the votes, so we ran with it, and the Old Man would have been proud.

But here's the thing. Of the twenty-nine, twenty-seven of us were White as ghosts, and two were right-minded Hispanics playing their cards close to the vest. Of the twenty-one, fifteen were Black, three Hispanic, and three White (two lake-front gadflies, and Gusman). Didn't play well in the press, you can imagine, got beaten up daily, frustrating the will of the people, Black progressive reform versus White dinosaur machine, we were racists overnight, poster boy Jim Crows, and as the *de facto* leader of the twenty-nine, overnight I became the symbol of White supremacy, keeping Black folks down after they finally found the Holy Grail, single handedly preventing the dawn of a new era.

Okay, so I didn't play the optics very well, but as anyone on the inside who knew anything about anything would tell you, the struggle wasn't about race, (the fact we were all White didn't help), but at its core, this was a political fight, a fight over power, and who would wield it, and we had it and they didn't, simple as that, and we knew, after having been in power all those years, that it wouldn't be good for us, our futures, or lastly, our constituents, if we were to let go, knew after all those years our foes would be ruthless in their own right, after all that's what they promised, what they ran on, and we had the power to prevent that, so who wouldn't, Black, White, Brown, whatever, in our shoes, and so we did. So sue me, and they did, but lost time and again.

Backlash for playing the game didn't bother me, I'd been playing a long time, trained by the best, most useful disciplines, could not have been better prepared for just such a moment, and there I was, once in a municipal lifetime, a perfect political storm that might never be replicated, so what the hell was I supposed to do but use everything I had learned, like no one else could have done, to wrest and exert political power, by the rules, by law, and do so responsibly, with a budget and laws that, if anyone bothered to read them, and report honestly about them, would tell you that by and large fairly provided for all neighborhoods in the city, Black, White, or Hispanic, but of course, no one saw it that way.

So I got beaten up pretty bad. Looking back, would I have done it differently? Probably not. I did my job and didn't let headlines do it for me. But I did pay a price. Nell was horrified. Not the power part, that she enjoyed, but what they said about me, how they demonized me. She didn't question me, didn't believe what people were saying, just thought it was unfair, undeserving, skin not as thick as mine, and it bothered her, greatly, and for that it bothered me. And we talked a lot about it, for her benefit more than mine, but what bothered us most was not the negative coverage, as bad as that was, but the back-slapping way to go hero worship from those in the twenty-nine wards who welcomed racial wars, about time, wanted a champion to right affirmative action wrongs, stop White flight, keep 'em down, show 'em who's boss, and protect our way of life, whatever that was. Me, the racial divider, for cheering Whites and cursing Blacks, who would have thought. It was malicious and sordid and at times made me think of a new line of work, I was trapped, to be sure, but I wasn't complaining, my fate, what I chose, and there was too much on the line, too many relying on me, and besides, for all of that, I was having too much fun.

Might have been hard on Billy though, cursed with my name, carrying my racist baggage among the lefties in the Latin School, neon sign of trashy privilege hanging around his neck, we know how he got here, parvenu, new money ill gotten, just a kid, but that stuff rubs off, must have, could have been part of it, I don't know what happened, but man, he and I were oil and water from the get go, never saw eye to eye on anything, even as a kid, cold toward me, loved his mom to death, bond I sure as hell never had, I don't know what it was, anything he wanted, only child I guess, but so was I, only thing we had in common. Took him to the Hall, showed him around, no pulse, introductions, this is my son, limp handshake, floor staring, no interest, my insides melting. Ward Night, one time, he sat in the corner, watching the clock, good folks telling life stories, their hopes and tears, nothing, nothing to say. And then high school, chrissakes, sullen, fatigue jackets, then leather, cigarettes, late nights, spoiled rotten, like all his friends I never met, roaming Lincoln Park, party time in the big city, like when I found his weed stash, threw it across the living room at him, he didn't flinch, nothing, smirk of what did you expect. New Year's bust at the condo, all underage, puffed-up cops, until, wait, who's your father?, two in the morning, phone rings, sir, respectful, sorry to bother, but your son, thought you should know, let it slide, let everything slide, one after another, year after year. Graduated from high school on a wing and a prayer, and plenty of phone calls from you know who, anything he wanted, any college he wanted, ended up in Madison, great town, close to the Property, far as I could tell, didn't learn a thing.

The one big thing in my life that didn't go right.

Right around the time Billy went away to college, we righted the ship in City Hall, brought the Council Wars to an end, and got rid of Williams, never had a chance to another term, we weren't going to make that mistake again, no splitting the White vote this time, but we had to be careful, everyone still pretty raw, but tired, so we ran a middle-of-the-roader, stiff of a Pole from the Northwest Side, guy named Jablonski, controlled him for four years, relative calm, box of rocks, godawful boring, and lucrative.

Billy spent the four years of Jablonksi's tenure in Madison, on what became the five-year plan, if there was a plan at all, out-of-state tuition, yours truly, changed majors, twice, three times, then, at last, Film Studies, great, great platform, plenty of jobs. At first he came home for winter breaks, spring breaks, never saw him, never around, one big party, pissed me off, couldn't help it, swearing, yelling, Nell crying, gratitude?, forget about it, clueless, angry, needed a break from each other, shitty grades, drugs, all kinds, looking for an excuse, didn't deserve that for all I'd done, world on a platter he didn't want. Busted selling Kool Aid at a Mifflin Street Block Party, but I knew somebody, of course, deep-sixed it, time after time, should have let them lock him up, but couldn't do that to Nell, who suffered, anguish, took its toll, for that could never forgive him, and it went on like that for five years.

Sick of Billy, for sure, but he's my son for God's sake, can't get rid of him, Jablonski, on the other hand, was a different story, we were all sick of him, and anyway, whether we liked it or not, the Council Wars had changed the city, and we had to look like we were changing with it, without changing at all, so as poor Jablonski was planning to extend his four-year footnote, I sat down with Gusman and hatched a plan to bury the hatchet and back Willie Jefferson, two-term county executive, in a run for mayor. Came as news to Willie. My kind of guy. First time we met, many years ago, handed him a $25,000 check in an unmarked envelope during a County Board of Commissioners meeting, for his role, not his work, as minority bond counsel on a big bond deal, handed it to him right there on the floor while the Board was in session, business as usual. Yeah, my kind of guy, old school machine, Old Man's black pocket, unscarred racial wars, lip service Williams backer, had to, I understood, no hard feelings, and up to his neck in debt, to me.

And from the moment Gusman and I made the deal, (the election anticlimactic), it's been a battle for Willie's one good ear. According to our deal, I kept Finance, Gusman Budget, and Gusman took over as floor leader. They figured I'd be better pissing out than in. They were right. But no one trusted anybody, need to know basis, and nobody needed to know anything, and it went on like that for four years, toughest years of my life, for other reasons.

It was a year after Gusman and I put Willie Jefferson on the throne that Billy finally graduated, and ruined our lives, having met a girl, Chicago girl, Jenny, from the South Side. Father, Dick, big-shot business guy, family friend of the Old Man turns out. Became a somebody, apparently. Old neighborhood in Bridgeport too cramped for him. Big house now in Beverly, lace curtains, country club, climber second wife, that sort of thing, waspirations. First wife, for whom the old neighborhood was enough, lived in a bungalow on Lowe Street that he paid for. Ran into Walsh a few times, condescending, legitimate businessman, unlike me, that sort of thing.

Jenny Walsh, long and lean, like Billy, little too lean, too vacant, half-second off, blonde, gorgeous, and pregnant. Jesus. Set them up in Old Town, place they couldn't afford. Dick, disgusted, wouldn't help, what she got for hanging with my kind, my kid. Billy started driving a cab, found out later Jenny worked a cash register at a porn shop on Wells Street. Far as I could tell, spent most of their time smoking cigarettes, going to clubs, cocaine, Quaaludes, what I heard, how should I know, never called, godawful.

Jenny delivered twins at Northwestern, my dime, boy and a girl, perfectly healthy, miracle, little blonds, beautiful. Dick and his wife, ambivalent at first, but Jenny's real mom, back in Bridgeport, took them under her wing, and she and Nell cared for those kids, day after day, together in the bungalow on Lowe Street, while the parents were God knows where.

What we should have seen coming happened when the twins were a little over two years old. One cold Saturday night in February, they dropped the kids off with Jenny's mom, spent the night freebasing, picked the twins up from Jenny's mom around nine o'clock the next morning, strapped the kids into car seats in the back of Billy's Marathon cab, and drove to the Jewel to buy Pampers. The Quaaludes on the way were Jenny's idea, and by the time they got there, she was fast asleep in the passenger seat. Billy stumbled in, and then out, with diapers, found Jenny and the kids fast asleep, started the car, closed his eyes, and he too fell asleep.

One hour later, a Jewel employee, collecting carts in the parking lot, noticed the Marathon cab running with the kids in the backseat, Billy and Jenny in front, all asleep. A half hour later, he checked on them again, still there, only now the kids were crying in the back. Police called, show up, crowd gathers, knock on the driver's side window, no response, front seat passenger window, no response, kids now howling, Billy stirs, wakes to a crowd of faces staring in the car, with cops on each side pounding and shouting at the windows. Jenny is non-responsive. An ambulance is called, rushes her to the hospital. Billy and the kids are taken to the district station.

Drug tests show cocaine, Quaaludes, marijuana, and alcohol, over the limit, in the so-called parents. Lucky to be alive. Billy calls me. Cops call the Department of Children and Family Services. One of the cops, Black guy, Williams voter, calls the Tribune. Nell and I go down to the station, film crew at the ready. Case worker releases kids to Nell's care, Billy's asleep in his cell, leave him there, and drive home with two of the cutest kids you've ever seen, cheeks working hard on sippy cups in the back seat.

Lead story on the ten o'clock news. And there we were, Nell and I, bright glare, fumbling with car seats in the back of the Eldorado. Front page next day, with photos, Trib, Sun Times, Defender, trifecta. Druggie son of clout-heavy hack endangers kids in drug stupor. And everybody gets the gist, silver spoon, powerful father, raised poorly, permissive, drugs, and it's not enough that he needs to screw up his own life but to risk the lives of toddlers? Lowest of lows, Billy and Jenny both. Cameras rolling next day as Jenny scrapes bedraggled out of the hospital, limp dirty blonde hair drooping, and cut to Billy leaving the station, with a smirk and a wave, a big joke, my God.

With my help, and it wasn't easy, DCFS allowed Jenny's mom to take temporary custody of the twins, with a promise of Nell's daily support. Billy went back to driving his cab. Never came around, never called, not a word. He'd meet Nell for coffee from time to time, so I'm told, but nothing for me, always my fault. Jenny stayed in Beverly with Dick for a week, but, needing a hit more than her families, cashed out her childhood bank account, skipped her bond, left without a word, and headed for the West Coast on an Amtrak out of Union Station.

Billy stuck around long enough to get probation on a child neglect charge, with the help of a lawyer I paid for, and a judge who, the press pointed out, was appointed out of my ward. Without remorse, Billy left the courthouse, and fled the city. Weeks later he surfaced in Lone Rock, Wisconsin, close to the Property, living above a bar called the Mad House Inn.

Apparently, he had forgotten he had children, any sense of respon- sibility, not a word, left them on a doorstep under cover of night. My son. How could such a thing happen? What had we done? Created a monster. Kids probably better off, God only knows how they survived with those two. The slinking off without a word was bad enough, but not even asking about them? Hey, could you guys care for them while I'm gone? Nothing. Did he just presume we would, or worse, did he give them a second thought? He just couldn't be bothered, his shitty life was all that mattered, never even told his mom he was leaving, and it tore her up, never forgive him, the leav- ing, shock of abandonment, heartless, soulless, and it began to take a toll.

We didn't know what to do, first time in my life, couldn't fix this one, no amount of chits. Nell and Jenny's mom did what they could, yeoman's job, but Nell began to slow a bit, lost weight, lethargic, and, as far as DCFS was concerned, Nell was part of the package, and she knew it, became anx- ious, apologetic, putting it off, nothing's wrong, it'll go away, not wanting to know, for fear, pushing through what was corroding her insides, a saint wasting away.

Over time there was no ignoring something very wrong, there was no getting better, and the doctor's diagnosis, pancreatic cancer, came the same day Jenny's dad, Dick, and his climber wife, served us with a subpoena and guardianship petition to take temporary custody of the twins, first we'd heard from them since the incident. Billy served, too, never showed. Little we could do. Nell was given months to live, Jenny's mom couldn't do it alone, and I was not an option, thought about it, thought about fighting it, but what chance did I really have, little to none, so I was told, and it was all just too much anyway, too much at the wrong time, I had lost my son, I was losing my one and forever only true love, slowly, painfully, and after six months, in an uncontested hearing, I lost my grandkids, to Dick.

One month later, Nell passed away in a morphine coma in our front room. Massive funeral, church bursting, everyone there, but her own son. Didn't deserve to be there.

And through it all, torn apart, I took care of business, didn't miss a beat, at least at first. Matter of pride, couldn't show weakness, just the opposite, no openings, no underbelly, no sign of humanity. Went through the motions, all on the outside, superficial anyway, nobody could tell, the detritus inside, scattered glass shards, repositioned, unrecognizable shapes and patterns, change in view, dimension, perspective, ponderous, morose, desultory, in private, alone, God I miss her.

Always thinking of her, these country roads she loved, open, pure, sadness in the beauty of these blue skies, the Eldorado, unleashed now, gliding up and down and along the hills, right at the old school house, left at the farm stand, past the Holsteins, a maze of twists and turns, honed over many such trips, many years of trial by error, short cuts and dead ends, adventures, exploring nowhere, into somewhere, the Eldorado a flash, from another time, place, slowing, squeezing, past John Deere combines, antique stragglers in beat pickups, Evansville, Belleville, the back way, steep climbs, scenic roads, river basin, watershed, winding, leaving the past behind, remembered, only to move ahead, set the stage, make plans, the future beckons, keep on, always, not much time left, to plow, to sow, to reap, as the dark amphibious shapes of the Blue Mounds surface on the horizon.

It was just about the time Willie Jefferson began running for a second term that I found, to my surprise, that I really didn't care, first time in my life. Saw things a little differently, after the twins were born, their parents ran away, and Nell died, began to feel the tremors, so I cut another deal, for Willie's second term, stepped back, gave Gusman Finance, but kept my office, took Budget, time to reconsider, recalibrate. As a young man, playing the game in and of itself was enough, to learn, laugh, and make mistakes, build, care, listen, walk out of the Hall after a long day with pride, direction, public service. Momentum, challenges, spheres expanding, learning by doing, impressing, excelling, always on the go, filling days, one after another, months into years, pride, headlines, ego, the Old Man, Tom McLean, my path, exciting, stirring, never a doubt, no time, what for, never why, always onward, upward, evolving, into family, responsibility, the best of reasons, providing, greater goals, never haunted, no questions, never why. And then you find yourself, after all those years, no family, no challenge, no reason, loss, suffering, alone, wondering why. New to me, the questions. Mortality, fear maybe, posterity, what will they say, what funeral lies told, celebrating my obituary, leader of the twenty-nine, great, great legacy, is that what I want, do I know? Nell would understand, cheer me on, for the world to see a side no one, but her, including me, had known, she saw something deep down, but is it there, a conscience, do I care, is it too late?

What was it Billy said, in our last knockdown drag out, I was a pawn, a tool, of self, greed, the system, never what might be best, only what serves me best, support the Old Man, preserve the machine, long live the machine, fuck everybody else, loyalty, blind, grease, money, clout, backrooms, smoke, mirrors, two-faced lying Luddites, but why, never smart enough, to even ask why. Not smart enough, that's what he said. Little shit. Never smart enough to ask why. Just didn't get it, didn't know me, never loved me. Why? Did I ever ask why?

And now, here I am, sixty-eight years in, power trip expert, top of my game, government guru, career broker, high stakes arbiter of the make or break, and wondering, for the first time, what for, (how could that be), and you'd think, after all that time, it wouldn't matter, I'd have figured it out, me, of all people, it would be enough, as it always was, but now wasn't. Course nobody could know, carry it around like that fox beneath the Spartan's cloak, eating away, bit by bit, growing cold, rare smiles, long walks, mulling it over. You know you go through stuff like that and you see the world with fresh eyes, anew, for the first time, after a baby is born, a parent dies, true love lost, returning from a long vacation abroad, all the conventional rationalized ways of the world, so important, so consuming, so, really?, the Emperor is naked?, really?, no longer, scales away, clearly now, does it have to be, wonder of all wonders, no, it doesn't, sky opens, north, south, east, west, possibilities, really?, I have a choice?, for the first time, really, I have a choice, and if I were younger I'd be scared, but not now, why not?, something different, radically, but what?

Didn't know, for a year or so, coalescing, first, something, had to do something, start somewhere, rejection maybe, no turning back, time to break down, December, Christmas lights, a beginning. My fundraiser, of all things, of all places, and there it was, bigger than ever, mayor, the governor, now there was a line, out the door, and I'm at the head, standing below the dais, waiting, greeting, the Man, city at my feet, bending a knee, kissing my ring, shaking my hand, with meaningless words, and as I stood there, in all my glory, it came to me, in a rush of disgust at what I had wrought, this farce, this spectacle of groveling for more, the rich, the powerful, doing their part, to preserve and protect a system, way of life, a machine, that worked to preserve and protect itself, spinning straw into gold for all but the uninvited, for the elites at court, the powerless nowhere to be seen. No one could notice the steam rising, bones aching, derision smoldering, bubbling beneath the surface, molten lava seeping from my Ferragamo shoes onto the lush Persian carpet, as the tawdry evening limped to its ignominious end. After the speeches no one listened to had ended, the music died, and the last check counted, as I sat alone in my condo dark, staring out at the blank slate lake, second bourbon in hand, car lights bending around the Oak Street curve, I vowed to make a choice, free will, not bound by youth, nurture, expectation, my choice, to dismantle and rebuild, conspire against everything I had worked for, and make a difference, before it was too late.

The mechanic, who maintains the machine, holds the wrench, knows how to break it, and I had some ideas. More of a program, a platform, a manifesto in motion.

Start out with something that's really bothered me. Okay, so it didn't bother me enough not to make a tidy commission, but sorta bothered me, a real estate deal I did about five years ago. That was a piece of work. Got a tip, insider information, guy who owes me, from DCMS, Department of Central Management Services, state agency handles state buildings, leases. Another state agency was about to go public on a plan to relocate and lease up to 100,000 square feet of space in the Loop. Lot of space, tough market. Timing is everything. A week before, owner of a down on its heels department store barely surviving in the South Loop, with 150,000 square feet of about-to-become empty space, comes to me in hopes of getting city financing for redevelopment once the store vacated. Then I got the tip from DCMS, then I call the owner, suppose I were to find you a tenant, would there be any value. Hell yeah. How much? Wow. What would we call it? Finder's fee. Finder's fee? Is that legal? Sure, do it all the time, real estate biz. What a biz. Finder's fee, hell yeah, let's call it that, and I give him the name of my guy in DCMS, and they do a deal, twenty-five-year lease, 100,000 square feet, nice finder's fee, for doing nothing, and everybody's happy.

So what do we do about that? Well, we could draft an ethics law, which, *inter alia*, bars all governmental employees from personally benefitting, directly or indirectly, from any business transaction of any governmental entity, and makes paying or receiving such compensation a criminal act. Disclosing non-public information for purposes of enabling anyone to benefit directly or indirectly from a governmental transaction, criminal act.

What about real estate taxes? Well, first, the Assessor cannot be elected, same with the Board of Tax Appeals. Take it out of our hands. Appointed would be better, some panel of citizens, do it all the time. Then, ban all patronage from the Assessor's office, everything merit based, shocking. Then, how about this, require that all assessments actually reflect fair market value, there's an idea. Create a separate division in the Circuit Court responsible to hear all tax appeals, by judges, with specific criteria of review, to replace the Board. Bar all governmental officers and employees from having anything to do with representing any person seeking an appeal of a real estate tax assessment. Require all representatives of persons filing real estate tax appeals to disclose the client, result, and fee in each such appeal.

Circuit court judges. Not elected, non-partisan. Selected by bar associations, criminal penalties for considering anything other than qualifications.

Patronage. But for mayor's top aides, and department heads, bar all governmental officers and employees from lobbying their or another governmental entity to encourage or discourage any personnel action, and bar all governmental officers and employees from considering anything other than the needs of the job and the applicant's qualifications with respect to any personnel action. Penalty? Termination.

Policing. Require that each rank in CPD reflect racial makeup of city as a whole. Period.

Minority Business. Establish a system within the purchasing department, by which city awards meaningful percentages of all city work to minority businesses. Enforce strictly, minority interest must be legitimate.

Bond Counsel. CBA (Chicago Bar Association) to develop a list of persons and firms qualified to provide bond counsel legal services. Selected on rotating basis. Minority firms required to meet definition of a minority business (no shams). Firms paid only for work performed, bill only by the hour (no percentages of multimillion-dollar bonds). All firms required to publicly disclose nature of work performed, hours worked, and fees charged. Firms may not charge more than $200 per hour, or make political contributions.

Slating. Kind of tricky. First thing we do, we kill all the committee-men (there are no women). Maybe all candidates for elected public office in the city, including the mayor, submit names to a seven-member panel of prominent citizens, former judges, etc., who review all applications and vote on the three most qualified, whose names will be selected two months before the election, and automatically appear on the ballot. Criminal pen-alties for considering anything other than qualifications. Others may run as well, but, not having been selected, will run under a dark cloud. Politics will surely play a role at the panel, but better the panel than hack pols, ped-dling the old *quid pro quo*.

Far as I got for now. Could be more. Not perfect. Plenty to be ironed out. Realistic? Course not. But that's not the point. The point is to make waves. Make no small plans. Throw the grenade. Just the beginning. And all together? All at once? Big splash, for sure. And coming from me? Press conference. Extravaganza. Massive wrench. Something to say at my funeral. What will that little shit son of mine say about that? Not smart enough? Shame he'll never know that little defer and publish trick I pulled back there yesterday. First taste of what's to come, shot across the bow, rock the boat, put them on notice, from here on out, business not as usual.

Little wound up you might say. Yeah, well, I get like that. Always had plans. Can't leave well enough alone. Driven, for bad or good. How it is. One thing for sure, blessed with energy, never my problem. Probably too much. Don't know how it happened. Not a choice. Wired that way, passed down, through generations, and thousands of years, resulting in me, playing my hand, as I am, like it or not, probably not, I get it, but there's more, as I head north, away from the urban madness, toward another home I've made for myself, another life, a double agent, unrecognizable, schizophrenic, but just as real, and for me, increasingly, perhaps the real thing, what I could have become in different circumstances, a different life, perhaps more suited. How many of us have them, lurking out there, our true calling, hidden talent, yearnings, waiting to be discovered? Sheer luck if we do, odds are we don't, because of the place or time in which we were born, but out there, somewhere, beyond the games and intrigue, beyond the here and now, is another universe to explore, a facet to turn, a soul to set free, where I'm headed, my new direction, as the Eldorado hurtles into the open fields and empty back stretches of road, closer to heaven and a benevolent God, if there ever was one, where my oasis awaits, my dual life, where time is arrested, and slowed to a reverent respectful crawl.

Out here, finally, my God, take a deep breath, look where I am, how far I've come, catharsis, so many times now, each time, the same rediscovery. Easy. Enough. Enough of all the rest, back there, for now. Deep breath. Let the transformation begin. Let the stress slip away, slowly, the machinations, furrowed brow, let the hard crust crack and peel into flakes that swirl in the wake of my rearview mirror, as it always does on this stretch of open road, the early summer sun, rows of corn, the aid of distance, the forgetting, anonymity, the cleansing, loss of self, giving myself up to it, as the flat prairie gives way to the rolling hills of the Driftless.

Getting closer now, just outside Barneveld, leave the main road, duck off the ridge and down, beneath the arc of lowing branches, into sheer coulees squeezed by tall wooded ridges, with ancient craggy limestone cliffs jutting out from cover of oak and spruce, sentries to a new land, thousands of years, rushing waters receding into bottom clearings, where narrow farms now nestle, with dairy cows and crooked creeks, with turkeys and white-tailed deer, disappearing into brambles and up the slopes, to watch from a safe distance the Eldorado and its cloud of dust, up and over and around each ridge, mile after mile, with sweeping views, into and out of each valley, jumbled together, randomly tossed, in a puzzle of bends and curves, blacktop over Indian trails, following streams toward the river, and the soft fields of Wyoming Valley. Take a left past Taliesin, grand upon the hill, comforting arms, shining brow, the Wisconsin River, a glimpse, glimmering through trees to the north, past Wintergreen slopes, closer now, climbing to the high overlook, plunging into the river valley, onto Lower Wyoming, Far Look, Bear Creek, and, just after a copse of pine, a bank down to the right onto Hilltop Road, at which point, over the years, any dog worth her salt, would begin to howl.

The road now rises along the southern steep edge of a north-south ridge, hugging the bottom curve, narrow field below to the left, old growth forest, primeval, blanketing the bluffs rising sharply on the right, the road narrowing as it bends along the curve, clinging to the edge along a last bend, the field below, pinched, disappears into a deep ravine, and up to the right, now into view, the cattle gate, moss-orange, lock and key, standing guard, waiting to be opened, to welcome, with bow and flourish, the grand entrance, our Property, the sanctum, kingdom of peace. Up the lush green grass of a farm road rising, angling up into the woods along the sheer ridge, spring water seeping limestone along the right under juniper and birch, sheer deep ravine on the left, one foot off the road, harrowing scenes over the years, one tire dangling on the cliff, just there, across the road from the first Buddha, lava stone, eyes closed, slight smile at our travails, resting in tufts of grass against the rock, wisp of vine around the ear and head, greeting, welcome home, you know the way, up the road, under the branches, the tunnels of beech and vine, to the hairpin rising hard to the right, below the second, larger Buddha up the hill to the left at the turn, benevolent, calm, looking down upon the curve, watching, praying the turn is made, the vehicle worthy, his gaze not returned, rushed, nerves, pick up speed, the

Eldorado leaps around the turn, up, and to the right, where the ridge is now a hill, a slope, negotiable, upward, past the poplars, the old pickup, woods thinning, and finally, the hard turn to the left, where the third Buddha sits, on the right, last guardian of the way, at the edge of the woods where the meadow begins, facing the setting sun in orange solstice glow, whispering a prayer, for the woods, the field, the in between, and those who pass, out of the woods and into the field, high grass, rising now, the little cabin in view up ahead, vast meadow surround, tall white spruce in formation on the right, relaxed, slowing now, only a slight rise left, to where the road and journey ends, just below the cabin, where a six-foot-tall metal Petroglyph Man raises a welcoming hand, you made it, congratulations, we've been waiting for you, to return, to where you belong.

The Eldorado parked below the log cabin, Amish built, faces down the hill to the south across the valley to the opposite ridge. Twelve feet (west to east), by sixteen (north to south), rough-cut pine logs inside and out, red metal roof, two steps up to covered front porch with wooden rails. Two windows each east, and west, one north. No electric, no gas, no water. Elk horns outside between the two western windows. Outhouse thirty yards slightly downhill to the east along the wood line. Work bench outside along the eastern wall, rusted wheel barrow tipped upside down against the bench next to a high grass mower covered in lichen tarp. The loft inside accessible by rough-hewn ladder, where cots, axes, hatchets, pots, pans, tools, netting are stored. Tall hutch tucked behind the front door, with card table, folding wooden kitchen table, bent rim chair and side table, folding rocker, Buddha head, rubber boots, souvenirs and turkey feathers, American flags, primitive country prints, bronze sconces along the walls, candlesticks on tables, flashlights, sundries, and Dalai Lama in the hutch ("Never Give Up"), strewn about, patiently waiting.

The wooden outhouse is just big enough, the walls decorated: Bear Alert notice (Yellowstone), "Inside Ancient Egypt" banner (Field Museum),

Forest Park liquor store calendar, Lincoln Park "Farm in Zoo" poster, with Holstein, Big Sky ski map and ski ticket, "I Closed Wolski's" sticker (Billy), Shakespeare likeness, Lone Peak picture, Acting Irish Festival handbill, Swedish road sign booklet (Volvo), bald eagle perched on branch eye to eye with one seated, last three paragraphs of The Dead, Joyce, "…snow falling faintly, through the universe…",[1] Buffalo Warning (Yellowstone), rake, shovel, wooden stakes, Lost, by David Wagoner, Taliesin ticket, FLW quote ("…but nothing that picks you up in its arms and so gently, almost lovingly, cradles you as do these southwestern Wisconsin hills."),[2] real estate listing: "Wyoming Wonderland" ("…breathtaking views in every direction. Rock outcroppings emerge from this wooded hillside of varied oaks, white pines, black walnut, birch and hickory. The hillsides culminate in an expansive, rolling grass meadow and some of the finest views to be found in the area… This is truly land to be savored."), Digging, by Seamus Heaney, Gillingham and Vicinity news article, by Mary A. Johnson ("Mary Johnson attended the Robert Aldinger estate auction on April 1."), Directions, by Joseph Stroud, Chico Hot Springs tickets, metal cup, thumb tacks, Einstein woodcut, Ford F-150 Shop Manual, Irish Druid stone circle, Sanitary Permit, Grateful Dead set lists (Billy), Rolling Stones set list (Billy), Satisfaction of Property Real Estate Mortgage, Art Institute catalog, Iowa County Fair ribbons: blue, red, yellow, five pound bag of lye, French enameled ladle in bag, various planks of barn wood, mosquito spray, flashlight, hand cleanser, toilet and paper.

The Property is fifty-two acres, a rectangle north to south, the meadow—with fallow fields, wildflowers, timothy, goldenrod—follows a ridge rolling up from west to east across the midsection to the top of the hill, ancient forests flank the meadow, north and south, impossible to clear, falling steeply away off the divide of the meadow ridge into wild ravines, slashing off the hill down to Hilltop Road to the south, into a deep gorge untouched by time to the north. From the top of the hill, looking west, the ridge and meadow undulates, along the broad back of a Titian nude, buttocks raised, sloping down to a wide waist, then up upon her broad shoulders, and then down again to the Duffy's tall red barn at the Property's western edge.

The cabin is in the meadow, tucked into the hill, close to the eastern edge. Above the cabin and outhouse, the one hundred wood, white pine and spruce, thirty-feet tall and almost as wide, in four neat rows, pinespruce-spruce-pine, stretch south to north, across the meadow, an eastern border, wind break, uniting the woods on either side. From seedlings, carefully planted, lovingly tended, protected from ravaging deer, year after year, raising tender children into towering adults, long soft paths of needles and cones through chapels of low hanging boughs, comforting, reverent, hallowed, golden in falling light, marking the years. At the very top of the hill, in the middle of a small clearing between the spruce and pine, stands a five-foot tall lava stone Ganesh, facing east, facing west, remover of all obstacles in line of sight, ten miles of ridge line and field to the west, one after another to the horizon, the setting sun, glimmering no doubt on the current of the river, flowing, out of sight, just over the ridge to the north, on its course west to the Mississippi.

You get the idea. Bet not what you expected. Not bad for a city kid. Not the acquisition, the fact of ownership (as if anyone could actually own such a place), but how, over the years, I've come to become, this place, these ridges, ravines, meadow, my trees, so distant, removed, from my world, so expanding with the universe, all-consuming over time, my other, real?, life, how foreign such a place could be called home, how possible that I, of all people, would find here. Jesus, little shit should give me some credit, fat chance of that, but that doesn't bother me here. Up here, it's not about me, I don't exist here, I am not who I am. Just another living thing, an organism, sharing the sun, the wind, the stars, with each songbird, tree, and blade of tall grass, one long moment, breath, at a time.

Hauled my stuff up to the cabin, Coleman cooler on the porch, cot down from the loft, unpacked my sleeping bag, pillows, the Hudson Bay tossed on the cot. Strapped on my boots, Danner, put on my Amish hat, deerskin work gloves, grabbed my hiking stick, and headed out to the path that leads from the cabin up to the one hundred wood. Slow stride, up the hill, past a Bodhisattva reclining in the tall grass, into the trees, with an hour left of sun, glowing through branches, spotlights on needles underfoot, mushrooms, spider's web, gothic canopy, silence, wind, bluebirds darting in and out as I pass.

Stuff of dreams, great plans. Everything clear, perspective. Inspiration. Hatched my rebellion up here. Seemed to make more sense here, the right thing to do somehow, until the drive back, when my life took over, for a time, until I returned, again and again, and slowly my future came into view. First leave my mark, shock and awe, then slowly ease out of the morass, the concrete, might take time, but would open time, time to build, something here maybe, little permanence, running water would be nice, ponder, manifesto maybe, who knows, who cares, maybe nothing, disappear maybe, on my terms, incommunicado, incognito, to all but hawks, turkey, coyote, and deer. Dreams. Space and time, to take stock, the years, the time left.

As I climbed through the trees to the Ganesh at the top of the hill, and looked to the west over the ridges, marking time with the Earth's slow turning, sun, low and orange now behind a ribbon of cloud, couldn't help but think of old Ray, his friendship, goodness, wisdom, irreplaceable, forever gone, and the spreading of his ashes tomorrow in the wide river he loved, and the small group who will be there to see him float downstream for the last time, the sadness of his loss, hollow certainty of death that awaits us, fills us with what feels like wisdom accumulated over the years, a knowing beyond the routines that engulf and define us unfairly to the world. God, no better place than here, take me here, unto dust you shall return, a willing sacrifice. Let the vultures swirl overhead. Let the coyotes howl with their young in the night.

Running out of light for the woods, I took the path down into the field, mowed in the meadow's tall grass, past the fire pit kiva, and echoes of voices singing with blazed faces around campfires long ago, Nell huddled beside me, Billy running as a boy through tall grass, fireworks, kites flying, silenced now in death and regret, the ones I loved, but holding out hope, just as the sun can dip below the cloud and light the field one last time, must have hope. Alone down the path, to the grassy veranda on the hill where the sunsets fall, as the last winds of day blush crowns of oak on either side of the meadow, birds make their last dips and climbs across the field, to the spot I have stood so often, gazing into the sun, where wisdom and knowing give way, to love, that last hope, that those you love in turn may love, may find in themselves the reason, to strive, to give of themselves, to love their children, my grandchildren, Nell's grandchildren, even if he won't, I will, but he must, my fervent wish, for him, for them, the gift, the deliverance, please God if you are at all out there.

When the sun makes its last stand, as always happens, I am last in light, field in shadow about me, total silence but for wind, and the random whoosh of wings overhead, the passing of day, but then a rustle, down the steep hill hidden by the tall grass, then louder, tips of grass dancing together, over there, coming here, this time, twilight, here before, not a move, closer, upwind, a shoulder, bent head in the grass, startled, antlers raised, alarm, buck, immense, regal, staring, at me, from the tall grass twenty yards away, he leaps, high above the grass across the horizon, when another noise, further down the hill, a flourish, rises, takes aim, and from the dusk rips a feathered arrow zinging through the air above the grass, missing the deer, hurtling, toward me, my God, I see it, in slow motion, ripping the air, sun dipping below the rim, arrowhead, sharpened blade, razors, twirling, rushing, toward me, upon me, thuds, into my chest, tears through my heart a gaping hole, legs give way, crumple to the ground, hat flying, what, who, is it real, could it be, can't be, like this, not close to done, but God, it is, a breath, last look, through tall grass, red orange wisp of cloud, the last, of everything, my loves, my son, the ones he left behind, the last wish, and nothing.

CHAPTER TWO

The Flow

Constant motion, rotation, spinning, from where space and time do not exist, coming together, swirling apart, closer, distant, waves upon waves, light years, unseen, unknowable, pulsating, beyond reach and close at hand, microcosmic, reflecting, black holes, grains of sand, fingertips touching, beginnings and ends, and the infinite interregnum, of each breath, drop, and joule, each cell, in and out and touching, dividing and growing in the gravitational warmth of stars, mitosis, meiosis, ocean deep and mountain wind, efforts and dreams, and the flow, in constant motion.

While there must be, there is no beginning, as far as we know it, the farther back we go the less we know, if we truly know anything at all, other than what we see and touch, and still in all likelihood do not fully understand, our history confined to a fingernail tip, prehistory, nothing at all unless written down, our vain conceit. Perhaps there is wisdom to be gained, but history would not repeat itself if we learned anything from it, accepting, choosing to remember what flatters us, discarding, conveniently forgetting, lying about, or never writing down the ugly truths, the horrible sins, the stains we all bear, who we are, have been, and perhaps always will be. But the past appears to have the advantage of making us less lonely, less meaningless, prideful, in our selective memory, an enriching we seem to seek out, and apparently need, to justify, rationalize, elevate ourselves over others, and explain the unexplainable.

However the story is told, however reconstructed, and for whatever reason, beyond all wants, needs, and rationales, is the undeniable flow, the constant motion in real time, of water and blood, in rivers and veins, the tumultuous heaving, languid repose, rising, falling, pulse, the random design of mutations, that happen, and cannot be changed, moments, infinitely strung together over billions of years, in the point of time we call now, the time you take to read these words, the warmth of the sun, the creeping advance from water to shore, seed to flower, eruptions, ice, meteors, the fierce storms and gentle waves of Cambrian and Ordovician seas, the Paleozoic, Mesozoic, warming and cooling, the Pleistocene's glacial advances, back and forth, time and again over millions of years, leaving markers upon the land, in Great Lakes, and small, brooks and streams, in sandstone and dolomite, and rushing water carving its course to the sea.

One such waterway, flowing just to the north of the hill on which Dan Hurley's body lies, begins humbly, as mighty rivers do, from small springs that bubble from aquifers below impassable swamps in the North Woods, filling a lake left by glaciers, overflowing in a brook, remote, unexceptional, out-of-the-way peaceful, where the waters escape into marsh and reed, and onward, gathering as they travel, mile after mile, swelling slowly with each tributary along the way, transforming, from brook to stream to river wide, over 430 miles, generally south to southwest, through meanders and rapids, oxbows and gorges, rushing, ebbing, past bluff and field, falling 1,067 feet along the way to its mouth, where it flows into the Mississippi.

The lake of the river's origin, its *veritas caput*, the Ojibwe (Chippewa) called *Gete-gitigaani-zaaga'igan*, Lake of the Old Garden, Lac Vieux Desert to the French, which it is known as today. The Woodland Sioux, precursors to the Ojibwe, no doubt called it a different name, as did all the other peoples over thousands of years who preceded the Sioux. The Ojibwe established a summer village on an island in the lake, as others had done before, a meeting place from which trails led through dense woods to the Great Lakes of Superior and Michigan, knowing that the Lake of the Old Garden gave rise to a great river, Ouisconsing, the Wisconsin, the River of a Thousand Isles,[3] water trail to the edge of the earth, blessed by the Gods, and formed, eons ago, by a gigantic manitou snake, that twisted and slithered across the land, forming deep grooves along the sandstone surface into which adjoining water rushed, scaring smaller serpents that scrambled away in terror, carving tributaries from their routes of escape.

As many as twenty-five glaciers advanced and receded across the north country over two and a half million years, plowing, compacting, absorbing, and depositing sedimentary glacial drift, over and through which most of the snake river passed on its descent south, through northern highlands, terminal moraines, sedimentary fans and aprons, outwash sand plains, glacial lake bottoms, sandstone gorges, sandstone lowlands, barrens, terraces, and the broad valley carved by the cataclysmic flood, until the river turns west toward the Father of Rivers, and passes through the Driftless, 10,000 square miles of high ridges and deep ravines, untouched by ice sheets for unknown reasons, and shaped by storms and wind and water washing over the hills for millions upon millions of years.

During the glacial era, recurrent lobes of ice invasions, several miles thick, pushed south in millennia of cold, consuming, engulfing all in their path, loss less than gain, until the warmth returned, slowly, over centuries, when loss exceeded gain, retreating, melting, into rivers and streams etching the land, only to freeze again when the cold returned, solid to liquid and back again, when the lobes reformed, marched south and reclaimed the land they had lost, hundreds of thousands of years of back and forth, freezing, warming, water flowing, water trapped, lakes contained by walls of ice that held until the temperature turned, when walls gave way to avalanche, flood, and torrents of destruction that carved wide the river gorges.

Around 18,000 years ago, as the earth warmed, the last of the glaciers, the Younger Dryas, began to retreat slowly back to the north, across the territory that would one day bear the river's name, and the frozen water and silt began to flow again down ancient riverbeds, marking the beginning of the end of the Pleistocene. In the thousands of years it took this last glacier to release its grip on the land, a stubborn wall of ice and quartzite rose to dam the river flowing in from the north, forming a large proglacial lake, about the size of Delaware and up to 160-feet deep, behind the massive wall. And in one of those moments in time when life goes on as you know it until it suddenly and drastically doesn't, the massive dam cracked and burst, sending waves of full steam freight trains rampaging downstream, altering the landscape in hours what would have taken thousands of years, and carving wide the river valley, filling it with up to one hundred and fifty feet of sand and gravel, sculpting the gorge with borders of steep dolomite and sandstone bluffs rising 300- to 400-feet above the valley floor, and forming the wide river valley as it appears today.

At around that same time, about 14,000 years ago, the receding glaciers across the continent exposed a land bridge that stretched from Asia to North America along the Bering Strait, and nomadic women and men, seeking food for their children, or driven by enemies, cautiously stepped into a new world of wonder and danger never before seen by human eyes. Over years, and decades, and centuries, bands of ice age hunters traveled ever deeper into the unexplored world the ice had left behind, tundra, deep woods, tall mountains, bogs, clear lakes, rushing rivers, eventually reaching what we now call the Upper Midwest, around 12,000 years ago, where they settled along the Wisconsin River, hunting caribou, muskox, mastodon, wooly mammoth, giant ground sloths, beaver the size of bears, and huge buffalo. They steered clear of dire wolves.

Imagine that. Imagine the life. Nothing but the land, and everything. Hunting with spears much larger and faster beasts. Do you think that was dangerous? Did they suffer tragedy? No horses, no wagons. When they traveled, they did so on foot, on trails the beasts had trodden, or by canoe, along highways of water. Any possession was carried, or thrown in the bottom of a canoe. Do you think maybe they were strong, resourceful, resilient, intelligent? Do you think you are smarter than they were? Better hunter, canoer, athlete? Did they dream, dance, tell stories? Did they sing, cry, laugh, and love? Did they suffer in the cold, and swim in the summer? Think of the insects, the mosquitoes. Did they celebrate life and mourn death, did they worship and fear Gods, and stop from time to time to see beauty, in sunrise and sunset, flowers and trees, constellations, rain storms and snowfall? Did they have poets and war mongers, shtarkers and schmucks? Do you think they had all our emotions? Did they tell jokes? Did they kill each other?

One thing we know for sure is they had what it takes. The large beasts came and went, unable to weather climactic change, the extreme seasons, but the ancient peoples somehow found a way, adapting to constant incremental change, hunting white-tailed deer, elk, and buffalo, catching fish, gathering mussels, moving from season to season, generation after generation, over 7,000 years.

Seven thousand years. Over the past 200 years, we've had Abraham Lincoln, Michael Jordan, Alexander Pushkin, Sojourner Truth, Albert Einstein, Henry Aaron, Susan B. Anthony, James Joyce, Frederick Douglass, and Aretha Franklin. Do you think over 7,000 years they did not? Over 155 generations of war and peace, these people survived, and prospered, and as the bands grew in size, their settlements grew, along river banks in summer, out of the wind in narrow river valleys and rock shelters in winter, more and more returning to the same sites time and again, marking their territory with graves of their dead, fashioning copper for weapons, ornament, and trade, and constantly battling to retain or expand what they considered their own.

They must have done something right, because their families grew, bands became tribes, with alliances and enemies. Over time, around 2,500 years ago, they began to make pottery, plant gardens. Some genius came up with the idea of making spears that flew through the air from taut bows, their gardens became fields of corn too valuable to let fall into the hands of others, populations grew, settlements along the rivers (where else), became more permanent, more of them, territories more defined, hunting grounds more precious, worth fighting over, and they did, and the dead they buried in massive earthen mounds, shapes of eagles and bear, landscape engineers, with architects, project managers, and crews, requiring organization, time, and skill.

Perhaps hunters became too skilled, game too scarce, competition from enemies too intense, harvests of corn and beans more reliable, but around 1,000 years ago, the prospect of staying in one place appeared more desirable than moving with the seasons, and the Mississippians arrived, eclipsing, or absorbing the Woodlands in large city centers, Cahokia, and Aztalan, inland river camps giving way to subdivisions along the Big Muddy, intensive agriculture the rule of the day, and then that too passed, as all must, after 500 years, when the Mississippians fade from view, the tribes consolidate, break apart, and move back to the uplands and inland rivers with their fields of corn, carrying all the lessons learned over the millennia, and roaming across the Wisconsin River territory, for another 500 years, across lands littered with the bones of their dead, living off the land as their ancestors had done for 11,000 years, until the late Sixteenth Century, when all hell broke loose.

There was a disruption in the force when Coronado, DeSoto, Cortez, Pizarro and their henchmen and priests showed up, with their disease and death, which flew on the wind from tribe to tribe across the continent, ravaging Wisconsin Natives long before a White man set foot in their land. Perchance to dream what the Incas and Aztecs could have done to Cortez and Pizarro. If only. But it was just a matter of time. Nothing stops the flow. The world was getting smaller.

The Europeans came from the south and west, and then from the east, where the French, Dutch, and English began to arrive, first a trickle, and then in waves, locusts, along the coast, pushing inland across the land, offering iron knives and trinkets, glass beads and axes, blankets, brass kettles, and guns, in exchange for pelts of beaver and bear. And business was good, at first, Natives got their guns, and the bourgeoisie of London and Paris their beaver hats, furnishing goods on credit, how thoughtful, which the Natives used to haul in more pelts, for more guns, and then liquor, and then debt, dependence, hunting a steadily dwindling resource to satisfy avaricious demand, for pelts and fisheries, metals, and eventually the land itself, and by then it was too late. As the Europeans pushed west toward the Appalachian Mountains, the squeeze was on, and the Natives fought, usurpers and each other, to retain what they had or make up what they had lost, decades of battles waged across the eastern continent, alliances made, broken, scalps taken, by all sides, prisoners hostage, maps redrawn, as the White wave moved west, pushing the Native tribes before it.

In the northeast, from 1640 to 1670, the Iroquois Confederacy: Mohawk, Onondaga, Oneida, Cayuga, and Seneca, moved further west into the Great Lakes territory and south into Ohio country, seeking fur to trade from forests unexploited, driving tribes before them in fierce fighting over great distances, with English guns, and settlers at their backs, pushing and being pushed, playing their part in the domino migration of entire tribes across the map of North America, driving French-allied Algonquian speakers west, the Huron to the brink of extinction, the Ojibwe, Ottawa, and Mesquakie (Fox) around the northern border of Lake Michigan, and the Sauk, Mascouten, Kickapoo, and Potawatomi, around the southern edge of the Great Lake, into the territory through which the Wisconsin River flowed, which the Sioux, Menominee, and Ho-Chunk already called home.

And then, to confuse matters further, the Europeans "discovered" the Great Lakes country. It appears, because no one is certain, that Jean Nicolet was the first European to set foot in the lands west of Lake Michigan, reportedly landing near Green Bay, in 1634. A believer in grand entrances, he arrived in a Chinese damask robe brightly colored in birds and flowers, brandishing a pistol in each hand. The Ho-Chunk called him *Manitouiriniou*—Man of Wonder. Over the next thirty years, the Man of Wonder was followed by Pierre Esprit Radisson; and Medart Chouart Sieur de Groseilliers, who may have been the first European to paddle the Wisconsin; René Ménard, Jesuit, who appears to have gotten close but then mysteriously disappeared; Claude Jean Allouez and Claude Dablon, Jesuits; Nicolas Perrot; and Pére Jacques Marquette, Jesuit, traveling with Louis Joliet, in 1673. The French *coureurs de bois* arrived in the name of Louis XIV, the Sun King, seeking profits in the fur trade; the Black Robes arrived in the name of Jesus, seeking souls in the trade of God.

Over the next ninety years, the French plied their trade, traveling by canoe from Montreal and Quebec, laden with goods to trade for beaver pelts, down the St. Lawrence, across Lake Ontario, Lake Erie, Lake Huron, into Lake Michigan, along its western shore into Green Bay, to the mouth of the Fox River, flowing northeast, then up the Fox, across a portage to the Wisconsin, and down the Wisconsin to the Mississippi, setting up trading posts along the way, networking with Natives, living with them, making friends, enemies, falling in love, having children, raising families, negotiating, haggling, encouraging, supplying with goods for winter, and welcoming when Natives returned with piles of fur the French stacked in canoes, and exchanged for gold when they returned along the waterway lifeline back to Montreal and Quebec.

But, of course, the French never got along with the English, forcing the Natives, now reliant on European goods, to pick sides or play one off the other, until the English won the French and Indian War, when, according to the 1763 Treaty of Paris, the Sun King ceded all French lands east of the Mississippi to the English. This came as a surprise to the Natives, whose land the English and French were fighting over, because the Natives were not parties to any such agreement, and were not happy about the Treaty's terms. But the English said not to worry; they didn't want Native land, they just wanted to continue the Native trade. Oh. Okay. So the English now canoed into Lake Michigan, up the Fox, across the portage, and down the Wisconsin to the Mississippi, carrying on the fur trade, alongside French woodsmen who never left.

And then, to make matters worse, or better depending on your point of view, a new group of people came into the territory. They called themselves Americans, after America, a place inhabited by Natives for almost 12,000 years, and the Americans called the Natives Indians, after a country in Asia that was 7,300 miles away. The Americans fought the English to be free of King George III, and won, leading to a second Treaty of Paris, in 1783, in which the English ceded all Native lands east of the Mississippi, south of the Great Lakes, and north of Florida, to the Americans. The Natives were not parties to that agreement either. They were assured that the Americans weren't interested in taking Native lands west of the Appalachian Mountains, even though the Americans' general, and future president, had already purchased thousands of acres of Native land west of the Appalachians from one of the kings across the Atlantic Ocean who had claimed the right to give it away.

The Americans began building forts in the new territories west of the Appalachians, from which they led raiding parties when the Natives misbehaved. One of these forts, Fort Shelby, was located at a trading post turned settlement the French called Prairie du Chien, just above the mouth of the Wisconsin along the Mississippi, where John Jacob Astor and his American Fur Company took up where the French and English had left off. The Americans were in the process of building Fort Shelby when the English and Americans went at it again, in the War of 1812, when, in 1814, the English assembled a war party of 650 redcoats, French *voyageurs*, and Natives, who traveled by canoe from Mackinac and Green Bay, up the Fox, over the portage, and down the Wisconsin to the Mississippi, where they surprised the Americans and captured Fort Shelby in the only battle in the Wisconsin territory ever fought by warring nations. The English held Fort Shelby until they were ordered to leave, after the English and Americans entered into the Treaty of Ghent, which ended the War of 1812. As you might guess, the Natives were not parties to the Treaty of Ghent, which returned to the Americans all lands the English had occupied during the war. As soon as the English retreated back up the Wisconsin, the Natives burned Fort Shelby to the ground, only to be rebuilt by the Americans as Fort Crawford in 1816, and Mr. Astor and his fur company were at it again, in lands now purportedly owned by Americans.

Setting aside for a moment these Treaties of Paris and Ghent, it surely is reasonable to ask, as a title company must, by what right did the Americans acquire title to these vast lands in the New World? Apparently, the issue was enough to cause King Ferdinand II of Spain, in a flicker of conscience, to ask his wise men whether taking land from Natives in the Americas was lawful. Two things, he was told: 1) under Roman law, government exists to protect property, and as the Natives had no government, according to Columbus, who never visited North America, they had no property, and thus did not own the land they had lived on for thousands of years; and 2) according to Aristotle, some people were just meant to be slaves, no fault of their own, just tough luck, and if they were by nature slaves, they were meant to have masters.[4] Enter Cortez and Pizarro, and the rape of the Aztecs and Incas, in the name of God.

But it remained over the centuries a nagging question, for people like the English and Americans, who prided themselves on the rule of law. John Locke, influenced by Thomas More, and on whom Thomas Jefferson relied in writing the Declaration of Independence, argued that Natives did not own their own lands because they did not grow anything on them, and if they didn't use the land, they didn't have any rights to them. At the time Locke came up with this excuse, unbeknownst to him, Natives in North America had been growing corn and beans for over 2,500 years, not to mention fishing and hunting game in these lands for 12,000 years, but then, fishing and hunting, and living off the land, and fighting and dying over the land, and burying your dead in the land, apparently, according to Locke, didn't count. That the Natives might have owned the land collectively, as opposed to a system in which a small minority owned all the land while others did all the work, apparently did not occur to liberal philosophers as a social and economic system worthy of the rule of law. After all, government existed to protect property, not people. The Europeans' inequitable concept of property was unheard of to the Natives of North America, to whom Jefferson referred in the Declaration of Independence as "merciless Indian Savages," the same Jefferson to whom marble monuments were erected, for having written "all men are created equal," when what he meant to say was "all White men with money," not poor White men, Asian men, African men, Hispanic men, Native men, and, of course, not women.

According to Locke, without citation, God, his God, did not want man to hold all land in common; he gave it "to the use of the Industrious and Rational, (and Labour was to be his Title to it)."⁵ So that's where title comes from. It comes from God, Locke's God, who gives it to the Industrious and Rational, according to standards which, while mostly held close to the vest, clearly exclude North American Natives. And suppose someone comes along who is more industrious and rational than the ones to whom God originally granted title. Should they not, according to the same logic, acquire title to the land from which they can achieve higher yields?

As a boy, John Muir, who grew up near the portage between the Fox and Wisconsin, overheard a discussion between his father and a neighbor. According to John's father, God could never have intended Natives to roam the land forever and never put it to good use, when productive Scots like himself could work the land and unleash its bountiful rewards. Then where would it stop, suggested the neighbor, when more industrious farmers came along and were able to "raise five or ten times as much on each acre as we did?"⁶

Well, no one was willing to go that far, surely not the colonists, who received their grants from the king and God, and that was good enough for them. And so there were initial land grants, and then treaties, lots of treaties, by which Americans entered into purportedly lawful contracts to acquire lands from Natives who, according to Locke, never owned them in the first place, and the treaties drew a series of imaginary lines in the sand across the continent, first here, then there, then a little further west, then a little further, lines ignored by settlers, voters, who kept coming, until the lines were redrawn, each time, further west, to protect settlers on lands they had trespassed upon, until finally Andrew Jackson, who had earned the nickname "Indian Killer," said enough of this nonsense, banished all pretense to hell, and exposed what had been the goal all along, passing the Indian Removal Act of 1830, which authorized the removal of all Native tribes to federal territory west of the Mississippi River, resulting in many Trails of Tears. Chief Justice John Marshall, speaking on behalf of the highest court in the land, ruled that the Indian Removal Act was unconstitutional as a matter of law, and therefore unenforceable. Like all imaginary lines, Marshall's opinion was ignored. So much for treaties, lines in the sand, and the rule of law.

The Indian Removal Act applied to all lands east of the Mississippi, which included the lands through which the Wisconsin flowed, in which but a handful of Whites, mostly fur traders and trespassing lead miners, lived at the beginning of the Nineteenth Century. That was the land of the Ho-Chunk, Menominee, and Sioux, and then, fleeing west, the Ojibwe, Ottawa, Mesquakie, Sauk, Mascouten, Potawatomi, and Kickapoo, battling each other for ever-scarcer resources: the Ottawa against the Ho-Chunk; the Menominee against the Ojibwe; the Ho-Chunk with the Menominee; the Mesquakie with the Sauk, Mascouten, and Kickapoo; the Mesquakie against the Ojibwe, Ottawa, and Potawatomi; the Menominee and Ho-Chunk against the Sauk; the Ho-Chunk against the Sioux; the Menominee against the Sioux, the Sioux against everyone, and everyone against the Americans.

The Sauk had been on the move for a century, from the St. Lawrence River, east into the Great Lakes, to west of Lake Erie, west of Lake Huron, then west of Lake Michigan, where, by 1766, they had established a large village along the Wisconsin, on a large plain shaped like a paw around which the river flowed, which Jonathan Carver, the first Englishman to write of the river, described as the "Great Town of the Saukies," the "largest and best built" Native town he had ever seen, with "ninety houses, each large enough for several families ... and streets regular and spacious."[7] But the Sauk kept moving, eventually traveling down the Wisconsin, and down the Mississippi to the mouth of the Rock River, where they settled at Saukenuk, one of the largest Native settlements on the continent, where up to 6,000 Sauk returned from various winter camps each spring. The fatal defect of Saukenuk, however, is that it lay along the eastern shore of the Mississippi.

In 1804, the Sauk had entered into a treaty, "skullduggery," per August Derleth, in which the Sauk and Mesquakie purportedly agreed to give up some fifty million acres, which included Saukenuk, in exchange for an upfront payment of $2,234.50, and annual payments thereafter of $600 worth of goods for the Sauk, and $400 worth of goods for the Mesquakie, with the assurance of the United States Government that the Sauk could continue to call Saukenuk home, until the government decided to sell it to someone else. Arm's length transaction to be sure.[8] After having continued to call Saukenuk home for twenty-five years, the Sauk returned to Saukenuk in the spring of 1829 to find Whites living in their town, fences around their fields, and lodges destroyed. The Sauk were told to leave and not come back, but some stayed, amidst quarrel, conflict, councils, and threats, feuding among chiefs, battles with other tribes, until the government sent troops, supported by local militias, mostly trespassing lead miners, and forced the Sauk west of the Mississippi.

Until April 1832, when a respected Sauk elder in his mid-sixties, *Ma-ka-tai-me-she-kia-kiak*, also known as Black Hawk, spurred on by a prophet's dream and the derision of Sauk women who wanted their cornfields back, led a band of around two thousand men, women, children, and warriors, east across the Rubicon, the Mississippi, in search of land to settle up the Rock River, into lands the federal government then called the State of Illinois, and the Michigan Territory, which at the time included the lands of the Wisconsin. So the Sauk were on the move again, as they had been for centuries, except this time, they were hunted by the United States Army, commanded by General Henry Atkinson, with Colonel Zachary Taylor, Colonel Albert Sidney Johnston, and Lieutenant Jefferson Davis in its ranks. The war cry swept across the land, among White settlers that is, who volunteered to join a militia, commanded by Colonel Henry Dodge, to support the army. Abraham Lincoln signed up for the militia for a brief time, his action limited to fighting mosquitoes. Up the Rock and over to the Four Lakes near present day Madison the Sauk fled, with their women and children, slower at first, then faster as the army closed in, leaving a trail of discarded pots and pans and blankets that slowed them down in the summer heat. They headed north and west of the Four Lakes toward the Wisconsin River, where the army and militia caught up with them, at a place now called Wisconsin Heights, along a high ridge overlooking the river from which Black Hawk, on his white horse, could see to the north the paw of land on which the Sauk had once thrived in the "Great Town" described by Jonathan Carver.

On the night of July 21, 1832, Black Hawk and his warriors fought a rearguard action, while the rest of the tribe slipped down the back side of the high ridge, across the sand barren terraces, and down to ford the river under cover of darkness and driving rain. A small group of women, children, old men, and warriors took to rafts to escape down the Wisconsin, while the majority of the tribe successfully crossed the Wisconsin, and headed west with the goal of recrossing the Mississippi. Jefferson Davis described the retreat as "the most brilliant exhibition of military tactics that I ever witnessed - a feat of most consummate management and bravery, in the face of an enemy of greatly superior numbers. Had it been performed by a White man, it would have been immortalized as one of the most splendid achievements in military history."[9] The Sauk had escaped, for the time being, but the army and militia regrouped, crossed the Wisconsin, and tracked the Sauk through thickets north of the Wisconsin River.

On July 29, 1832, those who had escaped by raft down the Wisconsin were massacred by a gunboat and soldiers waiting for them where the Wisconsin flowed into the Mississippi. Bands of Menominee and Ho-Chunk hunted down stragglers. Those who had crossed the Wisconsin after the battle of Wisconsin Heights made it to the Bad Axe River, and followed it down to the Mississippi, where they attempted to cross on August 1, 1832. They too were annihilated in the attempted crossing, men, women, and children, militia taking scalps for their collections. Those who escaped across the Mississippi were hunted down by Sioux warriors. During the entire exodus, Black Hawk had attempted to surrender three separate times.

Black Hawk slipped away from his tribe before the attempted crossing, (not exactly going down with the ship), and eventually was captured, imprisoned, then released, but as a condition to his release, he, his son, and a handful of renegade Sauk were forced to take a tour of eastern cities. In Norfolk, they appeared on a balcony before cheering fans, in Baltimore they went to the theater, one-upping President Indian Killer, also in attendance, with whom they shook hands, in Philadelphia they were guests of honor at a grand military parade, in New York they were feted at City Hall, with throngs of admirers, ladies yearning to kiss Black Hawk's handsome son, but by then the grand tour, having become too popular, had lost its appeal to their federal hosts, who cut short the traveling show, and sent them home back west, back to reality via Detroit, where ugly crowds burned their effigies, and then back to Iowa, where Black Hawk settled along the Iowa River to die. Shakespeare should have been around to tell the story.

And that brought an end to any Native resistance to manifest destiny in the lands through which the Wisconsin River flowed. The Americans' removal policy had reached its logical conclusion. Natives who had not accepted the plots of land to which they were confined were removed across the Mississippi, some of whom eventually returned, negotiating the right to purchase back from the Americans land that had once been their own.

And so the flow went on. Nothing is static. When a door closes, a gate opens, and as the Natives were swept away, White settlers rushed in. In 1800, only 200 some Whites had settled in what would become the Wisconsin Territory, primarily plying the fur trade. Starting around 1819, lead miners swarmed in to mine veins worked by Natives in what is now Northern Illinois and Southern Wisconsin, swelling to ten thousand by 1825. After the Black Hawk War, by 1840, the population in the Wisconsin Territory had risen to 30,000.

The White migration flowed in the opposite direction of the river. After the miners dug up all the lead to be had, and John Jacob Astor depleted the woods of profitable fur, the lumbermen moved north, upriver, where an "Empire in Pine,"[10] 16,000 square miles of 300- to 400-year-old trees, up to 200-feet tall, waited to be cut to size in the north woods of the Wisconsin Territory. By 1847, twenty-four sawmills operated on the river; six years later the number had reached one hundred, all along the water-way, the only means of transporting pine to market before the railroads came in the 1870s. Wing dams were built and towns and trading posts sprouted up along the river on sites of old Native camps, reaching far to the north to the river's source in Lac Vieux Desert.

And the lumberjacks came, in hordes, traveling upriver along Native trails, in heavy boots, blue trousers, red shirts and caps, rowdy and tough, melting pot of trouble, Irish, Swede, German, Norwegian, Finn, cossacks with axes and knives invading the woods, all winter long, harsh wind, freezing cold, deep snow, wielding sharp blades, felling tall trees, running, from the heavy, cracking, pounding crash of death, hauling tons of timber across the snow to the river's edge, each day, each night in kerosene camps, around blazing fires, with itinerant North Woods bards, one-armed blind Emery, and Shan T. Boy, singing and drinking, and fighting, and snoring, to wake before dawn and repeat the same day, over and over, until the spring melt came, when they emerged, grizzly and wild from the woods, hundreds at a time, with money in their pockets, pouring into nervous river towns, seeking booze, bawds, and battle.[11]

In spring, as the lumberjacks headed downriver, the raftsmen headed up, for work driving logs down the Wisconsin, settling logs into cribs, sixteen-by-sixteen foot square, up to seven cribs to a raft, ten to twenty rafts lashed together into a fleet, hundreds of feet long, carpets of hardwood afloat on the water, wet, icy spines to which the raftsmen clung on the harrowing ride downriver in the high water and ice floes of spring. If they had any choice, they would have chosen a better river. Studded with islands and sandbars, with cross currents and meanders, eddies, souse holes, rapids, falls, and boulders, the only difficulty was the Wisconsin itself, in high water and low. In high water in early spring, a good run could be made from the North Woods Pinery to St. Louis in about three weeks; a summer run could take months, if you got there at all. The languid days of summer made the Wisconsin almost too lazy to run, costing lumbermen a good deal of money; the raw rushing whitewater of spring made good time and money, but cost many lives.

As soon as ice started to break, the raftsmen would set off downriver, working, eating, sleeping on the long floating fleet of rafts that would be their home for weeks at a time, if they were lucky, the steersman, or star pilot, at the bow, the talisman at the rear, wielding oars sixty-feet long, with a crew of one to two men per raft, and the caravans moved downstream, slowly at first, thousands of fleets per spring, sometimes end to end for hundreds of miles, men preparing for battle, sleepless nights before shove off, quiet prayers, knowing that the falls, rapids, and crushing boulders, which Ojibwe and *voyageurs* had the good sense to portage, waited around the bend, knowing death for some was certain.

And they set off, picking up speed through Pelican Rapids, named after migrating white pelicans, past old Ojibwe camps, through the land of the menacing Hodag, into and out of Whirlpool Rapids, huge rafts of logs and men, caroming off rocks, rushing whitewater, through Grandmother Falls, Grandfather Falls, two miles long dropping ninety-four feet, Posey

Rapids, and Jenny Bull Falls, steep surges of white waves roiling, losing men in the icy water, crushed against boulders by heaving timber, to Big Bull Falls, dropping twenty-three feet in a third of a mile, around Lumberyard Rock, ten to twenty miles an hour, claiming fourteen lives in one spring freshet, and on to the most treacherous, Little Bull Falls, with its four granite islands, steeling against the torrent, deafening "roar of the bull," colliding ice and driftwood logs, rushing faster, past Kelly Rock, where 200 lost their lives, navigating the hard left turn, star pilot in front, clinging to the bucking raft, jerking the oar, through the Jaws of Little Bull Falls, rafts and men disappearing in the rocking waves, over a shelf, forty-five degree pitch, into a gorge thirty-feet deep, strewn with rocks, Scylla and Charybdis, Shoemaker Rock and a whirlpool eddy, swallowing men alive, ("And now the Old Wisconsin is rolling o'er his bones, his companions are the muskellunge, his grave a bed of stones"),[12] on through Shaurette's Rapids, Bloomer's Rapids, through the Hog Hole Bean Pot, then easing, mercifully, out of the Northern Highlands into the lowland marshes of the Central Plains, past cranberry bogs and blueberry fields, on through Grand Rapids, past Sugar Loaf Rock, and finally, through Whitney Rapids, the last on the river.

Followed by miles and miles of meanders, where the flow slows, through twists and turns, cattails and rice marshes, oxbows, bayous, and slough channels, past Pettenwell Rock, Castle Rock, past sandbars, and islands that float downstream, past the Yellow River, and Lemonweir Flats, draining swamps through sediment of proglacial lake, and as Louis's Bluff comes into view, the current begins to quicken again, approaching the Upper Dells, *Neehahkecoonaherah*, where rocks strike together, toward the Narrows, sheer walls of Cambrian sandstone, outlier rock formations, gorges, and glens, Stand Rock, into Witches' Gulch, Cold Water Canyon, faster now through the deep gorge, past Steamboat Rock, Ladies Slipper, Black Hawk Cave, where manitous live, past Artists' Glen, and Notch Rock, and the hard right turn through Devil's Elbow, where, in the 1850s, from the bridge spanning the river, spectators lined the rails, festive occasion, watching the danger, star pilots, dressed in costume, waving, navigating the Jaws, one raft at a time, racing past in whitewater, and settling into the Lower Dells, to cheers from the bridge, then faster again, past Romance Cliff, Angel Rock, Witches' Window, and Paul Bunyan's Heels, and then, once past Observation Point, the river and time begin to slow again, sandstone gives way to bottomland, the river widens, the current weakens, the bane of raftsmen, running aground, on islands and sandbars all the way to the Mississippi, logjams, busted rafts, driftwood, steamships run aground within the wide bluffs of the river valley, flowing into counties of sand, and sandhill cranes, where Aldo Leopold, naturalist poet, bought a shack to write an almanac, where thousands of migrant women pickers, on a lark and a spree, traveled by train during the Hops Craze, singing and dancing together at night, where millions upon millions of passenger pigeons were bludgeoned to extinction, and downriver past the portage, place of "Carry On Back," the two-mile carry, linking the Fox to the Wisconsin, the Atlantic to the Mississippi, the Mississippi to the Gulf, where John Muir spent his boyhood, "Oh, that glorious Wisconsin wilderness!,"[13] and on down around the paw of the "Great Town," past Wisconsin Heights where Black Hawk wept, and down into the lower Wisconsin Riverway, old Helena, where the army and militia tore down cabins to raft across on Black Hawk's trail, past the old shot tower, where the river dramatically dips, bottoms out in its southern descent, and turns hard to the west, on a calm current to the Mississippi, passing Taliesin high on the southern bluff, the domain of Driftless and Frank Lloyd Wright, fields, hills, ridges, and valleys, overlooking the river, with his Fellowship, wives, genius, and love of place.

And it is here, that the flow begins to subside, now that the history, more than you ever wanted, has been told, because it is here, just downriver, where vultures can now be seen, over a hill along the valley's southern ridge, circling above a body that lies sprawled in the high grass.

Around the bend where the Wisconsin turns to the west, on the northern bank, past what is now the Highway 23 bridge and the town of Spring Green, lies a large cove, protected by a wooded island, where Ray's Riverside Resort stands upon a grassy hill that gently slopes down to a makeshift beach, where a row of aluminum canoes are tipped over against a tree, and a group is forming along the edge of the water at high noon on a Wednesday in mid-June. Four men with shaved heads, in maroon robes, are setting an oriental rug along the shore, while another, watching, holds a brass urn under one arm. They are all smiling. Bright cumulus clouds are floating, reflected in the water, one of those bright mid-June days, too warm, not for the monks, for whom every day is a blessing, but for the mourners, for whom many days were cursed, in various forms of Sunday best, and worst, not certain what to expect or wear, most not caring for protocol or decorum, long dispensed with hereabouts, each to his own, some lives broken, some dreams forgotten, dreams of escape, each day, just another, in a long line of playing out the string, until they ended up like good old Ray, with folks gathering along the bank of the river, to say goodbye.

Most of the fifty or so mingling along the back side of Ray's Resort on the small slope of lawn leading down to the river had grown up in local townships carved from the river valley, flotsam and jetsam of long-dead Natives and pioneers, lead miners and farmers and loggers and raftsmen and railroaders and teachers and small shop owners and rascals and toughs, and the women forced into this hardship, heroines, all scratching out a living along the river, leaving their descendants with little choice but to do the same. Over the years, those who showed promise mostly left, leaving behind the hard core, committed, or snake bit, who for whatever reason never got away, and remained to eke out a living any way they could, two or three jobs, seasonal work, spending what they earned, no way out. The two small towns nearby were Spring Green and Lone Rock, Milwaukee and Mississippi Railroad towns built six miles apart in the 1840s for the line that ran along the north side and parallel to the river, westward through the river valley toward the Mississippi.

The town of Spring Green sat in the bend on the northern bank where the river ducked south and veered to the west, across the water from the old shot tower, still standing, and the ghosts of old Helena, and the valley of the God-almighty Lloyd Jones, over which, years later, his nephew the architect built a secular manse with a new age brow, theosophists, missionaries spreading prairie gospel throughout the world, bringing international acclaim and an air of sophistication to the little town of Spring Green, which it never wanted, probably resented, and never fully accepted, which is why, after Frank died and was buried per his wishes in his beloved valley within sight of his famous home, his vengeful wife dug up his bones and moved them to Arizona, which for years pretty much summed up the relationship between the town and its most famous son. Years later, a theater company formed, set a stage in a hollow between two tall hills in the valley across the river from the town, and the plays of Shakespeare could be heard there on summer nights, with owls and coyotes in the distance, and the players would come for the summer and live in the town, so the town had that going for it. But the town itself, on the other side of the river from all these fancy goings on, always seemed to keep its distance, the actors in fair weather would come and go, but by wintertime, the town returned to form, and folks scraped by as best they could, just as three generations of ancestors, and Natives for thousands of years, had done before them.

Lone Rock, on the other hand, had no such pretensions. Sure, Dr. Bertha Reynolds had given Lindberg a lift over the river, and one winter night its temperature had allegedly dipped to the lowest in the world, but mostly it was known for its enterprising townsfolk, who, as a sign of the times since the beginning of time, chipped away at its eponymous and prominent tower of sandstone to build basements for their homes, until the lone rock loomed no more over the river, and nothing was left but the town named after the rock they had shattered into wreckage. At one time the town had potential, only town in the county on the main line, shipping center for produce and pig iron, with a hotel and a good school and a drug store and a local band, but that was long ago, before highways and semis crossed the iron rails, and, as is so often the case with potential, it just didn't happen, and years later, after the local school closed down and then the feed mill, families and stores moved away, and but for the bait shop, branch bank, gas station, and a bar called the Mad House Inn, the old brick buildings along Main Street stood mostly empty. The town now boasted two mobile home parks, a Fourth of July parade with car show and tractor pull, an abandoned train station, and a smattering checkerboard of old houses and empty lots. And in its humble downtrodden state was the town's silver lining, for it was off the grid, out of the way, where the sheriff visited only if he had to, a place to hide out, escape, and become forgotten. And so long as there were folks who wanted to live beyond the pale, it had a snowball's chance, so long as those folks hung in there, but the odds weren't good. Dan Hurley's son, Billy, thought it perfect.

These were the towns and people with whom Ray, resort owner, had lived his life. The resort he fell into, which bore his name, hugged the river just west of Spring Green, his house, nestled on Long Lake, an elongated slough, that ran north of the river, just outside Lone Rock. Ray had been luckier than most. One brother died in a motorcycle accident, one drank himself to death, another ran away as far as he could, so that when his parents died two months apart, the pig farm went to him, and he sold it as fast as he could. He invested the proceeds in a beat to hell resort on the north bank of the river outside Spring Green, one of the few remaining private lots, grandfathers, to survive along the lower Wisconsin. Ray made a number of improvements over the years, doing most of the work himself. He rehabbed the old cabins and built a couple new ones, with river views. He dug out a swimming pool, attached a plastic water slide, paved a basketball court, expanded the parking lot, bought new canoes, cleared a field for an RV park, and extended and rehabbed the one low slung building into a shrine to knotty pine for bikers, campers, and locals, with a long bar facing out wide tall windows onto a wooden deck, the grassy hill sloping down to the beach, the river, the sandbar, and the island, framed by birch trees along the shore, with Nashville on the juke box, weekend blowouts, and drunken fights late on Saturday nights in the parking lot.

Renting out canoes was a sideline at first, but over the years the business took off. Ray's Riverside became a destination for urban refugees and pickup cowboys, and when the weather got warm and the river low, they came in droves, a summer time retreat of large groups and couples, families and rowdies, camping on sandbars, aluminum canoes with Native names, inner tube flotillas with overflowing coolers, laughing and lolling along on the same slow current, along the same route paddled by the ancients, French trappers, Marquette and Joliet. And Ray became an icon, tall, lean, cowboy boots, straight cut jeans, denim shirt, red bandana, thick brown hair tied back into a pony tail, full beard, back slapping, generous, judging no one, all welcome, no bias, no bullshit; the only thing he didn't put up with was nasty, mean people, who learned their lessons soon enough. Little League sponsor, Fourth of July fireworks contributor, police and firemen picnic supporter, host of the hungry for Thanksgiving dinners, leader of the Harley Riders' Christmas toy drive. Never gave money to politicians, avoided politics like the plague, which made his friendship with Dan Hurley a mystery.

Local employer of bartenders, cabin sweepers, groundskeepers, Econoline drivers hauling racks of canoes and ten inner tubes at a time, dropping off upriver, picking up downriver, the bedraggled, muddy, soaking wet, over served, sunburnt, modern *voyageurs* of the river. Over forty years, he had employed half the town when down on their luck, in need of a break, a second chance. Most everybody had a story or memory about Ray, and most were good ones.

Danny Redbird had one. Joey Larocca, too. Danny, short, pock-marked, long stringy black hair, just now headed out the door of the bar that led down the grassy hill to the shore, where the monks and ex-cons, farmers and bikers, shop owners and laborers, teachers and thespians, hippies and hardhats, a stray doctor and lawyer, and a host of aged delinquents in various shades of camouflage, all with a drink in hand, were gathering at the shore. Danny held a Cuervo on the rocks in a plastic cup, followed by Joey, sipping Southern Comfort, both van drivers for Ray several years back. Danny grew up, if that can truly be said, in one of Lone Rock's trailer parks, the one on the other side of the tracks. Petty thief under a bad sign, Danny's kicks were joyrides and burglaries. Never armed, never violent, always caught, never reformed, nothing in it for him, just liked the notoriety. But he was out now, heard about Ray, and called up his old pal Joey, stocky preacher's son, who, along with his girlfriend Judy, had the local meth market cornered until they got busted three years ago. They both were sentenced by Judge Ebersold, who, smiling, now graciously held the bar door open for them. Ray had given Danny and Joey jobs when no one else would. So they thought it best to pay their respects, to the only guy who ever gave them a fair shake, even though Ray fired them both, for pilfering a drunken tuber's purse.

Taking advantage of the judge's chivalry, Doris the librarian, coffee, Flo the hairdresser, double vodka tonic twist of lime, Marge, farmers' co-op business manager, PBR, and Mary Beth, third grade teacher, Cosmo, followed Danny and Joey past the judge, out the door, across the deck, and down the hill to the beach. Judge Ebersold, no cup in hand, followed them out the door into the sunshine, glittering river glare, smiling now at the assemblage gathering along the shore, inordinate number of women, bouffant hairdos, who came to pay their last respects to Ray.

Ray remained a bachelor till the end. Any other arrangement would have been self-defeating, for Ray had his own arrangement, with the community, or at least a substantial percentage of the women who lived in it. Simply, he loved well, truly, and often, and was loved in return, without strings. Wilt would have been a rival had Ray lived in a larger pond, it was all a matter of scale, the drive was the same. But for Ray it was not in the conquest. Improbably, Ray never made love to a woman he didn't love, and once loved, always loved, because Ray imbued love, for the land from which he came and the people struggling on it, seeing goodness and beauty where others did not, leaving all those he touched a little stronger, lighter, after talking with Ray maybe things weren't so bad after all, a little more reason to carry on, because here was someone who truly cared, with respect and dignity, who made those he loved, in the moment and each day thereafter, feel special.

And he did it all with pure honesty. All but one of the women in attendance on the shore had heard the same words from Ray before he rocked their worlds:

"My dear, I would love to make love with you, to please you, any way you want, any way I can, any way you've dreamed but were afraid to ask, and I'll be yours, completely, and I'll love you as well as any man has ever loved a woman since the beginning of time, but I can't do that without your promise, that you'll never expect anything from me, you'll never have me, because I can't be had, by anyone or anything. When I see you in town and say hello you'll see a good friend, forever, I'll help you if I can, lend an ear, a shoulder, but you've got to understand, you can't expect anything more. I won't be your boyfriend, your husband, or the father of your children. I'll never live with you. There won't be cards or presents or flowers. There'll never be any strings. So if you're looking for anything more than what I'm offering, then no hard feelings and best of luck to you. I hope you understand. I'm just trying to be honest with you. We need honesty to love. And so, with all of that, I would love to love you. So, what do you say?"

The words were memorized, remained the same, each time, holding her hands, staring into blue, green, brown, gray eyes, hair color, skin color, old, young, tall, short, large, small, didn't matter to Ray, non-discriminatory, he would love any woman, and did, so long as it was on his terms.

And, of course, invariably, they would agree to his terms, and he would rock their world, as he promised, and they would share that love, and friendship, for the rest of their days, through marriages and divorces, and in their small community his lovers knew each other, became friends, looked after him, and each other, protected him, and held interventions if a paramour strayed from her promise.

The one woman in the large group at the shore who had not heard Ray's terms of engagement was the one everyone suspected had been the lone exception. Mona stood now barefoot in the water, gleaming white cotton shirt tucked tight into blue jeans, sleeves and pant legs rolled up, copper golden skin lustrous in the sun, thick nest of black hair draped across her slight shoulders, not tall, but taller than short, lithe-wiry strong, high cheek bones, deep brown almond eyes, a dark jewel in the sun on the shore.

No one knew where she came from. They guessed her age between twenty and forty. One day about five years earlier she just showed up at Ray's as if she belonged there all along, another lost soul he had taken in, with no back story, no family, friendly enough, but aloof, not haughty, avoided conversation, foreign, forbidden, and over time the fantasy of every man in town. Rumors swirled, wife, daughter, cousin, niece, courtesan, if a lover, why the exception, why now, blackmail?, pregnant? Native American, African American, Lebanese, Armenian, Syrian, Hispanic, Italian, Jewish,

Greek, Turk, Iraqi, Tajik, Afghan, Uzbek, Aleut, Yanomamo, perhaps all of the above, swirling in a melting pot of intrigue and allure.

One thing everybody could see soon enough, she worked damn hard. She started cleaning cabins, whirlwind, pure energy, never breaking a sweat, working others out of a job, so Ray had her haul canoes, paddles, preservers, first woman to hold the job, denim shirt, tight jeans, blue bandana kerchief holding back her hair, hoisting aluminum canoes onto and off of flat beds down to shore for those setting off from the resort's beach, driving the old Econoline with chatty passengers upriver, towing the rig with rattling canoes, unloading for the trip downriver, to boat landings where hours later she would be waiting, always at the right time, saying only what was necessary, from early summer high water through autumn languor, and into the off season, when Ray discovered she was good with numbers, too, could work out accounts, and over the second winter season she cleaned up his ledgers, so for the first time since he could remember Ray had a handle on his revenue, costs, and margins.

Folks began to see some improvements around the resort, perennials planted, windows cleaned, back deck expanded, with new deck chairs, restrooms spotless, top-shelf liquor, well-run bar, updated electric and water hookups for the RV park, just a number of little things that made Ray's old resort look a little less run down than it had become, and lo and behold business picked up, and Ray and everyone else knew the only thing different was Mona, and not in a pushy sort of take over kind of way, very backseat, stayed in her lane, discrete, sensitive, respectful, never asked for anything, whatever Ray paid was fine, and Ray could not be more pleased, or grateful.

When she first arrived, Ray let her have the smallest of his cabins, one room, with kitchenette, wooden table, sofa, stuffed chair, twin bed, and there she stayed, content, with a view of the river. Visitors to Ray's house on Long Lake might find her doing dishes, reading in a corner, or fishing on the dock, and so they put two and two together, or so they thought, but they would be wrong, because she never stayed the night, and Ray never asked. You could catch her riding her little motorcycle back and forth to town, or on a remote country road, but mostly to see her required a trip to the resort, which some would do for that purpose alone, unless you were on the river, in which case you could catch her most every day, reading ripples, currents, sand bars, exploring back hidden sloughs. Far as anyone could tell, Ray had been her only friend for years, until Billy came along, but even then, it was hard to tell who or what was up.

Billy stood beside her in the water, in high black All Stars, no socks, commando in jeans, black tee shirt, tall, lean, thick brown hair, center part, draped his face like a hoodie, look of Jesus in him, without the aura, expressionless, tortured. Billy was a Ray project, though Ray never knew what to make of him. Tough to read, hard to know whether anything going on inside. Ray had seen drugs hollow a person before, suspected Billy was such a case, but no sign he'd been on anything since he arrived. That was two and a half years ago, just before the summer season, and Ray took him on doing odd jobs, hauling canoes. Ray owed it to Billy's dad, Ray's best friend for years, whom Ray deeply respected. Billy would never set the world on fire, Ray knew that much, more deliberate, steady, an ambler. If you want something done yesterday Billy was not your man, but if you weren't in a hurry, and Ray rarely was, Billy would do the job and do it right, at his own pace, in his own time.

Unlike Mona, everyone knew about Billy. His family had been coming up to Wyoming Township along the south bank of the river since Billy was in diapers. City folk might invest in the hills from time to time, but most preferred to squeeze in along a lake somewhere further north, and few stayed for any length of time, but the Hurleys were the exception, they were from the big city, but they were of the country, and for that were respected. Billy's old man, muckety-muck in politics apparently, as Ray would tell it, kingmaker in one of the biggest cities in the world, but you could never tell from what you saw in these parts, never held himself out, always courteous, respectful, of everybody, blended in, nothing special, not out here, and he was given space, and over time, became one of them. His wife, may she rest in peace, endeared by all, farmer's market regular, made pies for bake sales, one of the quilts she helped make with the Spring Green Women's Club earned a blue ribbon at the State Fair, of which the town was particularly proud.

The kid was a different story. As a boy, withdrawn, trailing his dad everywhere, didn't say much, limp handshake, no eye contact, background. As he got older, stories of wild parties on the hill, bonfires, shouts, screams, heavy metal, fireworks, and then there was that time he crashed his car into Parsons' field all alone at two in the morning heading back to Madison. But mostly what they knew came a couple of years ago when he made the local papers, big time, with news of his drug bust in Chicago, his girlfriend, his kids in the back seat, his conviction, and then he shows up with his tail between his legs, living in a single room above the Mad House Inn overlooking Lone Rock's deserted Main Street.

Stuck to himself mostly, since then. Hired on with Ray, free time learning and fishing the river, evenings on a bar stool, bottles of beer from Lee Anne at the Mad House Inn, punching songs on the juke box, nursing beers, keeping to himself and out of harm's way. Ray did what he could, tried to befriend him, the kid listened, but gave nothing up, and they just went on, dealing with each other, most that could be said. Over time, he could be seen speaking to Mona, furtively, as if the world was watching, listening, as if anybody cared. They began to explore the river together, disappearing into marshes and hidden ponds, returning with walleye, northern, panfish, and, as time passed, on occasional nights, you wouldn't find Billy at the Mad House Inn bar, and his room remained dark and empty. But even then, they never seemed together, keeping their distance, even when standing next to each other, as they did in the water at the shore, waiting for Ray's whatever you call it to start.

Whatever you call it was as good as it gets, the best one could say. After all, the celebration of life in death is a complicated thing, especially for Ray, who was not a non-believer, he believed in many things, just not religion, rituals, superstitions, which made planning his send off a challenge. The Buddhist monks were Marion's idea, knowing Ray wouldn't mind, probably closest to Ray's world view, beauty of the moment sort of thing, inside of us, not out there, and if for no other spiritual reason their maroon robes glowing in the sun gave much needed color to the proceedings.

Marion owned a barn, an oasis really, tucked into 200 acres along a remote turn of a back road, rough-hewn uneven stairs up four haphazard floors filled with Ikat weavings, shadow puppets, batik textiles, singing brass bowls, Bhutan temple drums, Timor fabrics, wax cast bronzes, Tibetan prayer chimes, wooden yak bells, bronze elephant bells, teak furniture, child protectors, Sasak figurines, lava stone Buddhas and bodhisattvas and Ganesh, and antiques and artifacts from artisans she had befriended over decades in corners of India, Indonesia, and Nepal, whose creations traveled around the globe huddled in dark containers, across the Pacific, halfway across America, into the remote hills of the Wisconsin River Valley, each to find their own comfortable resting place, each with their own story, along the walls, shelves, and floors of Marion's improbable barn. On the grounds of the farm, she founded a Dharma Center and Buddha Healing Center with resident monks to bring instruction and healing to the farmers and plain folks of the valley, if they were so inclined, and if not, that was fine, too, no proselytizing, no heavy hand, just kindness, and peace. She stood now next to the monks, little stocky, flowing white hair, white knit tunic over billowing brown skirt, broad smile.

If there was any structure at all to what was about to happen it was Marion's doing, having talked it over with Ray in his last days. It was her idea to mix Ray's ashes with grains of brightly colored sand from the mandala the monks had made, dismantled, and were about to offer to the river, and Ray figured that was as good a way to go as any, and, anyone's guess, might even help in the next life, so why not, and it would please Marion, whom he had loved for many years.

So there was Marion, surrounded by her monks, and fifty-some souls gathered in a semi-circle around her on a glorious day on the water's edge at Ray's resort, with flashes of blinding ripples in the constant flow behind her, standing before the expectant faces, a little nervous actually, waiting, wondering, because they were behind schedule, and most had no idea what they were waiting for. But as he stood in the water with his shoes on, Billy knew, and it filled him with dread and disgust.

They were waiting for his dad to show, the mensch of honor, as always, Ray's good buddy. He would know what to say, hit the right notes, capture Ray as no one could, crystallize his life, his virtues, his influence, tell funny stories, make everyone laugh, raise him from the dead, and into their hearts, all better having known him, and should carry on in kind. He would close with sorrow, a tear, not a dry eye.

It would be just fucking perfect, Billy thought.

Except Billy's dad was now almost a half hour late, and the crowd was restless. Ray was a great guy and all, but they all had lives, kids, jobs, things to do, get the show on the road, and finally, Judge Ebersold, who had a sentencing hearing at two o'clock, walked solemnly up to the rug where Marion and the four monks were standing, and whispered to Marion, who shrugged her shoulders, nodded her head, and made way for the judge, who cleared his throat before addressing the crowd.

"Hello, everyone. Sorry we're a little behind schedule. Ray wanted Dan Hurley to say a few words here today (he said in Billy's direction), and we were waiting for him to show, but it looks like he's been delayed, and with all due respect to Ray, I know he would understand if we went ahead under the circumstances. I really wasn't prepared for this, but I knew Ray well, as I know you all did, so I'll do my best, and feel badly that Dan wasn't here to say goodbye to his good friend.

"I guess the highest compliment I could give Ray is that he was, heart and soul, one of us, perhaps the best of us, though he would deny it. I know he touched all of us in one way or another (he regretted these words as soon as he said them, ladies blushing, everyone smiling), whether giving a helping hand, lending an ear, or making us laugh, he was always there for each and every one of us. We have lost a friend, a rock, a tall tree with deep roots and strong branches that reached into all of our lives. A guy like Ray doesn't come along often, and he will be impossible to replace, but we all have to pick up the slack, be there for each other as he was there for us, pick up where he left off, love each other as he loved us, and in that way try to keep his memory alive. Ray was not a religious man, but he had a great spirit, embodied in every cabin, canoe, tree, blade of grass, grain of sand, hope, and dream you see around us today. And his spirit will always be with us, in the strong current in the river behind me, in the colors of autumn, the eagles overhead, the islands, the sandbars, the harsh winter winds. As much as he loved all of us, Ray probably loved this river even more, his great respect for the constant flow, the lives and travels of the rivermen and women who came before us, over thousands of years, whether Native, *voyageur*, or logger, who lived and loved this twisting ever changing stream as he did, for whom the river was life itself, and death, and I am certain he is now taking his place and passing with them, down this great river behind me, leaving memories of that great warm light of his that we will carry with us the rest of our lives."

The judge thought he had rebounded nicely. He turned to Marion and nodded. Marion took the urn and, leaning down, began to pour what was left of Ray and the mandala into the flow, which accepted and carried the gifts downstream, and as she did so, the judge gave his parting words:

"And so, as we say goodbye to our dear friend, let's close as he closed, every night, closing time, one last time, let's give Ray one last call, and give it loud enough to scare the coyotes out of their dens, and let them know that Ray's spirit is now with them."

And with that Judge Ebersold raised his head to the sky and began to howl, and each of them at the shore did the same, even the monks, everyone howling as loud as they could, as they had done so often with Ray behind the bar, howling so loud coyotes trembled in their sleep, and the slumbering moon shuddered, howling and laughing and crying just as Ray would have wanted, in uplifted unified song, and with that the ceremony, such as it was, came to an end, the crowd began to disperse, the rug rolled up, and as the monks bowed in reverence to the ashes and sand swirling down river to the west, Billy could make out a vortex of vultures circling in the sky above the valley's southern ridge in the distance.

Conrad Wilcoxsin, the stray lawyer, paid his respects from the back deck, tall, thin, slightly bent at the waist, gray rumpled suit, white shirt, narrow black tie, tie clip, wisps of hair along the temples of his bald narrow head, floppy leather suitcase on the wooden deck leaning up against his leg. As the mourners left the shore, Conrad Wilcoxsin headed down to it, briefcase in hand, with the long careful steps of a sandhill crane, chin and Adam's apple vying for the lead. He came loping down the hill and on to the sand at the shore, where Mona and Billy still stood, in the water, adrift and a little stunned now that Ray, and nothing less than the lives they had led, in Mona's case for years, disappeared into the swift current downstream.

"Excuse me, Miss Mona," Mr. Wilcoxsin said. He was formal by nature, but more so in this case, confused as he was by the uncertain relationship between his client and the woman standing at the shore, to whom he had never spoken.

"Hello, Miss Mona, I am Conrad Wilcoxsin."

"I know that Mr. Wilcoxsin."

"I am, or was, Ray's attorney."

"I know that, too, Mr. Wilcoxsin."

"I need to speak with you."

"This is not the time."

"Oh, Miss Mona, to the contrary, this indeed is the time, quite necessary actually."

"Please, call me Mona."

"I think I'd be more comfortable with Miss."

Mona looked at Billy, said nothing.

"It's a matter of some importance."

Mona looked into the water and then at Mr. Wilcoxsin.

"Then what is it?"

Mr. Wilcoxsin looked into the water, around at the trees, back at the resort, then at Billy.

"Is there somewhere," he said under his breath, "where we might speak in private?"

Mona looked around. "Everyone's gone," she said.

"Well, not everyone," Mr. Wilcoxsin said, looking at Billy. "You see, this involves a legal matter, and you personally."

"I do not need a lawyer, Mr. Wilcoxsin."

"Perhaps not," said Mr. Wilcoxsin, "but perhaps you first should hear what I have to say before reaching that conclusion."

"What is it?" she asked abruptly.

"Well, first, this concerns only you, Miss," he said with a glance at Billy, "and is a matter of some importance…"

"Yes, you said that," Mona said, annoyed, not at all curious.

"And if it is to be disclosed in the presence of a third person," he said, as if Billy weren't standing there, "that third person should only be one in whom you have the utmost faith and trust."

These were the first words of Mr. Wilcoxsin that Mona really heard. She had not considered the issue as presented by Mr. Wilcoxsin quite in that way before. Did she? Had it come to that? Here? Now? She gave it some thought, awkward silence.

"If you have something to say to me, say it," she said, with a glance in Billy's direction.

Billy pulled his hair behind his ears, shifted feet.

"Here?" said Mr. Wilcoxsin. "Isn't there some place we can go?"

"Here, now," said Mona, fixing her eyes on Mr. Wilcoxsin in a penetrating stare to which he was not accustomed, "and make it short, no details."

Mr. Wilcoxsin had the feeling the tables had turned, he was at her mercy, unusual, just the way she looked at him.

"Well, then, so be it," he said, flustered, naked, without a desk. He rested the briefcase on his bony knee, pulled back the leather strap, reached in, and pulled out a document of several pages that was stapled at the top to a blue hem that covered the back side.

"I have here Ray's Last Will and Testament," said Mr. Wilcoxsin.

"Oh, for God's sake," said Mona, "this has to be done now?"

"Maybe you should hear what he has to say," Billy interjected, respectfully.

"Yes, yes, indeed," said Mr. Wilcoxsin, "quite right. A matter of some importance, you see, oh, yes, I did say that."

"Three times," said Mona.

"Okay, well then, not quite as I anticipated," Mr. Wilcoxsin said, shaking his head at the two of them standing in the water, "but, you see," he stammered, and then blurted, "according to Ray's will," which he brandished before them, "you, Miss Mona, are the primary beneficiary, of, well, most everything," his long outstretched arm turned in a broad embrace of the shore, the cabins, the basketball court, the RV park, the parking lot, the resort itself.

Mr. Wilcoxsin waited in vain for a response from Mona, but none was forthcoming, from either of them, stoic, unmoved.

"Did you understand what I just said?" asked Mr. Wilcoxsin.

"That is not possible," said Mona. "He never said anything about this."

"Oh, indeed, it is very much the case," said Mr. Wilcoxsin. "As I said, and as you said you know, I am, or was, Ray's lawyer. I drafted the document myself. I am the executor of his estate. I apologize for having to broach the topic under these circumstances, but as you can imagine, as far as the business is concerned," he said, looking back at the resort, "it is necessary to make arrangements for the continuation of the enterprise, or its liquidation, as you should deem appropriate."

Mona stood there, motionless, thoughts swirling like the current, grappling with the astonishing news.

"You mean, everything?" she finally asked.

"I'm afraid, yes, everything, the resort, the house, the canoes, everything."

"I am not a businesswoman, Mr. Wilcoxsin," said Mona.

"With all due respect, Miss, my client thought otherwise. I also was instructed to say, and as the document reflects," he said waving the will, "my client…"

"For God's sake you mean Ray," said Mona, irritated.

"Yes, my client, Ray, wanted me to express, as this document reflects, his wish, not his direction, mind you, there is no such obligation, his hope, if you will, that you will continue to run the resort. He also instructed that I express to you his confidence that, if you should decide to do so, he was certain that you would do so, in his words, 'a whole lot better than I (he) ever did.'"

Mr. Wilcoxsin, still nervous in her presence, not quite sure why, tried to smile.

Mona, stunned. This Mr. Wilcoxsin was not the joking kind. And Ray clearly was capable of doing something harebrained. Although, in its way, it did make sense. No one else came close to knowing the resort as she did, and it was a way to keep part of him alive long after his death.

"Well, wow, this is going to take a while to sink in, but, I guess, if that's really the case," Mona said, sizing up Mr. Wilcoxsin, "I think I may need a lawyer."

"Oh," said Mr. Wilcoxsin confused, "you mean, oh, I see, well, I would be reluctant to do so on your personal behalf, since you are the primary beneficiary, and I am the executor, conflict of interest, appearance of impropriety, that sort of thing, you know."

"No, I don't."

"But, if you mean the business, are you asking if I would represent the business, which you will own, of course, as a result of the bequests in my client's, Ray's, will?" he asked, uncertain.

"Yes."

"Well," Mr. Wilcoxsin straightened, inches taller, pleased with this unexpected outcome, "I would be honored to do so, Miss Mona."

"Mona."

"Conrad, then."

"Thank you, Mr. Wilcoxsin. I expect you will see to the details and not bore me with them. Give me what I need to know, and no more, always. You should know, if we are to work together, which frankly I am struggling with, and please don't take that personally, but you should know, I cannot stand people who love to hear themselves talk, and it's been said that lawyers in general like to do just that, so please, with me, going forward, know that I speak to communicate, and I expect that you will do the same. Is that understood?"

"Understood, Miss, uh, I mean, Mona."

"Well, Mr. Wilcoxsin, I think I'll need a couple of days to think this over, kind of a lot at the moment, but I guess I need to ask, what do we do in the meantime?"

"That is entirely up to you," said Mr. Wilcoxsin, "you are now, for lack of a more appropriate word, the boss, so to speak."

"Well, we can't just shut it down, we've got reservations, we'll keep on I guess," Mona said, looking at Billy. "I'll give you a call in the next day or so, Mr. Wilcoxsin, and I guess it makes sense that I come see you in your office sometime next week."

"Yes, that would be most appropriate, and I will very much look forward to your call," he said looking around. "Well, goodbye then, and, uh, thank you, thank you very much."

And with that, Mr. Wilcoxsin put Ray's documents back into his leather briefcase, and, stepping carefully, with long strides up the hill, disappeared around the corner of the business establishment that would remain his client, somehow enlivened after his first meeting with Miss Mona, a little thrilled actually, a little taller, a little younger.

Mona looked at Billy.

"Wow," she said in disbelief.

"Wow is right," Billy replied, as they walked together out of the water and up the grassy slope. "Smart move on Ray's part when you think about it, you are the one."

"Wow."

"You can do this."

"Will you help?" she asked, looking up at him.

"Yeah, well, about that faith and trust thing."

"Utmost faith and trust."

"Yeah, that."

"I haven't been the most faithful and trustworthy."

"I don't care what you've done before. My past hasn't prepared me for this either. I'm a little blown away, as you can imagine. But we're here now, and I'm going to need help. Will you help?"

As a rule, one that came naturally, Billy shunned responsibility, and suspected there was more to her question, but she was looking up into his eyes now, deep brown almond, with black hair gleaming against her white shirt in the sun, not plaintively, but directly, powerfully, with unmistakable imminence, on the bus or off, a linchpin on which a life may turn, anything other than yes an eternal recrimination, lost forever, and yet all of that, important as it may seem, didn't matter, because she was looking at him, with those eyes, and he couldn't say no to her, and so he said,

"Yes."

"Good."

That's all she said. He suffered tremors inside.

"Now, what about your dad? Odd he didn't turn up. Something must have happened."

"I could give two shits. He's always been the something-better-to-do guy, more important, never pin down, non-committal."

"He never would have done that to Ray."

"Yeah, well, he did, didn't he? He's done it to me my whole life."

"You should go check on him. See if he made it up at least."

"I really don't care."

"You should."

"You don't know anything about it."

Mona stopped before the door to the bar.

"You're right, but you still should. He's your father, he may need your help."

"That's hilarious."

Mona stood before the door, staring at him.

"Okay," he paused, "boss," with emphasis.

"I will never be your boss," Mona replied. "And you will never be mine."

"Deal," Billy said, and reached out his hand, which Mona shook firmly.

"Please check on your dad."

"Soon as I'm done, I'll head on up."

Took Billy longer than he thought, canoes coming in, lost kayakers needed a lift, late afternoon when he walked into the tool shed behind the last cabin on the river, changed from his sneakers into a pair of woolen socks and Red Wing boots, walked into the pole barn, rolled out the old Moto Guzzi Sport Ray sold him (more gave it away), tied his hair back with a blue bandana, put on his Ray-Bans, started the bike, and rolled off through the pines that lined the road into and out of Ray's Riverside Resort. When he reached the main road, he turned left, away from the town of Spring Green, down the long straight stretch of empty road, flanked by the railroad tracks on one side, river swamps and marshes on the other, the open road, all alone, with the rumbling engine and blue sky, cumulous shapes, leaning into rushing winds that cleared the way to assess and consider the looming circumstance of decisions made by others, excessive entanglements he vowed to avoid, meanings, principles, Gods, superstitions, morals, creeds, beliefs, values, conventions, rationales, fates, destinies, excuses, purposes, formulas, rhythms, answers, solutions, rights, and wrongs he was certain did not exist, leaving little if no point to accomplishment, effort, property, capital, responsibility, striving, ambition, accounts, deposits, pride, self-esteem, commitment, duty, obligation, anything that might restrict, constrain, or inhibit the pure unadulterated anarchic freedom in which he wallowed, the only sense and point of his current existence, a comforting purity, threatened in a moment, causing considerable unease, as he sped down the road toward Lone Rock, where his few belongings waited in his shitty room, to be bundled up in an instant, to escape, whenever he wished, carried far away to some new place of hiding, whenever the plastic bag started closing in, away from a future he just left, and a past just ahead, and as he reached the outskirts of town, the moment of truth breaking upon him, it crossed his mind, and, for no reason whatever, for there was no truth, he made a sweeping turn, away from his room on Main Street, and headed for the bridge across the river. The road across the old rusted bridge outside Lone Rock ran head long into a 100-foot high mass of million year old sandstone into which more than a handful of locals had sped with abandon to their fiery deaths, where Billy now downshifted, and turned left along Highway 130, which followed the sheer sandstone bluff along the river, and then banked to the right at Otter Creek, away from the river, into marsh land, barrens brushed with the green of early summer, rolling hills and valleys and farmland leading up to the ridges forming the southern bank of the river valley, and up the sloping roads to the hill where he hoped to God he would not run into his father.

He slowed when he turned left onto the gravel of Hilltop Road, now wrestling with the demons seeping in, years of subconscious practice, the familiar torture he had left behind, taking shape now before him, the disgust, nothing less, of his father's specter, awaiting him, the disapproval, the cold stare, abrupt words, the what the fuck are you doing now that you killed your mother and abandoned your kids in this shit storm of what you call a life subtext behind every word and question, derisive hopelessness, haughty unspoken look what I did with my life, no practice rounds, life is what you make it, give it your best shot, what can I do to help, (you can go fuck yourself ambivalence), think of your mother, your kids for God's sake, the inevitable silence, simmering anger, what the hell is wrong with you, what did we do wrong, we didn't deserve this, you're no son of mine denouement.

Billy wished he would just go away, really go away, he thought, as he steered his bike along a series of turns that followed the ridge, plunged into a coulee of deep ravines, slowed at the bottom, and turned left onto an old farm road under overhanging branches where an orange cattle gate guarded the Property that, despite his father, was the one place he ever wanted to call home.

He came to a stop before the gate, leaving plenty of room for the wide swing, flipped down the kickstand, walked up to the post where a lock held a rusty chain wrapped around the gate, and his spirits sank, because the lock still held the chain in place, but the bolt was not in the cylinder, which meant his father had made the trip, and was somewhere up on the hill, which made his absence at Ray's more detestable. Billy left the gate open and rode up the grassy farm road, past the lava stone Buddhas, showing no hint of trouble, made the hard right turn, climbed the last steep leg of the hill, and took the last turn out of the woods to the left into the open field, where he caught sight of his father's Eldorado, incongruous, proudly sitting below the old Amish cabin. Came all the way up here and still didn't go to Ray's funeral. What an asshole.

He brought the bike to a stop next to the Eldorado and called out dismissively. No response. He walked up to the cabin, and up onto the front porch, the door open, inside a Filson duffle bag lay on two lawn chairs under the window, the cot was down from the loft, sleeping bag and blankets and pillows on the cot, all ready to go, precision and order, as fucking always. From the front porch, he looked out over the field and down the slope of the hill to the south and west, and, everything in order, was about to get back on his bike and get the hell out of there, when from the east over the trees came a large turkey vulture, on a straight descending glide over the cabin to the west, shadow racing upon the field, and disappearing low into the high grass out of sight just over the hill. And then Billy noticed his dad's hiking stick was gone, and as much as he knew his father was capable of any indignity, things just weren't adding up, because his father really did like Ray, the only friend his father had, or could have, and he made the trip all the way up here, and was all set to go, and then doesn't show?

He walked down the steps off the cabin's front porch and walked up to the top of the hill, benches around the fire pit empty, forlorn, looked to the east where the pine and spruce stretched across the field, and then to the west, into the glare of the sun, the river valley spectacle unfolding over the hills in the distance, and then another vulture alighting in the grass, too many vultures, birds, portents, and from the deepest depths of a nowhere he never would have suspected came a creeping instinctive wave that began to break upon him, innate crescendo of total awareness, fear, that protects us and others from harm, all extraneous peeled away, leaving nothing but pulsing vibrations which quickened his steps into a flat out run down the path from the top of the hill toward where the birds had landed, rushing down the hill for no reason until he tripped, staggered, regained his balance, and burst upon a stand-off, coyote on one side, three vultures on the other, his father's mauled body between them, and he waved his arms as he ran and screamed and startled them into flight, the coyote into high grass, the vultures in air, and in that moment the Earth stopped turning, and he was left, alone, with his father, a gaping hole in his father's chest, his eyes open, searching.

Billy fell back into the grass on the hill above his father's body, waves breaking one after another, slowing into a deep throb at his temples, his head in his hands, looking down at the man just minutes before he had wished would go away. It was all he could do to absorb the blow, his entire life with his father rolled across the sky, came together, took shape, spread apart, and dissipated into nothingness. Slowly the vibrations imploded, and the webs began to clear, leaving a hollow from which he began to think of what he was supposed to do. Was he overcome with sadness? No. Shock, not sadness. Thought of his mother. That was sadness, and relief she was not alive to see, to know, of this. He was all that was left. Jesus, how could it have come to this? I mean he drove me out of my mind, but this? What the hell happened?

He looked down at his father's body, which he had tried to avoid, saw the places where the vultures had begun to have their way, and stared at the gaping hole in his father's chest. He's been shot. By what, a rifle? Not that rare, read about it all the time, hunting accidents, sons killing fathers, mistaken for a deer, drinking, but in June? Out of season? Of course there are poachers, always poachers, any time of year, not uncommon, spotlighting deer at night, routine, but Jesus, right through the heart, my God what an end, larger than life, and now in death, never missed a beat right to the very end, martyrdom, for the record books, the newspapers, Jesus, if he had to pick a way to go, probably right here, but not like this.

And anyway, what the hell now? None of it made any sense, but he still had to do something. Classic his dad would do this to him, leave him, of all people, with his dad's final mess. Too perfect. But really, what? Why couldn't it be someone else? The sheriff, he'll have to get the sheriff. Yeah, but what about the body? The scavengers will be back. Have to move the body, wrap it somehow, what the hell. Move the body? They'll think he did it. He had a motive, hate's a good motive. Maybe he should hightail it, never saw. Idiotic. Mona. Okay, the sheriff, the body. What.

Blankets, picnic table, chicken wire, a plan. Billy retraced his steps back up the hill away from the body, saw the vultures circling over the trees, and broke into a run, when he saw the arrow lying in the middle of the path, what he must have tripped over on the way down. He picked it up, inspected it, dried blood, his father's, immediately dropped it, fingerprints, Christ, he was a suspect, he thought, as he ran to the cabin. He grabbed two old blankets and a rope from a plastic container in the loft and ran back to the body before the vultures returned. He rolled his father's body in the musty blankets, tied a rope around the blankets, and then, pulling the rope, he dragged his father's body up to the top of the hill to the picnic table, where he hugged his father one last time, first time in years, struggled to stand him on end, Christ, wrestled with him there, and then guided the stiffened bundle onto the top of the picnic table, out of the insects' reach. He then ran down to the outhouse, grabbed several long wooden stakes, and the ax from the loft, and then ran up to the tree line, pulled out of the grass several rusted rolled up chicken wire enclosures his father had used to protect young pine from hungry deer, and brought everything back up the hill, pounded stakes around the picnic table, wrapped chicken wire around the stakes and over the body, and then ran down to his bike, got on, started it up, and left to get the sheriff, with whom he returned about an hour later.

As soon as Walt heard Billy's story, Billy was the prime suspect. The sheriff liked Billy's father, Billy not so much. Except the sheriff also knew that Billy was capable of just about nothing, let alone shooting someone through the heart with a bow and arrow, and then coming down to report it. Although not a hint of sadness in the kid, that's for sure, kind of matter of fact about the whole thing, just wasn't right, not normal.

When Walt got to the top of the hill, and looked at Dan Hurley's body wrapped in blankets in a cage of chicken wire, he scratched his head, looked at Billy.

"You moved the body for chrissake," he said, in disgust. "And what was the plan, set him on fire?" he asked, looking at Billy's father atop the picnic table.

"I told you about the coyote, and the vultures," Billy said.

"Yeah, that's right, a Mexican stand-off."

"Well, what was I supposed to do?"

The sheriff shook his head and thought about it. Jesus, he thought, it actually made sense, in a twisted way. But whatever this weird kid was up to, the sheriff knew he had to get this one right, and it didn't help that the sun was about to go down. This was not his first rodeo, and this was not your ordinary crime scene. This right here could make or ruin a career; he couldn't fuck this up.

The sheriff and Billy looked down the hill at the sound of vehicles coming one after another up the road, as a squad car, a pickup truck, and an ambulance made the turn out of the woods into the field and up the hill.

"Well, you can take this contraption down now," Walt said, jerking his thumb at the chicken wire, "and don't touch the goddam body."

As Billy got to work, the sheriff waited for the arrivals to reach the top of the hill. Ben Halvorson drove the pickup truck and owned the archery shop on Highway 14, the sheriff's deputy drove the squad car, and the EMT driver drove the ambulance with the county coroner, who once he got wind of what was going on didn't want to miss out on the action. They huddled for a moment out of Billy's earshot, then went to work, the sheriff checked out the arrow, its location, where Dan Hurley fell, the coroner and EMT unwrapped the blankets and examined the body, the deputy, with his camera, rummaged through the tall grass down the hill from where the body was found, Mr. Halvorson, self-important, all knowing, took it all in, the approximate location of the shooter, the body, the wound, the arrow, all in the last light of day. Billy just hung around, fielding stray questions lobbed his way, without answers.

The dark cut short the investigation after about forty-five minutes, but there was little left to do for the time being.

"Why don't you go down to the cabin," the sheriff said to Billy, "we're going to talk it over."

Billy left the top of the hill, the sheriff looked at the coroner.

"Well, guys whaddya think. I'm not lookin' to hold you to anything here and now, but I've got to decide whether I'm gonna hold this kid overnight. I know you've got to cut poor Dan up and look him over," the sheriff said to the coroner, "but do you have any idea when this might have happened?"

"Well, the vultures didn't help any," the coroner said, "but I'd say at least a day, best guess, I'd say maybe evening yesterday."

The sheriff turned to his deputy.

"I think I found the place where the shooter crouched in the grass," the deputy said, Mr. Halvorson nodding with approval. "Would have made sense given the location of the arrow, and the wound, about thirty yards down the hill."

The sheriff turned to Mr. Halvorson.

"But I also found something else," the deputy said, looking at Mr. Halvorson, who nodded for him to proceed.

"About halfway between where the shooter might have been and where the body was found," Mr. Halvorson nodded again, "is like a one foot berm that a farmer must have built across the contour of the hill, like my father did on our farm growing up, kind of like a terrace, hard to see in the tall grass, but it's there, and on the far side, or near side, or, I should say, the body side of the berm, is kind of like a low trough, that catches water going down the hill, kind of muddy now given all the rain we had earlier this week, and there are pretty clear hoof prints in the mud there."

"Where are the hoof prints?" asked the sheriff.

"On a direct line between the shooter and the body," said Mr. Halvorson.

"Any idea how old?" the sheriff asked Mr. Halvorson.

"Probably about a day," said Mr. Halvorson. "Big animal, too. Buck for sure, eight-, ten-pointer, but mature, heavy."

"Right in the line of fire?" the sheriff asked Mr. Halvorson.

"Right in the line of fire," Mr. Halvorson replied.

"Did you get pictures?" the sheriff asked.

"Yep," the deputy replied.

"Anything else?" asked the sheriff.

"This guy was no rook," Mr. Halvorson broke in, "toxic broadhead arrow, carbon shaft, probably a high-powered compound bow, blades'll rip through just about anything."

"Mr. Hurley's heart?" asked the sheriff.

"You can see for yourself," Mr. Halvorson nodded toward the body. "Looks to me like Mr. Hurley got himself in the way of an errant shot," Mr. Halvorson said with authority.

"Yeah, but right through the heart?" asked the EMT, all of twenty-one years old, "and out of season?"

"You just stick to your knitting," the sheriff said to the young EMT, the deputy now nodding.

"You have no idea how much poachin' goes on," Mr. Halvorson said to the EMT, "all times of year," he said, not to be trifled with.

"Okay, boys, thanks for your help. It's my call, and I don't see any reason to keep this kid overnight, any of you?"

"Don't believe this kid would know a toxic broadhead from a whittling stick," said Mr. Halvorson dismissively, looking down at the cabin where Billy sat on the steps of the front porch.

Everyone laughed.

"Okay, well then, I guess we're done up here for now. This is long from over, but good work fellas. Let's get this body off the hill, and call it a night."

The EMT pulled the ambulance up to the top of the hill, and he and the coroner loaded Dan Hurley's mangled body into the back, strapped it in, headed down the hill, steered onto the road in front of the cabin, and headed down the hill into the woods, red lights flashing through the trees.

"For God's sake, he doesn't need those lights on up here," the sheriff said to his deputy.

"So you think it's a hunting accident, Walt?" the deputy asked.

"Looks that way for now."

Later that night, the boys in the Mad House Inn bar weren't so sure. They were sitting on barstools at the bar's front curve under the window that looked out through the Miller High Life neon sign to the street, and they were talking about the body that was discovered on the hill that day, all of them burly in one form of camouflage or another. As soon as the sheriff had left with Billy for the crime scene, Trudy, the sheriff's secretary, civic duty and all, did her level best to spread the news, so the bar was busier than normal for a weekday night, and abuzz, because nothing ever happened around Lone Rock, and nothing quite like this since the temperature dropped that one cold night back in 1951. Not that people didn't die in Lone Rock, it's just that this particular guy was kind of like famous, and they would surely be splashed all over the Chicago papers, maybe even New York, and the Mad House Inn was ground zero, because of the guy who happened to live upstairs, who everyone had come to see, not talk to, he never talked to anybody, just to see, he was kind of like famous now, too, maybe even a suspect, a murderer.

The sheriff made Billy cool his heels, not for any particular reason, for the hell of it mostly, but also, because the kid didn't seem too fazed, and should be, too matter of fact, wasn't right, time to sink in. Billy phoned his dad's assistant, Dorothy, who would know what to do, handle everything, if she could ever stop crying, and then he sat and waited, couple hours at least, until around midnight, when the sheriff finally let him go. He hopped on his bike, rode to the Mad House Inn, parked in back, walked through the back door, past the stairs which led to his room on the second floor, past the restrooms, and took a seat on his usual barstool, at the dimly lit back end of the bar, as if it were any other night, as if the presses in Chicago weren't already feverishly churning out headlines with the news.

Lee Anne opened a bottle of Pabst Blue Ribbon, placed it on the bar before him.

"Oh, honey, I'm so sorry."

Billy looked up at her, weak smile, took a long sip from the cold bottle of beer, as Lee Anne stepped respectfully away.

The patrons had ceased all conversation, the juke box quiet, everyone staring at Lee Anne serving the beer at the back of the bar, and then at Billy, sitting alone, no one knowing him well enough to say anything.

Couple of barstools down from where Billy sat, drunk Joe Gilliam sipped and spilled his brandy old fashioned, poisoned, not feeling much of anything, let alone respectful.

"Justice," he slurred into his drink, loud enough for Billy to hear, "is done. Big city fuckin' big shot meets his de-mise," stretching demise for effect, "in the middle of fuckin' nowhere, fuckin' fitting, don't ya think?" he said, turning to Billy.

Billy smiled into his beer.

Lee Anne leaned over the bar.

"Shut up, Joe, or I'm throwin' you out."

"Sure, Lee Anne honey, I'm gettin' to go anyways," he said, as he took one last long sip from his drink, "but, ya know, that's all I'm sayin'," lurching from his barstool, looking over at Billy, "justice was done!" he said, making a wide flourish with his left arm, and about to go, when he was struck upside the head from behind and knocked to the floor by a long haired bearded fire plug of a man in a camo vest, Dean Crook, Deano to everyone, who just leveled Joe Gilliam at the Mad House Inn bar.

"What the fuck, man, what's the matter with you," Deano said to Billy over Joe Gilliam rising from the floor, "you shouldn't take that shit."

Deano raised a fist at Joe, who scrambled through the barstools, past the juke box, and out the door.

"I don't blame him," Billy said into his beer.

"What the fuck, man, you should stand up for your old man, he didn't deserve that shit. You gotta stand up for somethin' man."

All eyes were on Billy and Deano.

Billy paused, then picked up his beer, took a drink.

"Deano, you're right, I'm gonna take a stand," he said as he got to his feet, "and say good night, to all of you," loud enough for everyone in the bar, "it's been a long day," and he turned to go, but then stopped, and turned back toward all the faces.

"You know, if any of you gave a shit about my dad, I guess I should say, I appreciate that, for him anyway, so good night."

And with that he took his leave, and his beer, up to his room above the bar, another day in paradise, while one floor, directly below, Deano and the Camo boys huddled at the bar, ordered more rounds, and argued, hashing out theories, conspiracies, to explain the mystery, of Dan Hurley's demise at the top of the hill.

CHAPTER THREE

The Funeral

"So what do you plan on doing now?" Colleen asked.

"Oh, I've got some plans," replied Mona.

"Path of least resistance," said Billy.

Mona sighed.

"If he plays his cards right, he can come along for the ride," Mona said, smiling.

"Not goin' anywhere," said Billy, with pride, noncommittal, annoying really, never a rise, a laugh, a spark. No affect, no sign anything had happened. No loss, no sorrow, no hint of mourning or shock. Stoic to a fault, Colleen thought.

"I'll say," Colleen agreed. Her husband gave her a slight, didn't need to say that under recent circumstances grimace, but she couldn't help it, didn't care for Billy much, knew he wouldn't care, because he didn't seem to care about anything. Had no idea what Mona saw in him. Affinity of lost souls, all she could figure. Maybe that was all it took. Maybe that was enough, except Colleen didn't believe it. She believed lives took the form of an arc, or line, or parabola, or some geometry suggesting movement, direction, requiring effort, achievement. This guy, as he loved to admit, was going nowhere.

Colleen's husband, Ben, too, was into effort. In complicated circumstances told elsewhere, he had learned to trust his talents, and apply them as best he could. Simple as that. No more searching, for truth, himself, or America, it's all right before us, every day. He had made his choices, paid some dues, and busied himself with the stuff of life.

They were sitting on the front porch of Ben and Colleen's farmhouse, tucked into the woods down a dirt road off County Highway C, watching the chickens dance and peck around the legs of Ben and Colleen's two kids, a boy ten, Dirk, and a girl eight, Bonnie, in a large yard that separated the house from the old red barn, a little down in the mouth. Six months earlier, Mona had suffered from a gastrointestinal issue that wouldn't go away, and no doctor could figure it out, until Ivy, a bartender at the resort, suggested Mona go see a young woman doing her residency in pediatrics at the UW Medical Center in Madison, who happened to live nearby in Iowa County with her husband and two kids, and in two minutes' time on the front porch of a farmhouse Colleen diagnosed giardia, set Mona on the road to recovery, and in due course became a good friend. Ben, turns out, graduated from UW's law school, worked pro bono from time to time, but didn't practice, preferring farm work to courts of law. It was Ben's side practice which led Billy and Mona to the farmhouse porch.

"Well, we've got some things to sort out," Mona said, "with Ray's passing and all, and," she said looking at Billy, "Billy's dad's passing and all, and there's some things that need attending. Blown away at what Ray did to me, or, I guess, for me, I should say, the responsibility, kind of overwhelming, you know, that's what really gets me, can't help but wonder if I can really do this, but then I think, why not me? If he'd given it all away to some half-wit guy, no one'd think twice about it, and I'm sure they all think I took advantage of him somehow, that I'm just a girl, really, didn't deserve it, not up to it, but you know, deep down, I know I can do this, and do this well, as well if not better than anybody, and I'm going to show them all, prove that to everybody, show them we won't miss a beat, and, as I said, I've got some plans, improvements, first class, we'll see, if the money's there, I've got some things I want to do."

"Doesn't matter what anybody thinks," Billy muttered.

"Well, yeah, it's a business, so yeah, I'm sorry, Earth to Billy, it does," Mona shot back.

Billy shrugged.

A gesture, Colleen thought, fit for his tombstone.

"But really," Mona said, "we wanted to stop by because Billy has an issue, a legal issue he wants to run by Ben."

Billy cringed.

"Wasn't exactly my idea, more yours," he said to Mona.

"Whatever, we're here now."

"So, what's up?" asked Ben.

Mona looked at Billy.

"Well," Billy said, as he reached into his back pocket and pulled out several scraps of paper, "I got these," he said, handing the papers over to Ben, "and Mona thought I should show them to you."

Ben unfolded the crumpled pages and began to read them over.

"It's a summons," Billy said, "and some kind of petition."

"I can see that," Ben said.

"Has to do with my kids."

Ben read through the papers, slowly, one time through, then turned back, and read various passages over again.

"Well, looks like you've been summoned to appear at a hearing, on a guardianship petition, filed by Richard and Mary Alice Walsh, who are seeking permanent custody over two children, Sam and Kate, five-year-old twins, who are the children of a certain," he said looking at Billy, "Jenny Walsh and William Hurley, the respondents."

"That would be me," Billy mumbled.

"Really," Colleen said.

"When did you get this?" Ben asked.

"The petition a couple months ago, the other thing, about three weeks ago."

"Well, the reason I ask is that, the other thing, is a copy of an order, entered by the court, a Judge Wozak, which says that neither parent appeared at a mandatory court appearance, and that if they don't appear by the next status, which appears to be, let's see, that would be, next week, next Friday, a default order will be entered granting the petition."

"What've you done about this?" Ben asked.

"Nothing really," Billy replied.

"Nothing?" Colleen asked, "Aren't these your kids?"

Mona shook her head, embarrassed.

"Where's the mother?" Ben asked.

"No idea," Billy said, "somewhere in California, strung out probably."

"Will she contest this?" Ben asked.

"No way, probably doesn't even know about it, or care," Billy replied.

"Well, do you plan on doing anything about this? Why show it to me?"

"Nothing I really can do," Billy replied. "Like I said before, showing it to you was Mona's idea."

"Can't he fight it?" Colleen asked her husband.

"Sure he can, he's the father," Ben replied, "the question is, does he want to?"

They all looked at Billy.

"Look, I know what this looks like," Billy said, in particular to Colleen, "I'm not stupid, it's not like I don't know what this is about," he said looking at Mona, "but, fact is, I was, and would be, a shitty father, I already put them in danger once, and I'm no better now, except, without the drugs. I've got a shitty job, I can't afford a lawyer, couldn't afford to take care of two kids, no decent place for them to stay, no idea how to be a parent, let alone a good one, I mean look at my dad, he had everything going for him, and he was still a shitty parent, look at me for chrissakes."

Colleen nodded.

"'The petitioners, as it says, are their grandparents, Jenny's father and his wife. They've got money, nice house, do a lot better job than I ever could, kids'd be better off, not like I don't care at all, just they'd be better off without me in their lives, I'd just fuck it up, and I don't want to do to them what my father did to me."

"What did your father do to you that was so bad?" asked Colleen.

"With all due respect, that's none of your business," Billy said, evenly, without anger or offense.

"Well, I don't know about all of that," Mona said looking at Billy, "but this whole default thing," she said to Ben, "isn't there a downside to doing nothing?"

"Yeah, well, it's never a good thing to completely ignore something like this," Ben said. "Not too familiar with these, these guardianships, but it's never a good thing, for example, at the end of the petition, it says they're looking for the court to grant whatever relief the court thinks is necessary and proper, boilerplate stuff, but you just never know what the court will do, especially after it hears the evidence, because even if you don't show, there'll still be a hearing, still be evidence, and after the court hears what you did, I don't know for sure all of what it could do, I do know that if you're not there, there won't be anybody there to protect you, make sure you don't get screwed. I mean, maybe someday you might want to see your kids again, and the grandparents won't let you, and the order that's entered might prevent you from seeing your kids without the guardians' consent. I mean, I'm not sure about any of this, but, bottom line, you never want to just ignore this stuff, because you never know what bad shit might happen if you're not there."

Mona nodded. Billy shrugged, again.

"Thanks, Ben, we do appreciate it, don't we?" Mona said suggestively to Billy.

"Yeah, I guess, I do appreciate it," Billy said, sincerely, in Ben's direction, "I just don't think it's worth the effort," Colleen rolling her eyes in disgust, his kids not worth the effort, not understanding that what he really meant was that the cost of spending any more time enmeshed in the big city, its anxiety, rat race, and sordid entanglements, from which he had escaped and from which he vowed to forever free himself, was much greater than the speculative benefit of avoiding some remote consequence of a court order that might never happen.

"But I'll think it over," Billy said. "If I go to the funeral, I may be down there anyway."

"If?" Mona asked.

"Haven't decided," Billy responded, looking at Mona.

"You haven't decided whether you're going to your own father's funeral?" Colleen asked.

Mona and Billy got to their feet; Mona took Billy's arm.

"We're talking about it," she said, hopefully, "I think it's the right thing to do," Billy was just about to cut in but Mona cut him off, "and I know you don't care about that kind of stuff," she said to him, "but I think you should go, and that I should go as moral support, and I've never been to Chicago, two funerals in a week, that's something, isn't it, doesn't always happen, and I'd really like to go, and…"

Mona looking up at him, Ben and Colleen nodding in support, Billy held out his arms, a plea for silence.

"Okay. I get it." He took a breath, knowing what he had to do, knowing they were right, didn't like it. "Oh God, you have no idea," he said with a sigh, shaking his head, "but okay, you see," he said, gesturing to Mona, "she's my weakness, have a hard time saying no, so I guess we're goin.'"

Colleen thought that the one sensible thing he had said the whole time, a decision he might want to think about though, a little, some, kind of important in the grand scheme, one you can never take back, but he was decisive, hand that to him, and he did make the right call, along his path of least resistance, which apparently led downstream, to Mona, which, Colleen could see, was not a bad thing.

And so, Billy and Mona went to the big city. Could have taken Ray's old Cadillac under the tarp in the pole barn, but Mona and Billy just didn't feel comfortable laying claim to Ray's favorite toys, at least not yet. So Billy packed a sport coat he borrowed from Ben, and Mona her little black dress, and stuffed them in a backpack that Mona carried, hanging tight to Billy going seventy miles an hour on the Moto Guzzi down Interstate 90 that

Friday morning, which at first had been sunny and pleasant, but which all changed around Rockford, when a mass of dark clouds began mustering in the west, crept across the flat farmland toward the highway, and overtook them with what turned out to be the first wave of heavy rain, one after another, all the way from outside Belvidere to the Fox River, where Billy finally pulled over under a highway underpass, soaking wet, and shivering.

Mona climbed up to sit on a concrete embankment, while Billy turned away, and started walking, up and down, back and forth along the shoulder of the road, from one end of the underpass to the other, semis whooshing and spraying by.

And Mona knew exactly what he was thinking. No good deed, cold, wet, and a front-row seat to an infinite rush of hot metal under a concrete roof. This was what you got, he was thinking. It takes you forever to get somewhere down here, and the getting there is such a hassle, that when you finally get there you're miserable. And that's just the beginning, God on this trip, that's just the beginning. That's what he's thinking. That he was right, that I don't know what he knew all along, and even though he might be right about a lot of that, he also, to his credit, won't be mad, because he doesn't seem to get mad, far as she could tell, equanimity, remarkable, really, never disappointed, if expectations are low enough, and he won't be upset with me, because I think he loves me, doesn't even know it, never admit it.

Mona stared at him as he walked right past her toward the far end of the underpass, reaching the curtain of rainfall, looking out, not letting up, he turned and walked back toward her, past her, toward the other end, calm, without accusation, knowing he was right and that it didn't matter, looking out, another sheet of rain, turning again, back toward her, and as he came to pass again he looked up at her, rain dripping from his hair, and he smiled, barely, and kept walking.

Mona let him walk away about twenty paces, and with eighteen wheelers roaring in the background, she yelled out to him.

"Hey," her voice echoing under the concrete span.

He turned.

"Want to get married?"

Couldn't have heard her, thought she said.

"What?"

"I said," she yelled out louder, "do you want to get married?"

He heard her this time. Thought for a second. Looked at her dripping wet on the concrete embankment, her dark hair a mass of curls falling on her shoulders, arms propped stiff, leaning backward, broad mischievous smile, with those lips.

He paused, turned away, looked out at the rain, shook his head, then turned back.

"Yeah, sure," he called back over the semis.

Just couldn't say no, didn't know why, more time wouldn't help, and so, he kept walking.

Mona smiled. She thought as much.

Eventually, after the rain passed, without another word, they got back on the bike, and rode into the vast inner workings of urban mechanics, swallowed up by the hustle, pulling into town as the sun broke upon tall sleek glass boxes, Mona very happy, Billy, not exactly happy, but as happy as he got.

Billy took the North Avenue exit east to the Gold Coast, turned on to the Inner Drive, then south a couple of blocks, and into the drive of the garage beneath his father's condo building, where he explained himself to the suspicious attendant, showed his ID, got the attendant's sincerest condolences, and brought the Moto Guzzi to a stop in the Eldorado's reserved space. Billy led Mona into a freight elevator that rose to the twenty-third floor, twenty floors higher than she had ever been before, and opened the door with a key he thought he would never use again, with Mona entering an altogether new world, high in the sky, staring out tall windows at ribbons of cars curling around Oak Street Beach, the Drake, Playboy, the mass of Great Lake, hypnotic constant motion, a trance, disbelief, Billy's revulsion, exhaustion, falling, into comas of sleep, Mona in the guest room, Billy on the living room floor, because it was hard being there at all, let alone sleeping in his father's beds.

Mona woke late the next day, to Billy, steeling himself for the worst. He was dressed in Ben's dark brown suede jacket, slightly wrinkled, black jeans, black tee shirt, and All Stars, high and black. Mona smoothed out her little black dress, sleeveless, little short, little clingy, she thought, as she looked herself over in the mirror, heels, olive skin glowing, no stockings. Billy thought she looked fabulous, she thought Billy underdressed, but knew better to say anything, miracle enough he agreed to go, and anyway, she knew there was no change of clothes in the backpack she had carried all the way from Lone Rock.

They took the elevator down to the main lobby, aglow in full sunlight bouncing off the lake across Lake Shore Drive. Bob the doorman, round, bald, Bridgeport Irish, revered Billy's dad, stood up from his welcome desk in surprise when Billy and Mona stepped off the elevator, wondering when they showed up, how they got in. He remembered Billy, more his parties.

"Good morning, Mr., uh, Bill," he stammered, looking the unlikely couple over, not at all impressed with what he saw. "You going to the funeral," he said to Billy, "like that?"

"Mornin', Bob," Billy said, ignoring the question, striding past, with Mona, smiling at Bob, on his arm.

"Around for a while?" Bob asked as they reached the revolving door.

"Only as long as I have to," Billy said, and they swung out the door.

Bob retook his seat, shaking his head, miffed his life required he stand for such an asshole, and his old man such a great guy.

Billy and Mona put on matching black horn-rimmed sunglasses and headed south toward Michigan Avenue, arm in arm down the Magnificent Mile, secret agents on a mission, Mona in awe, past the Fourth Presbyterian Church, stopping at the windows of Bonwit Teller, to the Water Tower, where they took a right onto Chicago Avenue, toward Wabash, and the Holy Name Cathedral, where the funeral service for Daniel Hurley was to commence promptly at 11:00 a.m.

Of course, Dorothy—black and white large floral print, espresso complexion, straight brown hair tied back, not thin, not large, kind smile, motherly, with hips—had taken care of everything, funeral home, notifications, obituary, funeral, flowers, scriptures, music, burial, expenses, everything, knowing Billy would be no use at all, and everything gold plated, mahogany casket, Cadillac limos, abbondanza bouquets, Lyric sopranos, even the cardinal for God's sake, all lined up and ready to send off the most wonderful man she had ever known, and all the work turned out a blessing, a distraction, because she'd taken it hard, very hard. She was pacing in front of the Cathedral steps in the bright sun as large cars with well-dressed passengers disembarked, gave keys to valets, and walked, respectfully, with somber masks, into the Cathedral.

Anyone who was anyone, and many who thought they were, converged on the Cathedral steps that bright Saturday morning, in echelon, the governor and his wife, the Democratic senator, a majority of the Illinois Supreme Court (four Democrats; one Republican), the mayor, his wife, son, his son's wife, at least twenty-nine alderpersons, committeemen, city commissioners, state representatives and senators, the city clerk, city treasurer, county executive, executive staffs of all of the above, the deceased's entire law office, a quorum of the County Board, corporate titans, almost every judge in the Circuit Court and First District Appellate Court, and wannabes to all of the above, (minus the US Attorney), most of whom, recipients of Hurley's largesse, his cajoling, wrath, and ownership, he who taketh must giveth, and they had all given, one way or another, because they had all taken, Hurley's dole, and they were all here now, dressed to the nines, with their wives and husbands, paying their respects, relief, not reverence, writing off debts, first thought how best to fill the void, best for me, eyeing each other suspiciously in the Cathedral's pews, world's largest collection of pinky rings, egos, ambitions, and indictments, circling in the waters as they said their prayers, for the grace of God in Dan Hurley's passing.

Most had taken their seats by the time Billy and Mona turned the corner onto Wabash Avenue, and saw the long black chrome gleaming hearse parked prominently along the curb outside the Cathedral steps, where Dorothy nervously paced, until she spotted them walking down the block, heaved a mighty sigh, opened her arms, rushed up to Billy, and threw her arms around him, in tears.

"Oh, dear, I was so worried you wouldn't come," Dorothy whimpered.

"Hello, Dorothy, we are here," he said, "and this is…" he said, and stopped short, noticing, on the other side of the steps, Dick and Mary Alice Walsh, keeping their distance, standing together, shoulder to shoulder, concealing a commotion behind them.

Mona took off her sunglasses.

"Hi, I'm Mona," she said, taking Dorothy's hand.

"Hello, dear," Dorothy said, looking at the two of them, confused by the sight of this striking girl at the side of this…

"Well, one way or the other," she said looking Billy over, "you are here, and just in time," she said, as the pallbearers, old pals and precinct workers from the neighborhood, struggled to remove the casket from the back of the hearse.

"You better head on in now," Dorothy said, as Billy looked over the steps into the cavernous Cathedral, overflowing with heads turned, waiting for his perp walk down the main aisle, but as he turned to the steps, he saw, hiding behind the Walshes, two five-year-olds, boy and a girl, twins, blonds, peeking at a man they had not seen in two and a half years, creeping out from behind Mrs. Walsh to get a better look.

Mrs. Walsh opened her arms to hold them back.

"Come on now, children," she said, grabbing their arms as they eyed Mona, "we have to go in now."

Mrs. Walsh handed the kids over to her husband, who led the children up the steps into the church, and then turned on Billy in a hiss.

"We have a court order, you know," she sneered at Billy, "you're to have nothing to do with those kids," she said, turning a cold shoulder and following her husband up the steps.

Billy, unfazed, Mona didn't know how, kept his distance, and waited, as Dick, his wife, and Billy's two kids disappeared into the Cathedral.

The pallbearers reached the first of the steps, a little uneasy, surprised by the weight.

"You two got to go," Dorothy said to them, "before your dad beats you to it."

"Welcome to my world," Billy whispered to Mona, as he took off his sunglasses, took Mona's arm, and began their long walk, one of shame for Billy, if he had any, up the steps and into the sacred gothic space, epicenter of the Chicago Catholic Church, lofty, threatening, divine, with the full scrutiny of the Illinois political world upon them, all eyes, sanctimonious, watching Billy and Mona walk arm in arm down the main aisle, sinners, not a sound, past saints and statues and stained glass windows and committeemen and aldermen and representatives and senators and commissioners and justices and judges and executives, eyeing Mona, imperious, pious, and smug, judging, every move, the little dress, the All Stars, please, must he really, hasn't changed, disrespectful to the last, should have known, and his kids, what an ass, poor Dan, and that girl, disapproving, salacious looks.

Billy and Mona stepped into the first pew on the left side, stripped naked by stares, where Aunt Audrey sat, ninety-four and still at it, smiling, welcoming, across the aisle from the pew in which Dick and Mary Alice Walsh were standing, nearer the aisle, with Billy's kids on the far side, peeking behind their grandparents, at their father, and that pretty woman.

The pallbearers walked alongside the mahogany casket, blanketed in roses, up the aisle, stopped at the center of the main aisle just off the communion rail, and took their seats. And everyone waited.

A little too long, most everyone thought, governor and senator especially, not accustomed to waiting, but this was all in the plan, for ultimately, even Dan Hurley had to wait, for God, and his emissary, his eminence, the cardinal, who, after several minutes, emerged from the sacristy, scarlet head to toe, skull cap to socks, flowing cassock, white embroidered surplice, flowing shoulder cape, regal, all-knowing, all-powerful, and all controlling on the altar of his sanctuary festooned with flowers.

Well into his seventies, the cardinal had lost something in his step but not his grip. Old school, doctrinaire, minister to the Gold Coast, the well-heeled, expert at spreading fear of God and eternal damnation, hope and charity, not so much. Overweight in his old age, in his opulent mansion on Astor Street, he ate well, went out less, ministered little, and, well satisfied, grew old, with his housekeeper, Lincoln Continental, and penchant for bad temper. He had taken to falling asleep during meetings, or in the evening on his throne before warm fires, in large rooms with high ceilings, gold frames, dark wood, crystal chandeliers, and thick rich oriental rugs of deep reds and blues, which, if taken together with all the other expensive oriental rugs owned by the Catholic Church would alone be enough in the years to come to pay settlements and claims of abuse to which the cardinal had turned a blind eye for years, trading kids for deviants, but by then it'd be easier, and less expensive, to declare bankruptcy.

But that was a long way off, and by then he'd be long gone, buried with his sins, difficult enough to live in the present, with his gout, weak heart, aches and pains, it was enough now to indulge in the comfort he so richly deserved, he had fought his battles, earned his rest, these days it was a matter of saving himself for just the right moments, to summon lost energy, and faith, and rise to the occasion, like this one, to hit just the right notes, console and heal families, dress in flowing robes and stride across his stage, God's altar, beatific, albeit heavy steps, in all his scarlet glory, before his kind of flock, governors and senators, kissing his ring.

And he raised his outstretched arms, and asked them to join him in prayer, over the body of Daniel Hurley, whose spirit now rests with the Lord Jesus Christ our savior, etcetera, etcetera. He walked down to the coffin, aspergillum in hand, sprinkling holy water indiscriminately, on the blanket of roses, the coffin, on Billy, sizing up Mona, on the Walshes, and the twins, intoning this, that, perfunctory, heart not in it, this part at least, and one last flick, and, that's enough, turning and, with some difficulty, climbing the few steps back up onto the altar, where he commenced to celebrate the Mass, wished it were Latin, with operatic voices soaring from the choir loft, scripture from the senator, scripture from the governor, and lights, camera, action, now is his time, the cardinal climbs heavily to the pulpit, to pay tribute, inspire, and address the august crowd.

He looked out upon them, pausing on Billy, the Walshes, smiled, and said:

"Please be seated."

Chorus of wooden pews creaking, groaning.

"I wish to welcome all of you who have come to worship on this mournful day, in particular the family of the deceased, relatives, friends, and elected officials of our great city and state, I welcome you all to Holy Name Cathedral, to pay our respects and say our last goodbyes to this fine man, a hero really, Daniel, Dan Hurley, a true giant of our time, and for me personally, as I am sure for many of you, a good friend." Dorothy, who knew all her boss's friends, raised an eyebrow.

"I am honored today to open up this grand house of worship to all, Catholics, Christians, and the rest, and as we hope and pray that you may feel the presence of the Lord in our faith, our services, and our hearts, we trust you will respect the holy foundations of our Catholic faith, our blessed sacraments, on which this edifice and the one true church rests, which are gifts from God, in particular the sacred gift of Holy Communion, in which we eat of the body of Christ, and which is reserved for those who have confirmed their Catholic faith."

"Inclusive, nice," Billy whispered to Mona.

"As for our brother in Christ, Dan Hurley, it is unlikely there is anyone in this church who has done more, for more of you, in ways big and small, than Dan Hurley. A mentor to us all, a father figure if you will," he said looking down on Billy, "for Dan offered his wisdom, his energies, encouragement, a helping hand, his pocketbook, his common sense, to any and all, without recompense." Without recompense? Who was he talking about? Knowing smiles from the aldermen. Aunt Audrey blew her nose. "A man of such diverse talents is indeed rare, too rare in our lifetimes, and at this time of his passing, it is right and just that we recognize his accomplishments, his achievements, the service he has given to his ward, his neighborhood, and the city he loved, but as important as his service may be and certainly was, he was so much more than just a public servant, for he was a man of great faith, great empathy, who loved as much as he was loved," Billy fidgeting.

"He was a man of high ideals and lofty purpose, wielding the tools of government for those whose voices could not be heard, and turning to the law for those in need," of tax breaks on commercial properties, thought Billy, "because he was born to serve, a soldier of Christ, a selfless man of the people who believed in an open door and a large tent," muffled guffaws, cleared throats, "and yet was not afraid to stand up for what was right, when the city was suffering, and the city that works broke down, when it most needed a guiding, forceful hand, Dan Hurley stood up, stood up for the people," "he means White people," the mayor whispered to his son, "and steered the ship of state to stable, and prosperous shores.

"Now he could not do these great things over so many years without faith, in our God, our savior, Jesus Christ," Billy's fingers started to shake, "and without a deep consuming love, for his city and its people, for Dan Hurley had the biggest heart," more than one thought of that big heart ripped out of its chest by an arrow, "and a love that knew no bounds, as best reflected in his love for his dear wife, Nell, may she rest in peace, with whom he no doubt is celebrating in a better place today, who left a void in his heart that could never be filled," Dorothy, sputtering, "and yet, through all his suffering, he never showed his pain, and instead gave us his love," Mona grabbed Billy's twitching arm, "the love of a father for his family, a father for his son, for he so truly loved his son, William, prodigal though he may be," the cardinal said, smiling paternally down on Billy, "and just as I am certain in the grace of God," he said raising his voice, "I know it must truly and without doubt be the case, that in his heart of hearts," lowering his voice for effect, "his son," looking down on Billy, "must too have so loved his father."

Billy, erupting, about to explode. Who does he think he is? I've never met this guy. He doesn't know me. Billy gently took his arm from Mona's grasp, and rose from his seat, he and the cardinal, only ones standing. Wooden pews creaked with stiffened backs and craned necks, five hundred sets of eyes, on Billy, standing now in the front pew, directly below the pulpit.

They could tell from the cardinal's reaction this was not part of the script. The cardinal stopped, shocked, dumbfounded, as Billy stepped out of the pew, turned his back on the cardinal and the altar, and walked slowly away from his father's casket, with head bowed, down the main aisle, past the governor, senator, mayor, aldermen, judges and justices, mouths agape, walking out, of his father's funeral, the cardinal aghast, at the blasphemy, in his church, ruining his moment, before this crowd, how dare he, Mona holding her ground next to Aunt Audrey, and all the mourners, watching Billy's silent protest, a final rebuke, his long defiant unplanned march, past saints and statues and horrified disgusted judgments of anyone who was anyone in his father's home town. They all watched as he passed, and as he reached the back of the church, they all turned back to the cardinal, cheeks the color of his cape, hand to his heart, speechless, struggling for words for such an affront.

And they all sat in the grand Cathedral, uncomfortably, in silence, waiting for the cardinal to speak, when a high pitched howl erupted from the vestibule at the back of the church, a coyote's howl, loud, jarring, haunting, one after another, bouncing off the marble walls, ringing in their ears, filling the church with the sound of deep woods, full moons, and death upon a hill, sending shivers up the spines of the cardinal and his flock, and then, just as it started, it stopped, God, what an asshole.

Mona, not knowing what to do, everyone looking at her, wondering what she would do, glanced at the twins, giggling, having enjoyed the coyote, staring at her behind the Walshes' backs, and, looking at the twins, she decided to stay put, for the duration, and she looked at the cardinal, who was looking at her, and nodded to him as if to proceed, which he did, with some difficulty, heavy breathing, and may that young man burn mercilessly in hell.

After the service, Mona found that young man sitting on a park bench under a tree next to the elegant limestone Water Tower on Michigan Avenue.

"Well," she said sitting next to him, without another word, calm after the storm.

They sat and watched the tourists, and shoppers, and beautiful people, strolling through the little park along the Magnificent Mile, light years away from churches, and cardinals, and public servants.

"You don't have to apologize…"

"I wasn't going to," Billy said.

"I'm the one who should apologize," Mona said, "I pushed you to go."

"Just as well."

Long silence.

"Proud of you," Mona said, giving him a gentle nudge on the shoulder.

"For what?"

"Your stand against hypocrisy."

"He was telling lies up there, and everybody knew it."

"He may have meant well."

"Does it matter?"

"Probably not."

"Makes it worse."

"I get that."

"Sorry you came?"

"Not at all, you?

"No, not really."

"They did their thing, you did yours. I liked yours better. Especially the coyote. Your kids liked the coyote, too."

"My dad loved the sound of coyotes."

"Your kids are cute."

"Yeah, well, that's out of my hands, as you heard."

Billy looked out at the procession of buses, cars, and pedestrians, the constant flow, the urgent pulsing beat of somewhere to go, rushing here, to get there, to places that matter until crossed off the list, been there done that, places never the same after having been there.

"God, I used to love this city," Billy said, "but all their bullshit, my dad's bullshit, all that bullshit in there," he said jerking his thumb in the direction of the Cathedral, "it's all so transparent, using each other, clawing, climbing, for what, egos, power trips, the lust for more, and they dress it all up, like, well, I'm doing it for the church, or I'm doing it for the people, or I'm doing it for my family, or, I'm doing it for the country, or I'm doing it for prosperity, or I'm doing it for, bullshit, themselves, all the rest is bullshit, they're not saving lives, they're not protecting the planet, they're getting ahead, making money, going places, and none of it matters. There's no point in getting ahead; there's no such thing, none of that means anything, it's all right here in front of us, everything else is bullshit, we'll all end up like Ray, or my dad, with a hole in our chests where our hearts used to be, reputations, legacies, it's all bullshit, which is why I can't live here anymore, why I chose Lone Rock, where I'm not caught up in the circle jerk, where I can simplify, everything, where people can't afford pretenses, they just are who they are, trying to get by, warts and all, full display, and when they die, they die, and the world moves on."

Mona got a little nervous. She had not been simplifying his life.

"So here's what I have to say about you…," he began, but just then the wail of an ambulance came echoing down the glass and steel canyons from the south, two ambulances, a fire truck, two police cars, lights flashing, honking loudly, ear splitting, everyone turning to look, chaos on the street, cars angling toward the curb, making way, decibels shaking as the screaming convoy passed the park bench where Billy and Mona sat, and headed off to the north past Oak Street onto the Inner Drive.

Mona waited in dread for Billy to continue.

"So what is it you have to say about me?"

"All of what I just said is who I am, to the core, and you," he paused, "was not what I was looking for, cuz I wasn't looking for anything. You, to tell you the truth, I can't explain, other than to say, for some weird reason, for me, there isn't really a choice at all, you are just, it, for me, I just feel it, I know it, I can't tell you how, or why, I'm just, totally into you, best I can say, it's not passion, or reason, it's like two spirits, connected, an unknowable truth, meant to be, don't believe in much of anything, but I believe the truth in that, so when you ask me if I'll help you out with the resort, or go to this goddam funeral, or even marry you, it's like those decisions have already been made somehow, in the stars maybe, I don't know, but the simple fact of the matter is, you shake my soul, so I may not have much of a life, know I'm no grand bargain, but what I have I know I want to share with you."

Mona took his hand and smiled. She knew exactly what he was saying. She knew about spirits, and stars, the unknowable truth, thought he'd described it as well as could be done, and there was nothing more to say about it. They would live with and love each other, simply, the rest of their lives; there would never again be any question about that, so they rose from the bench, put their sunglasses back on, and, holding hands, walked north up Michigan Avenue, toward the place Billy's father called his home away from home.

Billy couldn't wait to get the hell out of there, but that guardianship thing was still six days away, and he'd decided to take Ben's advice, make sure nothing happened that might screw him forever, like the court order that conniving woman gloated over. They spent the next day, Sunday, at the beach, sun hot, water cold, Mona golden, diving down into the world of blue, erupting from the deep into cityscape, the Drake Hotel, Lake Shore Drive, the mouth of the Magnificent Mile, infectious, the life. That night, Dorothy called to ask Billy to a meeting requested by his father's lawyer for ten o'clock the next day, which Billy had no desire to attend, but Mona was catching a Greyhound back to Madison that afternoon anyway, so Monday morning, he and Mona grabbed a cab and headed down to City Hall, like his father had done every Monday for the past forty-five years.

They hopped out on Clark Street, walked through the county side of the building, under vaulted ceilings aglow in globe lights, and walked up the broad marble steps off the main hall, to the second floor aldermanic offices outside Council chambers, infested waters, through the outer door, the lobby, up to the first heavy glass and oak door, which bore his father's name, and into the reception area, where Dorothy jumped up from behind her desk to greet them.

"Oh, my goodness," she said, flustered, rushing up to Billy, "are you okay?" she asked Billy, giving him a concerned hug. "It's not right what they're saying about you, it's not like it was your fault."

Billy and Mona looked at her a little confused.

"Well, I did walk out."

"Yes, yes, of course you did, and that was almost unforgivable, but I mean, you weren't *responsible* for his death."

"Oh, for God's sake, Dorothy, I didn't kill him."

"No, of course not, it wasn't your fault, well, maybe, sort of, but not really."

"Jesus, Dorothy, I've never shot a bow and arrow in my life."

"No, not that, my Lord, I wasn't suggesting, no, no, the other thing, just horrible."

"What other thing? asked Billy.

Dorothy looked the two of them over.

"You haven't heard?" she asked in disbelief.

"Heard about what?" asked Billy.

"The cardinal."

"What about the cardinal?"

"He's dead!"

"What?"

"He's dead. Went back to his mansion, after your father's service, after you walked out, suffered a massive heart attack, and died, no more than an hour after."

"Jesus," Billy said.

"They're saying it's your fault," said Dorothy.

"That's ridiculous," said Mona.

"I know, I know," Dorothy reassured them, "doctors said it was a coronary infarction, but, well, we were all there, we saw how he took it, especially that awful noise, most folks believe you had something to do with it, although a lot of folks think he had it coming. He shouldn't have said those things about you."

"And maybe God struck him down for lying on the altar," Mona suggested.

Dorothy, deeply religious, seriously considered the remark.

"That's true, that's very true, Miss Mona, I hadn't thought of it that way."

"Divine retribution," added Billy.

"Yes, maybe," Dorothy said, "but all the same, bad business all the same, seems to just follow you around Billy, doesn't seem fair. But anyway, nothing can be done about that now, come," she said, motioning to the inner office, "you can wait in your father's office until Mr. Carlisle arrives."

Over the years, many a beating heart and sweaty palm had taken those same few steps Billy and Mona now took from Dorothy's reception area into the sanctuary of clout, if they were lucky to have been invited at all, millions of dollars on the line, high-rise projects, public works, city contracts, airport concessions, political ambitions, black robes, entire careers, the make or break of hopes and dreams, all riding on the half hour following those few steps into the inner sanctum, where the utter stillness of death now hovered, the absence, void of power, the loss, of significance.

Only one alderman could boast such an office, dean of the Council, Finance chairman, for so many years, the size, the cherry wood paneling, the Italian leather sofa and high backed chairs, credenzas laden with glass commemoratives, bowls, awards, Man of the Year, bond deals, Waterford crystal, mementos, mahogany end tables, Tiffany lamps, satellites, arranged in deference, orbiting the nerve center, the large walnut desk of former mayor Anton Cermak, from which Dan Hurley dispensed favors, dashed hopes, and ruled his world. It was the photographs that caught Mona's eye, as intended, gilded frames along the walls, Dan Hurley, with John Kennedy, Bobby Kennedy, Ted, Jimmy Carter, Lyndon Johnson, Humphrey, Eisenhower, Everett Dirksen, (the one with Nixon had been taken down), Garret FitzGerald, Taoiseach of Ireland, Frank Sinatra, Zsa Zsa Gabor, Louis Armstrong, Ernie Banks, Dolly Parton, Ron Santo, Sid Luckman, Bobby Hull, Stan Mikita, and on and on, all smiling, enjoying an inside joke, with their good friend Dan Hurley.

"Wow," Mona gushed.

"Finest room in City Hall," Dorothy said with pride, wistful.

Billy noticed a few boxes out of place, stacked in the corner, thought about Dorothy, knew how it worked, cut adrift now with his old man gone, not an easy time.

"How're you doing, Dorothy?" he asked.

"Oh, I'm holding up," she said, and burst into tears. "I do miss him so."

Mona turned from the walls of honor, taken by Dorothy's sadness, giving Billy a do-something look, returned by confusion, Mona walked over and gave Dorothy a hug, and Billy a disapproving look.

"What's going to happen to all of this now?" Billy asked softly.

"I was going to ask you the same thing," Dorothy faltered.

"Well, I sure as hell don't want any of it," Billy said abruptly, which brought on more tears.

"Oh, I just don't understand you, Billy," Dorothy said a little cross, "you caused your father such endless pain."

"Oh come on…," Billy started, but cut short, by Mona, shaking her head.

Silence followed Billy's father's endless pain.

"So what's going to happen to this place now?" Billy finally asked.

"Got the news last Friday," Dorothy said, "couldn't even wait for the funeral, Gusman's moving in, and that shrew of a secretary, boils my blood to think of it…"

"Gusman?"

"Sure enough, Gusman's been the Finance chair since Mayor Jefferson got reelected, all your dad's doing of course, the mayor and Gusman that is, your dad wanted it that way, arranged the whole thing, stepped back since you've been gone, just wasn't the same, now it never will be," she whimpered.

At the sound of the outside door, opening and closing, Dorothy went into the reception area, and came into Dan Hurley's office with a tall graying man in a dark gray pin striped suit carrying an oxblood briefcase.

"Billy, this is the man who wanted to meet with you, your dad's lawyer, Mr. Carlisle, Mr. Carlisle, Billy Hurley, and this…," but Mr. Carlisle was not interested in this or that or anyone else, nor in shaking Billy's hand.

"W. Foster Carlisle the Third," he announced to Billy, with a nod of his head, "and I'm not your father's *lawyer*, per se," he said tilting his head to Dorothy, "I am his *probate* lawyer, to be precise, your father no doubt counseled with a number of lawyers," he said in correction.

"So?" Billy asked.

"So," Mr. Carlisle replied, "I have a need to speak with you."

"So, go ahead."

"To you privately."

"Of course," Dorothy said, "certainly," and whisked out of the room.

"Privately," repeated Mr. Foster, in Mona's direction.

"I've nothing to keep from her," Billy said, "go right ahead."

"I am not at liberty to do so," said Mr. W.

"I'm giving you permission to do so," Billy said, getting angry.

"You are not my client," said Mr. Third.

Mona interjected.

"Look, of course, no problem," she said, Billy and W. Foster Carlisle the Third staring bullets at each other. "I'll just wait outside, with Dorothy," she said, giving Billy a knowing look, she exited the office, and closed the door.

"Well, now," Mr. W. Carlisle said to Billy once they were alone, "my client, for whom I had the greatest respect, directed that I communicate with you in the event he should meet an untimely death, which, under the circumstances, I must say, I find a particularly odious task, after your despicable display of last Saturday, and its shocking aftermath," he said moving around Anton Cermak's desk, opening the one button of his suit coat exposing his identical pin-striped vest, and taking a seat in Dan Hurley's chair, which he never would have thought of doing in a million years if Dan Hurley were alive. "Although, I must say, the disgust I feel for the necessity of this meeting is mollified somewhat by the subject matter of my communication."

"What the hell are you talking about?" Billy asked, still standing.

Mr. Third Carlisle spread his arms and placed his hands on top of Dan Hurley's desk.

"Yes, well, your father, no doubt deservedly so, as I can see now," he said with some satisfaction, looking at Billy's All Stars, "must not have been very fond of you."

"Is that what he directed you to communicate to me?" Billy asked mockingly.

"No, not exactly, not in those words, he never used those precise words, but the gist, I suppose it would be appropriate to say, the proof, as my litigator partners might say, is in the documents, the trust documents, which I drafted, at his direction, and which he most assuredly signed, evidencing his assent."

"I really don't care about any of this," Billy said. "I don't want any of my father's stolen goods."

"Stolen goods?" Mr. Foster Carlisle asked incredulous. "Preposterous!"

"If that's what you came to talk about, you've wasted your time, and mine, I don't give a shit about my father's blood money, and I don't care who gets it."

Mr. W., the Third, taken aback, did not expect Billy's ambivalence. He had hoped to be delivering some very bad news.

"Well then, whether you like it or not, and, for the record, I must say, I highly suspect the veracity of this act of yours, I am duty bound, and personally quite happy, to tell you that you will not be receiving any of your father's funds, his condominium, his home, his personal property, investments, pensions, accounts, stocks, or bonds. But for contributions to well-deserved charities, which I will faithfully administer, everything is to be liquidated and held in trust, for your children, whom, I understand, by court order, and for no doubt good reason, you are prohibited from seeing or having anything to do with."

"I really don't care about any of this," Billy said softly, believably, to Mr. W. Foster the Third's disappointment.

"Now, however, there is one exception," Mr. Foster went on, "your father did see fit to leave you a certain tract of land, consisting of fifty-two acres of undeveloped and unimproved property located in Wyoming Township, Iowa County, in the State of Wisconsin, which, as I understand it, in comparison to the rest of the estate, is of somewhat relative and marginal value."

"He left me the Property?" Billy asked.

"He did, but that is all," Mr. Carlisle replied.

"But that's everything, you fool," Billy said in shock.

"It most certainly is not everything, relatively speaking, not much of anything," said W., confused.

"Are you done?" Billy asked.

"Yes, quite," Mr. Carlisle said, quite satisfied behind Dan Hurley's desk.

"Then get the hell out from behind my dad's desk."

"Really, and what will you do now, assault me?" W. Foster Carlisle asked, smugly smiling as he got up from behind the desk.

Billy made a slight feint toward the desk, the kind Deano made at Joe Gilliam in the Mad House Inn when Joe tried getting to his feet after Deano slapped him upside the head, and Mr. W. Foster Carlisle, the Third jumped back, around the other side of the desk, sidled away from Billy, and rushed out the door, oxblood briefcase in hand.

"That man is crazy," he said as he raced past Dorothy and Mona, and ran out the heavy door in a huff.

Billy shook his head in surprise at the fifty-two acres, brushed off any memory of Mr. Whatshisname, and took a seat in his father's chair, just like when he was a kid, except now his dad was gone, and all of this, looking around the room, is history, and no one's really going to care, except maybe Dorothy, and what for, Dad, what the hell for, he thought, as he looked at twenty-five photographs of his jovial father staring back at him, all that leverage, know how, chits, and angles, all vanished, gone, in an instant, drifting toward others to fill the void, because nobody owes you anything anymore, Dad, you don't own anybody anymore, and if you had any more plans, advice, or hopeless dreams for your son, well you can just forget about it, they're no longer, you're done, and I'm free of you once and for all.

Billy looked down at his father's desk, wondering how many millions, billions in city business had passed over that gold inlaid surface, now empty, but for a City of Chicago zoning book, map after map page after page, forlorn and out of place, off to the side, with a bookmarked page. Billy picked up the zoning book, opened to the bookmark, each page a separate zoning map for several blocks on the west side, one property circled in pencil, 2620 West Jackson, not even close to his dad's ward, curious, Mona peeking into the office, to find Billy sitting behind his father's desk.

"Everything okay?" she asked.

"Guy's an asshole," Billy said, "but, oddly enough, I'm getting the Property. Early onset, all I can figure."

"Well," Mona smiled, and lowered her voice, "nothing better in the whole world could happen other than that, is there?"

"Yeah, it's okay..."

"Yeah, it's okay, your favorite place in the entire world, it's okay all right," Mona said, as Dorothy walked back into the office.

"Well, he left in a hurry," she said.

"Dorothy," Billy asked, holding up the zoning book, "why would my dad, alderman of a North Side ward, care about a zoning issue on the West Side?"

"Heavens I have no idea, but he sure did raise a ruckus about it before he left, he D&P'd a zoning item, never saw him do that before. Calls the next day from the Alderman, Buildings, Zoning, and they weren't happy."

"Yeah, well, that's all over now, the hell with this," Billy said tossing the zoning book back on the desk, "the good news is that I will never have to deal with any of this bullshit again, now let's get the hell outta here, and maybe we, the living, can get on with our lives."

And they did. Dorothy busied herself in the following days cleaning out Dan Hurley's office, Mona headed back home to take the reins of her new business, and four days later, Billy found himself in court, making his first appearance in the case of *Walsh v. Hurley et al.*

"Call the next case," the judge muttered to his clerk.

From the four rows of benches at the back of the courtroom, Judge Wozak looked bent and beleaguered, perched up on his bench, threatened on all sides by leaning piles of papers and court files, as he looked out over his glasses, rubbed what was left of his hair back over his head, and waited with displeasure for the clerk to call the next case, one after another, day after day, year after year, godawful boring most days, street smart justice in his inimitable way, tough, impatient, gruff, but ultimately fair. Got his start working precincts, Southwest Side, blue collar, worked for years, scrap yard during the day, undergrad, law school at night, where he met Dan Hurley, who helped him get a job in the State's Attorney's Office, where they stuck him in misdemeanors, for five years, and kept him there, smart enough, but no bright light, until it came time to appoint a Polish judge, and with the help of his committeeman, and Dan Hurley's blessing, they put him on the ballot, beat back opposition, and elected him a Circuit Court Judge, assigned to traffic, where all judges started and eventually moved on, except for Judge Wozak, who languished there, passed over, for eight years, until he ran into Dan Hurley at a funeral one day, told him his story, and less than one month later was reassigned to the Probate Division, where he presided over estates worth more than he would see in twenty lifetimes, sons suing fathers, mothers, daughters, disgusting really, could have grown resentful, but he'd worked hauling scrap long enough to be grateful, the law was a calling, and a black robe an honor, and so, despite the piles of paper, petty squabbles, and condescending silk stocking lawyers, he always tried his best.

His courtroom was spare, modernist, tall ceiling, warm oak predominant, in the four rows of back benches, where the public sat, in the jury box rail, the judge's formidable bench, the entire wall behind, in the two counsel tables, and tall doors to jury room and chambers, with green marble ledges along the periphery of the judge's bench and clerk's box, clean lines, not fussy. For the judge's ten o'clock motion call, the clerk sat at his desk to the left of and below the judge's bench, deluged in court files, announcing each case on the call in turn, handing each court file up to the judge, which he did when he called the case, of *Walsh v. Hurley.*

Billy sat in the back benches with a smattering of lawyers waiting for their cases to be called. He perked up at the sound of his case, but did not rise, as a white-haired lawyer in an elegant dark blue three-piece suit rose from one of the counsel tables, called out "petitioner," and approached the judge's bench, followed by a middle aged African American woman, neatly dressed, in a matching gray wool jacket and skirt.

Upon hearing the name of the next case, the judge straightened in his chair, and shed his beleaguered mien, looking out at those approaching the bench, and beyond to the back benches.

"Any respondents in the courtroom?" he called out.

Billy rose from his bench. The judge recognized him.

"Then, get up here!" the judge yelled out.

Billy slid down the bench row, passed through the swinging low brass gates, and stepped up to the judge's bench, alongside the woman in gray.

"Good morning, Your Honor, William Hanneman, from the law firm of Stone, Doherty & Hanneman, on behalf of petitioners."

"I know what law firm you're with Mr. Hanneman," Judge Wozak growled, turning, and smiling, to the woman at Mr. Hanneman's side, "Good morning, Ms. Beecher, nice to see you."

"Good morning, Your Honor, Margaret Beecher, appointed guardian *ad Litem*."

"And I know who you are," Judge Wozak said dismissively to Billy, dressed in his one change of clothes, black tee shirt, jeans, sneakers, "but state your name for the record."

"Billy Hurley, respondent, I guess."

The other lawyers waiting for their cases to be called all realized who had just approached the bench, they had read all about him in the papers, they stopped reading their materials, the clerk stopped shuffling papers, the courtroom silent.

"Of course, I knew your father," Judge Wozak said to Billy, "but then everybody knew your father. That's not gonna be a problem is it Mr. Hanneman?"

"Of course not, Your Honor," replied Mr. Hanneman, knowing full well that if Judge Wozak had a conflict then so did every other judge in the Circuit Court.

"Do you have a lawyer?" the judge asked Billy.

"No, Your Honor."

"Then you better get one."

"Well, I, I don't want my kids," Billy began to say, and then caught himself, and shook his head, "wait, no, that's not what I meant to say," Ms. Beecher looked up at him, "I mean, I'm not contesting…"

"Custody's not all that's at issue here," Judge Wozak declared, "you need a lawyer, but at least you're here, that's miracle enough. What have we got this morning, Mr. Hanneman?"

"Your Honor, we're up this morning to set a date for a hearing, a full evidentiary hearing, at which we intend to prove that the petitioners, my clients, Richard and Mary Alice Walsh, the grandparents of the two children, and the current temporary guardians, who have done everything in their power over the past two and a half years to provide for the children at issue because of this man's contemptible neglect, and who are willing…"

"Mr. Hanneman, just tell me what we need to do today."

"Set a hearing date, Your Honor," said Mr. Hanneman.

"Thank you, and Ms. Beecher," he said, directing his attention to the guardian *ad Litem*, "where are you in your investigation?"

"I have spoken with the children, Your Honor," Ms. Beecher said, "and I have interviewed the Walshes, in their home. All efforts to locate the mother have been unsuccessful," she said, Mr. Hanneman nodding, "but I have not yet had the chance to speak with Mr. Hurley, Your Honor, and wish to do so before submitting my report to the court."

"Of course, understood, Mr. Hanneman?"

"Well, Your Honor, if, as Mr. Hurley has indicated this morning, he has no intention of contesting my clients' petition for permanent guardianship, and of course, really, how could he, I don't see the necessity of wasting any more time just to allow Ms. Beecher to interview Mr. Hurley, I mean, really, I don't see the point…"

"Ms. Beecher, when do you think you will be in a position to submit your report?"

"Well, if I can set up an appointment to speak with Mr. Hurley, I can complete my report and submit it to you, within say, two weeks thereafter."

"Your Honor," Billy interjected, "I'm going home this afternoon, out of state, so I won't even be around…"

"Not until you talk to Ms. Beecher, you're not."

"Look, I don't even want custody," Billy said, "what's the point, I mean what happens if I just leave anyway?"

"If you ever want to see your kids again, you're gonna stick around and talk to Ms. Beecher," Judge Wozak sneered down at him. "You see, son," the Judge barked, "I was there last Saturday," pausing for effect, "I had the utmost respect for your father, and I watched you walk out of your own father's funeral," he said in disbelief, "I saw the look on the cardinal's face, we all read about his death, so it's a good thing you don't want your kids, as you say, but this case is going to be handled according to the letter of the law, with your cooperation, whether you like it or not. If you don't want to show up for the evidentiary hearing, that's your decision, but in the meantime, you're going to talk to Ms. Beecher."

Billy felt all eyes in the courtroom on him. He thought of what he would have to say to Mona if he went back.

"Okay, I'll stick around."

"Big of you," the judge said. "Okay, now, I'm going to set this for another status…"

"But judge, my clients, the petitioners, have been more than patient, they're entitled to a hearing…"

"And they're going to get one, Mr. Hanneman," the judge interrupted, "now when can the two of you sit down and talk?" he asked Ms. Beecher.

"Well, I'm going out of town for my aunt's funeral this weekend, Your Honor, so it won't be until mid-next week at the earliest," said Ms. Beecher.

Billy rolled his eyes.

"Okay, you," the judge said to Billy, "will meet with Ms. Beecher at a mutually convenient time next, Wednesday?" a nod from Ms. Beecher, "and I will give Ms. Beecher two weeks after that to submit her report. That will take us," the judge said looking at his calendar, "into July and I have a trial scheduled for the last two weeks in July, so we're looking at August."

Mr. Hanneman rolled his eyes.

"How about we schedule the next status for Monday, August 6, how does that look?" the judge asked Mr. Hanneman, thumbing through his own calendar.

"Yes, Your Honor, yes we can make that work."

"Thank you, then we're done here for today, prepare the order," the judge announced.

"Next case," he growled, and slumped back into his chair.

CHAPTER FOUR

The Trail

"Okay, so I just got out of that goddam guardianship thing, and I've got to be back here next Wednesday, too!"

"What for?"

"Gotta talk to some lady, she's doing this quote, investigation, close quote."

"All you've got to do is talk to her?"

"Yeah, that's not so bad, but next Wednesday? Really? Now, if I go home, I'll have to come right back, this is a pain in the ass, and there isn't even a point."

"Ben explained the point."

"Nothing I do's gonna matter, the judge hates me already."

"Why, what did the judge say?"

"He was at the funeral."

"Oh."

"The whole goddam town was at the funeral."

"I don't think that's true."

"You're not much help, should I stay or go?"

"Well, I'd love you back here, but I don't like the idea of you on the road so much, on that bike, with all those trucks, if anything should happen to you…"

"I'm comin' home."

"But if you come home, you might not go back."

"That's the idea, it's all bullshit."

"Your kids aren't bullshit. You've got to stop saying stuff like that."

"That's not what I mean, it's the whole process, the lawyers, the judge, an investigation, Jesus, what, now I'm being investigated?"

"You just have to answer some questions."

"It's nobody's business."

"I think you should stay. It'd be a mistake to come home and not go back."

Silence.

"Billy, you need to do this. You've already done the hard part."

"Yeah, that went well."

"It's just a couple more days, then you'll be able to come home saying you did the right thing."

"I'm gonna go crazy in this hellhole."

"Oh, come on, you've got a doorman."

"Easy for you, in God's country."

"I think you're going to live; I'm doing fine by the way."

"Sorry."

"Weather's nice, river's low, reservations are steady. Meeting with Wilcoxsin again tomorrow, see where we are, figure out what we can do, what not."

"And I'm not around to help."

"You will be, soon enough. Just take care of your business down there, and get back here, I miss you."

"Miss you, too."

"Hey, I had an idea."

"Yeah?"

"Did you mean what you said on the highway in the rain that day?"

"Let's see, you mean when you asked if I'd marry you and I said yes?"

"Yeah, that part."

"Yeah, I remember that."

"Good, cuz I've been thinking…"

"Uh-oh."

"Given any thought to how that might happen?"

"No, but I bet…"

"I have an idea."

"Figured."

"Don't see the point in putting things off. If we're gonna do it, I think we should just do it."

"That's fine, something small, maybe, understated…"

"Well," Mona paused, "not quite what I had in mind."

"Oh, God."

"There's a full moon July 16."

"You're talking July 16 like next month July 16?"

"Yeah, why too soon?"

"No, well…"

"I thought we could have a little ceremony, out on the island, invite a few friends."

"We don't have any friends."

"Well, actually, I was thinking of, well, kind of making it an open invitation."

"What does that mean?"

"Well, I was thinking of spreading the word, whoever wanted to come could come, be good for business, let everybody know we're in it for the long haul, together. Open bar, bluegrass band, the works."

"On the island?"

"Yeah."

"Wow." Silence. "Is there money for that?"

"I'll find out tomorrow."

"But, open bar? You know how many'll show if there's an open bar? Up there?"

"Well, I figure not everybody's gonna want to go out to the island, that should keep the numbers down, anyway, it's just an idea."

"In a month?"

"Yeah."

"Wow."

"Can't tell if that's a good wow or a bad wow."

"I can't either."

"We'll start out with a bang."

"Sure hope you know what you're doing."

"Got a good feeling about this. I'll talk it over with Wilcoxsin."

"Good idea, let Wilcoxsin plan our wedding."

"So, you gonna stay?"

"Yeah, probably, since my future wife doesn't want me home."

"Come on."

"Actually, I did get a call from Dorothy, said she wanted to see me, so maybe now I will."

"City Hall?"

"Yeah, says she found something in my dad's papers she needs to show me."

"I trust her."

"More bullshit."

"Be nice, she's doing all that work, plus, she was really into your dad, this is hard on her, you're the closest thing to him she's got."

"Yeah, great."

"By the way, Deano stopped by the other day."

"So?"

"So, he was talking about your dad."

"Yeah?"

"Well, you know Deano's a pretty good hunter, and he was saying, he's really not sure it was an accident."

"Great, Deano conspiracy theories."

"Well, you should talk to him about it, when you get back."

"Hey, babe, that's on him, I really don't care. What happened, happened, he's dead, accident or not, and nothing's going to bring him back."

"But don't you care…."

"Not really."

"Okay fine, but you be careful down there, if somebody wanted him dead, it was probably somebody down there."

"Bob, the doorman, maybe."

"Seriously."

"I'll be careful."

"Chin up, see you soon, in one piece, love you."

"Love you, too, and thanks."

"What for?"

"Everything."

Monday morning Billy went back to City Hall, last time ever, solemn vow, climbed the stairs, walked into his father's reception area, boxes everywhere.

"Holding up?" he asked Dorothy.

"Lord help me, they want me out by next week, but I am making progress, as you can see," she said pointing to the boxes. "They're letting me put them in storage for now, until you change your mind," she said smiling.

"Not a chance. So, what's so important?"

"Okay," she said rising from her desk, "I was going through everything in his office last week," she said as she made her way into Dan Hurley's office, Billy following, "after you left, all his papers, desk drawers, credenzas, file cabinets, tried to organize them best I could," she said pointing to the boxes in scattered columns about the office, as she made her way behind the desk, no more photographs on the walls, no more Man of the

Year awards on the credenza, a lifetime, erased, stowed in boxes that may never see the light of day.

"The photographs and crystal, anything valuable I'm gonna keep separate, but there was one drawer that was locked, this one," she said pointing to the lowest drawer on the right hand side of Anton Cermak's desk, "for some reason, never even noticed it was locked before, must have been somewhat recent, and I found this," she said, as she leaned down and took a thin manilla subfile from the lowest right hand drawer and handed it to Billy, "and after looking it over, I couldn't figure what he was up to, I mean, I know about the one, the big one, the one with the clip, because I got it for him, from the State, it's a lease or something, but he never told me why he wanted it, made no sense to me at all, until he D&P'd that zoning matter, don't know why he'd want it locked up, though, and, well, after looking at it, the only person I could think of to show it to was you. I think you'll see what I mean," she suggested, "and so you take your time, I'll leave you to it," she said as she left the room, a little proud at getting another Hurley to sit behind the old man's desk one last time.

Billy held the file, looked at Dorothy suspiciously as she left the room, and sat down in his dad's chair, behind his dad's desk.

"What is this bullshit," he muttered, as he opened the file, and began to examine its contents.

The first set of papers consisted of about forty pages held together by a black binder clip at the top left hand corner, the first six pages of which appeared to be a lease, typed onto a State of Illinois Real Estate Form, for 200,000 square feet of space to be leased by the Illinois Department of Public Aid as a warehouse from the New Life Blessing Corporation for a term of ten years, at five dollars per square foot, for a total rental over the ten-year life of the lease of approximately $10,000,000 on property located at 2620 W. Jackson Boulevard, Chicago, Illinois, and dated April 2, 1983.

Also attached were multiple pages of building and program specifications for construction of improvements, i.e. the warehouse, on the premises. The lease was signed by 1) the Illinois Department of Public Aid, which would be using the warehouse; 2) the Illinois Department of Central Management Services, servicing agency for all state property; and 3) the New Life Blessing Corporation, signed by a Sydney Black, as power of attorney for the President of the New Life Blessing Corporation.

The second document was a copy of a page from the Committee on Zoning Report for the City Council meeting held on June 6, 1984, with a circled item, Item No. 34, which appeared to seek a change in zoning for property located at 2620 W. Jackson Boulevard, Chicago, Illinois.

The third document was a copy of a page from the City of Chicago Zoning Code. He looked down at his dad's desk, at the zoning book which lay where he had tossed it the week before, and opened it to the bookmarked page, the same page in the manilla subfile, showing the zoning map for property which included 2620 West Jackson Boulevard.

Okay, so it's the same property, Billy thought.

The fourth and last document in the subfile was a yellow page from a legal pad, with what looked like his dad's handwriting.

There was a scrawled heading, which appeared to read, "Grenade," followed by a harder to read handwritten list, in blue ink, of bullet points:

1) - Ald. Prerogative

2) Bench - Elected; Merit

3) - Patronage

4) Elctds, Emplees - Govt business

5) Ass Office; - elected; appt.; Court appeals

6) CPD rank, race %

7) Bond counsel, - inside; appt; real work, MBE; bill - %, hourly

8) MBE, Govt. K's; %'s

9) - Committeemen, "first thing we do…"

The final item on the list was written in pencil, at a slant, an after-thought, which simply read "10) D&P."

The last entry, without a number, appeared to read, "Press, all of above."

Hieroglyphics, inscrutable, except for maybe the D&P, which he knew now related to a lease of property on the West Side he couldn't care less about. Couldn't make out the rest, really didn't care.

"Dorothy?"

Dorothy came running into the office.

"So why was I supposed to give a shit about any of this."

"Billy, you should watch your language in your father's office."

"Okay," Billy started over, "Dorothy, why did you think this was so important that I had to come down here. This has nothing to do with me, don't know why I should care about this lease, or these notes, which, best I can tell, is a summary of how my dad and his cronies stayed in business all these years."

"Yes, well, I don't know, I don't know what it means, it's just, it's just not like him, locking stuff up like that, must have been important to him somehow, but I don't know why. And why is that D&P on there, he never did anything like that before, not in somebody else's ward, why would he do that?"

"So what do you think it is?

"Goodness, I don't know. He was real thoughtful like, toward the end, like he didn't care as much anymore, like maybe he was having, I don't know, like, second thoughts."

"About what?"

"I don't know, about everything," Dorothy replied. "I don't know, I'm sorry, I just thought that you should see this, I don't know what any of it means, I thought you might, I just want you to know about your father I guess, he was a good man, and I'm really, really sorry you don't think so, and I think you should give him…"

"Thanks, Dorothy, but you can spare me. That's between him and me, actually, just me now, I guess. He's gone, and whatever he meant by any of this doesn't matter anymore, we just have to deal with that," he said, tears welling in Dorothy's eyes.

"Okay, fine, Billy, you have your own life, that's fine, but I know where that property is," she said seriously. "That building is right next to the First Missionary Baptist Church near the railroad viaduct on West Jackson, I drive by it all the time. Reverend Simmons is the pastor there. Wonderful man, truly blessed, spirit's in him," she said. "Your father knew him, went to see him the week before he died. You might want to go talk to him, he's a healer, do you good."

"Why would I want to do that?"

"Because, he's a good man," Dorothy said, unable to hold back tears, "and somebody you should know, he's the good side of this town, a side you know nothing about. I know what you think about your father, all of us, big city, fightin' over spoils, no goodness, but not everybody's like that, you just don't know cuz you've never been out there, you don't know about *us*, *our* community, your dad cared more about us than you think, you know about your Latin School and your big house and your dad's condo, and all your wild parties, and those awful clubs, no wonder you feel like you do, you think you know it all but you don't know nothin' 'bout 'nothin,'" she said, tears now streaming, "you don't know where the heart is, there's real goodness out there, on the streets, and 'til you know about that side you'll never know 'bout what you think you're so sure about. You want to find out what this city's about, do yourself a favor, before you turn your back on us, and your father," wiping tears away, "you go see Reverend Simmons, then you tell me this place I call home is a hellhole."

Billy stared at Dorothy. She'd never said a cross word to him, while his dad was alive. She was right, of course. He deserved it. He didn't know anything about her world, where she came from, her family, her church, her neighborhood. Had a mental picture, a bias, and it wasn't pretty, because he didn't know, didn't really know where or how three million people in his home town carried on their lives, how they scraped by, raised families, dragged their asses out of bed every morning and went to work, to school, dodged bullets, gangs, cops. Most of which he didn't want to know, didn't need to know what might shake what he thought he knew, but if he knew that much he knew enough to know he really didn't know, no right to be so sure, any of us, easier to be sure, that's for sure, then it's all right there in a neat little box, that doesn't exist, it's the stuff you're not so sure about, that's the challenge, the stuff that doesn't fit your world view, hard, confusing, and not worth your time, except it's what you need to know, to know anything. Yeah, she was right, of course, he thought, as he gave her a parting hug.

And so he left his father's office for the last time, humbled, and a good thing. Took the file with him. Walked out into the long pink marble hall, saw an elevator light halfway down, ran to jump on, had to reach out his arm to stop the doors, and hopped in to one other rider, staring, impatiently.

"Well, Hurley," the passenger said, surprised.

Billy didn't recognize him at first.

"It's me, Jefferson."

The space in the elevator, plenty big, tight for the two of them.

"Oh, hey Johnny," Billy said. Hadn't seen Johnny since graduation, Latin.

"What're you doing here?" Johnny Jefferson asked.

"Just checkin' out my dad's office, one more time."

"Awww, that's so sweet, and after what you did in front of that cardinal," Johnny said laughing.

"You were there?"

"Everybody was there, you fool."

"What were you doing there?"

"You haven't heard?" pride, fake surprise, "I'm in the biz these days, man. Course you know my dad, the mayor, and I, well, I am the newly appointed Commissioner of Buildings."

"Didn't know," Billy said, checking out Johnny Jefferson's silk suit and alligator shoes.

"Yeah, I guess you could say shoe's on the other foot now, eh Hurley?" Johnny said looking at Billy's one set of clothes.

"What's that supposed to mean?" Billy asked.

The elevator reached the ground floor, the two stepped into City Hall's main concourse.

"Well, back in school, your old man was always the big shot, and you along for the ride, but things have changed since then, man."

"For the better I can see."

"Damn straight," Johnny said smiling.

"Nepotism, alive and well."

"Read 'em and weep, buddy," Johnny said slapping Billy lightly on the shoulder.

"Don't really care," said Billy.

"Yeah, right, well, s'pose I should say sorry about your old man, guess we all have our time, things'll be a lot different around here now, though, won't have to worry about him stickin' his nose where it don't belong, for one thing."

"That been a problem for you?"

"Yeah, well, let's just say it won't be a problem anymore," Johnny said smiling.

"Well," Billy said turning away, "wish I could say it was great to see you, Johnny, but I've got to go, reality calls."

"Don't get more real than this," Johnny said, with outstretched arms, smiling, as Billy walked away, waving his hand holding the file, out of the Hall one last time, Hurleys waning, Jeffersons ascending, what a loser, Johnny thought, looking down at the shine in his alligator shoes.

Next day, nothing else to do, Billy did the unthinkable. He went to see Reverend Simmons at the First Missionary Baptist Church, Madison Avenue bus, due west out of the Loop, hot, no air, windows don't open, shades of black everywhere, Billy, a sore thumb. Discount liquor, hair salons, vacant lots, storefront churches, wigs, seafood, convenience stores, taverns, soul food, a school, barber shop, converted church, Catholic to Baptist, forward or backward, all the same, barbecue, a fire house, empty shops, bungalows, walk-ups, some tidy, some not, nevertheless, neighborhoods, families, getting by, home is home, block after block, carved up checkerboards of gang territory, boundaries drawn down alleyways, gotta know who's who and what's what.

Got off at Rockwell, and walked south along the east side of the railroad viaduct, to Jackson, where he turned right, walked through the littered viaduct underpass, darkness, and into the light of day, upon a large, relatively new, two-story stone nondescript rectangle of a building that ran north to south along the west side of the viaduct, fronted by a large parking lot. But not a church at all. Billy looked down the street to the west, saw a church at the end of the block, and what looked to be some kind of warehouse in the middle, but no, this was the address, this must be the place. He turned into the parking lot, walked up to the glass doors of the building, and walked inside.

"Hey, brother, can I help you?" came a deep voice from a large man in what looked like a security office toward the back of the reception area. Billy looked lost. Through the doors to his left he could see a large, looked brand new, gymnasium, with squeaks and shouts of a full court game going on, and straight ahead several folks in the security office, eyeing Billy.

"Is this the First Missionary Baptist Church?"

"This's the place, brother, who you lookin for?"

"I have a meeting with Pastor Simmons, at ten o'clock," Billy said.

"Well, do you now," said the security guard, "come to see the Reverend," he said getting up from his chair, "well, welcome brother, he's on the second floor, the elevator's broken, so you'll have to use the stairs," he said pointing.

At the top of the stairs, Billy came upon an open landing, with windows to the west, and a clear view of the warehouse building next door, turned the corner, through a door into a large room, chairs along the walls, metal desk, prominent against the facing wall, no greeting from the middle-aged woman behind the desk. Billy and she were the only ones in the room. She ignored him, preoccupied with papers, dissembling contempt.

"Hi, I'm here to see Reverend Simmons," Billy said stepping up to her.

Still ignored him.

"I have an appointment, at ten o'clock, is he in?"

"Have a seat," she said, not looking up. "He'll see you when he's ready."

Billy took a seat, began reading through a pamphlet describing everything offered by something called, Reverend Simmons' Saving Grace West Side Community Center, laundry list of lifelines, programs, for the needy, impressive.

An older thin man with a cane walked in.

"Blessed day to you, Julius," the Reverend's assistant greeted the older man, warmly, for Billy's benefit, let him know where he stood. "You go right ahead in," she said to Julius.

And it was like that, one after another, ten-ten, ten-fifteen, ten-thirty, a parade of visitors, just stopping by, chairs starting to fill, Billy a lighter shade, everyone except the receptionist, smiling, friendly.

Around ten-forty, the Reverend himself opens the door from his office, ducks his head out.

"Blessed mornin', everyone," broad smile, big teeth, looking around the room, "Althea, have you seen…"

"Ah, Mr. Hurley," the Reverend said, spying Billy sticking out in the corner, "been waiting for you," he said, "come on in."

Althea scowled. Billy rose from his chair, walked up to the Reverend, big welcoming smile, "You come right on in," the Reverend said to Billy, "and folks," he addressed the room, "you all sit tight. I'll be right with you," he said with a wave, and walked into his office after Billy, "here now, son, take a seat."

Billy looked around the room. Wooden desk old, veneer chipped, large stenciled picture of what looked like the Reverend and a woman in a gold cap, on an easel, in the corner, cushioned red Naugahyde chair for the Reverend behind the desk, red floral stuffed couch against the wall, wooden chairs facing the desk, small circular writing table, with papers, to the side, discount furniture, relatively new, showing its age.

"I am so, so, sorry about your father," the Reverend began, in a low, serious, genuine voice, shaking his head, "he was a fine man."

The Reverend wore a burgundy suit with narrow gold pin stripes, coat a little spacious, little long, wide lapels, matching vest, textured white shirt, pointed collar, large cuffs with gold cufflinks, wide tie, goldenrod, sky blue stripes, pocket kerchief, goldenrod, pointed light brown polished shoes. About fifty years old, five-feet ten, two twenty, round bald head smallish in proportion, shoulders somewhat stooped, bent forward, for listening, caring, round brown eyes, knowing flashes of kindness, empathy, tell him anything, unburden, we're all sinners, you're not alone, give me your hand, we'll walk together through the valley of death, in the light of Jesus, which on the West Side was no small thing, to know there was somewhere to go for help, without judgment, to make it through, to make sense, of trials and tribulations, drive-bys, and drugs and maximum prisons, which Lord knows there's plenty enough to go around, we're all in the same boat, you're among friends, don't be afraid, we've got each other and the spirit of Jesus, all we need, Hallelujah, we'll all be blessed in the kingdom of heaven. That's what his eyes said.

And Billy saw all that, felt it, remained skeptical. Nice front, good show, see how it works, but what's with the suit, the shoes, the Benz parked in the first space outside the front door. What's in it for him, for them, the outward show, the smooth talk, ulterior motives, he'd seen that routine before, makes the world go round. Peddle the Lord, live large on the fear of God.

What Billy didn't know, how could he, the Benz was leased, and the Reverend had missed the last two payments. The suit was old, as any of his church members could tell you. The new building they were in was the first phase of an ambitious building project the Reverend had undertaken, on the advice of trusted advisers who had since disappeared, to demolish the old crumbling red brick church three blocks away and build a new church on vacant land near the viaduct, with a brand spanking new community center, all financed by the Christian Ministries Finance Corporation, on the most reasonable terms, reserved for the faithful, in the name of Jesus, and the Reverend's personal guaranty, and so the old church was razed, and the community center built, way over budget, with cheap materials, unscrupulous subs, and the Reverend ran out of money, with no new church, counting every last dime from Sunday offerings, and coming up short to pay interest on the loan, for which the community center was collateral, on which the good folks at the Christian Ministries Finance Corp. were threatening to foreclose, and by the way don't forget the personal guaranty, praise the Lord.

Billy, of course, didn't know any of this. He didn't know, that when somebody at the Christian Ministries Finance Corp. finally asked the Reverend to update his personal financial statements they found, to their surprise, he had a negative net worth. His wife, the smiling woman in the gold cap, had been seriously ill for months, hospital bills were devouring his high deductible, and the home equity credit he took to make ends meet all but wiped out any equity in his modest three-bedroom home. Just before his wife had fallen ill, they had taken in two crack babies, whose custodial grandmother had suddenly passed away, for whom he was now responsible. Each Sunday, after preaching the gospel above a basketball court, he'd huddle in his office, personally counting each bill and coin in the offering baskets, praying it would all add up, cover the nut just one more month, wondering how he could keep all these plates spinning, when they would come crashing down.

And a lot was riding on it, on him. While it would have been nice to have the church, the community center was doing its job, literally, the center, of the community, Bible study, all hours, job training, computer literacy, food for the hungry, public aid seminars, public housing services, summer job programs, after school programs, nutrition classes, reading tutors, career counsellors, legal counseling, financial counseling, mentors, neighborhood block meetings, all of this he, they, tried their best to make available, open to anyone, an oasis, where kids shoot hoops instead of each other, where felons find work, and all of it pretty much riding on him, driver of the bus to the tent revival, son of a minister, boy to man in these same streets, self-effacing, soft spoken, on his back, wings fluttered.

Billy couldn't see any of this, because the Reverend didn't let on, to Billy or anyone. No one knew or could tell what he carried around with him each day, because he kept it to himself, he wasn't the one with problems, he was the one to whom everyone brought problems, he was the answer, because he was in with the Lord, God's ear, had his back, and together with the spirit of the Lord he rose each day to spread the good news, with a smile and an open heart, and the faith that it would all work out, somehow, because each day was a blessed one.

The Reverend settled into the cushion of his Naugahyde chair, leaning slightly forward and to his right, with a kind smile, the kind you could trust.

"To be honest Reverend, I didn't care much for my father, to me he wasn't such a fine man."

The Reverend sized him up.

"I'm sure you have your reasons, son, but do they really matter anymore?" the Reverend asked.

"Well, they don't just disappear."

"True enough, true enough, but maybe a little distance, some time, will help, heals all wounds."

"Saw him up close for a long time, didn't like what I saw."

"Well, sometimes, you get too close, you lose focus."

Billy nodded his head. That made some sense, bird's eye view.

"You know, in my work," the Reverend said, "I've found, grudges, kinda like yours, just bring us down, make us angry, unhappy, and we start lookin' at everything with these dirty glasses on and it's no wonder we don't like what we see, but it all starts in here," he said pointing to his heart. "To make things better, we have to start here," he said.

"We were talking about my dad."

"I think we're talkin' about you. Your father, may he rest in peace, is no longer with us."

"Yeah, well, to everyone out there, he was this back slapping what can I do for you kind of good guy, but when you got up close, like I did, had to, my whole life, you could see how it was all just for him, there wasn't anything behind anything he did that wasn't based on greed, what was in it for him. He didn't believe in anything except the game for the game's sake, it's like he was going through the motions his whole life, nothing behind it, all a prop, nothing like this," Billy said, stretching out his arms, meaning the Reverend and his works, "there was no reason for anything other than self-gratification, there wasn't any soul in anything he did. It was all, it was just all, bullshit," Billy blurted out, and regretted, "sorry, Reverend."

"I've heard the word before."

"And it's not as simple as saying well, he's gone now, get over it, because we are who we are, I'm my father's son, that's the rub, because I feel like, growing up with them, my folks, all that time, I feel like they gave me everything except, I don't know, everything except a soul, somehow."

"And you think that's your parents' fault," the Reverend said smiling.

"Yeah, well at least his fault, for sure."

"So what are you going to do about that, the rest of your life," the Reverend said, stabbing the air with the two fingers of his right hand, pointing, thumb tucked behind, "blame your old man because you feel like, like, well, a word you would say but I would prefer not to, if you know what I mean."

"You mean because I feel like an asshole?"

"That's the one."

Billy fell silent. His rage, carefully constructed, rationalized, over the years, had come to define him, an addiction, a crutch, the anti-father, everything he was not, but saddled with the same blood, the same wiring, the same lost soul.

"I have a pretty good eye for people," the Reverend said, leaning back in his chair, "and you strike me as exceptionally honest, confused, but honest."

Billy did not respond, never thought of it that way.

"Honesty is a virtue, to be sure," the Reverend continued, "but it's a tough world for the truly honest," he said, with a shadow of regret, fault, a far-away look replaced his smile.

"The trick is to find a path that is true to yourself," the Reverend said softly, twinge of vulnerability.

Billy saw it.

"Yeah, well, you found yours," Billy said.

"Yes, I was lucky," the Reverend replied. "My daddy was a minister, and his daddy before him. My, wiring, as you say, I was made for this, this is who I am, I just want to help people, that's all I've ever really wanted to do, but really, it's not about me at all. On my own I don't know where I'd be, but I don't face it alone, because I have a savior, it's all about Jesus, all of this," he said motioning with his arms, "is all about Jesus, and if you open your heart to him, son, I do believe you will find the strength you need to shed those dirty glasses and see the world with all his blessedness, in Jesus' name."

"I don't think you give yourself enough credit," Billy said. "You're the one doing all this good work, not Jesus."

The Reverend laughed.

"But I'm not the son of God, Billy, my flesh and blood, it's not enough, my flock needs more than me to get through their days, they need to know there's a reason they suffer so, they don't come here to see me, they come to see the spirit of Jesus, find a new life, one worth living, in his name, in the name of the father, and the son, who carried out the works of the father."

"No offense, Reverend, I don't buy it."

"No, I can see that, that's fine, son, you didn't come here to become a Baptist, just can't help myself," the Reverend said with a broad smile, "so, was there something, in particular, you wanted to see me about?"

"No, although I can see why Dorothy wanted me to come."

"Your dad's Dorothy?"

"Yeah, it was her idea, seems anything good I end up doing is some woman's idea."

"True, since the beginning," affirmed the Reverend.

"But she did tell me that my dad came to see you, week before he died."

"That he did, came to see me about that warehouse next door."

"What about it?"

"He was asking who owned it."

"Why?"

"Don't know, don't know who owns it, either. It was ours couple years ago, got it from the city, for a dollar, urban renewal program, thought we could do something with it, but we were over our heads, code violations killing us, and one day couple years ago this fella comes along, didn't know him, South Side, says he'd give us $10,000 to take it off our hands, and I thought, well, the Lord does act in mysterious ways, manna from heaven, just when we needed it, so we sold it, felt sorry for the guy at the time, and then he kinda disappeared, and the owner, on the deed anyway, is some kinda land trust, one of the banks downtown, so I don't know who owns it really. Lot of work done to it, though, looks right nice now, somebody put some dollars into that old warehouse, money we never had, don't know what they plan on doing with it."

"So that's what you told my dad?"

"All I knew. Would've helped your dad any way I could. He helped us out over the years."

"My dad?"

"Regular contributor, your father."

"To you?"

"Not me, our church."

Billy looked surprised.

"See, things you didn't know," said the Reverend.

"Guess so," said Billy, rising to his feet.

"Well, you've got a full house out there, I should leave you to it, Reverend."

"Yes, my flock awaits, but I'm glad you came, good to meet the son of my good friend."

Billy shook hands with the Reverend.

"Good friend?"

"I thought so, best of luck to you, son."

"Thanks, Reverend, and to you."

When he left the Reverend, and the Saving Grace West Side Community Center, Billy walked across the parking lot to take a closer look at the three-story warehouse. Long building, dark gray bricks, newly tuck pointed, new windows, new doors, new barrel-vaulted ceiling on the top floor, new loading docks, broom clean, complete rehab, real nice, and now empty, just waiting, for something. But what, Billy wondered, and then didn't, because for Billy, but what, really didn't matter, as he turned his back on the warehouse, the West Side, and headed back downtown. What mattered was getting the hell out of town, and he was almost free, one more day.

When Wednesday finally came, he called to set up the appointment with Ms. Beecher, but didn't hear back from her until noon, and when she finally did call back, she couldn't meet until four, the whole day practically shot, his exodus slipping away. It wasn't until early afternoon that he took the elevator down to the lobby, where Bob rose from behind his desk.

"Got something for you," Bob said looking around his desk, "here, this came around eleven this morning," Bob said handing Billy an envelope. "Some Black guy comes in lookin' like he just crawled out from under a rock," Bob said in his wrinkled uniform, "said to give you this."

"Was he really a Black guy, Bob, in your lobby?"

"Fuck you, Billy. I don't want any part of your drug deals, you hear me?"

Billy took the envelope, entered the revolving door, over his shoulder.

"Have a nice day, Bob."

Billy opened the envelope and began reading the note as he walked down the Inner Drive toward Oak Street, cryptic, some guy needed to see him, no name, said it was important, urgent, yeah, right, what is it with these people, Art Institute gardens, south side, six-thirty, urgent, really? Why him? Whole town stricken with a sense of urgency, not one thing it's another, angle upon angle, hidden agendas, trip wires everywhere, no thank you, with any luck, he'd be long gone by then, get away from all this, leave it all behind, soon enough, he thought, as he put the note in his back pocket, but the timing wasn't good, could run out of daylight if the meeting goes late, didn't want a night ride, interstates at night, on a bike, Mona right about that, better in the morning, but still a chance, if she's on time, and then, the great escape, concrete to field, room to move, open air, freedom, at last.

It was around one o'clock when he hopped on the 151 bus heading south down Michigan Avenue, past the Drake, George Jensen, the church, Bonwit Teller, John Hancock, Fields, Lord & Taylor, Water Tower, Saks, Nieman Marcus, Tip Top Tap, Hotel Continental, Tribune Tower, Wrigley Building, Michigan Avenue Bridge, Chicago River, Fort Dearborn, Jean Baptiste Point Du Sable, Grant Park, Cultural Center, Streetwall, Chicago Athletic Association, the Art Institute, where he got off, and went inside to kill time, with Turner, Bellows, the Impressionists, Rodin, Sunday Afternoon on the Island of the Grande Jatte, The Old Guitarist, Georgia O'Keefe, Chagall's American Windows, and the shining suits of armor.

Around three-thirty, he walked out upon the wide steps of the Art Institute and took in the view, no, Lone Rock had nothing that came close, and walked west down Adams Street, past the Palmer House, Peacock Jewelers, State Street, the Berghoff, Van der Rohe's courthouse, Calder's flamingo, Clark Street, to the Rookery Building on LaSalle Street, where Ms. Beecher had her office on the seventh floor. Twelve story red marble terra cotta Burnham and Root load bearing steel skeleton Chicago school floating raft masterpiece, with Wright's skylight lobby, ironwork Carrara marble oriel staircase, bronze elevator doors etched with birds. Elevator still had an operator, with a cage, and a stool, and took Billy up to the seventh floor, where he found Ms. Beecher's office, and opened and walked through the glass door stenciled with her name.

The tight waiting area had two old frame chairs, a small table with old People magazines and a Daily Law Bulletin, a glass ticket window with a silver bell, and a door leading back to Ms. Beecher's office. Billy tapped the bell, took a seat and waited. Ten minutes later, he tapped the bell again. Ten minutes after that he tapped the bell again, and five minutes later Ms. Beecher opened the inside door, wearing a navy cotton skirt, matching fitted jacket, and a silk scarf of bright red, yellow and navy tied about her neck.

"I apologize for making you wait, Mr. Hurley" she said, "I had a call I couldn't get rid of, come on back," and she led Billy through the door, past gray file cabinets, and into her spacious office, lined in walnut, with two large windows facing out into the Rookery's open core.

"I do believe you made the right decision by agreeing to speak with me," she said, "and I am sorry I was not available earlier, but family funerals deserve our attention, as I am told you understand."

"It gets around."

"Yes, unfortunately, our reputations do precede us."

"Yeah, well," Billy said, feeling the afternoon, his ride home, slipping away, "let's go then, what is it we have to talk about?" matter of fact, not mean-spirited.

"Your children," Ms. Beecher said, an accusation.

"Okay…"

"I believe when you were in court, you said, something to the effect," she said looking down at her notes, "that, quote, I don't want my kids, end quote, which, quite frankly, is not something I hear very often," she said, expecting a response.

Billy did not.

"You know that this guardianship proceeding will in all likelihood decide the fate of your children for years to come, if not the rest of their lives."

"So I've been told."

"So how can you not care about them?"

"I didn't say I didn't care about them."

"Sounded like that to everyone in the courtroom."

Billy looked down at his hands.

"You know I'm this close," he said calmly, with finger and thumb extended, almost touching, "…well, let's just say, that's the wrong button to push with me, you see, I really don't care what everyone or anyone in that courtroom thought, okay? Really. I don't live my life for them. Nobody in that courtroom knows anything about me, you don't know anything about me. Maybe the judge and you and all those suits got a charge out of rushing to judgment about me, makes everybody feel better when there's somebody to kick around, but I don't do that, I've given up judging people, or caring about what they think."

"You don't do that?"

"Do what?"

"Judge people."

"I try very hard not to."

"You judge your father."

"Yeah, well, that's something I know something about."

"And now I'm trying to get to know something about you, for the case, for the judge."

"Okay, well now you know something about me."

"You know why the judge is called a judge, right? You know that's his job?"

"Some job."

Ms. Beecher thought a moment.

"Well, what if that judge tried his best to first understand all the relevant facts that applied to a particular situation and only then judged the case, do you have the same problem with that?"

"Didn't sound like that's what he was doing."

"Well, the reason I'm here, the reason I'm doing this, talking to you, is to do just that, determine the relevant facts that pertain to your children and report on those facts so the judge can make a reasoned decision about who should be responsible for your kids."

"Well, we can cut this short, cuz I can tell you right now that ain't me."

"Why not?"

"Look, I assume you read all about what I did to them didn't you? You wouldn't be worth your salt if you didn't."

"Yes, I did."

"Then isn't this case closed?"

"Not necessarily."

"Okay," Billy shrugged his shoulders, "why don't you just ask what you need to ask so we can get this over with."

"Okay," Ms. Beecher looked down at her notes, "have you done any drugs since the incident with your children that the whole city read about two years ago?"

"No."

"None at all?"

"I said no, didn't I?"

"How do I know you're telling the truth?"

"Because I don't lie."

Ms. Beecher raised an eyebrow and looked at him. In her legal experience, a juror's job is to figure out who's lying least.

"About anything?"

"About anything."

"Okay, then what do you think about your in-laws, the Walshes?"

"They have a nice house, money, and they probably love my kids."

"Probably?"

"Don't know for sure."

"That bother you?"

Billy thought about it.

"Hadn't thought about it."

"Think you should?"

"Probably."

"Okay," expectantly.

"Well, first, I'm not really sure I know what that word, love, really means, to you, to anyone, used so often, by too many, too loosely, I have a higher expectation I guess, but second, what's more important, is that my kids'll be taken care of."

"So what's your definition?"

"Not sure. I think if you've been living with someone happily for more than thirty years you might know, something lasting, unshakeable, not disposable or undoable, so that you might be willing to do something for somebody that might not be good for you because you think it's more important."

"Okay, then apply that definition to my question about the Walshes."

"In that case, maybe, probably, I mean they did file the petition."

"What about you?

"What about me?"

"Do you love your kids?"

Billy knew the answer, just didn't think it best to tell her, but he did anyway.

"Okay, believe it or not, I think the answer is yes."

"The answer is yes, it meets your high standard, okay, so how can that be, if you don't want to care for them, don't want to," Ms. Beecher looked down at the note she had just taken, "do something for somebody that might not be good for you because you think it's more important."

"Because I don't think it would be better for them."

"Or maybe you just don't want the hassle."

"Okay, then, if that's your judgment, can I go now?"

Ms. Beecher did not respond, waited for Billy.

"Yeah, fine, sure, that might be part of it, if that makes you feel better, but really, I think it's more about them, I'd be a shitty parent, not good at it, not ready for it, can't even take care of myself, look, I live in a shitty room over a bar, I have a shitty job that pays bupkus, I have no ambition, I just killed a cardinal for God's sake, and so I guess you could say I'm a fuckin' mess, okay, write that down in your notes," he said smiling, "and then maybe I can leave," without rancor.

Ms. Beecher smiled, less prosecutorial.

"Yes, I will most definitely take that down," she said writing on her legal pad, "I-am-a- fucking-mess," she said, drawing out each word.

"You know it's all in the effort," she said, "none of us know whether we're any good at it. We just do the best we can and hope it turns out all right. And in the process, you might find doing all those things for somebody else all those years was actually good, for you."

"Not if they become serial killers."

"Yes, there's always that, but I don't think we're dealing with that here."

"Low bar."

"Do you love anyone else?"

"Don't see why that's any of your business."

"Because part of my job is to ascertain the relationships of interested parties."

Billy didn't like it.

"I am, well, in a relationship, you could say, well," he laughed to himself, remembering, "yeah, well, I have to get used to remembering, actually, fact is, I'm gonna get married."

"Well," Ms. Beecher said surprised, "I'd say that's a relationship. Congratulations, facts please."

"I'm marrying a girl, Mona, who I've known about two years now. The marriage part came on a little sudden, don't know it's necessary, really, but, in answer to your question, I can see myself living with her, happily, for more than thirty years."

"What does she do?"

"Well, she just inherited a resort on the Wisconsin River, if you can believe that, total shock, outside Spring Green, plans on running it."

"How old is she?"

"Don't know."

"You don't know how old your fiancée is?"

"No."

"Does she know how to run a resort?"

"She'll be great."

"Is it a successful business?"

"I guess, she'll make it better."

"And will you be living with her?"

"I guess so."

"What does that mean?"

"We haven't really discussed it. I'm sure we'll be living together."

"So you may not be living in a room above a bar."

"Haven't thought about it, I suppose, maybe, doesn't change anything."

"Would you have an objection if I were to come up to take a look?"

"Why would you wanna do that?"

"Maybe just because I need to get away. When's the wedding?"

"Next month."

"Did you love your mother?"

"Jesus Christ, where's the couch?"

"Did you?

"Aren't there any limitations on these things?"

"Did you?"

"Yes."

"I'm told you didn't go to her funeral."

Billy winced.

"That's more between me and my dad."

"How about your father?"

"What about my father?"

"Did you love your father?"

"Please."

"What did you think of your father?"

Billy looked at Ms. Beecher, well put together, tad matronly, light-skinned African American woman who'd lived in Chicago since the thirties, ground up, rose above, lots of things, to an office in the Rookery Building, no small feat.

"I think my father was a racist, among other things."

"I agree," said Ms. Beecher, Mayor Williams supporter, wholehearted, dreams of her own black robe spurned by Alderman Hurley, and his gang of twenty-nine. "Good thing we got those things turned around."

"Yeah, well, we'll see if your guy's any different."

"I expect he'll take care of us like your dad took care of his."

"Us? His?"

"You know what I mean."

"I'm more into we."

"Yeah, well, when White cops kill Black kids, it's us versus them."

"That's not the problem."

Ms. Beecher, animated.

"White cops killing Black kids not a problem?"

"Sure it's *a* problem, it's not *the* problem."

Ms. Beecher, heated.

"Well, then, why don't you tell me what *the* problem is?"

"*The* problem," Billy said, "is that Black kids are killing each other."

Ms. Beecher, little stunned.

"And what would you do about it?"

"Well, for one thing, I believe in reparations," Billy said.

"You do?" Ms. Beecher asked, greatly surprised.

"Yes, for Native and African Americans."

"That would be a lot of money."

"Money well spent, deserved, crimes against humanity."

Ms. Beecher had not anticipated this turn, little off guard, beginning to like this young man.

"I don't suppose you're willing to stick around and do something about it."

"Can't stand the bullshit."

"Maybe you're just lazy."

"True, very true, but it's equally true I have a physical aversion to bullshit, avoid it like the plague, doctor's orders, bullshit, from anybody, any time, anyone peddling bullshit, which is most of the people in this town."

"So it's bullshit and judgmental people," Ms. Beecher, writing down.

"Yes, that's right, that's accurate, for your report, make sure to tell the judge that," Billy said, all in all kind of fond of Ms. Beecher.

Ms. Beecher, in conclusion, flipping her legal pad to its first page.

"As I said, I've spoken to the Walshes, they have a nanny, you know" she said, looking seriously at Billy. "And from what I can tell, the nanny knows more about your kids than they do."

"At least they have a nanny."

Ms. Beecher shook her head and placed her materials on her desk.

"Well, thank you for coming," she said, rising to her feet, "that will be all for now, I may think it best to take a look at your situation, up there, at some point, I don't know, it'll have to be after my report's submitted, but before the final hearing, we'll see."

"So I guess I'm free to go," Billy said reaching out his hand, and they shook hands, smiling.

"Yes, well, congratulations on your wedding, this wasn't so bad now was it?" Ms. Beecher said, and Billy left her office, walked through the marble corridor, down the spiral staircase seven floors to Frank Lloyd Wright's lobby, through the revolving door, and out onto La Salle Street, into the bustle of businessmen and women leaving their offices on a Wednesday evening in the Loop during the summer, walking fast toward commuter trains, and cocktails.

Good to get that over with, but no point in heading home now. He was downtown. Take two hours to get out, easy. Just not as pumped, after talking about his kids, his mother, his father. Hostage, one more night. He could handle it. Eventful couple weeks, but still alive. Parts were interesting. He was getting married. How did that happen? Seems so far away now, up there, from down here. Could've been worse all in all. Maybe not so bad, he thought, at the corner of LaSalle and Adams, where he turned east toward the lake, and headed down Adams in the direction of the Berghoff stand up bar, where he spent the next hour lubricating, thinking about his city, what he might do in the hours left, and the note in his back pocket.

He walked out of the Berghoff into a flood of gold from the evening sun, filling the corridor of buildings down Adams Street, tall windows flashing, cornices, ornate, blinding Billy as he stepped into the orange glow, floating on a smooth buzz, with a smile, on his last night, alive, with all these strangers, all as one, each a destination, a journey, joining together, separating, moving, in unison, apart, straight, intersecting, lines, yielding, rights of way, ebb and flow, each a place to go, each a route to get there, all the same, each different, but alive, and warm and glowing and sure of the next big thing, around the corner, on the subway, at the end of the line, pulse, after a few drinks, in the big town, sun going down, glass half full, Billy made his way, to the east, toward the Art Institute steps, awash in light, stick figures, origami shadows, sitting and standing, talking, and watching the world go up and down in the gilded frame of Michigan Avenue.

Billy crossed between cars cooling jets, anxious, at red lights, skipped up the steps in the late sun, past the bronze lion, up and around the beaux-arts facade to the south, to a wide walkway running east to west along the southern limestone wall, capped by Van Dyck, Rembrandt, Teniers, Murillo, Wren, Hobbema, Reynolds, and Gainsborough, above Corinthian column, goddess, and Parthenon frieze overlooking the southern garden, canopy of low cocksure hawthorn, red in winter, stepping down, ducking thorns, to the long blue reflecting pool, at the far end of which, flanked by honey locust, gold in fall, stands the Great Lakes Fountain, sculpture of the flow, Superior, Michigan, Huron, Erie, Ontario, each a bronze nymph, holding a shell, into which a trickle spills, from one to another, great waterway of the north, down the St. Lawrence, and out to the wide ocean.

On the low wall holding back the pool into which the fountain waters flowed, sat a young man, in a hoodie, jeans, lean face, five-six, thin, dark skinned, alone, in the entire garden. Billy walked the length of the reflecting pool, dodging hawthorn tentacles, up to the fountain under which the man sat, fidgeting, and sat down next to him.

"Didn't think you were going to show," the hoodie said, agitated.

"I didn't either."

"But you did, so I guess you want to know what I got to say," little cocky.

"Not really."

"So what'd you come for?"

"Well, truth is, I've got nothing else to do in this godforsaken town."

"God hasn't forsaken this town, he's forsaken you."

"So I'm told. So, who are you?"

"Doesn't matter. Look, we can make this quick, I've got information," he said, looking around the empty garden, "inside information, if you know what I mean, about your father."

"And what makes you think I care about that?"

"Well, first, he's your father, second, you came out to the church."

"How'd you know that?"

"My aunt works there, for the Reverend."

"His receptionist?"

"She's the one."

"Surprised she even remembered. Not very nice."

"Oh, she's real nice, just not to crackers."

"Crackers?"

"Yeah, like you folk," he said waving his hand in front of his face.

"Oh, I see." Billy thought a moment. "*All* crackers, or just me?"

"All."

"So she doesn't discriminate then, among crackers, I mean."

"Look, you want to hear what I gotta say or what?"

"Shoot."

"It's about that warehouse. It's a bad deal. I work for the State, Public Aid, downtown, physical plant kind of stuff, stuff we need, space, equipment, forms, that kind of stuff. For a long time, we were all spread out, stored shit here, shit there, made no sense, so the higher ups decided to put it all together, in one place, one huge fucking warehouse, here in town, in what they call," he said, lifting up his fingers in quotes, "'an economically distressed area,' which means, of course, where *we* live, if you know what I mean."

Billy did not respond.

"So all of that's supposed to be hush, hush, need to know basis, until time comes to make the announcement, when we're supposed to tell everybody what we need, this much, in this area, best if a minority gets involved, and we're accepting proposals, by such and such a date, make it all fair, so the taxpayers get the best deal," he said laughing, "'cept it doesn't work that way, never works that way, your dad'd be the first to know."

"I get it."

"So we're all workin' on the specs, the announcement, takes six months, way too long, getting it all ready, and the day comes and we put it out there, and lo and behold, the very next day, I'm telling you, the *very next day*, we get a detailed proposal with just the right property, just the right amount of space, just the right part of town, just the right people, my kind of people, too good to be kosher, couldn't possibly work that fast, and thirty days later, they get the contract, and we've been workin' on it ever since, for over a year now, and it's that goddam warehouse sittin' right next to the Reverend."

"So it's just another inside job," Billy said, with a shrug.

"Yeah, but this time I'm pissed, because it coulda been the Reverend doin' this deal, makin' the do-re-mi, but they got him to sell, he was set up."

"So who's the lucky insider this time?"

"Yeah, well, that's the thing. I don't know. I thought it'd be your dad, so I got in his face one day, in the parking lot after he left a meeting with the Reverend, my aunt tipped me off, and I could tell he didn't know anything about it, probably pissed because it didn't come his way, and then I hear he does something in City Council to hold it up, prob'ly cuz a deal's goin' down he doesn't know about, and that's all I know, above my pay grade, and the way they work it, prob'ly never know, with these land trusts, and limited this and limited that, all under the table, all that bullshit lawyers do."

"And so why tell me all this shit? It's the same old thing, man. Why do you think I live so far away from this town?"

"Thought maybe you'd care."

"Why?"

"Heard what you did at that funeral."

"Oh God, you too?"

"Most of the folks *I* know thought it was pretty cool."

Billy, surprised.

"Look, I'm sorry, you seem like a decent guy, not that I liked your aunt very much, but you seem all right, and I'm sorry to say, I'm just not the guy to help you, I've been embarrassed by my old man since I was old enough to know what was going on, I can't stand the way this town runs, but I just don't want anything to do with it anymore."

"So, what, you just run away?" the hoodie asked, standing, upset.

"Yeah, as a matter of fact, I'm very happy to say, that as of tomorrow morning, I'm going far away, where nobody, especially me, gives a shit about any of this."

"Nothing's ever gonna change."

"That may be," Billy said getting to his feet. "But I'm sorry, I'm not your guy."

The hoodie threw up his hands. "Man, what a waste," he grumbled, and stalked off, away from Billy, and the fountain, and the gardens, into city streets, toward the Green Line, and the West Side.

Billy watched, listening to the hoodie's fading footsteps tromping over loose stones under the trees, leaving Billy alone in the garden, gazing onto the cobalt pool toward the low hum of traffic along the avenue, Great Lakes trickling from shell to shell behind him, distant siren, the quiet, no more voices, accusations, entreaties, encouragements, from well-meaning people, alone, in the dignity of the garden, with nothing but the reckoning, soul searching, if he had one, taking shape, perhaps, the form, of all forms, from nothingness, taking account, the march of days, from one to another, from where he came, to where he's going, how well moments are lived, whether honestly, or not, alone, with the judgment of the only one who matters, well, almost the only one, and for that one instant, the snapshot, is of a young man, standing by a fountain, in a beautiful garden, disappointing almost everyone, but trying his best, making strides, slowly, but surely, he thinks it's true, these last few weeks, one world to another, surfing the wave, falling, to be sure, rough spots along the way, but getting back up, getting better, learning how to live, all over, on his own, and to love, in his own way, without judgment, or bullshit, yes, it was time, he thought, as he began to walk, very slowly, hands behind his back, out of the garden, on his first few steps on his way back home.

He came out of the garden onto the corner of Jackson and Michigan, trailhead of Route 66, great highway to the west, Chicago, Funks Grove, St. Louis, Albatross, Joplin, Riverton, Tulsa, Oklahoma City, Amarillo, Tucumcari, Albuquerque, Gallup, Winslow, Flagstaff, Rancho Cucamonga, to the beach at Santa Monica on the Pacific shore, a world of adventure, possibility, unspooling before him across the great American West, fading into the setting sun, but he wasn't even tempted, he turned east, toward the Great Lake, on his way to little Lone Rock, along the river, all he wanted, the only place he really wanted to go.

Billy decided to walk back along the lake, through Grant Park, past the bandshell, in shadow, across eight lanes of traffic on Lake Shore Drive, past the marina and yacht club, still in sun, and the Great Lake of deep greens and blues, with low clouds along the horizon, white and soft against an azure sky, up and over the river, reversed, past Navy Pier and the great white ship at anchor, skyline view from its prow. Outside Olive Park, he took a tunnel under the Drive back into city streets, past the Holiday Inn, into Streeterville, beneath the hospital window where he was born, through the University, turning at each block north and west, until he came upon the entrance to the Drake Hotel, where he pushed through the revolving door and stepped into the warm shelter of the Coq D'Or, up to the polished bar, plush red leather, cherry wood paneling, far from the Mad House Inn as you could get. Ordered a Manhattan that cost as much as Ray used to pay for a half day's work, thought maybe he deserved it, conspicuous, among the well-heeled, just as well, silent protest, stares all around, as he finished his drink, plopped the cherry in his mouth, and walked out into the hallway, past the grand staircase, past George Jensen, the Cape Cod Room, and exited the side door onto Oak Street, directly across from the beach, where he took a tunnel back under Lake Shore Drive, and walked out onto the sand, all in shadow, the last of the sun falling far out upon the water, clouds blushing the day away.

Billy sat cross legged in the sand at the water's edge, gazed out at the water, and resumed his accounting. All in all, he was glad he came, she was right about that, of course. Maybe a turning point, after all, if he wanted, an intervention with the past, confront and banish demons, discard heavy baggage, and begin again, renewal, a second chance, out there before him, in the waters of the Great Lake, as he rose from the sand and stepped into the water, tee shirt, jeans, All Stars, no socks, right into the water, scaring the Mexican family down the beach, wondering if he was coming back, the water warm, pleasant, washing away the days and nights, the years, mistakes, regrets, he plopped under the water, closed his eyes, held his breath, submerged, withdrawn from the world, an ancient creature, from the beginning of time, starting over, learning to breathe, to crawl, absolved, and surfacing with a whoosh into twilight, the city lights in the tall buildings around the Oak Street curve, into a future of his own making, with a woman, he was quite certain now, he truly loved.

CHAPTER FIVE

The Wedding

The bride awoke, in tears, because it was raining, hard, and the rain would ruin everything. Well, almost everything, it was possible, she supposed, a marriage might survive a first day of foreboding omen, impending doom, clouds dark as night, sheets of rain pounding the roof, only gloom visible through the small cabin's window, except, the problem was, she believed in omens, alignment of stars, what's meant to be, and not, and knew, in her heart of hearts, which was now broken, that fate and destiny defied all good intentions. On a clear day, from the window in Mona's cabin, she could look across the inlet, to the island in the river across from the resort, to the broad beach, where hopes and dreams would come alive, vows, music, dancing, bonfires, joyous, community, memorable, uplifting, under a cloudless sky, bright stars, full moon, the best laid plans, all now washing away in taunting oppressive torrents falling heavily off the metal roof onto sand into mud. In a small corner of denial, she had considered the bar a backup, but who wants to get married in a bar, what kind of send-off, nothing but ruin could come of it, so she refused to think of it, it wouldn't happen, and now it had, and there was nothing left to do, but put her head in her hands, and cry, which she had not done for as long as she could remember.

Billy looked out into the same night sky in the morning rain over Main Street in Lone Rock and really didn't care, so it's raining, didn't believe in fate, believed in her, in them, get married in the tool shed if need be, didn't matter, didn't need the rest of it, except that now, thinking for two, it did matter, and he did care, because he knew it would matter to her, which satisfied his definition after all, and for that, despite the hard rain, he was quite pleased, without any doubts, he was doing the right thing, even his father might have been surprised.

Ivy, the maid of honor, or the best man, take your pick, one of two witnesses, all you needed, stood outside the passenger door of her pickup truck in the rain, buckled her two kids into car seats on the bench seat, ran around the bed of the truck, hopped into the cab, soaking wet, and backed away from the mobile home she rented in Lone Rock's upscale trailer park on the main highway north of town.

"Mommy, we don't wanna go to grandma's; we want to go to Mona's wedding," her daughters whined.

"Look, you little monkeys, I told you I'm gonna be busy all day, and the wedding's going late tonight, and besides, no kids are allowed, so to grandma's house you go."

"But Mona said we could…"

"It's not up to Mona, it's up to me, and this is the way it is."

Ivy steered the pickup onto the back road which led along the pine forests and railroad tracks on the north side of the river toward Spring Green, where she had grown up and gone to school as a girl. Never knew her dad, mom, waitress at the diner on Highway 14, lived hard, two packs a day and a bottle at night, Ivy raised herself.

Ivy'd been a tall scrawny little girl, pale skin, black hair, parted in the middle, never stood out, average in everything, kept to herself, few friends, preferred the fringes, shadows, out of the way. Entered a goth stage at 14 she never left, first tattoo at 15, nose ring at 16, pregnant at 17, dropped out of school, pregnant again at 19, the father a meth addict, Ivy lucky, just dabbled, he was long gone now, suspicions of abuse in the relationship, although questions remained as to who abused whom.

Ivy now stood six-feet tall, lithe, no longer scrawny, long tattooed arms on alabaster skin, swaying willow branches, still in black, always, but, improbably, somehow elegant, as she grew into life, each twist of her hand, bend at her waist, turn of her head, unwitting choreography, unpracticed, unwanted, really, unexpected, that Ivy, of all people, short black hair, black leather choker, spike bracelets, black leather laced up boots, opened up her dark shell and emerged a black pearl, and no one, least of all her, could tell where it came from, it just was, who she was meant to be, and it took her awhile to understand, still struggling, embarrassed really, playing it down, but she had reached a point, for the first time in her life, when she began to stand out, people, men in particular, began to notice, and it made her uncomfortable, more reserved, more withdrawn, more careful, of a world she had grown to know, over a short time, was just one kick in the teeth after another.

Ivy drove into the drive of her mom's ranch home that backed up onto the golf course west of town, and shuffled her two girls out of the cab, into the rain, and into the open garage, where Ivy's mom sat in a lawn chair smoking a Marlboro with an ashtray and mug of coffee at her feet.

"Some day your friend picked for a wedding," she growled.

"Not her fault."

"There's fate in these things, you know."

"Like you would know."

"I see you got dressed up for the occasion."

"Thanks."

"Don't know how you do it, but you still look good. Different some-how, though," she said looking her over, "can't tell what it is."

"Grandma, what are we gonna do today?" one of the girls whined.

"How the hell should I know?" exhaling a large burst of smoke into the garage behind the curtain of rain, "I haven't even finished my first cup of coffee," she said, exasperated, "we'll figure it out, we always come up with something now, don't we, you little tramps," she said to the girls, grinning, "but, you gotta remember, grandma's rule number one: and you know it," she said raising a finger, "no whining, you whine, I drop you off in the woods."

"Oh, for chrissakes, Mom."

"I mean it," she said smiling, raspy.

"Okay, look," Ivy said, looking hard into her mom's eyes, "*my* rule number one: *please*," she said, "*please*, be careful, no bullshit, and you know what I mean," she said, and her mom knew what she meant, "I might be late…"

"How late?"

"Does it matter?"

"Just so I know."

Ivy turned away,

"Oh Christ, late, I don't know, gimme a break, whatever hap-pens happens."

"Okay, okay, you can all sleep here tonight, if it comes to that, so go, have a good time, you deserve it, really, you do, I'll take care of these knuckleheads," she said, taking another drag of her cigarette and blowing a puff of smoke into the damp air.

Ivy looked out into the rain to make a run for the cab.

"But now, I'm telling *you* something, babe," Ivy's mom said, starting to wag her finger, and Ivy turned to see her mom, and two girls, all three, wagging their fingers at her in the garage, "before you go, you be careful out there, we need you around here."

Ivy smiled.

"I can take care of myself, love you guys, see you tonight," and she was off, into the rain, into the cab, and off to see poor Mona.

Across the river, on a makeshift stage at one end of a large pole barn at the foot of a hill which led up to the summer theater stage, a group of actors, listless, resentful of the early morning rehearsal, stood in place, listening to another of the director's ill-timed and unnecessary interruptions. A chorus of rain beat upon the metal roof, and streamed outside the open bay door at the far end of the barn, as the director struggled out of his chair.

Cecil Hampton, f/k/a, Ralph Spotnitz (it's pronounced Sessil, he would say, often), middle-aged, lumpy, did his best to get the attention of what he derisively referred to in private as his middling troop, an otherwise spirited winsome group of young talent laboring under his direction. They were lucky to have him, Cecil thought, the others, not so sure. Cecil's resume boasted Hollywood directing credits, movies so forgotten no one knew how bad they were, and off-off Broadway productions, which few had ever seen, but together they looked good enough on paper to appeal to summer stock companies in a pinch, like his current gig, directing A

Midsummer Night's Dream, after its original director died of a heart attack weeks before the opening. In such circumstances, Cecil, always available, would waltz in, ascot and tweed, assume control, prey on the young and aspiring, if he were lucky, and hope his players were talented enough to obscure his inevitable misdirection. Happen in any industry, schlubs who thrive, with remarkable luck and a sense of timing, against all odds, schlub doctors, lawyers, directors, whole careers, getting by, with outsized egos and undersized talent.

"No, no, no, how many times must I repeat myself?" he moaned as he got to his feet from a chair below the stage, rubbing long strands of hair back over his bald pate, "I'm looking for ambiguity here, uncertainty, you understand? It's a new take, I'll grant you that, but that's what makes it special, and more importantly, that's what I want, I want conflict, internal conflict, you say you don't want her, but you're riven by lust at the same time, you say your lines, but you must find a way to communicate that somewhere, deep inside," he said, bowing and grasping at his heart, "you want her, you need her, I mean look at her, how could you not?" he said pointing to the actress in question, a twenty-three year old from Chicago, blushing now, strawberry blonde, shoulder length, blue-eyed, slender delicate features, thin, well-proportioned, embarrassed.

"But it makes no sense!" Demetrius wailed back, "I enter, my first line is, 'I love thee not; therefore pursue me not,' and then, 'get thee gone, and follow me no more,' and then 'I am *sick* when I do look on thee,' what's ambiguous about that? There's no uncertainty, there's no pathos, he can't *stand* her, he wants nothing to *do* with her," he yelled, pointing at the actress, a little unnerved at the emphasis, "his disgust is palpable, and it needs to be clear, at this point, there is no conflict, and it must be, because the one extreme highlights the final reconciliation."

Meredith Fairweather, the actress in question, not thrilled at the attention, silently cheered him on, as did the other players. Demetrius was right, it made no sense, ridiculous really, reinvent Shakespeare, sure, reinterpret, done all the time, but there had to be a line somewhere, and Cecil had crossed it, and she couldn't help but wonder if she had anything to do with it.

"Who the hell do you think you are?" Cecil stormed back, crossing his arms across his chest and grabbing the leather patched sleeves of his tweed jacket. "I'm the director here, and who are you? You're nobody. You want to be somebody? You want this?" he said pointing to the stage, "Best part you've ever had? Then follow direction, or you'll be dismissed!"

Meredith dearly hoped it didn't come to that. She was playing the part of Helena, who loved Demetrius, played by Demetrius, a too cute choice by the casting director, and, as it turned out, much to Meredith's distress, life imitated art, because Meredith thought Demetrius the most dynamic elegant man she had ever met, had fallen hard for him, but Demetrius hadn't noticed, and if he had it wouldn't have mattered, having fallen, just as strongly, for someone else, Ivy, it turns out.

Demetrius, too, was from Chicago, twenty-four, six-foot four, powerful arms and chest, slim legs, booming voice, crisp speaker, brown glowing skin, destined for standing ovations over a long successful career, obvious to everyone, including Cecil, hence the resentment.

"So, now, you have anything else to say?" Cecil fumed.

Demetrius weighed the challenge. The role had been a break for him, be just like him to screw it up. The players waited, nervously, for Demetrius to reply, storm out, something dramatic.

Meredith broke the silence.

"Maybe this might be a good time to break for the day," she offered.

Cecil and Demetrius stared at each other.

Cecil opened his script, officiously turned several pages over in disgust, as if he were looking for something, a way out.

"Okay," he finally said, in a voice to suggest he was not backing down, "okay, we can break for the day," he said in Meredith's direction, to everyone's relief, "and we're off tomorrow, but you all better come back here first thing Monday morning, committed to making this play work, my way, or you can be assured I will find any one of a number of worthy players eager to take your place."

Cecil took his seat, feigning interest in the script, until each of the players left the stage, tread lightly past him, and walked out to the open bay door, where they gathered, peering out at the rain, and the rivulets streaming into the gravel parking lot.

"No way Romeo's happening tonight."

"Saturday night, who's having the party?"

Cecil left his seat and walked back toward the open door, keeping a respectful distance.

"That wedding's going on tonight, at Ray's" Meredith said, hopefully, in Demetrius's direction, "heard it was open invitation."

"Yeah, was thinking about it," Demetrius said, "might go, might not, never know," although he did know, wasn't going to miss it, knew she'd be there.

One by one, the actors peeled away from Demetrius and Meredith, into the rain, on a dash to their cars.

"Couldn't help but overhearing, who's getting married?" Cecil asked.

Demetrius looked at Meredith.

"Gotta go," he said, and ran out into the rain.

Meredith watched Demetrius reach his car, and turned to the director.

"Oh, just a girl from town, works at a place we go for drinks. Don't know her that well, groom either. They're not theater people."

"Why would you be going if you don't know them that well?"

"Well, kinda funny, actually, it's open to anyone who wants to go, no presents, kind of a community event, I guess."

"Communal wedding?"

"Yeah, well, I guess," she said looking out into the rain, "some of us might be going, if this rain ever stops."

"Think anyone would mind if an old director tagged along?"

Meredith hadn't thought that was where this was going, immediately regretted saying anything at all.

"Well, you'd have to find a boat to get to the island," she said over her shoulder, "looks like it's letting up a bit, see you Monday," and she rushed out into the rain.

Cecil watched her, running in the rain in her jeans, a little excited, about what might lay in store.

By the time Ivy turned into the long lane bordered by pine leading into Ray's Resort, the rain was letting up and the sky lightening, just a bit. The wheels of her pickup splashed violently into puddles scattered like land mines across the gravel parking lot, where she pulled around to the left of the main building, skirted the motley collection of pop-up campers, Airstreams, tents, and Winnebagos, forlorn in drenched misery of dashed hopes, pulled down the path along the river cabins, and pulled up into a large mud puddle in front of Mona's cabin. Not a soul in sight, huddled in makeshift shelters, damp, testy, and thinking of alternative plans. Ivy brought her truck to a stop, took a deep breath, and prepared herself for what she surely would find inside the little cabin.

She stood outside Mona's cabin door, rain falling softly now, and looked out at the shoreline of the island fifty yards away, formed by an inlet, that made a ninety-degree turn to the north off the right bank of the river, swirled past the cabins and beach at Ray's Resort, and then turned west, circling the island and rejoining the main channel downstream to the west. The island itself was wooded, with a clearing and rise in its center, bordered by a grassy bank perched five feet above a beach, more of a sandbar, that ran along the eastern edge of the island facing the resort. The island's sandbar ran seventy yards along the entire eastern width of the island, crawling gradually out of the water on the inlet side, seventy feet of sand stretching from shore to island bank, directly across from the resort, tapering as it wrapped around the island to the south into a point that stretched out into the main channel. The inlet between the island and the resort was chest deep, and easily waded with drink in hand, making the island's sandbar a favorite site for blowout bashes on hot summer days, for boaters, campers, and the RV set.

Any other day it would be the perfect setting, Ivy thought, as she looked across the inlet, at the makeshift wooden stage, recently built among the trees upon the grassy bank, sodden portent of what might have been. She knocked on the door.

No answer.

"Mona, it's me, open up."

She knocked again.

"Go away, I'm going to kill myself."

Ivy opened the screen door, tried the inner door, unlocked, and stepped into the one room cabin, where she found Mona sprawled face down across the bed.

"Oh, Ivy," she whimpered into the bed. "This can't be happening."

"Well, it is honey, so dry your eyes, you'll look like hell."

"There's fate in these things, you know."

"Yeah, heard that before, it's all bullshit, and you know it."

"What are we gonna do?"

"Well, you're gonna get married, and I'm gonna see you to it."

"But this ruins *everything*," Mona moaned.

"Come on, I'll make you some breakfast, the rain's stopping."

"It is?"

"If you'd stop crying, you'd notice, not like you," Ivy said, sitting on the bed. "Come on," she said, reaching across Mona's shoulders, "come on, girl, you're a fighter, you and me, come on we're gonna see this thing through."

Mona sat on the bed next to Ivy and looked out the window. The rain really was letting up. She reached her arms around Ivy, put her head on her shoulder, and gave her a hug.

"I still do want to marry him," she sniffled.

"Of course, you do, now stop acting like a goddam princess, and get a move on."

Mona watched as Ivy got up from the bed, opened the refrigerator, took out some eggs and butter, and began making Mona scrambled eggs and toast.

"You look a little different," Mona said, getting to her feet, sizing up Ivy's long black tattooed presence cracking open the eggs.

Ivy scowled at her.

"Very funny. If you thought I was going to wear pink or something, you had the wrong girl."

"No, there is something," Mona said, quizzically, managing a smile, looking into Ivy's face, "and it's not the black eye liner."

"Wait a minute, oh my God, I know what it is!" Mona shrieked. "You're not wearing your nose ring!"

Ivy blushed, first time in years.

"Yeah, well, thought I'd give it a rest, just for today, my little wedding gift."

"I wouldn't have cared."

"I know," Ivy said, "cuz you're a good egg, but for some God knows what fucking reason, I thought it might be the right thing to do."

"Well, I'm honored," Mona said sincerely.

"Yeah, right, well, you better start getting yourself together girl, you've got things to do today."

"Yes, m'am," Mona replied, and looked out the window, to see the rain had actually stopped.

Lee Anne had closed the Mad House Inn for the day to prepare for the festivities, but made an exception for the groom, who sat on his usual bar stool in the darkened quiet bar, as Lee Anne shuffled around the back kitchen flipping Billy's hash browns, sausage patties, and over medium eggs, to set him on his way, in her trademark knee braces, Bermuda shorts, sleeveless blouse, with short tinted hair and firm jaw.

"Biggest mistake everybody makes on wedding days, nobody eats. I'm gonna make sure you start out right, the rest is up to you, God help you," Lee Anne called out from the dark kitchen.

"Preciate it. Lee Anne, I…"

"As if I don't have enough to do, you know, how the hell you roped me into all this I'll never know, out back I've got the sweet corn, I've got the beans, I've got the potatoes, I've got the cups, the plastic ware, the napkins, the trash bags, the garbage cans, the tables, the chairs, what in God's name don't I have, lamb, pigs and chicken, that's what I don't have, thank Otto for that, fine enough butcher, never gets anywhere on time though, late for his own funeral, hopefully not your wedding, just one more thing to worry about, course I could've done that, too, you know, then it would have been taken care of, handled right, nothing to worry about, but your bride thought different, she thinks of everything, she's whip smart you know, you don't deserve her, you got real lucky…"

"I know she's…"

"Any one of a hundred guys round here would give their eye teeth to be in your shoes today, you know that don't you, and that's without that whole resort thing going to her, boy that Ray, full of surprises, I'd say she got lucky but she deserved it as much as anybody, and if it means we get to keep her around here I figure that's a good thing, maybe Ray knew what he was doin' after all, I do miss him, hell, half the ladies in this town miss him, but it's a good thing, what your bride's doin', keepin' the resort up and run-nin' I mean, she'll do that place proper, where you fit in's a different story, what she sees in you I'll never know, can hardly tell what you look like with that shaggy dog thing you got goin', thought at least you'd cut it for your own wedding, should have known, and those clothes, for God's sake can't you find something other than black, I mean, really, doesn't that get old…"

"Well, actually I was thinking…"

"But of course not, wouldn't think of making the *sacrifice* I suppose, just like my old man, may he rest in peace, you're all the same, goin' round thinkin' it's all about you when nothin' happens without us, only reason

anybody gets from point A to point B round here is cuz of us, we're the
glue, you know, always around to pick up the pieces, best vow you can
make: don't leave your pieces lyin' around, keep it together for chrissakes,
all that stuff in your past, keep it there, now's your chance, turn over a
new leaf, make something of yourself, for God's sake, you've got everything
goin' for you, you're a smart kid, I think, if you'd ever say anything, so don't
mess it up, and don't you dare do anything to hurt that beautiful bride of
yours, so help me God, if I hear you do anything to her I'll…"

"Lee Anne, you don't have to…"

"And this rain! My goodness, what the Lord giveth, is it still raining
out there?"

Billy looked across the bar and tried to tell if it was raining through
the Miller High Life sign in the front window.

"I think it might be…"

"Looks like it might have finally stopped, could start right up again,
Lord knows, with our luck, my God nothing but sunshine for weeks and
now this, heard on the radio this morning it's supposed to clear up, but
what do they know, whatever they say, expect the opposite, that's what I
always say, but it would be nice, if it cleared up I mean, your bride deserves
it, even if you don't, this much rain this hard never a good thing though,
just all runoff, and the river gets high, and no sandbars, and nobody wants
a canoe, bad for business, God help us if they got as much rain upriver,
wash away the whole sandbar, and then what'll you do, get married in the
bar?, romantic, rained like hell my first wedding day, too, see how that
turned out, son of a bitch, but that was my mistake, can't blame that on
mother nature, it's all what you put into it I always say, and I'm saying that
to you right now, you understand?," she said as she gathered the plate of
eggs, sausages, hash browns, and whole wheat toast, walked out of the dark

kitchen in the back of the bar, and clanked the plate down on the bar in front of Billy.

"There you go now hon, you eat up, don't make the mistake I made my second time around," she said turning back behind the bar and grabbing a pot of coffee, "passed out right on the altar," she said as she refilled Billy's cup, "middle of the service, out cold, fell off the kneeler in a lump, second husband, should have known, didn't even help me, just, boom, down I went, at his feet, where he thought I belonged, turns out, but anyway, that was my fault, too, passing out I mean, well, the marriage, too, I suppose, shoulda known better, shoulda walked outta there as soon as I came to, but the Lord has a plan, everything for a reason, cuz for me the third time was a charm, despite all his faults, and he had plenty, but deep down, Tom was a fine man, unlike those other two jokers," she said wistfully, "he treated me like I was somebody, knew how lucky he was, so for me, like I say, third time was a charm, suppose I had to pay my dues first, life's like that, God only knows why, shouldn't have to be that way, and it doesn't have to be that way for you, rain or no rain."

Lee Anne walked to the front of the bar and looked out the window onto Main Street.

"Yessiree, looks like the monsoon might have come to an end, just in time," she said to the window as she looked across the street at a car pulling into the gas station, "you might get lucky after all, and I don't think we'll have to worry much about the river rising," she said, turning and walking back along the length of the bar, "cuz the radio said we were the north edge of this storm, which means no rain upriver, which means they won't have to open the dam, which means you might just have your sandbar after all, full moon tonight too, you know, could get a little crazy, why in God's name you opened it up to everybody is anybody's guess…"

"Well, Mona thought…"

"Yeah, of course Mona thought, Mona thought of everything, what have you thought about, that's what I wanna know, one thing, you better be thinkin' 'bout one thing, sickness and health, young man, you think about that, good with the bad, thick and thin, times'll get tough, there'll be times you'll want out, believe me, I know, all men are like that, but you just remember, sickness and health, young man, *sickness* and health, you hear what I'm sayin'?, you say 'I do' later today and you're in it for the long haul, you understand?, I'm not doin' all this work for some short-term arrangement, I put in all this work, I've got certain rights, like an investor, so I hear you take off on this beautiful girl of yours and I'm tellin' you right now I'm gonna track you down, I'm gonna find your straggly ass, I'm gonna take you by the ear, haul you back, throw you at her feet, and make you beg her to take you back, capisce?"

"Capisce," Billy said, finishing his breakfast, pushing his plate away.

"Well," Lee Anne said, "here it is your big day, and you sit there like you lost your tongue, don't you have anything to say for yourself?"

Billy smiled.

"I don't think you have to worry," Billy said, "I'm in love with this girl."

Lee Anne smiled back.

"I know you are," she said, patting his hand affectionately on the bar, "I know you are, and she's in love with you, but a little wisdom on a big day never hurts. Now let's wash ourselves up and get all this stuff over to Ray's, get the show on the road, get this party started."

Danny Redbird, Joey LaRocca, and a small band of long-haired scrawny urchins old enough to know better filed out the broken screen door of Danny's trailer.

"Man, I gotta get outta there," Davey moaned out the door, "I'm like a wet rag already, and this is what I'm wearing."

"Like anybody's gonna give a shit about what *you're* wearing," Rose said, exiting the trailer behind him.

Rose was followed by Nick, the tallest, pale narrow face, black stringy hair, pointed nose, hanger shoulders, long, wiry.

"Like I'm tellin' you man," Nick was saying over his shoulder to Joey, "this takes strategic thinking, a day like this, ..."

"Yeah," Joey said, "I get that, Genius," which is what they sometimes called Nick, because he'd done well in school before meth came to town, "I'm just not diggin' your *strategy*, man," Joey said, stretching, drawling the word strategy for emphasis, an elocution trick of his, "like, the *strategy*, man, is to get *wasted*, man," Joey said, stepping down into the carport, taking a seat on a bench of the picnic table, and bouncing right back up.

"Awww man, I'm all wet" Joey groaned.

Nick the Genius, Davey, and Rose laughed.

As did Danny and his girlfriend, Judy, last out the door, Judy, who used to be Joey's girlfriend, but now Joey didn't mind, really. All laughing now at Joey the clown. Danny tossed paper towels around, the five of them wiped off the table and a couple of lawn chairs, smoked their cigarettes, took their seats, and looked out over the field and trees to the south toward the river, where they could clearly see the back side of the storm.

"Might you have thought that perhaps the bench may have become wet as a result of our recent precipitation?" Nick asked.

"Shut the fuck up, Genius," said Joey.

"You know, Danny," Rose, dirty-dyed blonde, pale, waif, sharp features, "you got a piece of shit crib but the outside does have a nice view," she said, looking out at the last of the dark clouds.

"How nice of you to say, your highness," Danny, long shiny black hair, Ho-Chunk, short, hanger shoulders, Iron Maiden tee shirt, hang backer if there ever was one, staring in Davey's direction, because it was Davey's idea to bring Rose.

"Like I'm some princess," Rose said, disparagingly, believing it to be true.

"Okay, now look, Joey, like I was saying," said Nick, resuming the conversation that came out with them from the trailer, "a day like this takes strategy."

"What are you assholes talkin' about?" asked Davey, unkempt red hair, hanger shoulders, short, bent, wild eyed.

"The optimal prescription for today's festivities," Nick replied. "A day like this takes planning."

"You guys really sure we've been invited to this thing?" asked Rose.

"I received a personal invitation from the bride, man," Joey said proudly.

"Me, too," said Danny.

"Me, too," said Judy. "And she said we could bring along friends, and that would be you, fool," she said to Rose.

"Okay, now, look, listen you guys, this is what I'm saying, dig this. Let's just assume, for the sake of explanation, that each of you is carrying something today, just an assumption."

"You can assume that all fuckin' day," Joey bellowed, satisfied grin.

"And let's also assume, that you may be carrying more than just one thing, doing a little bit of this, a little of that," Nick said, with one hand, and then the other.

"Or a fuckin' lot of this and a fuckin' lot of that, man" said Joey.

"Exactly, the point I'm trying to make,"

"Taking you a while," said Judy, blonde wastrel, nice smile.

Nick gave her a look of exasperation.

"Assuming all of that," he went on, "the question is, to get the most out of what no doubt will be a day long blow out, how is it that you plan to use those items, that you might be carrying, to achieve the ultimate high for the longest time, without crashing."

"Now that," Davey said, "is an important question."

But no takers.

"Answers, idiots?" Nick challenged.

Danny sat in a lawn chair with his back to the field, a bit lower, and off from the edge of the picnic table.

"Amphetamines," offered Danny.

"That would be a reasonable answer," Nick agreed, to nods around, "necessary perhaps, under the circumstances."

"But I believe, and what I'm saying is, there's a process," Nick said solemnly, "so it might come to that, will come to that, but first, you start off slow, cigarettes, coffee, for starters."

"Shit, I forgot the coffee," Danny said, got to his feet, squeezed around the picnic table, and went back inside.

"Well, he'll just miss it," Nick said, frustrated.

"No, I can hear you," Danny said, through the screen door.

"Okay, first, coffee and cigarettes, then, maybe a little blow...," he said, lowering his voice, as if the sheriff lived next door.

"Who's got the blow?" Davey asked softly.

"I-do," Danny replied in a sing-song voice from the trailer.

"Nice," Davey muttered from the other lawn chair. "How'd you manage that?" he called out.

"None-of-your-fucking-business," Danny sang out the kitchenette window.

"...little bit of blow, then we smoke a little weed, so now we've got a good buzz going, we're high, but we've got that hard edge, know what I mean, that motor in your temples telling you to keep going, and it feels good and so we do more of that, so that by the time we get to the wedding later this afternoon, we're flying, but flying straight, if you know what I mean, none of that hard liquor yet, plenty of time for that, and then, we let 'er rip. Open bar, are you kidding me? Mona's gone mad!"

"God bless her," said Judy.

"Fabulous," said Davey.

"Let's do this," said Rose.

"So, let me get this straight," Joey said from the picnic table, arms spread before him, "you're saying," he said, waving at Nick, looking into the table, "that, according to your plan, we do things in moderation, one thing at a time, with a purpose."

"Exactly," said Nick.

"You're an asshole," Joey said, more difference of opinion than insult. "Day like today, you gotta dive into it, man, like those Mexican cliff divers, man, you gotta just dive off that cliff, man, and let it come to you," reluctant nods, suggesting a reasonable point, around the table, "that way, it's an adventure, you don't know what's gonna happen, because you haven't planned anything, so you don't know where you're gonna end up..."

"Sounds like your life," said Judy.

"Love you, too, babe," Joey replied, "but really, we're more fun that way, you know it, babe, you're more fun that way," he said to Judy, Judy smiling, "you just gotta take that dive, man."

"What about rocks?" asked Nick.

"Rocks make it exciting, man."

As Danny came out of the trailer with a pot of coffee and a bottle of Wild Turkey, a ray of light crept into the sky, announcing the sun's first appearance on Mona and Billy's wedding day.

"Well, how do you like that?" Danny said placing the coffee on the table, handing the bottle to Nick, and nodding at the field, drops shimmering on blades of grass in the sun. "We may have ourselves a party after all."

Smiles around.

Joey looked at Nick, hunched his shoulders, as if to say, "well?"

Nick held out his arm, examined the dark gold liquor of endless possibility swirling in the clear bottle, respectfully unscrewed the cap, and addressed the urchin band.

"Not quite the plan," he said, to cheers, "but hell, To Billy and Mona," in a loud voice, raising the bottle toward the sunlight, "To Mona and Billy," he took a long gulp, and passed the bottle around.

Each in turn toasted the bride and groom, took a long gulp, and then took a dive, passing the bottle around a second time. Let the party begin.

Toby Miller, Aryan poster boy, walked out of his Winnebago trailer into the sunshine and surveyed the damage.

"Think we've finally got ourselves a day," he yelled back into the trailer, to his wife Doreen, primping herself in the mirror above the Winnebago's sink, generally not listening to a word her husband had to say.

Doreen didn't much like what she saw, at first. Wrinkles. God she was too young for that, hair, pixie, bottle blonde, acceptable all in all, she concluded, turning from side to side, cute highlights, too, stepping back, full-length view of her new jeans tucked into her red cowgirl boots that pushed her well-shaped derriere up into the mirror's view, yes that will do, she thought, looking over her shoulder with a little moxie, never quite tall enough, but she made up for that, other ways, oh hell, she heard Toby's voice from outside the trailer, what in God's name is he yelling about now?

Toby stood among a passel of lumbering metal beasts taking shelter in the open field which passed as Ray's RV campground, parked helter-skelter, latest in motor homes and travel trailers, all hooked to electrical outlets, generators humming, playing country western, hard rock, top forty, cacophony of radio stations and cassette tapes, occupants shaking off the rain and preparing for the day. Toby and Doreen had come up from Lake County in Northern Illinois with three other couples, each with their own motor home or travel trailer, a sort of pleasure group they had come to form over the years, fueled by kids the same age, alcohol, and, at special events, like today, when a little abandon was called for, the willingness to throw car keys in a fish bowl, why Doreen was wearing those red cowgirl boots and new form fitting jeans.

Toby surveyed his domain, the space his rig took up in the RV park, and took pride in what he saw, brand new Winnebago trailer, sleeps four, kitchenette, television, stereo (playing Johnny Cash), a chrome beauty shining in the sun, hooked on to a brand new two-toned, red and white, Chevy Silverado 4×4, with a decal behind the driver's seat of Calvin pissing on a Ford logo, a gun rack, and a flag decal on the rear bumper. Yes, now that was something to be proud of, Toby thought, as he looked around at his neighbors' rigs, each coming up a little short, pop-up camper? Please, motor home? Too expensive, Toby's was just right.

And paid for, too. Paid for by him, to be precise, and his hard work, no idle claim, because Toby worked hard, first for his dad, hauling, building, anything, rough carpentry, to cabinetry, not exactly artisanal, but real good work, the kind of work folks can count on, knowing he'll deliver as promised, and in the unlikely event something went wrong, which it rarely did, he'd make it right, no questions asked, and Toby had worked in Fox Lake that way for twenty years, so it wasn't a surprise that now, at forty years old, he had plenty of work, starting to make real money, like to buy that beautiful rig, he thought. Maybe in a couple of years they might have enough to start looking at a little cabin, maybe on a nice lake somewhere up north, something classy, like the one his neighbor the plumber had, he thought, looking around at Ray's campground.

What Doreen wanted all along. Man, was she pissed when Toby surprised her with the travel trailer wrapped in red ribbon in the snowy driveway last Christmas. All that money on a trailer they could have used on a down payment for a lake house and she could have finally escaped this noisy godforsaken campground. Not saying she didn't have great memories of her times here, hell, she'd practically grown up at Ray's, where she met Toby, when they were four years old, in that shitty old swimming pool Ray used to have, because their parents liked Ray, and the little he offered was really all they wanted, if only what they could afford, and sure they never had a lot of money, but man when they got in that car and knew they were on their way to Ray's they were all squealing with glee, another adventure, the great escape, the great unknown, because you never really knew who was going to be at Ray's or what you were going to get, but you always knew there would be something to do, in the river, in the sun, hanging on sandbars on hot summer days, nighttime parents drinking and dancing their hearts out, while kids swam naked and made out in the woods. Good times had by all.

But by the time Doreen started seeing wrinkles in the mirror she was ready to move on from Ray, God bless his soul. And yes, it would be with Toby, no matter what he was yelling to her from outside, because he wasn't bad looking, he worked his ass off, he was strong, made money, good father, what more could a girl ask, but, well, how about a little passion, maybe, now and then, might be nice, just a *little* fucking *passion*, in a forever relationship, would that be too much to ask? But that just wasn't his way, never would be. So these little excursions, she thought, giving herself a saucy look in the mirror, they work for me, they work for us, keep us honest, together, hell, whatever works, it's all hard enough as it is, so let's go out there and have a fine time, she thought, looking at herself with approval one last time, and she opened the screen door, looked out into the sun from the top step of the Winnebago travel trailer like some hot American fox and called out to Toby:

"Hey, Baby, let's have ourselves a real good time."

The last of the clouds had gone, the sun shining brightly on the buzz of activity at the back side of Ray's Resort, where the grassy lawn stretched down to the beach, vehicles pulling around to the north of the main building along the dirt road that circled down to the shore, under trees dripping the last of the rain, unloading, and pulling away, to let another follow, unload, pull away, one after another.

Otto had arrived with his trucks and equipment around noon, only to sit, frustrated and anxious, listening to the rain pelt his cab and threaten the entire enterprise, wondering how he would ever get all his spits up and running on wet sand in the little time left before the feast was to begin, feeling increasingly sorry for Mona, and her big day. He was bumping up against it, and starting to give up hope, wondering how the hell he was going to get three pigs, three lambs and assorted chickens cooked to perfection in the time he had left, when the hard rain started to lighten, and then, miraculously, stop altogether, which wasn't exactly a green light, he had heard the forecasts, too, but you never knew, and he didn't want to ferry all his goods over to the island just for it to start raining again, but when the rain finally stopped and he got out of his cab and looked to the west over the island downriver, he could make out a clear line between dark and light marking the backside of the storm, knew he'd have to hustle, but knew it was a go, and motioned to his guys in the trucks behind to get the hell out and get to work.

Ben and Billy had come up with the idea of building two rafts to get everything across the inlet from the beach to the island. Each raft consisted of four canoes, fastened with lines, together side by side. On top of each set of canoes they lashed sections of an old sturdy fence stored behind the tool shed, placed face side up, on which to rest the pots, and pans, and food, and equipment, and tables and chairs, and quarter barrels, and bottles of top-shelf booze, and musical equipment, loaded onto rafts maneuvered in the shallow water along the shore, and pushed slowly over to the island, by a flat prow Tracker boat, with a ten horsepower motor, one for each raft, each side of the raft gently guided by someone wading across from shore to shore, slowly, carefully, with each valuable load of cargo, until they reached the island, where the waders unloaded the cargo, and returned in the Tracker for the next load.

Looking out from his cab at the rafts on the beach in the pouring rain, Otto had been skeptical, but in the light of the sun, after inspection, tight, no give, he was kind of impressed. With the help of Deano and a few of the Camo boys, who'd been waiting in the bar for the action to start, Otto and his recruits loaded the rafts with Otto's generator and spits and charcoal and pigs and lambs and chickens and tables and pots and tools, made the maiden voyage, without a hitch, and the wedding was on.

By the time Lee Anne and Billy arrived, in separate trucks, with open flatbed trailers piled with provisions, Otto had ferried everything he needed over to the island, and was already hard at work, raking furiously, one man grounds crew, turning wet sand into a smooth dry base wide enough for his fires.

When Mona saw Lee Anne pull up, she burst from the door of the bar and jumped onto the deck above the hill, throwing her hands in the air, shaking air maracas, and jumping around in a circle, yelling.

"Yippeee, my rays of sunshine," she squealed at the top of her lungs, so that Otto looked up and smiled from the island shore.

Ivy followed her out from the bar, as did Ben, Colleen, and their two kids, Dirk and Bonnie.

"It's a miracle," Lee Anne said, coming up the hill to give Mona a hug.

"It was in the forecast," Billy said flatly.

"God, what a creep you are," Ivy said to him. "You sure about this, girl?"

"Oh, I am, I am," Mona said flinging her arms around the smiling groom.

"Okay, hey, we got a lot of shit to do here," Billy said, "and I'm not even supposed to be seeing you."

"Fuck that," said Ivy.

"Come on, group hug," Mona said jumping up and down, "it all starts right here, with a little bit of luck, and fabulous people, come on Deano get over here, you, too," and Deano, bearded overgrown fireplug in camo pants, reluctant but pleased, joined the circle, next to Dirk and Bonnie, excited, ear to ear, "okay it all starts with us," she said, looking around the tight circle, arms over shoulders, "so let's *seize* this day," and they all joined her in a whoop and a holler that carried across the water and echoed off the island.

"Now let's get to work," Billy insisted.

And they all went down to Lee Anne's trailer, loaded with huge pots of potatoes and lettuce and spinach and carrots and onions and sweet corn and green beans and baked beans and sauerkraut and cranberries and God knows what else, and hauled them up to long tables on the deck outside the bar, to prepare the loaves and fishes, a salad for 200, potatoes in foil, beans mixed with Lee Anne's special sauce, husks of corn peeled back to strip the silk, fixings for Colleen's coleslaw. Mona, Colleen, and Lee Anne went to work on the deck, bathed in sunshine, Ivy went back into the bar to inventory the bottles of Chardonnay and pinot noir and gin and bourbon and vodka and scotch and rum and tequila, which Ivy thought a bad idea, the tequila that is, but Mona insisted, and tonic, and mixers, and sodas, and bottled water, and limes and lemons, all boxed up and ready to go, with many large coolers full of ice, all hopefully in sufficient quantities to satisfy what would no doubt be a very thirsty crowd on a hot summer day at an open bar, which was also something Ivy didn't like, the open bar that is, but Mona insisted on that as well, and while Ivy looked over her charges, Ben, Billy, Dirk, and Deano unloaded Billy's trailer of long tables and set-up tables and chairs and tiki lamps and pots and pans and cooking spoons and ladles and knives and carving tables, loaded them on a raft, put Dirk on for the ride, which meant Bonnie had to go, too, and escorted the raft over to the island, Deano at the helm of the puttering Tracker boat, Billy and Ben wading alongside.

And it went on like that, all afternoon, one trip after another. Billy, Ben and Deano loaded a pile of two by fours and sixes, and battery powered drills, and hammers and nails and wood screws, onto a raft, and over the water, and they set out to build a bar ten feet long, four feet tall, with its back to the fire pits, for a little separation, looking out a safe distance upon the sandbar kiva forum which would host the celebration. From the beach at the resort, looking across the inlet to the island, to the right, Otto was working at the north end of the sandbar, off to the left of Otto, the boys were hammering away at the bar, which would face to the south, onto the forum directly across the way, the makeshift stage centered and up on the bank, five feet above the forum, tables and chairs for eating unfolding into place left of center, and the rest of the sandbar stretching out elegantly off to the left on a curve toward the main channel.

About four o'clock, about the time the bar took shape, the bluegrass band from Madison ferried over, with their equipment, amps, generator, instruments—banjo, guitar, stand up, mandolin, dobro, fiddle—talented, versatile, penniless, and then all the pots of potatoes and beans and salad and coleslaw and sweet corn, and serving tables, and then all the coolers of ice and boxes of alcohol, soda, and bottled water, set out neatly on tables behind the bar per Ivy's dictates, blue and green and brown, bottle upon beautiful bottle, and then Marion arrived with her four monks in tow, with a canopy of maroon silk attached to four long poles, and red and gold pennants attached to even more poles to encircle and define the forum, and finally, the Pabst Blue Ribbon quarter barrels arrived, which Mona insisted come last, and once she saw the barrels of beer safely reach the shore, Mona took her cue, and with Ivy and Colleen went back to her cabin, and Billy and Ben retired into the resort, to prepare themselves for the evening, the night of their lives, not noticing the last ferry that Deano loaded and unloaded once they were gone, and it was about time the bride and groom got out of the way, because slowly, at first, but then steadily, the parking lot began to fill, and the guests began to arrive, and a steady stream began to descend to the beach, to the flotilla of canoes lined up along the shore, and one by one, they clambered in, some with difficulty, oars clanging on aluminum sidings, heralding the armada, an island invasion, of Natives lead miners lumberjacks river runners hop pickers and *voyageurs*, blood-lines, all mixed up and flowing together, Camo boys at the helm, laughter on the water, passengers alighting, excited, on the island shore, and then making the return trip, one after another, a group of actors from the theater arrived, with Demetrius and Meredith, a handful of Taliesin architects and students ferried over, a bunch of old hippies, Ray's dear friends, emerged from the hills, Cecil Hampton made an appearance, sharing a canoe with drunk Joe Gilliam, a bevy of regulars from the Mad House Inn arrived together, there were families of farmers, mechanics, and shopkeepers, a cadre of girls from the mercantile, the nine o'clock coffee klatch of retired codgers from the diner on Highway 14 motored over in a caravan of rickety pickup trucks, an impressive showing from Lone Rock's two trailer parks graced the event, lifetime members of Ducks Unlimited and Pheasants Forever, Vietnam Vets from the local VFW, Ray's Harley buddies and their bleach blonde girlfriends, River Valley High grads home from college for the summer, the boys from the reclamation center, a/k/a the dump, dressed to the nines, campers and recreational royalty from the RV campground sauntered over, anyone ever employed at Ray's Resort, none of whom would miss this for the world, and all of these folks, or most anyway, Cecil Hampton was an exception, arriving well lit.

Which included the group that had just come from a pre-party hosted by none other than Judge Ebersold, who no one could remember ever doing such a thing, the guest list including what those in attendance believed to be the upper crust of their small pond, Joe Fletcher, the Democratic State Representative, was there with his wife, as was Jimmy Fitzgibbons, the Republican State Senator, who, when he heard Joe Fletcher was going to the wedding, decided it would be good to make an appearance, Doris the librarian, spinster, eyeing the judge, bachelor, stopped by, with, to the judge's surprise, several members of her bridge club, Flo the hairdresser was there with her successful HVAC husband, the Superintendent of Schools was there with his much younger girlfriend from Madison, Walt the sheriff attended with Dottie, the owner of the diner on Highway 14, the Township Supervisor showed up, Mary Beth the third-grade teacher was there, feeling a little out of place, Marge the co-op business manager showed up with a very large man from Richland Center no one had ever seen before, and Conrad Wilcoxsin, in his gray suit, white shirt, and narrow black tie, with tie clip, proudly made an appearance. One week before, when Mr. Wilcoxsin got wind the politicians were planning to attend the wedding as an opportunity to work the sandbar, he dutifully advised his client, who instructed him to tell the public officials they were more than welcome to attend on the firm condition they not engage in any political activity, i.e. politicking, arguing, glad-handing, etc., during the wedding celebration, and if they agreed to that condition, and agreed to come to her wedding for the sole purpose of having a good time, they would be welcome, so Mr. Wilcoxsin was a little put out at Judge Ebersold's pre-party when he saw Messrs. Fletcher and Fitzgibbons in an argument on Judge Ebersold's patio, and felt the need to step outside and intervene to protect his client's interests, when he was assured by Messrs. Fletcher and Fitzgibbons that they were not arguing about politics at all, but about which of them would attend the wedding without the sport coat each had worn to the pre-party, the sport coats, Mr. Wilcoxsin duly noted, being identical, navy blue with gold buttons, worn over what looked to be identical gray pants, with white shirts that looked identical except that Mr. Fletcher's sported short sleeves, which was a problem for Mr. Fletcher, because he'd decided on a short sleeve shirt, against his wife's wishes, only because it would be more comfortable under his sport coat on a warm evening. Sizing up Messrs. Fletcher and Fitzgibbons in their identical attire, Mr. Wilcoxsin understood that the problem required a solution, so he attempted to mediate the dispute, by suggesting that Mr. Fletcher wear his sport coat during, but remove it directly after, the wedding, because all three agreed with Mrs. Fletcher that short sleeves during the wedding proper might look a tad tawdry, and then, after the wedding ceremony concluded, Mr. Fitzgibbons would have the right to wear his sport coat, to which each party agreed, tensions calming all around, and with that Judge Ebersold's pre-party ended up being quite enjoyable for all in attendance, after which they all drove down to Ray's, where Mr. Wilcoxsin had the occasion to admire his handiwork, watching State Senator Fitzgibbons help State Representative Fletcher's wife settle, with misgivings, into an aluminum canoe, for the first time in her life, and then perhaps see it all unravel, when State Representative Fletcher stumbled, and landed in his dress shoes, socks, and gray pants, in six inches of water, much to the delight of Senator Fitzgibbons.

For a long time, Bonnie sat on the edge of the stage, in her overalls, and her mom's old American Beauty tee shirt, supervising all the back and forth of canoe and raft and hauling and lugging and maneuvering and swearing, tables and chairs squeaking into place, never having seen such a commotion, and then she watched the band lug their instruments and equipment up the makeshift steps leading to the top of the river bank and the stage where she was sitting, and they were real nice and everything, but she was getting antsy anyway, so she stood up, went to the center of the stage, which she would remember later, flung her arms out wide to all the activity, and took a bow, maestro of the whole shebang, for one fleeting moment, one of the female singers applauded, as Bonnie skipped off the stage, time for a little recon, and ducked into the woods behind the stage, where she found a path that took her through the woods along the bank of the sandbar to the north of the island, where she could look down on Otto and his minions sweating over his simmering spinning meats, stoking the low glowing fires in long rows, with spits and basted brown skin, those poor things, is that how it all ends, on a spit over hot coals, it was too much to watch, so she reversed course, south, where she could see, through the trees, Lee Anne and her minions in full form, stirring pots over fires, shiny wrapped potatoes, cobs of corn, Lee Anne yelling at Otto to add more coals, itching to throw some on, lining up long buffet tables just behind and off the bar toward the shore, and the bar, came out pretty nice, Bonnie thought, surprised, more substantial, good for dad, solid, sturdy, and placed perfectly, a respectable distance from Otto and looking south upon the large kiva dance floor that Marion was creating just below the elevated stage, and as Bonnie double-backed behind the stage she could see through musician silhouettes a circle forming before the stage, of colorful pennants on tall poles, thrust into the sand, red and gold in the wind, which Bonnie liked best, and as she took the path to the south toward the main river channel she could see past Marion's circle of life, to where the tables and chairs were being assembled for the feast, with table cloths, hurricane candles, even, wow, Mona thought of everything, and the path led to a point on the bank at the southern edge of the island, overlooking the swirls and eddies of the river's wide flow, constant motion, thousands of years, and she looked out into the deep blue sky upriver, and her eye caught a fluttering in the seventy foot pines, regal at the river's edge, and Bonnie was the first to notice the bald eagle nestled in evergreen within the boughs of the tallest pine, spying on, taking in, like she was, all the activity below, the two of them, sharing a connection, and she thought of the heavy morning rain and the eagle and thought you just never knew how things can change from bad to good, you just gotta keep at it, which she would remember forever. She took the path around the bank of the island to where it turned to the west, where it followed the main channel until half the length of the island, where one path veered off into the woods to the north, and that was about far enough anyway, so she took it, as it sloped gradually upward to the rise in the middle of the island, closing in through dense bushes, and hearing a man grousing ahead, metal clanking, she reached the clearing at the top of the rise in the center of the island, where she ducked under a heavy spruce branch, saw Deano with his back to her, bent over what looked like a bed frame, and called out, a little too suddenly,

"Hey, Deano, whatcha up to?"

Deano jumped as if he'd seen a bear, turned in fear, to Bonnie.

"Jesus, girl, you scared the hell outta me," Deano said, shaking his long curly hair.

"Whooof," he exhaled, shaking it off, "you'll be a good hunter, Bonnie girl, but hey, now that you're here, come on over here and help me with this thing."

Most of the guests had arrived by the time the band of urchins showed up, feeling no pain, parked in the trees, they came down to the beach from around the north side of the resort, while, unfortunately, at the same time, Toby, Doreen, and their cabal of swingers, having shut down the margarita mixer, came floating through the maze of recreational vehicles, through the parking lot, and down to the beach around the south side of the building, where, across the grassy slope at the back of the resort, the two groups surprised each other, Joey Larocca holding out his arms to hold back his tribe, Toby stopped on a dime, stiffened in full manhood. That two such groups, as different as they might be, should meet suddenly on the grassy slope at such a large gathering ordinarily would not seem unusual, or anything in particular to be concerned about, except that the drunken tuber whose purse Joey and Danny pilfered happened to be Doreen, and Toby was the one who'd caught them red-handed. Good memories.

"Hey, you little fuck you wanna steal somethin' offa me?" Toby called over.

"Fuck you," Joey yelled back, from a distance, noting the Aryans' size advantage, conceding the right of way, Doreen pulling Toby and the cabal down to the beach.

"Yeah, get over it, man," Danny yelled out after them, "we paid for our crimes."

Joey turned back to Danny, "We did?"

"You haven't paid for shit," Toby called back, climbing into the canoe, a little unevenly.

Judy and Davey and Rose and Joey and Nick and Danny all watched the canoes push off into the water.

"Who the hell was that asshole?" asked Rose.

"Short story," said Danny, "me and Joey got caught, by him, stealing money from his wife's purse."

"Wow, you guys are a class act," Rose grumbled, Judy nodding.

"Well," Joey said, turning his back to the swingers, now safely off to the island, "it is fair to say, that the whole purse thing, was not, a shining hour." Danny nodding. "But, we've changed all that now, haven't we Danny boy," arms wide, "we're re-ha-*bil*-i-tated now," swinging his hips, "we were invited to this party, close friends of the bride, low table number for sure, and here we come," and he turned to the water, and led his band of urchins down to the canoes, and they climbed in skillfully, laughing their asses off all the way to the island.

Billy knew the story, telling it to Ben as they looked out the resort windows onto the confrontation taking place on the grassy knoll, couldn't stop laughing, maybe a little nervous, granted, but it felt good, hoping all the while those idiots didn't come to blows, afterward, fine, not before. And, when all clear, Billy and Ben walked out the resort door onto the deck, to the last of the canoes departing for the island, the sun commencing its decline, and knew it was time, time for the stars to shine, and at that moment, down the beach at the last cabin under the tallest pine, the three Graces appeared, with purpose, bounding out the door into the sunshine, Colleen, sprite, in yellow floral sundress her mother would have worn, bright in the sun, thick-flowing curls of red hair tied back in a chiffon scarf splashed in green yellow and orange, Ivy, taller, long, sultry, short sleeveless black cotton shift, tattoos, black eye liner, short black hair, swept back, black leather choker, spike bracelets, and by then everyone on the island was watching, as the bride stepped out of her cabin, gleaming white knee-length flowing pleated chiffon and lace, sweetheart neckline, lace overlay, cap sleeves, tanned skin glowing on white lace, nest of dark curls untied, dancing on her shoulders, and the owner no less, and the crowd on the opposite shore began to applaud, as she stepped between the maid of honor and best woman, interlocked arms, and together they strode, with great confidence, all as one, laughing through the trees up the road to the resort deck, where her future husband waited, watching the whole affair, thanking his lucky stars.

When the ladies reached the deck, there were kisses all around, and then Billy, black Italian suit his dad bought him years ago he swore he'd never wear, open collar white shirt, hair actually combed back, barefoot, and Ben, white dress shirt, chocolate suede coat, bolo tie with turquoise stone, long black pony tail, black jeans, also barefoot, walked down to the shore, right into the water, hopped into a waiting canoe, and shoved off, Ben at the helm, Billy standing at the prow, George Washington pose in bright sun, restrained smile, all the way across to the island.

"He's gonna fall in," Ivy said to her sisters on the deck.

It had crossed Mona's mind, but she had more confidence, thought he struck a handsome pose, never seen him in a suit, liked what she saw.

"Well, come on now ladies, it's our turn," Colleen said, and she took one of Mona's arms, and Ivy the other, and led the bride down to the beach, where all three of them took off their shoes, walked into the water, and deftly climbed, with Deano's assistance, onto the carefully laid blankets on the benches of the Tracker boat, Mona at the prow, seated. In his camo pants rolled up to his knees, thick white calves, Deano started the Tracker motor, and, very slowly, chest out, puttered his precious cargo to the island, as the band played Clapton's *Wonderful Tonight* above the heads of the guests, standing now together in the kiva below the stage, on either side of a sandy aisle, watching the bride and her retinue arrive in their processional across the water.

Billy and Ben climbed out of their canoe and walked up the aisle between the assembled guests, back slapping, "way to go," "don't fuck it up," all the way up to the steps climbing the river bank, and then up the steps to the stage, where Marion's four monks, four corners, stood solemnly apart, grasping wooden poles fixed to a crimson canopy slightly rippling in the wind.

After Deano steered the boat onto the beach, he shut down the engine, and jumped out to help Mona, then Colleen, then Ivy, onto the sand, where Mr. Wilcoxsin was the first to greet the bride.

"You look absolutely beautiful," he whispered.

Mona leaned up and gave him a kiss on the cheek.

"And you're sure all this is deductible?" she whispered back.

"Too late to worry about that," Mr. Wilcoxsin assured her, "now go have yourself a good time."

Mona reached down to retrieve something out of the boat, and as she did so noticed one lonely soul, an unassuming older African American woman, now standing on the opposite shore, looking helpless across the

217

water, Billy saw her, too, as Mona whispered something to Deano, and Billy watched as Deano jumped back in the boat and sped to the opposite shore to retrieve the stranded guest.

"Make sure she's comfortable," Mona whispered to Mr. Wilcoxsin, nodding toward the beach, "her name's Harriet."

"Now, let's do this," she declared, as she and her maid of honor, and best woman, readied themselves, lining up in single file, as the band played a sweet little intro to *Can't Help Falling In Love*, and the lead female and male voices sailed above the smiling faces turned toward the water, and upon hearing the opening lines to her favorite song, Mrs. Fitzgibbons began to cry, as first Colleen, and then Ivy, and then Mona, holding a framed picture of Ray, stepped off onto the sand, each of them floating, one bare foot after another, down the aisle, *Can't help falling in love...*, through the beaming crowd, more tears, no words, divine.

Bonnie, standing along the side of the stage, tried to get her dad's attention as the three Graces walked up the aisle, but he shushed her off, important and preoccupied at center stage before the gathering, but she wouldn't give up, and he kept ignoring her, until she had no other choice, and while everyone watched the bride walk down the main aisle, Bonnie snuck up on the stage to her dad's side, and whispered up to him.

"Sorry, Dad, but it's important."

Ben looked down, surprised, annoyed, which was nothing compared to her brother Dirk's disgust from across the stage.

"If you look up in that tall pine next to the river," she whispered, not looking so as not to give it away, "there's an eagle up there," and that was all she wanted to say, and she retook her place along the side of the stage, and her father, quite fond of eagles, pretended at first that she had not told him anything, until his wife reached the first of the steps leading up to the stage, when he stole a look across the water into the trees, at the unmistakable shock of white gazing down from on high, as first Colleen, and then Ivy, and then the bride, stepped up onto the stage, dappled in sunlight glancing through the trees, as the song came to a close, to rousing cheers and a thunderous ovation.

Mona walked across the stage, handed Ray's picture to Dirk, blushing, and the wedding party took their places under the canopy. Ben, having sent twenty-five dollars in the mail for a purportedly legal certificate of ministry, took center stage, and faced the crowd. His wife, the maid of honor, off to his right, the bride facing the groom before him, the best woman off to his left.

Ben smiled at the bride and groom, cleared his throat, and addressed the crowd.

"Hey, everybody, thanks so much for making this such a beautiful and special day," he projected out to the crowd, "the bride and groom are grateful that you're all here to share with them these first steps of their lives together, on this humble little island, in the middle of this river we love. In the thousands of years these waters have flowed past this holy ground there no doubt have been moments of great joy, great tragedy, and everything in between, the stuff of life, passed down, generation by generation, to all of us who stand here today, and the bride and groom are hoping, that today, tonight, as the sun sets and the moon rises, that we take up the cause of all those who have come before and all those who will come after, and represent them well, by kicking up our heels, raising the roof of stars, and savoring our good fortune, to be alive, and well, and excited, at this precise moment in the history of time, in the here, and now, on this humble island, in this great river, on this day of love, community, and friendship."

"What'd he say?" Rose asked Nick, who, unlike Rose, was tall enough to see over the heads of the crowd.

"He's talking about the here and now, how lucky we are," Nick whispered down to her.

"Well, of course it's the here and now," Rose said shaking her head.

"Luckier if they'd open that bar back up," Davey muttered.

"Shut *up*, you cretins!" Judy hissed.

"So," Ben continued, "we are gathered here today, as friends of Mona and Billy," no family present, "to celebrate and support the forging of a bond, the tying of a knot, and their commitment, to share their lives together, which, those of us who have made this leap of faith know, is no small thing, that word, commitment, tough word really, should scare you a little, because it suggests something we need to do even when we don't want to do it," Ms. Beecher, standing next to Mr. Wilcoxsin, smiled, "and we do that out of love, for a greater good, because two is better than one, when facing the wild and wooly times ahead, and so Billy and Mona stand here before you, to make that commitment, and take that leap of faith, to share their hopes and fears and dreams and heartaches, to support each other, and forgive each other, respect each other's uniqueness, accept each other's weakness, and love one another, and we all hope and pray," he said smiling, putting his hand on Billy's shoulder, "that old Billy here is ready for all of this," to a smattering of laughter from the crowd.

No shit, Ivy thought.

"And for all those reasons, as they have said in churches for hundreds of years," looking down at his book, "this honorable union is not to be entered into unadvisedly or lightly, but reverently, discreetly, advisedly and solemnly, and if any person can show just cause why they may not be joined together, let them speak now or forever hold their peace."

Joey the clown straightened, as if to say something stupid, but Judy, knowing him all too, well, kicked him hard in the shin.

"Owwww," he wailed, to turned heads.

"It's nothing," Judy called out, "please continue," to laughter, because everybody knew Joey, and Judy.

"Okay, well, dodged a bullet there, good sign," Ben said, "so let's have a song, a song chosen by the bride."

And at that, two female singers came to the front of the stage, stood alongside the monk standing behind Mona, and in pure clean acapella voices layered one atop the other, began to sing, Mona's song, *Boulder to Birmingham*, the longing to find, halfway across country, over mountains and rivers, canyons and prairies, how far we would go, for that one forever face, and Mona teared up, and Emmylou would have been proud, to hear her song sung with such heart and soul, to small town folks on a little island in a wide river, as the sun began to fall behind the trees overhanging the stage, and a line of shade began to ever so slowly move across the crowd, and their voices streaked across the water, *...Boulder to Birmingham...*, echoed off the hill on the opposite shore, and returned, softly, to the last notes, and Mona, reaching up, tears welling, to touch Billy's face.

Mona turned, applauding, with Billy and Ivy, and Colleen, crying, amid raucous cheers from the guests, as the singers bowed and took their places at the back of the stage.

"Well, now, we've come here for Mona and Billy, so let's hear if they have anything to say for themselves."

Ben stood back, and Mona took center stage facing the crowd, to louder cheers.

"Oh my gosh," she said humbly, "thank you all so much for coming, and helping us celebrate this, once in a lifetime," she said, pointing at Billy and smiling, "occasion."

"You know, I never really did have any family," she said looking out on the crowd, "never really knew what it meant, most I ever felt at home was in that little cabin across the water there, but from the moment I ended up here, I felt, somehow, that I belonged, and you can think about it and analyze it and rationalize it all you want, but sometimes these things that happen to you in life, these most important things, are just meant to be, they might be hard to understand, you don't know why they happen, or how, but all of a sudden you find yourself somewhere, and you don't know how you got there, but you just know it's the right place, which is how I feel, in his arms," she said, looking fondly at Billy. "I have never been so sure of anything in my whole life," she said taking Billy's hands and looking into his eyes, "and I am so very excited, to start my own family, and spend the rest of my life, with you."

Ben looked at Billy, as did the crowd, most, if not all of whom believed, as Lee Anne did, he didn't deserve her.

There was an awkward silence in the moments Billy steeled himself to find the right words, but, with a little nudge from Ivy, he took one step to center and looked out on all the expectant faces, who, in the aggregate, might have heard fifty words from Billy in their lives.

"I know there are a lot of you wondering how a guy like me got to be standing in a place like this next to this beautiful woman."

Nods of general agreement in the crowd.

"I think he's kinda cute," Rose whispered to Judy.

"I'll be the first to admit, I haven't done much in my life so far, other than maybe screw it up, truth is, I haven't tried very hard at it either, I know that, and I know I've let some folks down along the way," a good number in the crowd could relate, "but through it all I never really saw myself as a lost cause, just never really found a good reason, to care, about much of anything, and there was some comfort in that, rejecting everything, kind of a safe place when you're alone, and then she came along," he said looking at Mona. "So when she looked me in the eyes one day a while back and asked if I wanted to grab a canoe and go explore Bakken's Pond, I wanted to say no, wanted to go back to my room at the Mad House, but somehow just couldn't, and another day, when she said let's grab some poles and go fishing down by Otter Creek, I had other things to do, but for some reason, all of a sudden, they could wait, and it went on like that for a while, and I found myself getting accustomed to saying yes to things for the first time in my life, so that by the time we got off the motorcycle sopping wet under an overpass on Interstate 90 outside Chicago, and she asked me to marry her," no one in the crowd knew that detail, although none were surprised, "I looked into her beautiful brown eyes, and there was no hesitation, no doubt, just, yes, of course, and that was that, because for the first time in my life, I knew something to be true, I had found a reason to make the effort, for me, for her, for both of us. So here, before all of you, I pledge my love to you Mona," he said looking into those eyes he could not resist, "and I say not only yes, but, *hell* yeah!"

Ivy leaned up and gave Billy a kiss on the cheek. Colleen still crying.

"All right, wow, so, I guess it's my turn again, no, wait," Ben said, a little flustered. "Let's see, oh yeah, how about another song," he said turning backstage, and one of the same women and a man came out, took their places alongside the monk standing behind Billy, adjusted their microphones and began to sing, Dylan's *Girl From the North Country*, traveller's lament, chosen by the groom, the version with Bob, and Johnny Cash, singing together, deep haunting memories, moaning, longing, for that one girl, far away and long ago, lost in the sweep and breadth of aloneness, somewhere, in silent lakes and forests, bare branches on a winter's day, small towns scattered about the great North Woods, and found in Billy's homage, clear voices melding, over and around and through each other, and everyone, flowing, back and forth and back again, stirring the north country deep in their bones, and swaying now, on a warm summer breeze, in a song, that ends, with a long brown strand of Mona's hair, waving across her face.

Bows, applause, Billy, pleased.

"Well, now, that brings us to a pretty important part of the ceremony," Ben announced, and he turned to Billy. "Are you guys ready?" he whispered to Billy and Mona, more than ready.

"Then, Billy," Ben proclaimed to the audience, "do you, take Mona, to be your lawfully wedded wife, to love her, comfort her, and honor her, for better or worse, for richer or poorer, in sickness and in health, for as long as you both shall live?"

Billy looked at Mona and said in a low voice, "I do."

"What'd you say, we couldn't hear you?" someone yelled from the back of the crowd.

"I said I *do*," Billy yelled out.

"Just wanted to make sure," the voice yelled back.

"And now, Mona, do you, take Billy, to be your lawfully wedded husband, to love him, comfort him, and honor him, for better or worse, for richer or poorer, in sickness and in health, for as long as you both shall live?"

Mona looked at Billy and in a loud voice said, "I do!"

Billy started bending down to kiss the bride, but Ben thrust his arms between them.

"Wait a minute, wait a minute, you're jumping the gun," Ben laughed, "we're not there yet."

"The rings, please."

Ivy stepped up and gave Billy Mona's ring, and Billy placed it on Mona's finger. Colleen stepped up and gave Mona Billy's ring, and Mona placed it on Billy's finger.

"Now?" Billy asked Ben.

"Almost," he whispered and then raised his voice to the crowd.

"And now, it is my pleasure, and honor, to say to you, Billy, and to you, Mona, and to announce before all these witnesses, that by the power vested in me," and he paused, and looked up into the trees across the way, which everyone thought was for dramatic effect, but, in fact, Ben panicked for a second, thinking he didn't really have any power vested in him, that his mail order certificate was probably a fraud, and just at that moment, the silence was shattered by a high-pitched whistling sound from the tallest tree across the water, and Ben looked up, as did Bonnie, and then Mona and Billy and Colleen and Ivy, and then the entire assembly turned to stare, as the great bird decided it was time to come out of hiding, and make her presence known, and they all watched as she launched herself into the air high over the inlet, wheeling into a tight loop over the bride and groom, the gathering on the shore, the inlet, over the resort, above the trees, and then out west over the river into the descending sun. Ben looked over at Bonnie, then down upon the throng, mouths open, goosebumps, watching the eagle fly off over the river, and then he raised his arms wide, and this time, with confidence, he grabbed their attention, and announced, "And so I say," and they all turned back, in awe, to the bride and groom, "by the power vested in me, and all our spirits, I now pronounce you, Mona and Billy, man and wife. You may finally kiss the bride."

Wild applause, as Billy took Mona in his arms, and kissed her.

"Hello, my name is Conrad Wilcoxsin," Mr. Wilcoxsin said to Ms. Beecher.

"Well, that was nice," Doreen said to Toby.

"It was okay," Toby, replied, watching the exodus to the bar.

Davey, who'd been edging toward the bar the entirety of the service, made a mad dash.

"How'd they get the eagle to do that?" Joey asked Nick.

"Wasn't that just beautiful?" Mrs. Fitzgibbons said to Mrs. Fletcher.

"Really, you thought so?" Mrs. Fletcher replied.

Danny took Judy, shocked, in his arms, and kissed her.

Rose looked around for Davey.

Demetrius couldn't take his eyes off Ivy, Meredith stared at Demetrius, Cecil at Meredith, Doreen at Demetrius, Ivy at the bar, Lee Anne at the coals, Otto at his meats, Colleen at Ben and Ben at Colleen, Dirk at his parents, Bonnie at Dirk, the sheriff at Billy, Senator Fitzgibbons, putting on his sport coat, stared at State Representative Fletcher, taking off his, Nick stared at one of the women standing next to Toby, the judge at Mary Beth, the third grade teacher, Joey at the empty sky, looking for the eagle, the wedding party left the stage, the band stepped up, a banjo took center stage, started pickin' *Foggy Mountain Breakdown*, guitar bass and fiddle kicked in, collective holler burst from the crowd, arms started shaking, bodies jumping, shoes flew off, and the party was on.

The cool shadow of the sun falling through the trees crawled across the water, the gathering, the dancers, those at the bar, everyone with drink in hand, and then another, and another, cooling off in the shadow as the party heated up, drawing shade and some relief, finally, upon the furnace of Otto's fire pits, Otto, full throttle, too busy to notice. He had removed the pigs, lambs, and chickens from the spits as soon as the ceremony began, and now that the meats had cooled, pig on the cutting table, herbs, rinds, and garlic removed, apple in its mouth, the carving began, Otto, cleaver in hand, first the shoulder, front leg, falling off the bone, back leg, peeling crisp brown skin, back meat, pork loins, back shoulder, back jowl, spare ribs, flip her over, repeat, assistant slicing serving pieces as they go, then another pig, Otto's bald head, sweating, thick arms, rolled up sleeves, white apron over bow tie, Mona tiptoes up to give him a kiss, Otto smiling, then one of the lambs, then a couple chickens, then another pig, then a lamb, steaming pink perfect slices piled in growing mounds on serving platters under foil, stealing looks out onto the sandbar, frenetic dancing to *Black Mountain Rag, Whiskey Before Breakfast,* into *Man of Constant Sorrow,* the hoi polloi tippling, on gin and tonics on ice with limes, rum and cokes, shots of tequila, many of them, ginger and bourbon, vodka and anything, cold beer, chilled bottles of Chardonnay, Deano and a buddy, first shift behind the bar, madmen, feverish, three deep, Davey still waiting for his drink.

Rose squeezed, elbowed through the throng before the bar, ducking under tall shoulders, parting the sea, to the front row, looking down the bar at Davey, no respect, at the opposite end.

"What'll you have, Rose?" Deano half shouted to her over the din.

"I'll have a Brandy Old Fashioned," Rose said affirmatively.

"Oh, Jesus, Rose, gimme a break, you see what's happening here?" Deano, exasperated, waving his arm at the pressed bodies.

"Okay then, gimme a shot of Cuervo and a PBR, and for God's sake get him the same," she said pointing down the bar at Davey.

"He can wait, he's an asshole," Deano said.

"Yeah, but he's my asshole."

"Don't think that's what you wanted to say," Deano said laughing, pouring two shots, tapping like an artiste.

"Yeah, didn't come out right."

"You didn't mean to say that either, Rose, now get outta here," he said handing over the drinks.

"Okay, who's next?"

"I'll have a Brandy Old Fashioned," the judge piped up, grinning.

A loud harmonica groaned a long locomotive moan, followed by another, and another, huffing down the tracks, and the *Orange Blossom Special* came round the bend, and the Taliesin folks and the theater folks, Demetrius, Meredith, couldn't resist, jumped on board, pumping arms and legs, kickin' up a sandstorm, total abandon, *Deep River Blues*, *Cotton Eyed Joe*, *Shady Grove*, one song after another, dancers oblivious, of Mona and Billy, making the rounds, of the feast, in preparation, of Toby, Doreen, and their Lake County cohorts, lounging around a dining table looking out on the dancers and the bar across the way, sipping strong drinks, men talking football, women, sex, invariably more fun.

Toby and Doreen, Fox Lake, Bob and Carol, Waukegan, Eddie and Joyce, Round Lake, Doug and Betty, Mundelein, had spun the bottle on the picnic table outside Toby and Doreen's Winnebago after several margaritas earlier that afternoon, Doreen sort of pleased that hers pointed to Eddie. Sort of, because Eddie was the tallest of the group, six foot five, respectable two hundred pounds, not bad looking, endurance an upside, foreplay a downside. Carol was happy with Doug, who she'd been seeing on the side anyway, and Betty thrilled with Bob, a born pleaser, but Joyce, frankly, was disappointed, and there was no way of disguising it, because she'd had Toby before, wooden, she called him, cigar store Indian, just wasn't fair, and Toby caught her drift, bad mood.

"Who the hell are those people?" Toby muttered looking out at the barefoot dancers in the sand.

"Well, they're havin' a good time, that's for sure," said Betty.

"Not quite what I'd expected," said Toby.

"Makes two of us," said Joyce.

"I think the whole thing's awesome," said Carol, smiling at Doug.

"Who's the Black guy?" Toby asked.

"Think he's an actor," Doreen said, dreamily.

"Figures," Toby replied.

"I think the bride and groom make a handsome couple," Carol said.

"Well, thank you," came a voice from behind.

Betty and Bob and Carol and Doug and Doreen and Eddie and Joyce and Toby all jumped to their feet, big smiles, as Mona and Billy stopped to say hello.

"Thank you so much for coming," Mona said, sincerely, "Yes, thank you," Billy, for the twentieth time, not so much. "We were so lucky with this weather," Mona said, "I was crying my eyes out this morning."

"Oh, you poor girl," Doreen said, standing and giving Mona a hug, "we were so worried for you, but you deserve this, you do, and I mean it, and, you have a very handsome husband," she said, sidling up to Ben, moving slightly away.

"And you look so pretty," collectively, sincerely, more emphatically from the men, hugs, kisses, handshakes.

"Well, we do so hope you have a good time," Mona said. "Dinner will be ready soon. Too bad Ray wasn't here to see this, with all his old friends," she said, referring to the Lake County couples, "we really appreciate your coming back all these years, place wouldn't be the same without you."

"Wouldn't miss this for the world," said Doreen, "now go have a great time, and congratulations!," seconds around.

Billy took Mona's hand, and they walked, barefoot, away from the sandbar dining hall, across the sand, toward the pennants, the circle of dancers, the crowded bar further on, meats sizzling across the way. As they crossed the outer pennant ring into the kiva, the band launched into *Rosalie McFall*, and Mona and Billy, holding hands, joined the architects, players, and college kids, and twirled and leaped and skipped and laughed and stomped their feet and slapped their knees, pure Americana.

"She sure as hell should be thanking Ray," Toby offered, watching the bride and groom dance in the sand, "weren't for him this whole shebang never could have happened, two ways, first he off and dies, then he gives it all to her. Wonder what she had to do to make that happen?"

"Oh, don't be an ass," said Doreen.

"Well, it is a little suspicious," Joyce said, "she's like what, fifty years younger than him."

"Who says that had to be part of it?"

"Oh, come on," Eddie said, wanting a part of Doreen, "it's human nature, they seemed pretty close, we all knew Ray, and she is a hot thing."

"Well, I don't know how it all happened, and frankly, I don't really care," Doreen said, "I'm glad it all went to a woman, place started looking better the day she got here, so it makes sense to me, whether they did it or not, but look, bottom line, for me, I'm not going to sit around here and bash the bride on her wedding day, it's just not right," Doreen said looking around the table, "I mean we're having a good time aren't we, it's a beautiful night, the bar's open, and we've got each other, right?"

"You know what?," Toby said, waiting for their full attention, "Doreen's right, I'm sorry, let's give the bride her due, she's damn cute, and nice, and he, well, he's just lucky, and I am happy to be here with all you guys," he said looking at Joyce, "so here's to the bride and groom," he said, holding his near empty cup above the center of the table, "may they always be happy," and the couples from Lake County all rose to their feet and toasted the bride and groom.

"Come on, let's get some refills," Eddie suggested, and they all pushed their chairs in and moved away from the table, Doreen, lagging behind, bringing up the rear, with her red cowgirl boots, strolling across the dance floor, stealing a glance at Demetrius, in rhythm, to *Roll in My Sweet Baby's Arms*.

Walk on Boy slowed things down a bit, dancers pairing up, Meredith, turning to Demetrius, playfully, hopefully, Demetrius, sensing trouble.

"I think I'm going to get a drink," Demetrius said abruptly, and walked over to the bar, leaving Meredith, to herself, alone among the dancers in the sand, embarrassed, little humiliated, nowhere to go, hoping no one noticed.

She walked over to the tables Toby and his gang vacated and slumped in a chair, as the evening grew long, heralding the night, shadows stretching to the opposite shore, windows of the resort bar across the way reflecting bright glare of the setting sun. Maybe he's just not ready, she thought, might not mean anything, could mean everything, but, maybe it's okay, just thirsty, little awkward, maybe that, these things take time, just because she fell hard, maybe he wasn't like that, maybe slow hand, cool customer, for sure, little hard to read, give him a little time, little space, usually the other way around, she was the catch, always had been, beauty, really, best in a spotlight, sought after, just not by the right ones, but plenty of time, so buck up, the night's just begun.

Don't want to hurt her feelings, Demetrius thought, as he walked away from Meredith toward the bar, really good actress, great dancer, beautiful voice, good to work with, pretty, smart, but, I don't know, just not my thing, too good somehow, best nip it in the bud, last thing I need on a night like this, free rein's what I need, for the wild, off beat, little miss wickeds of the world, suffer for it in the long run maybe, but that's a long ways off, short run I'm interested in, like tonight, like those red cowgirl boots, like that tall stick of licorice standing near the bar, yes, I could definitely use a drink.

A monk passed him by, striking a wooden mallet on a singing bowl, the pure tone calling all for dinner, Mona announced the same from the stage, the band took a break, Ben played the first of his pre-recorded mix cassettes, all Dylan, for the dining hour, *When I Paint My Masterpiece, Highway 61 Revisited, Don't Think Twice It's All Right, New Morning, Maggie's Farm, Twist of Fate, Buckets of Rain, Just Like a Woman, Shelter From the Storm, Visions of Johanna, I Shall Be Released, Tangled Up in Blue, Queen Jane Approximately, A Hard Rain's Gonna Fall, It Ain't Me Babe.* Ivy relieved Deano from behind the bar, Billy and Mona donned aprons to ladle out the food, Lee Anne in charge of the serving tables, Otto the platters of meats, honor of first in line: Deano and the Camo boys, all their hard work, long line, hour long, behind them, ecstatic, drinking, laughing, hungry, patient, behaved, snaking past plates of steaming sweet corn and baked potatoes, huge wooden bowls of lettuce spinach tomatoes walnuts goat cheese vinaigrette, green beans and cauliflower, baked beans with bacon, coleslaw, glazed rolls, blocks of butter, tubs of sour cream, pork, ribs, lamb, and chicken, Otto's secret barbecue sauce, the long line, edging along, heaping plates, carried through the line, across the sand, dance floor empty, bar still crowded, dining tables across the way, filling up, as the brink of night and day crept up the pine trees, only the tips golden in the last light, leaving the sand bar in gray shadow, time to light the hurricane lamps, on the serving tables, the dining tables, candles flickering in the gloaming, lighting animated faces sitting for dinner.

"What is that awful music?" Mrs. Fletcher complained, whispering to her husband before the bowls of salad.

"It's Bob Dylan," Rose answered, totally buzzed, standing behind Mr. Fletcher.

Mrs. Fletcher, embarrassed to have been overheard, looked over her husband's shoulder, at Rose, who gave her a warm wasted smile, no offense taken.

"Thank you, young lady," she said, "not familiar with him."

"My name's Rose," leaning slightly.

"How do you do, Rose. I'm Genevieve Fletcher, this is my husband, the State Representative."

"Nice shirt," Rose said to Mr. Fletcher, standing barefoot, in his short sleeves, tie, and rolled-up gray pants. Mr. Fletcher caught Rose looking down at his plump white feet in the sand.

"Got a soaker climbing in the boat," Mr. Fletcher explained.

"Hey, it's cool, man, far out." Rose said, with admiration.

"Really?"

"Yeah, man, you look like you be-*long*."

They moved on to the green beans and cauliflower.

"Well, how do you like that?" Mr. Fletcher whispered over Mrs. Fletcher's shoulder, "bet nobody's said *that* to Fitzgibbons," he said with pride, Mrs. Fletcher, rolling her eyes.

Meredith waited a long while for the line to make its way, thought of waiting for Demetrius, who was preoccupied at the bar, so finally, she joined what was left of the line, close to the rear, and inched her way, night approaching, step by step to the tables, behind a tall thin young man in a Ramones tee shirt, staring up, lost in the last colors of the sun high in the sky, until he finally turned around, surprised, to find Meredith standing behind him.

"Oh, hi, my name's Nick."

"Hi, Nick. Meredith."

"Wow, I didn't see you there."

"Been here all along," Meredith said smiling.

"Yeah, well, I'm a little high," said Nick.

"Good for you," said Meredith.

Meredith and Nick had just approached the first serving table when Joey came up, grabbed a plate and cut into line behind Meredith.

"Hey, asshole," came Toby's voice from behind.

"Hey, yourself," Joey yelled back.

"My name's Joey," he said to Meredith, white residue on his upper lip, difficulty standing.

"My name's Meredith," she nodded back to him.

"Don't recognize you," Joey slurred.

"That a problem?"

"No, no, not at all, just that, I know everybody."

"I'm an actor, here for the summer."

"Shoulda guessed, you're beautiful."

"So are you the mayor or something?" Meredith asked, passing over the baked beans.

"Mexican cliff diver," Nick said over his shoulder.

"Really?"

"Just for today," Joey said, large helping of baked beans.

"Wow, never met a Mexican cliff diver."

"It's an art form," Joey assured her.

"Dangerous business," Nick offered, "had his share of scrapes."

"I can see that."

Joey listing toward the sour cream.

"So what's the play?"

"Shakespeare."

"I like Shakespeare," Joey said.

Nick stopped moving in line, turned, confronted Joey.

"When have you ever read Shakespeare?"

"Four score, and eleven years ago…"

"Oh, Jesus," scoffed Nick, turning to the meat platters.

"In high school, I think, hey, mind your own business, I'm talking with my friend the actor here."

"Less talk, more food," Toby called out over four heads behind Joey.

"Yeah, yeah, we're movin', man, speed a light," Joey said.

Meredith helped herself to some chicken, a dab of Otto's special sauce, and turned away from the serving tables, toward the dining tables across the way, hurricane candles in the dusk, faces aglow, Nick holding back to see where Joyce might end up, Meredith, judicious, waiting for Joey to find his way.

"See ya 'round, nice talkin to ya," Joey said, walking past, almost stumbling.

Meredith surveyed the scene, plate and plastic ware in hand. Now what, she thought, walking slowly across the sand, avoiding the tiki lamps, scanning the possibilities, waiting for Joey to find his table, evasive action, actors and architects filled a table, burly guys in camouflage another, tables filled with laughter, families, goings on, locals who knew each other, Demetrius still at the bar, tables with two or three, hoping for company, risky bets, everybody might know something she didn't, there was one, where drunk Joe Gilliam sat by himself, think not, and then she spotted one toward the back, where one of the monks sat with a stocky middle-aged woman with flowing white hair, full face, broad smile, the kind that would never steer you wrong. Meredith approached the table.

"Do you care to join us?" asked Marion.

"Hi, I'm Meredith," placing her plate next to Marion, across from Gessho.

"My name's Marion, this is Gessho."

Gessho placed his hands together in a prayer position in front of his heart, and made a small bow.

"Bride, groom, or both?" Marion asked.

"Ashamed to say, none of the above."

"Well, you're not alone in that department."

"I'm just here for the summer," Meredith said, "I've a part in a play."

"Well, you're more than welcome here," Marion said, Gessho smiling, not understanding a word.

"Where you from?"

"Chicago."

"The groom's from Chicago. Maybe you know the name."

"Chicago's a pretty big town."

"Dan Hurley's the groom's father."

"Wait a minute, I do know who that is, wasn't he killed recently, hunting accident wasn't it?"

"Yes, more than likely, others feel differently."

"Wow, what are the odds, wasn't the kid, I mean the groom, a suspect?"

"Ruled out pretty quickly."

"Seems pretty cool."

"Not a bad young man, sticks to himself, mostly, maybe one or two of all the people here know him at all, troubled to be sure, but if that girl loves him, his future's bright."

"What about you?" Meredith asked, "what do you do around here?," curious about the monk, one eye watching Cecil Hampton make his way across the sand, plate piled high, heading her way.

"Oh, I'm just a shopkeeper," Marion said, "I own a barn over on…"

"Excuse me if I'm interrupting, mind if I join you?" Cecil asked, approaching the table.

"By all means," Marion said kindly, the monk bowing, Meredith sighing.

"My name is Cecil," not asking Marion's name, ignoring the monk. "Quite a feast, I really must say, not at all what I expected," Cecil said, settling in a chair next to Meredith.

"Low expectations, I take it," Marion said.

"Well, I'm from LA," he said.

"Really," said Marion, ignoring the non-sequitur.

"Low expectations common in L.A.?" Meredith asked, one eyebrow raised, toward Marion.

"Well, of course, it's just so different, other side of the world," Cecil pronounced, with an accent, unknown origin.

Gessho, nunchi expert, no longer smiling.

Ms. Beecher walked across the sand toward the tables, followed by Mr. Wilcoxsin. She spotted Gessho, what passed for diversity, and decided to take a seat next to him, Mr. Wilcoxsin setting his plate down next to hers.

"Hello, Marion," said Mr. Wilcoxsin.

"Hello, Conrad," said Marion.

"This is Ms. Beecher," announced Mr. Wilcoxsin, "she's from Chicago."

"Please, Harriet," Ms. Beecher said to the table.

"I'm from Chicago, too, I'm Meredith."

"Nice to meet you, where in Chicago?"

"Old Town, how about you?"

"Pullman."

"Oh," Meredith said, having no idea where Pullman was located, Ms. Beecher figuring as much.

"My name's Cecil, I'm from LA."

"Seesil or Sessil?" asked Mr. Wilcoxsin.

"Sessil, Sessil Hampton, I'm a director, and this," he said putting his arm around Meredith's chair, "is my star."

"Oh God, hardly," Meredith said, leaning, Ms. Beecher noticed, slightly away from her director.

"How do you do? My name is Marion, and this is Gessho; he's from Nepal," Marion said pointedly, toward Cecil, now disinterested in geography.

Gessho smiled and bowed to Ms. Beecher and Mr. Wilcoxsin.

"Marion and I are locals," Mr. Wilcoxsin said, with some pride, as Joyce, trying to avoid Toby, and then Nick, following Joyce, took seats at the table.

"Hi, I'm Joyce."

"Hi, I'm Nick," Nick said, to Joyce.

"Marion was just about to tell me about her barn," Meredith said.

Mr. Wilcoxsin laughed.

"Marion is entirely too humble," Mr. Wilcoxsin said, "she happens to own what may be the most unique barn in the state, or anywhere for that matter."

Marion smiled broadly.

"Well, that is nice of you to say Conrad," Marion said, "we do what we can, you see dear," she said to Meredith, "our barn has four floors of Tibetan and Asian artifacts, textiles, jewelry, statues, prayer flags, singing bowls, brass and wood carvings, puppets, child protectors, Buddhas…"

"Oh my God, it's amazing," Mr. Wilcoxsin interjected.

"We're all super proud of Marion around here," Nick said to Joyce.

"Each spring, gosh for at least fifteen years now, I travel to Dharamshala and Nepal and Ladakh and Lombok and Java and lots of places in between, and meet in huts with old friends and we drink tea and they show me these amazing hand-crafted objects that've been made in their families for centuries, and I purchase a nice variety and bring them back to display and sell in my barn."

"Yeah, but it's much more than that," said Mr. Wilcoxsin.

"It's really far out," offered Nick, to Joyce, Cecil mangling a chicken wing.

"Well, yes, so we have the gallery, but we also have a library of Buddhist books, and music, we offer meditation instruction at our Mahayana Dharma Center, we put on Tibetan culture festivals and dances, and we offer Tibetan healing options from trained doctors in our Medicine

Buddha Healing Center; Gessho here is one of our doctors, visiting for the summer."

Gessho smiled.

"Around here?" Meredith asked.

"It's all tucked away in a barn in the hills you'd drive right by if you didn't know what you were looking for," said Mr. Wilcoxsin.

"It's fuckin' amazing, really," Nick said, forgetting he was not with his usual suspects, "oh, sorry, shit, but it is," little embarrassed, getting a laugh from Joyce.

"That is very nice of you to say," Marion said to Nick.

"Well," Cecil interrupted, "Meredith and I are putting on *A Midsummer Night's Dream*."

"I'd like to go see your place," Joyce said to Marion.

"My play?" asked Cecil.

"No, her barn," said Joyce.

"Me, too," said Ms. Beecher.

"Me, too," said Meredith.

"Opening night is next Saturday, you should see her perform," Cecil said gesturing to Meredith, "she really is magic."

Ms. Beecher eyed Cecil.

"Were you born in L.A.?" she asked, suspicious.

"Well, no."

Ms. Beecher, the lawyer, pressed the matter.

"Where'd you grow up?"

"Buffalo."

"So you're *not* from LA."

"Marina Del Rey, if you know where that is," Cecil said, haughtily, "beautiful views, right on the water. Love for you to come see it sometime," he said to Meredith, blushing, in the candle light.

"I bet he would," Ms. Beecher said, under her breath, to Mr. Wilcoxsin.

"You know I think I remember reading that play," Nick said to Cecil, from left field.

Cecil looked down the table, amused, at Nick, scrawny, long black hair, beak, Ramones tee shirt.

"Isn't there a director in that play?" Nick asked Cecil.

Cecil, the entire table, for that matter, taken aback.

"Well," Cecil replied, having to think about it, "well, now that I think of it, yes, there is a director, of sorts, in the play."

"He's an ass, isn't he?" Nick followed.

"Well," Cecil smiled, "as a matter of fact, he does have an ass head."

Nick, in a low voice only Joyce could hear,

"You mean ass *hole*," and just as Joyce began to giggle, the attention of the table, and all tables, turned, to see Joey Larocca rise suddenly from the darkness two tables over, stand uneasily on his chair sinking in the sand, and open wide his arms to the eastern violet sky, as the bulbous radiant full moon, in all its glory, began to rise above the trees, shining its spotlight on the gathering at the shore.

"La Luna, La Luna," Joey roared on top of the chair, welcoming the moon, in awe and homage, and all the guests turned to the sky, faces glow-ing, collectively, in the good grace of moonlight, in hushed reverence, in the transformation of night to light, the audience casting aside their masks, becoming players in the night, and the blind shall see, upside is down and inside out, once in a blue moon, the ancient sense of wonder, mysterious grand forces from the great beyond, unknowable, visceral, a tingling chill, a shift in the wind, felt by all, altogether, from the judge to Joey and everyone in between, all as one, with the spinning and exploding and tilting and expanding and contracting monstrous and contemplative universe, celebrating the moon rising full to the brim at that precise moment, never before and never again, in the history of the universe, when the planet turned to reveal the moon, shining on this gathering, of these people, celebrating this wedding, to revel and rejoice for that one fleeting moment in the unique eclipse of beauty over the anxiety and boredom and addiction and hunger and pain and heartache and tragedy ever present in all their lives, all forgotten, in just that moment, when they all rose into the sky like the moon above the trees, totally and consciously aware, of each other, and the absolute and incredible miracle of life, their existence, their lives, as the moonlight fell like a mist upon their eyes, and they were changed, changed utterly, each and every one, for one midsummer night, in a dream, hot ice and wondrous strange, as the curtain rose on their island stage, and they assumed the roles they were meant to play, their better natures, spirits free, fairies straying from the deep wood, and they saw it all in the moonlight, with perfect clarity, for once in their lives, spirits joined with the river and the moon and the island and all living things, animists all, loosened from tethers, unfettered, swaying slightly, all together, with the island floating on the water downriver in the summer night.

"La Luna," Joey called out, and as he fell backward off his chair onto the sand, his head barely missing an exposed rock, the guests erupted in applause, and the band burst into their second set, rocking the ground.

"Stir up the Athenian youth to merriments, Awake the pert and nimble spirit of mirth," Cecil declared.

"What he said, come on," Nick said, taking Joyce's hand, "let's dance," and he pulled Joyce's long arm to the dancing sand, and Mr. Wilcoxsin reached out for Ms. Beecher, and Meredith took Gessho's hand, and they joined the exodus, of the newly baptized, electric, flocking to the tiki circle sand, hands reaching for the night sky, hips twisting, music blaring, shoes airborne, bar hopping, bare feet jumping, kicking up a storm, kicking up their heels, like there was no tomorrow, because there never would be one, quite like this.

And they danced, possessed, for two whole sets, and when the second set came to a close Deano came to the stage, and gave instructions in a voice not to be messed with, on how everybody could help put the food away, sealing everything in plastic bags, nothing behind, before the music began again, and each worked as hard as the next, doing their part, Deano conducting the enterprise, all together, in everything, mobilized, energized, Deano instructing, here, over there, the judge obeying orders, Deano cheering from the stage, imploring, applauding, until, after the work was done, and the last of the black plastic sea lions was thrown upon the shore, Deano made an announcement.

"You're all fucking awesome!" he yelled, a little too loudly, into the microphone.

"Okay, we have a little surprise, where's Mona and Billy?" he asked peering out into the crowd.

Cheers came from a small group off to his left, which included Mona and Billy, cleaning up the last of the serving tables.

"Okay, you guys," he said, referring to Mona and Billy, "and you too, Otto and you too, Lee Anne, get over here, hey, everybody, let's give a hand to Otto and Lee Anne, all their hard work, absolutely awesome, man, they're the *best*, fuckin-*A*," he yelled, raising a fist in the air.

Lee Anne and Otto beamed, little pat on the back, all they needed really, God bless Deano, and the crowd roared, without a doubt among them, that what Deano said about Otto and Lee Anne was the absolute God's truth.

"Okay," Deano announced in his gruff voice, "we have a surprise for the bride and groom, if they would please come up to the stage. And after they do that, you are all invited to come on up after 'em, cuz we're all gonna take a walk in the woods back here, in the moonlight, where you never know what you might find."

A few held back, Mesdames Fletcher and Fitzgibbons, for fear of the woods, Cecil Hampton, for fear of darkness, Lee Anne, exhausted, sore knees, Otto, well-deserved rest with a tumbler of Cutty over lots of rocks, some of the Vets, starting a fire down past the dining tables, and a handful of the older, overweight, or infirm, but in general, the crowd, over served, intrigued, followed Billy and Mona up the steps to behind the stage, where Deano held a lantern, and started down the path like a king of shadows, under the trees toward the middle of the island, followed by Bonnie, and the bride and groom, and the best woman, and the maid of honor, and Dirk, and all the faithful, following Deano and his lantern in single file like ghosts trooping home to churchyards, teddy bears home late from picnics, and they did not need to walk far, far enough into the cool darkness of the woods, when up ahead on the turns they could begin to see what looked like flames shimmering in the trees ahead, and as Deano reached the clearing in the middle of the island he led the group into a circle around the perimeter, around what Deano and Bonnie had constructed earlier that afternoon, and what Deano had ferried over on the last run of the day, and as Deano's followers reached the clearing, one by one, flames of four tiki lamps came into view, and in the center, on a slight rise in the middle of the island, stood a four poster bed on a metal frame with box spring and double bed mattress with white cotton sheets and pillows and sheer white netting draped like lace curtains over the highest posts and waving softly to the ground in the slight breeze.

Mona gasped, and took Billy's hand, Billy took Colleen's hand, and each in turn a hand, as they made their way around the perimeter to make way for the rest of the guests, arriving one by one, holding hands around the white lights of the wedding bower, and when they had all assembled in a large circle around the edge of the clearing, Deano, completing the circle, first to last, holding hands with Bonnie, addressed the crowd.

"So I didn't think this was gonna work this morning when we all woke up in the goddam pouring rain, been thinkin' about this for a couple of weeks now, Lee Anne helped, with the sheets and stuff, but miracles do happen sometimes, and we wanted to make this one happen, for Billy and Mona, so we hope they don't mind we took matters in our own hands, did it for Mona really, thought Billy might need some help, so we set up, me and Bonnie here, this newlywed suite for the bride and groom."

Mona and Billy were speechless.

"If you don't want it, me and Judy'll take it," Danny Redbird called out.

"No, don't get excited, Danny," Billy said, and looked down at Mona, "wow, I just gotta say," looking around the circle, "to all of you, that this," he said pointing to the marital bed, "and all of you, have been amazing. I'm not much for speaking my mind, but I don't mind telling you this has been the best day and night of my life. I thought Mona was nuts when she told me what she wanted to do today, but as usual she knew exactly what she was doing, and I want to thank you for being a part of it, and for giving me a chance, but after today, I think I get it, that whole community, safety in numbers, thing, and it's thanks to you, and I'll never forget that. Now, as far as this bed goes, I've gotta say, as the one who wears the pants in the family," and anyone who knew Mona got a laugh at that, "I'm gonna make a command decision, and say, I'm sorry darlin', I know you had your heart set on spending our first night on your saggy little twin bed in your hot little cabin, but," Mona nodding vigorously, "I just don't think we can pass this one up, and I would be honored," he said, with great sincerity, "to make wild love to you right here, all night long, on this magical bed in the middle of the woods on our very first night as man and wife," to howls from the crowd, "but," he said looking at Deano, "you guys," he said pointing around the circle, "are gonna have to go…"

"But not anytime soon," Mona cried out, "come on, it's time for our first dance! Better late than never," and she grabbed Billy's hand and skipped into the woods.

At the sound of voices from the middle of the island, Ben, who had stayed back at the stage, turned the speakers around into the woods, pressed Play, and Patti Smith's voice came floating through the trees, singing *Because the Night…*, as the circle of arms broke into single file, following Mona back down the path toward the music, into a potion of soft dew lurking in the woods, the perfect cocktail, the song through the trees, of lovers, of moon and woods and island and water and temperature and music and spirits and opportunity and abandon and desire, a breath of aphrodisiac in the woods, a surge, unbridled, wild, was what he said, that was the spirit, that, was what they felt, the answer, deep within their timeless wiring, magnetized, drawn to opposites, if not in common, mattered not, only one thing mattered, and they all took deep breaths of it, *Because the Night…*

Toby looked around for Joyce, but couldn't find her, Doreen jumped on Eddie's back for the short trek back to the sand, so Eddie didn't see and probably wouldn't have cared that his wife Joyce had ducked into the bushes with Nick, the judge secretly grabbed hold of the third grade teacher's hand in the dark, Mr. Wilcoxsin bravely led a smiling Ms. Beecher through the trees, Davey had Rose pinned up against a tree, and Judy was biting Danny's neck under a tiki lamp flame.

Ivy did not follow the crowd, pulsing, as much if not more than the lot of them, stunned, by the notes of her favorite song, she wanted to be alone, sort out her feelings, come to grips with them, accept them, she couldn't ignore them any longer, live a lie, not who she was, maybe this was the night, and she ducked through the bushes where Bonnie had scared Deano earlier in the day, and took the other path that led toward the main river channel and then around the river bank back to the party, Demetrius followed her, Meredith, who had not seen Ivy, followed Demetrius, and Demetrius caught up with Ivy where the moon rippled in the current of the river, good a place as any, and, throwing caution to the wind, he bared his soul, told Ivy he loved her, said he knew it didn't make sense, they hardly knew each other, but wild love looks from the heart not the mind, an innocent child, and who was to question the current, the power, and he was a beautiful man in the moonlight, and they would make a beautiful couple, and Ivy kissed him, because a kind soul lurked in her hard shell, and they walked back to the party, holding hands, Ivy determined, now with purpose, Demetrius's feet never touching the ground, Meredith, just as in love, following, seeing, watching, crushed, a safe distance behind, *Because the Night…*

By the time Ivy and Demetrius reached the steps leading down to the sand, Ben had turned the speakers back to the beach, Mona stood at the microphone, and announced, "This one's for Ray," and she ran down the steps and jumped into Billy's arms, as Ben pressed Play again, and another song rang out, Billy and Mona's first dance, a special song Ray came up with, that he liked to play late on Saturday nights before the last howling began, and anyone who worked there or whoever closed the bar on a Saturday night knew the words, knew it was all about Ray, and his buddy Bowie, and they all joined together, knew what was coming, a smooth electric miracle of silver and blue, pure through the speakers, a bass bottom beat that grabbed their hips in the opening lines of *Let's Dance*, a song you can dance to, thin black ties, white shirts, long black jackets, and you know what color shoes, to the beat and twist and joyful sway, the bride and groom, and partners in crime, dancing, as one, together, collective, swirling, joyous, in the sand, *Let's Dance*, celebrating Ray and each other and the bride and groom and their little towns, singing each word, outside themselves, Mona and Billy and Danny and Judy and Joey and Nick and Joyce and Davey and Rose and Ben and Colleen and Bonnie and Dirk and Demetrius and Ivy and Deano and the Camo Boys and the Vietnam Vets and the actors and actresses and architects and college kids and girls from the mercantile and Eddie and Doreen and Carol and Doug and Bob and Betty and Toby and drunk Joe Gilliam and Meredith wiping tears from her eyes, together they danced in the moonlight, beneath blue sequined stars, toward the end of the last chorus, where Ray's magic kicked in, where he spliced in Freddy Mercury, pleading for forgiveness in the lead in to the last stanza of *Under Pressure*, wailing, pleading, for one more shot, *Under Pressure*, and the kiva began to sing along, with Freddy, and Bowie, the last chorus, a slow wave crescendo of voices and hopes and notes rising up the scale to the stars and the moon, the moment the dancers were waiting for, to stop their dancing, and crowd together in a circle upon the sand, united, stiff standing, buzzed, religious, all they believe, all together, once in their lives, maybe never again, with everything they got, raising voices, anthem to the heavens, every atom alert, singing, the last chorus, you know it, and if you don't, look it up, sing along, for nothing more than hope that things will work out after all, not just for you but for all of us, that people might come together from time to time and celebrate each other, with song, and dance and memories and hopes, the rise, and then, inevitable, slow fall, ebbing softly, as everything must, come to an end, *Under Pressure*, *Last Dance*, lower, *Under Pressure*, whispering *Under Pressure*, and the music stopped, and the choir bowed their heads, Mona crying, Colleen crying, Deano, tears in his eyes, and en masse the dancers hugged, and drifted apart, some to the bar, like Demetrius and Ivy, some to the chairs around the dining tables, where Meredith took her troubles, some across the way to folding chairs strewn haphazard between the bar and shore.

As she walked across the sand, with Demetrius's arm around her shoulder, Ivy decided to change the way she cared about herself. She stopped, turned to face him, took his hands in hers, smiled up at him, whispered something in his ear, and walked away, leaving him, stranded, shocked. Meredith didn't see, Doreen, eying Demetrius all night, did. Demetrius stood, frozen to the spot. Heaven to heartbreak, in a flash of a girl's whisper. In an instant, claustrophobic, nowhere to go, Ivy at the bar, Meredith across the way, only Black man in a sea of White, what did he expect, simmering, bullshit, same old same old, thought she was different, how to get away, eyeing the exits, the water, make a break for it, when he saw one red cowgirl boot bouncing up and down on crossed legs in tight blue jeans in the chairs near the water, eyes staring, back at him, and he knew that look.

After a breather, time to regroup, recalibrate, find a second wind, the band kicked into another set, launching into *Friend of the Devil*, as some of the guests began to peel away, the Fletchers, the Fitzgibbons, most of the judge's pre-party guests, early-rising farmers, saying their good-byes, slipping away, one canoe after another. Ben took his turn behind the bar, Ivy joined him, Billy and Mona went and stood in the water, holding hands, taking a breath, cooling off under the moon, waving to departing canoes, Deano took a seat next to the sheriff in the chairs next to the bar, Lee Anne and Cecil nearby in earnest conversation, the Vets around their fire down the sandbar past the dining tables, college kids went swimming near the fire, Toby and his crew plopped down at a dining table, Meredith found herself seated alone, at one of the tables, and, as it turned out, between two factions, Toby and Eddie, Capulets, at a table near the shore, an empty table, then Meredith, then directly on her left, the urchin tribe, the Montagues, slumped around a table, Sharks and Jets, trading drunken barbs over Meredith's head, wasting idle breath, too busy to notice Doreen, grabbing a table cloth, and heading up the steps into the woods behind the stage, Demetrius, close behind.

Something came over Mr. Wilcoxsin upon hearing the first notes of *Friend of the Devil*. Leaping to his feet, he excused himself from a surprised Ms. Beecher, and said,

"I'm sorry, but I've got to dance," and he strode out to the sand, and, singing every word, with his gray suit coat still on and his tie still clipped, he began to dance, possessed, like a mad stork, twirling, and leaping about in long vertical graceful angles, a thin gray silhouette, he sang about the devil, on the lamb, and too many women, his arms erect, hands bent down, prancing, dancing like he was alone, which he was, with everyone watching, astonished, and he encouraged them to join him, which they did, starting the third set off with a bang.

Ms. Beecher saw an opportunity, while Mr. Wilcoxsin danced with the devil, and she left her chair, and with amazed, over the shoulder glances at Mr. Wilcoxsin, she walked up to Billy and Mona at the shore, and stepped into the water, barefoot, having lost her shoes.

"I don't know what's got into Conrad, but he does know how to have a good time," Ms. Beecher said.

"That's my lawyer," Mona said proudly.

"Well," she said looking at Billy, a little nervous, "I hope you didn't mind my crashing your party, shown me a whole different side of you Mr. Hurley."

Billy looked at Mona.

"I suppose you had something to do with this."

"No, actually, no," Ms. Beecher said, rising to Mona's defense, "this wasn't planned at all, I did call to see if this would be a good weekend to come up and have a look around, and I was told it would be as good as any, so I decided to make the trip, I had no idea this was your wedding day, really."

"You didn't happen to tell the person you spoke to who you were."

"Well," Ms. Beecher said defensively, "I did speak to your bride, your wife, that is, and I did state my business, but I swear she didn't say anything about a wedding."

"Look, it's okay," Billy said, squeezing Mona's hand, "I hope you're having a good time."

"My Lord, the time of my life!"

"It doesn't change anything," Billy said, with conviction.

"Well, it's a wedding, it's a pretty big change," Ms. Beecher said.

"You know what I mean," said Billy.

"And Mr. Wilcoxsin, did he take care of you?" asked Mona.

"He's a delight!" said Ms. Beecher.

"Well, it looks like he might need to be taken care of after that," Mona said, looking over her shoulder at Mr. Wilcoxsin, leaping into the air.

"Yes, I will most certainly do that," Ms. Beecher said, "but first, let me say, thank you, both of you, I didn't know what to expect, not a lot of us up here in this country, if you know what I mean, but I've been pleasantly surprised, and I just want to say, Mr. Hurley, that I think you've done quite well for yourself, and I wish the two of you all the best for many years to come," and she shook Billy's hand, gave Mona a hug, and walked across the sand, *Friend of the Devil* coming to a close, Mr. Wilcoxsin taking a bow, almost run over by Ben's son Dirk, running across the dance floor, and up to his father tending bar.

"Dad, Dad," he said excitedly, trying to get Ben's attention.

Ben served up several shots of tequila, which proved, to Ivy's chagrin, a most popular drink throughout the evening, and leaned down to his agitated son.

"What's up Dirkie?"

"Dad," he said trying to catch his breath, "some kids have taken their clothes off, and they're going into the river and doing weird stuff."

Ben shared a look with Ivy.

"Thank God, one of us hasn't been drinking," Ivy said, "he's the only adult left."

Ben looked down at his son's eager face, laughing patrons looking at Ben, wondering what you say to that.

"Well, Dirk, I'll tell you what," he said, all serious, "I'm glad you let me know, you know, we've talked about this, swimming in the river, especially at night, one of 'em might slip off a sandbar, and then where'd they end up?"

"I know, that's what I thought."

"Okay son, I'll tell you what I want you to do," the whole bar listening.

"I want you to get back there as fast as you can, and your job, is to watch those naked swimmers like a hawk…"

"But the girls…"

"Especially the girls, make sure they don't do anything stupid, they've all had too much to drink, make sure they stay in shallow water, their lives are in your hands, is that clear?"

Dirk saluted his father.

"Yes, sir," he said, and galloped back across the dance floor, on direct orders to watch naked girls frolic in the water.

"Oh, God," Ivy said.

"He'll never forget this night," the judge said, ordering a drink.

Deano and the sheriff watched Dirk run back across the sandy dance floor, through the dining tables, past Meredith, past the fire, to his lifeguard post, the band mellowing a bit, *Sweet Virginia.*

"You don't still think it was an accident," Deano said to the sheriff.

"It's an ongoing investigation, Deano, can't talk about it, you know that."

"Oh come on, Walt, off season? Right through the fuckin' heart?"

"Shit happens, Deano, you know that."

"Not like that it don't," Deano replied.

"How many people round here could hit a mark like that from thirty yards away?"

"Okay, but maybe he wasn't from around here?"

"And what are the odds of that, somebody from not around here, doesn't know the lay of the land, walking around in daylight with a bow and arrow, in the summer. Have to be really stupid."

"Or desperate, or really good. I mean, bottom line, somebody shot that arrow."

"I know Deano, bothers me, too."

"Hell, they could be right here at this party," Deano said seriously.

"Yeah and I could be talkin' to him right now."

"Not funny."

"Look," Walt said, leaning closer to Deano, "if it'll make you stop crappin' on me and my investigation, I'll tell ya, shouldn't, but I will, since last fall there've been reports of a huge buck in the area around the Hurley property."

"Heard that, everybody knows that."

"You know the Hoffman's farm, just north of the Hurleys?"

"Sure."

"He's got trail cameras. We've looked at the footage, one from last fall?, huge buck, twelve pointer, and then he brought us one for the day Hurley died, same buck, hoofin' it down the trail at a clip, spooked, right around sunset, footprints we found at the scene would match the size, makes me think somebody almost bagged him."

"Yeah, but then what would they have done with it once they got it?" Deano asked, unconvinced.

"We found tire tracks, Deano, to a pickup, in the ravine between the Hurley and Hoffman property. Tried to trace em but so far no luck."

Deano considered the sheriff's intel, shook his head.

"Not buyin' it, Sheriff."

"Not askin' you to, Deano, just sayin', there's more to this than you know, all I'm askin' is that you gimme a break, and stop shittin' on my office all over town, for God's sake, I'm up for reelection next year."

"Okay, Walt, I get it, but Jesus…," Deano said, as he and the sheriff now watched Bonnie run across the sand in the opposite direction of her brother, "…man, those Gold kids are in a lather tonight."

Bonnie ran through the dancers and up alongside Mr. Wilcoxsin, ordering two waters from her dad.

"Hey, nice tee shirt," Mr. Wilcoxsin said to her.

"Thanks. Dad," she blurted out, "Dirk's watching naked girls in the river."

Ivy burst out laughing.

"And he's on strict orders to do so," Ben said to her, "now you go watch Dirk, make sure he's doing his job."

And Bonnie saluted, "Yes sir," and she ran across the sand, dodging dancers to the strains of *Luckenbach, Texas.*

Ben turned to Mr. Wilcoxsin.

"So, I guess you like *Friend of the Devil*?"

"Yes, I am fond of that song."

"And the Dead?"

"Yes, the band, too."

"Never would have guessed."

"Saw them a few times."

Ben looked at Mr. Wilcoxsin, in his gray suit and clipped black tie.

"Really."

"In the Haight, in the beginning Benjamin, if you know what I mean," he said leaning over the bar, lowering his voice.

Ben not quite sure he heard correctly.

"We are both lawyers, are we not Benjamin?"

"Well, yeah, I guess we are."

"Both well-acquainted with the attorney-client privilege?"

"Sure."

"Is this a privileged conversation counselor?"

"I guess."

"Okay then, nobody around here has a clue, and it needs to stay that way," he said with a look, "but I suspect that you, of all people, might appreciate, I was at a couple acid tests," he whispered, "back in the day, saw the band a few times, knew Cassidy, best time of my life, when I decided to become a lawyer, and here I am."

"Wow."

"Privileged conversation?"

"Absolutely."

"I hope you don't think less of me."

"To the contrary, profound respect, sir."

Mr. Wilcoxsin slicked his hair behind his ears, adjusted his rumpled suit, grabbed the two bottles of water, and walked over to join Ms. Beecher, sitting in the bar bleachers alongside Deano and the sheriff, all three discussing the Hurley case.

Meredith had watched Bonnie run past her, through the dancers, up to the bar, and then back through the dancers, and the dining tables, and as Bonnie passed a voice called out "Hey, fuck, you!"

Bonnie froze. Meredith got to her feet, put her arms around Bonnie's shoulders.

"Not you Bonnie, sorry," Danny Redbird yelled to her, "I was talking to that asshole over there," he said pointing to Toby, very drunk, hurling verbal grenades Danny's way.

By that time, Toby had nothing going for him but a boatload of tequila. What was worse, his penis felt the size of his little finger, Joyce wanted no part of him, and why would she, he was a shitty lover, and he knew it, Joyce was hanging with Nick and the Vets around the fire getting high for the first time, Doreen was missing, Eddie hung with Toby, but only because Eddie couldn't find Doreen, Doug and Bob were nowhere to be found, because unbeknownst to Toby, and better that way, Doug was banging Carol for the third time back in Doug's pop-up trailer, and Bob was getting down on Betty in the sand on the other side of the island. Toby didn't like the music, he couldn't see straight, and these scrawny little assholes were looking his way, laughing, mocking, and having a great time doing it, which bugged the hell out of him.

Meredith thought it best to get out of harm's way. She saw to it that Bonnie went on her way, and then, discreetly, ducking insults in the line of fire, walked away from the tables, around wild dancers, envious of their delight, wheels wobbling off her life, and badly in need of a stiff drink, she walked up to the bar, to where Ben was serving a drink, but Ivy saw her first.

"Can I help you?" Ivy asked.

"Are you a psychiatrist?" Meredith asked.

"No honey, a rocket scientist."

"Then you can't help, me. Can you make me a Cosmo?"

Ivy leaned down, placed her elbows on the bar, and looked directly into Meredith's eyes.

"You know, that's the first Cosmo order I've had all night, and it's funny, because, believe it or not, I have what it takes to make a Cosmo back here, which you had no right to expect, but for some God knows what reason I actually thought that tonight some crazy bitch might actually order one, and I'll be damned if you're not the crazy bitch."

"That would most definitely be me. So can you make me one?"

"Sure," Ivy said, grabbing the bottles, "so what's eating you?"

"The course of true love does not run smooth."

"So you're an actress."

"Yeah, you see that guy over there in the tweed coat and ascot?" she said, pointing to Cecil, listening to Lee Anne, "he's my director. He wants me badly."

"Ouch."

"I know, and I know you know that handsome hunk of a Black guy who's been gracing these shores with his beautifulness?"

"Seen him around."

"Fell hard for him, but I just realized, here, tonight, for the first time, that he's sick when he looks on me."

"Doubt that."

"Well, he's not into me, that's for sure, God, it's embarrassing, I have to work with the guy. You see, I've got this problem…"

"We've all got personal problems," Ivy said, handing Meredith her drink.

"The guys I fall for, they're always too cool for me," Meredith said, as she raised her cup, and drank it all down. "It makes no sense."

"Love has nothing to do with making sense," Ivy said.

"Another?" Meredith asked, holding out her cup.

"Sure, sister."

"I'm just not cool enough, too run of the mill, I'm not exotic, like you are," she said waving her hand at Ivy, to make her point, "I mean look at you, you're tall, tattoos, sleek, and freakin' gorgeous."

"Wow, really?" Ivy stopped and stared, "are you drunk? You don't seem drunk."

"No, really, you are, if I was a guy, you'd be just my type, hell, you are just my type, but you'd be too cool for me, too," Meredith said, Ivy setting the second Cosmo before her.

"Here, now take this one slowly," Ivy counseled. "And try and have a good time; there're only a few songs left, find somebody to dance with."

"Thanks for listening, sorry I'm such a crazy bitch."

"I charge by the hour," said Ivy.

Meredith turned to check out who might be available to change her life. The band started playing *Wild Horses*, Mick's baleful wail of hopelessness.

"Oh Jesus," Meredith mumbled, taking a sip of Ivy's Cosmo. She turned around to look at Ivy, who was looking at her. Maybe she's right, Meredith thought, I need somebody to dance with.

"Colly, come on over here," Ben yelled over his shoulder to a table behind the bar, where his wife Colleen sat with a bottle of Cutty, Otto, and two full glasses, with ice.

Colleen excused herself, and with Otto's wave of a hand, she sidled up to her husband behind the bar, swayed a loose hip into him, threw her arm around him and said,

"Hey, my man," in a seductive, be it not, slurry, voice.

"Do you see that sad pretty girl standing there watching the dancers with a Cosmo in her hand?"

"Do you love her?"

"No. Ivy and I think you should go dance with her."

Ivy, surprised, said,

"Yes, I think that would be a fine idea."

Colleen threw her arm off her husband's shoulder in a cavalier fling.

"Then off I go," she said, with a sassy sway, and she walked, dramatically, up to Meredith from behind, joined arms with her and said,

"My dear, I would very much like to dance," and Meredith turned, to see Colleen's freckles, dimples, red waves of hair, and over her shoulder, Ben and Ivy, behind the bar, pushing with their hands.

And so they danced, to *Wild Horses*, and at Colleen's urging, Deano joined them, and the band played the old country song *I'll Fly Away*, with high harmonic voices, and Lee Anne rose unsteadily on her aching knees and joined Colleen and Meredith and Deano, because she loved that song, and they tried to get the sheriff to come out, but there was no way in hell Walt was going out there, and then they all danced to *Angel From Montgomery*, and then *Momma Don't Let Your Babies Grow Up to be Cowboys*, which was when Toby finally had enough, and he walked up to the stage, and when the band wound down its song, he slapped a piece of paper on the stage in front of the guitar player, and said, "Play this," affirmatively, drunk, pointing to the piece of paper, which the guitarist picked up when they finished the song, looked at, and then shared with the rest of the band, all of whom were half in the bag by then, and they thought, yeah, it's a rowdy fun song, might be right for the occasion, but they were wrong, it wasn't, because it was too late, and the bar was too open. Before Toby even got back to his seat, the band began to play *Up Against The Wall Redneck Mother*, which proved to be an unfortunate choice, because what Toby could have used most at that moment was a soft bed and a pair of headphones listening to the sound of waves on a go-to-sleep cassette, but what he got was *Up Against The Wall Redneck Mother*, and he smirked as he looked over at those delinquent fucks who stole his wife's purse, who were this close to getting the shit kicked out of 'em, and what was worse, at just that time, Joey LaRocca, getting high with Nick and Joyce and the Veterans by the fire, speech a tangled chain, impaired and disordered, made the mistake of deciding, well, that might be pushing it, deciding is too strong a word, more like psychically lunging, Joey psychically lunged toward the water, for the cool relief of water on his toes, raising his arms over his head, as if he were diving, "Shoooom," he said, and then another dive into the air, "Shoooom," and then he was "Shooooming" up the beach in the shallow water, away from the fire and back toward reality, where he found it, coming face to face with Toby.

"Fuck you, you sick fuck," Toby said to Joey.

Joey was in no condition to recognize his own mother, much less Toby.

"Shooooom," Joey said, and began to dive, but in doing so, Joey raised his arms from his side, which Toby mistook for an assault, and in self-defense he pushed Joey, not that hard, under the circumstances it didn't take much, but he pushed Joey hard enough that Joey fell onto his side in the water.

It looked worse than it was, from a distance, if he could have remembered it the next day Joey would have said it was far out, but it didn't look that way to Joey's good buddy Danny, or to Davey, or to Nick, who'd been watching from the fire. Davey was the first to round the table where Toby had been sitting, where Eddie still sat, now with his leg out, which Davey ran into, tumbling into the shallow water, and when Nick ran up after Davey, Eddie leveraged his considerable height advantage, jumped from his chair, pushed both hands hard into Nick's chest, and Nick too, fell in the water. Danny, strategically, went around Toby's side of the table, where Toby looked down at him, laughing.

"What do you want acorn dwarf?"

And with a quick right upper cut that Toby never saw, Danny punched Toby in the jaw, sending Toby reeling backward, and falling hard into, it so happened, one of the college kids, a former high school defensive lineman, a naked swimmer, drunk, and now pissed, and he charged at Eddie, who began wrestling with the college kid, whose brother happened to be one of the Vets at the fire, who then ran over and charged at Eddie, Danny spinning, fists raised, lethal, and then Rose jumped on Toby's shoulders, like a mermaid on a dolphin's back, and put her hands over Toby's eyes, and as the simple misunderstanding devolved into a full scale melee, as so often happens, with bodies flying, water splashing like schools of stingrays, the band singing *Up Against the Wall Redneck Mother*..., and finally, Walt, who'd been watching from his chair near the bar, and who would have left much earlier had he not suspected just such a contingency, strolled over to the scene of the crime, took his gun out of a holster at the back of his belt, raised his gun into the air, and fired one shot out over the river. Everything, the pugilists, the band, came to a halt.

"You fellas are disre-*spec*-ting the bride and groom," Walt yelled into their drunken faces, his deep voice booming across the water, echoing off the bank on the far side of the river.

The fighters stood, ashamed, dripping wet, the college kid, naked.

Doreen, who'd been waiting in the woods behind the stage for just the right moment, skipped down the steps into the crowd of dancers, all staring at the altercation.

Danny turned his head up to the moon and yelled out, sincerely, "Sorry, Mona."

"Sorry, Billy," Nick yelled out after him.

"Shoooom," Joey said, diving down the beach.

Walt put his gun back into its holster, turned toward the band, and yelled out,

"Why don't you try another song."

The band stood, confused, a little responsible, when Ben came up to the stage with a suggestion, and the band huddled, seemed to agree, started playing, *The Weight,* upbeat, good sing-along, and everyone carried on, as if someone pressed Play, from a dead stop.

Billy wasn't at all surprised by the turn of events, kind of figured it might happen, Mona, hoping for a night to remember, kind of pleased, so the bride and groom thanked Walt for his smooth handling of the situation, and took to dancing to the last songs in the band's final set.

But there was no getting around the fact that the gunshot over the river took the wind out of most everybody's sails, more and more taking to the canoes, where the Camo boys waited to ferry folks to the far shore, Doreen and Eddie shared a canoe, Betty and Bob, who'd returned from the other side of the island, Cecil and Lee Anne, Marion, Gessho and the monks, Otto and his gang of butchers, the mercantile girls and the coffee codgers, the Harley riders, the hippies, the dancing architects, the college kids, wading across. Toby, not feeling well, especially after Danny's humiliating blow, wandered off to lie down in the sand near the main channel, Demetrius sat back in the woods next to the river watching the moon ripple in the current, the sheriff, thinking it was finally safe to leave, said his goodbyes, and soon, just a handful of stalwarts, diehards, remained, Deano and Meredith and Ben and Colleen and Dirk and Bonnie and Nick and Joyce and Danny and Judy and Davey and Rose and Joey and Mr. Wilcoxin and Ms. Beecher and all of Ray's former employees and the Camo boys and to everyone's surprise, the judge and the third-grade teacher, Mary Beth Shaughnessey.

For the second to last song, the band swayed into a soft lovely version of *Ripple*, Billy, Ben, Colleen, Dirk, Bonnie, and Mr. Wilcoxsin, singing along, and when Ivy heard the notes of a slow song, at the end of the night, she thought it was now or never, she mustered up her courage, stepped out from behind the bar, out from behind a lot of things, walked up to Meredith, and, hesitantly, fearing a colossal mistake, asked,

"Would you like to dance with me?" as if Ivy were in seventh grade.

Meredith, surprised, looked up at Ivy, tall, tattoos, sleek, freakin' gorgeous, and said,

"I think you might just be my type."

Ivy took Meredith's hand, placed her right arm around Meredith's hip, and the two of them began to dance, slowly.

"Maybe a little closer," Meredith said, and Ivy and Meredith shared a dance the two of them had been waiting for all night long, if not most of their lives.

And the dancers began to pair up, Colleen and Deano, Ben and Joey, Ivy and Meredith, Rose and Davey, Billy and Mona, Nick and Joyce, Dirk and Bonnie, Danny and Judy, Mr. Wilcoxsin and Ms. Beecher, the judge and Mary Beth Shaughnessey, and all the rest, until the last *Ripple* note faded into the trees.

And the moon looked down with a watery eye, with Venus in her glimmering sphere, and the wolf behowled the moon, time to honor the shadows and the light, time for sweet friends to bed, as Deano and Joey and Dirk and Bonnie and the urchins and the old resort hands left the dance floor, drifting off to gather their shoes, and in the softness of the early morning the band played one last song, in honor of summer, and the night, and the woods, and the moon, and the eagle, and magic, and friends, and lovers, and new beginnings, and the flow of the river over thousands of years, Mona's choice, set weeks ago, *Summertime...*

The dancers swayed, each couple their own space, Mr. Wilcoxsin, leaning far from Ms. Beecher, dramatic, long, outstretched arms holding hands, twirling, slow motion, Ms. Beecher a pirouette under his arm, the judge and Mary Beth, slowly, a bit apart, like their ages, contented, smiling like neither had in a long time, Ivy and Meredith close, very close, Meredith's head on Ivy's shoulder, arms wrapped around, Ben and Colleen, always together, through a summer very different from that long ago, and the King and Queen of Fairies, over the moon, on the first night of a lifetime they would share, a *Summertime* to savor, in the fading melody of a long midsummer night, and a last song, coming to a close.

The musicians packed up their instruments and equipment, and the scattering began, hugs and goodbyes all around, Ray's gang of employees, the judge and Mary Beth, Mr. Wilcoxsin and Ms. Beecher, Nick and Joyce, Danny and Judy, Davey and Rose, and Joey and drunk Joe Gilliam, who Deano found sleeping under one of the tables. The Camo boys ferried the musicians back to the resort, returned, said their goodbyes, waded back through the water, got in their cars, and drove away, leaving the core behind, who knew it was time, but just didn't want to leave.

After weeks of preparation, and anxiety, and planning, and the incredible hours of work and contributions made by so many, now that her dream had been realized, and had now come to an end, and looking at those most responsible for pulling it all off, Mona could not hold back her tears.

"Oh, my God, you're all so wonderful," she said, embracing Ivy, Deano, Colleen then Ben, not wanting to let go. "I'll go to my grave thinking about this day and all of you," she sputtered, giving Dirk, and Bonnie, and even Meredith big hugs.

Looking at them, all in a circle, she blurted out through tears,

"Oh, this is just like when Dorothy woke up in her room with Auntie Em and the farmhands standing around…"

"Oh, for chrissakes, get a grip girl," Ivy said, "we love you terribly, now go to bed," and she stepped up and gave Mona a big hug and kiss, "and you," she said to Billy, "don't fuck this up!"

"Thanks, Ivy," Billy said, gave them all a hug, and sent them on their way, in the last of the canoes waiting on the shore.

Billy took Mona's hand and led her back across the sand, up the steps, onto the stage, and they sat down at the front of the stage, feet dangling over the edge, Mona curled under Billy's arm, watching the little armada paddle across the water in the moonlight. They watched as the canoes scratched into the gravel on the opposite shore, paddles bouncing off aluminum sides.

"Good night!"

"Good night!"

"Love you!"

"Good night!"

"Love you!"

Back and forth across the water.

Billy and Mona, Mona whimpering, listened to the last of the muffled engines in the distance, and watched as the last of the headlights caromed through the trees and disappeared down the lane, blinking red taillights in their wake.

"Too bad your father couldn't have been here," Mona whispered.

"He would have found something he didn't like, me, most likely."

"Well, then it's too bad your kids couldn't have been here."

"Don't know if it would've been right. Don't even know them. Just don't know."

"You could try and do something about that."

"Don't go there, please, not now."

"Well, if you don't go there soon, and do something about it, you might not ever be able to."

"I've made my decision, it's enough for me to work on us."

Mona had a funny feeling that what his father would have disliked most was that his grandkids weren't at his son's wedding. But it was no use pushing, not now.

They looked about the sandbar, and what was left to be retrieved the next day, plastic lumps of tightly sealed perishables along the shore, bottles behind the bar, tables and chairs, covered plastic bins of tools and equipment and utensils and garbage bags, as neatly ordered as they were delivered.

"Lot of work tomorrow," Billy said.

"Rest of our lives," Mona said.

"But we'll do it together, won't we?" Billy said, holding Mona tight.

"Oh, we will," Mona said cuddling into him, "and for that I am so happy."

And they looked out on what they had wrought, on their little sandbar, aglow in moonlight, all quiet, but for an occasional coyote howling in the distance, and they were about to rise and turn to bed, when far off to their right they saw a movement, someone wandering across the sand, around the bend by the main channel, and they watched him, oblivious of their presence, walking, heavy footed, stumble here and there, past glowing embers, through empty dining tables, across the dance floor, in silence, as he made his way across the sand to where the canoes should have been to get him across to the other shore. They watched as he realized his predicament, saw him sit down at the shore, head in his hands.

"What the fuck," Toby mumbled.

And as Billy and Mona looked out on the seated figure at the shore, they heard something, coming from behind, footsteps through the woods, at the back of the stage, where Demetrius stepped through the trees, around the side of the stage, to the steps leading down to the sand, where he saw Billy and Mona.

"Hey, there's a nice bed waiting for the two of you back in the woods."

"Yeah, thanks, "Billy said, "'fraid you're gonna have to wade across."

"Is it over my head?"

"No, chest deep, you'll be fine."

Demetrius stepped down to the sand, turned up to Billy and Mona.

"Then we're all good. Man, you two know how to throw a party, may all the rest of your days be as splendid as this one."

"Thank you," said Mona, "and thank you for coming."

"Wow, my pleasure," Demetrius said, "best wedding ever."

"It looks like he might need a little help," Billy said, pointing to Toby at the shore.

"Got it, will do."

Demetrius walked away from the bride and groom and down to where Toby sat, forlorn, in the sand.

"Hey, buddy, you okay?"

"We're fucked," Toby said, pointing to the water.

"No, man, we're okay, we just have to walk across."

"I can't swim," said Toby.

"It's not that deep, we'll be fine."

"I don't feel so good," Toby said, not ready to move.

Demetrius looked back at Billy and Mona, then took a seat in the sand next to Toby.

"Man, what a night," Toby said.

"Too much to drink?"

"Too much of everything."

"Too much fun."

"Not for me. My life's coming to an end."

"Hey, man," Demetrius said, looking Toby over, "you might be messed up, but you don't look so bad."

Toby looked across the water.

"I'm fucked up, all over."

"How so?"

"I mean, I always thought the older you got the more you got your shit together, but here I am, halfway through, stranded on a beach with... what's your name anyway?"

"Demetrius."

"What kind of a name is that? So here I am stranded on a beach with a guy whose name I can't even say, and I realize I'm more fucked up than ever."

"Wow, man, mid-life crisis?"

"What's that?"

"What you got."

"Well, at least there's a name for it."

"Come on, man, I'll help you across."

"No, really, always been on top, always the guy to beat," Toby said, shaking his head, waving his hands, "work my ass off, but what do I get out of it, man, you know what I mean, done everything I can, to get to just this point," he said, pointing down to the sand, "good job, nice truck, nice RV, but, is that all there is, I mean, am I just gonna do this the rest of my life, and then die? What the fuck?"

Jesus, I could be here forever, Demetrius thought.

"Maybe you need someone to share it with."

"Yeah, and that's part of the problem."

"Well," Demetrius said, thinking about his own night, his own life, "I think, when it comes right down to it, we need people to share the journey with, all the rest might come and go, but love might be what it's all about."

"Yeah, but what if you're bad at that? You're really fucked then, right?"

"Bad at what? At love? What do you mean?"

"You know what I mean."

"You mean making love?"

"Yeah," Toby said, almost whispering, seriously, looking at Demetrius, for help.

Wow, Demetrius thought.

"I think you're suffering from cognitive dissonance."

"What?"

Demetrius thought it over. Just wanted to go home, but this, this guy, he looked back at Billy and Mona, owed it to them, but how the hell, had to get this guy to shore, this guy needed help.

"So, you're having trouble with the big nasty?"

"Man, I'm just a failure."

"Okay, look," Demetrius said, different tack, "I'll let you in on a secret. It's a can't miss."

Toby all ears.

"Okay, well, first of all you gotta get a grip, cut out all this baggage, all this whining, all the awkward, fumbling around, strip it all away, grab the reins, start all over, forget who you are, what you fear, doesn't exist anymore, you're just another animal in the kingdom, a rack of horns, a raw nerve, of desire, abandon, and lust, for her scent, her breath, her nectar, put your nose in it, brush your teeth in it, bathe in it, get lost in it, you exist only for that, try everything, and if you fuck it up, try something else, but never stop exploring, and don't give me that 'ooooh I don't like that,' or 'ooooh that's disgusting' bullshit, cuz if you do you're done, pathetic, hopeless, you've gotta be willing to try anything, and you'll find there'll be things you don't like, but if you keep trying, you'll find things you'll like that you never thought you would, but here's the most important thing, bottom line, what you like doesn't really matter, it's not about you at all, all that matters, your total commitment, your one true goal, is to please your lover, it's all about him or her…"

"Her."

"Okay, it's all about her, you must embrace her, give yourself up to her, get down and dirty with her, find out what pleases her, and when you've got that down, find something else that pleases her, and then do that, lose yourself in her, become one with her, she will love you for it, and you'll feel better about yourself. You said you're the one to beat, for chrissakes act like it."

"Down and dirty?"

"Embrace the down and dirty."

Toby looked at Demetrius.

"You know, you're all right. What's your name again?"

"Doesn't matter," Demetrius said, "can we go now?"

"Yeah, we can go now," Toby said, struggling to his feet. "Sure we won't drown?"

"No, but we don't have a choice. Come on, let's go."

Toby and Demetrius carefully stepped into the cool water, feeling a slight current.

"So what do you do?" Toby asked.

"I'm an actor."

"No shit, say something."

"What do you mean?"

"Act something."

Demetrius thought about it, waist deep, why not, keep this guy quiet, thought about something appropriate.

"Well, okay," Demetrius said and he started out, chest deep:

"If we shadows have offended…"

"No, in your actor's voice, so the moon can hear you."

Demetrius raised his voice, loud enough so that Billy and Mona could barely make out the words across the water, as they watched the ripples of Toby and Demetrius wading side by side, in the moonlight.

"If we shadows have offended," Demetrius intoned, waist deep, "Think but this, and all is mended, That you have but slumbered here, While these visions did appear, And this weak and idle theme," words fading as they approached the shore, "No more yielding but a dream, Gentles, do not reprehend, If you pardon, we will mend…," but the rest of the words faded in the distance, inaudible, just a voice, as the two shadows made their way out of the water onto the sand, appeared to shake hands, and go their separate ways.

Billy and Mona took a deep breath of the cool night air, rose from their seats, held each other close, kissed, and walked off the stage, back through the woods, and into the clearing, where Billy drew the netting back from the bed, and he and his wife slipped out of their clothes, crawled under crisp white cotton sheets, and into each other's arms.

Mr. Wilcoxsin followed Ms. Beecher in her car to see that she made it safely to her motel on Highway 14. He walked her to the door. Ms. Beecher, barefoot, fumbled for her keys.

"I had a very nice time, Harriet, I'm glad you came."

"Me, as well, Conrad, me as well."

"I hope you don't mind my asking, but, if you would be so inclined, and if I happened to be in the Chicago metropolitan area any time soon, perhaps you might not think it inappropriate if I were to ask you to accompany me out on the town somewhere, maybe a dinner, or a show or something."

"I think I would like that very much, Conrad, good night," she said, and she smiled up at him, and she kissed him on the cheek, and he kissed her on the cheek, and Harriet opened the door, and stepped, beaming, into her little room, while Conrad, saying "good night," walked away, beaming, into the moonlight.

The judge dropped Mary Beth Shaughnessey off at the door to her apartment above the local newspaper, thanked her for the evening, and asked if he could see her again sometime. Mary Beth responded in the affirmative, age being just a number, after all.

Cecil went home with Lee Anne to her big empty house on Long Lake, Johnny Walker in hand, looking out tall windows through pine trees at the moon glancing off the lake, Cecil accepting Lee Anne's invitation to stay during the run of his play, and though it wasn't Marina Del Rey, he did have a view of the water, and Lee Anne could tell anyone who would listen that a Hollywood director was living in her house, so there was consideration, in the legal sense, and the best part, for both of them, was the purely platonic nature of their relationship.

Nick walked Joyce to her recreational vehicle with her telephone number in his pocket, kissed her, and then left with all the urchins back to Danny's trailer, where they did a few more lines, stayed up all night, and watched the sun rise.

Instead of going inside the RV, Joyce lay down on the picnic table, very high, and looked up at the sky, tracing shooting stars in the moonlight.

Demetrius walked all the way back to town, had a really good time all in all, pleased with his life, proud of his advice.

After walking Meredith to her car, and a kiss, Ivy walked down to Mona's cabin, having asked Mona for the key. Meredith then drove her car down to Mona's cabin.

Dirk and Bonnie, kissed and tucked into bed, each in their own room, identical look of wonder, unable to sleep, wide eyed, in the moonlight shining through the windows.

Billy and Mona: love. Wild.

CHAPTER SIX

The Documents

"All rise."

Creaking wood. Judge Wozak walks with a flourish through the tall oak door from chambers, pile of documents in his hands, plops the papers on the bench, and looks out into the courtroom, exasperated, always.

"Please, be seated," he says from his perch, to no one in particular. "Call the cases," dismissively, to his harried clerk, perpetually fed up voice.

"Walsh v. Hurley, 84 P 1349."

A young woman, looked old enough to be in high school, rose officiously from one of the lawyers' tables, called out in a piercing voice, "petitioner," the judge looking at her over his glasses, raising an eyebrow.

Billy, now familiar with the routine, rose from his seat in the visitors' gallery, stepped into the aisle, held open one side of the swinging gate for Ms. Beecher, who had stepped out from her seat in the back benches, and Billy and Ms. Beecher walked up to the judge's bench, Billy to one side of the young woman, Ms. Beecher to the other.

"Mary Anne Topinka, for the petitioner, Your Honor."

"Harriet Beecher, Guardian *ad Litem*."

"Mr. Hurley, it does not appear you have a lawyer," the judge said.

"Well, actually, I do have a lawyer, Judge, in Wisconsin."

"You *are* aware we are not *in* Wisconsin, Mr. Hurley."

"Yes, Your Honor."

"Has your lawyer entered an appearance?"

"What's that?"

"If he's a lawyer, he should have told you about that. Is he licensed to practice in Illinois?"

"Not that I know of."

"Is he familiar with guardianship proceedings at least?"

"I don't believe so; in fact, no, he told me he wasn't."

"Well you're batting a thousand, Mr. Hurley, you have a lawyer who's not here, from an out-of-state jurisdiction, who's not licensed to practice in this state, and who is not familiar with the matter before the court."

The young woman standing next to Billy snickered at his dressing down.

"And who are you?"

"Mary Anne Topinka, Your Honor, associate of Mr. Hanneman."

"Are you licensed to practice in Illinois?" the judge asked.

"Yes, of course, Your Honor," she said proudly.

"Are you familiar with guardianship proceedings, young lady?"

"Well, no, not really," she answered, flustered, off guard.

"Are you familiar with this case?"

"Well, not exactly, Your Honor, I'm standing in for Mr. Hanneman, who's on vacation."

"Well, then, what are you snickering about? Can you get Mr. Hanneman on the phone? He specifically agreed to this date the last time this case was called."

"Mr. Hanneman wanted me to express his apologies, Your Honor, but he mis-docketed the date, and can't be reached."

"Can't be reached? Where is he that he can't be reached for a status that was set for a date he agreed on?"

Mr. Hanneman had hoped it would not come to this, Ms. Topinka knew he would be displeased by the news, and a red splotch began to appear on her neck.

"He's on a sailboat in the Caribbean, Your Honor."

The judge looked down at Ms. Topinka, the splotch reddening, growing.

"Well, isn't that nice, I do hope he's having a wonderful time," the judge said, raising his voice, "while we're here wasting ours because he didn't have the common courtesy of letting us know he was unavailable. Were you aware that we were supposed to set a final hearing date today?"

"Yes, Your Honor," Ms. Topinka's spirits rising a bit, "and I do have dates from Mr. Hanneman."

"Good morning, Ms. Beecher," tone turned on a dime.

"Good morning, Your Honor."

"Does anybody here have any idea how long this hearing should take?" the judge asked Ms. Topinka.

"Yes, Your Honor, Mr. Hanneman believes the hearing should take at least two days."

"There's no way you're getting two days," the judge quickly replied. "Mr. Hurley, has your position changed?"

"No, Your Honor."

"Then one day should do it. When is Mr. Hanneman available?"

"Any time during the last two weeks of August," Ms. Topinka said, with authority.

"Is he? Well, isn't that convenient, because I'm on vacation the last two weeks of August. Of course, I didn't clear that with Mr. Hanneman, I do hope that's okay with him?"

Ms. Topinka, thinking on her feet, declined to answer.

Silence in the courtroom.

"Mr. Hurley, I suppose you came down from Wisconsin for this status."

"That is correct, Your Honor."

"And Ms. Beecher, while it is always a pleasure, I take it you have better things to do than to come over here this morning for the sole purpose of hearing that Mr. Hanneman is on a sailboat in the middle of the ocean."

"That is correct, Your Honor."

The judge takes his measure of Ms. Topinka.

"Counselor, when will Mr. Hanneman return?"

"I believe this Thursday."

"You believe?"

"Well, Your Honor, he will be back in the office on Thursday, but…"

"Be careful what you say next," the judge said.

Ms. Topinka did as the judge suggested, she reconsidered what she was about to say, stiffened her spine, tired of making apologies for her boss, taking the fall, maybe she needed to find another job.

"He's back in the office on Thursday."

"Then this coming Thursday, Mr. Hanneman will report to this courtroom at 10:00 a.m. sharp, is that understood Ms. Topinka?"

"Yes, Your Honor."

"As will you Mr. Hurley."

"But Your Honor…."

"Will you be on vacation, too, Mr. Hurley?"

"No, but…"

"Then, I will see you, *and* Mr. Hanneman, on Thursday, at 10:00 a.m. Prepare the order."

Ms. Topinka stepped over to the clerk and grabbed three blank order forms and two sheets of carbon paper, as Billy and Ms. Beecher walked away from the judge's bench.

"Remember what I said to you about bullshit?" Billy whispered to Ms. Beecher, holding open the swinging gate.

"Welcome to our civil justice system," Ms. Beecher whispered back.

That evening, Billy sat in a plush stuffed chair in his father's condo on the twenty-third floor looking out on the white and red lights of the cars navigating the Oak Street curve on Lake Shore Drive, as his mother liked so much to do in the months before she died, sipping some of his father's bourbon, on ice, in a Waterford tumbler. W. Foster Carlisle, III had not been particularly aggressive in opening Billy's father's estate, so the condo locks had not yet been changed, extending Billy's squatter rights another week at least, much to Bob the doorman's dismay. So here he was, again, powerless in a power town, with time to kill, and not a damn thing to do, he thought, as he looked down at the material on the end table, the file from his dad's office, Gold Coast News, Chicago magazine, a Tribune sports page his dad had been the last to read, Cubs making a run, wonders never cease.

He reached down for the file, opened it, and looked at the lease, thinking about what they had told him, the hoodie, Dorothy, Reverend Simmons, what the hell was his dad doing with that. Knew enough to know that nobody in City Hall deferred and published a zoning matter, just wasn't done, if it's not in your ward it's not your business, show some respect, get out of the way, let it go. But defer and publish, at the meeting, in front of everybody, cameras rolling, only do that if you're a rookie, had no idea what you were doing, or, you wanted to fuck with somebody, send a message, and his dad was no rookie, his dad knew exactly what he was doing.

He looked at the lease, the New Life Blessing Corporation, please, a warehouse in the name of the Lord, God must have been on somebody's side. Maybe the hoodie was wrong, maybe there wasn't a tip, maybe there was no inside information, maybe the Lord came to the President of the New Life Blessing Corporation, in the shower maybe, in a ray of light, and said, by the way, thought you should know, the Illinois Department of Public Aid is going to be consolidating all of its warehouse operations, needs such and such an amount of space, near good transportation, so you might want to be on the lookout, and if you have to screw Reverend Simmons out of a valuable piece of land and a multimillion dollar business opportunity, well, so be it, to the riches go the spoils, praise the Lord. Billy started getting a little upset, God the bullshit in this town, he thought, but what was his father up to, the king of bullshit, probably wanted in on the action, but if that was the case, why the D&P, why not just weasel his way in, quietly, piece of the pie, not someone you'd want to turn down, much better on your side, but the D&P meant that was not happening. Did he try to get in and get turned down, unlikely, but he didn't want this thing to happen, that's for sure, was he trying to kill the zoning change, the lease, who would he want to fuck like that, that was the question, interesting question, Billy thought, who did his father not control in this town? Apparently, the New Life Blessing Corporation.

But ultimately, the best question, Billy thought the next morning, was whether he had anything else to do, and the answer was no, not really, he had three days to kill. No harm in poking around, little puzzle to work on in his spare time, and it was a puzzle, best he could figure, his father trying to throw a wrench in some inside job, totally unlike him, intriguing actually, given his father, and as he had the time, maybe he should check some things out, start out with corporate records, so he hopped on the Moto Guzzi and rode down to the Secretary of State's Office in the State of Illinois building on LaSalle Street, parked in the alley near a garbage dumpster, and rode the elevator up to the fifteenth floor, with, as chance would have it, Saul Bellow, Billy in awe. The elevator ride alone was worth the trip. The Secretary of State's records, however, were not as thrilling, because apparently the Secretary of State doesn't believe the public is entitled to much information on companies that apply to the state for corporate status so they can insulate their shareholders from any meaningful liability for corporate misdeeds. What the records did reveal was that the President of the New Life Blessing Corporation was a Mr. Virgil Davis, its Secretary, a Ms. Viola Jones, and its registered agent, on whom corporate notices were to be served, was a Mr. Sydney Black, whose offices were located at 180 West Randolph Street, Chicago, Mr. Black being the signatory on the lease document in Billy's father's file. The date of incorporation was April 2, 1983, less than two months prior to the date of the lease. The address given for the President, Mr. Davis, and the Secretary, Ms. Jones, was the same: 3523 South Martin Luther King Drive. The names were not familiar, no surprise there, he thought Viola rang a remote bell, but he had no idea why, probably just liked the name, maybe from Twelfth Night.

So now what? Sydney Black's office was right around the corner, on Randolph, so he left the State of Illinois building by the Randolph Street entrance, walked past Cardozo's Pub, and stepped into the lobby of an old Class C office building, long past its prime. The building registry, unkempt, neglected, out of date, identified a Sydney Black, Esquire, lawyer, of course, on the 11th floor, number 1150. Billy took the creaky elevator up to the 11th floor, walked up to office number 1150, opened the door, and peeked in. Cramped reception, two chairs, one old wooden end table, one cracked glass window, desk call bell, one door, no receptionist, shoe string, solo practitioner. No great shakes. Billy took the elevator down to the lobby, stepped out of the elevator, walked out onto Randolph Street, and looked east toward the lake, past the tall columns of City Hall and the County Building.

The City of Chicago and the County of Cook shared the monolithic stone building hunkered on the entire city block bordered by Randolph, Washington, LaSalle, and Clark. The city offices took up the west side of the building, mayor on the fifth floor, aldermen and City Council on the second, various admin offices, Buildings, Law, Zoning, Purchasing, scattered throughout. The east side of the building belonged to the county, County Executive, County Board, Treasurer, Recorder of Deeds, Comptroller, numerous agencies, and ghost payrollers.

Much to the county's chagrin, the building was generally known throughout town as City Hall, even for those having business with the county, in all likelihood because city government had been more famous, and infamous, throughout the years, the county, second fiddle, after-thought, unless you had business there, like the Blues Brothers, or Billy, who, looking down Randolph at the building's tall columns, remembered his summer job at the Recorder of Deeds office, and figured, since he was downtown anyway, he'd pay a visit, look up the skinny on 2620 West Jackson Boulevard.

The Office of the Recorder of Deeds was located on the first floor on the county side, a large high ceilinged open space, tall windows looking east onto Clark Street, Daley Civic Center across the way, rows of tall metal shelves and cabinets, stuffed to the gills with papers, and books, and index cards, with every address and residence and two flat and townhouse and warehouse and office building and apartment building and manufacturing plant and high-rise and vacant lot, all accounted for, each with its own set of scrawled notations of each and every above and below board real estate deal ever transacted in Cook County over the last more than one hundred years, guarded in front by a long high gray counter, behind which cousins and in-laws of aldermen amble back and forth, taking slips of paper with addresses written on them, disappearing back into the stacks, and emerging, if you were lucky, with the book that matched the address, after two or three tries.

Billy wrote out 2620 W. Jackson Boulevard on a piece of torn pink paper and waited his turn, looking for a familiar face, knowing the drill, watching the clerks back and forth, not exactly energetic, still an hour to lunch, when an overweight unfortunate slouch of a gnome approached, hand out, no words necessary, took Billy's piece of paper, shuffled off into the deep recesses of the Recorder's shelves, and returned with a large bound book which included entries for 2620 West Jackson Boulevard. Billy took the book over to the long wooden tables across from the counter and took his place with stooped law clerks, paralegals, and title officers, squinting into inscrutable tract books. He opened the book, found the page for 2620 W. Jackson, and began poring over the notations, abbreviations, fewest words possible to describe each transaction, different language, making it

CASEY

all the more difficult to figure out exactly what happened, by design no doubt.

During the Twentieth Century, in the early 1920s, the property had been sold to a corporation named the West Side Yards, so, from its age, it's fair to assume the warehouse dates back to the twenties. Various mortgages over time, but the property never changed hands, until 1979. A notation dated August 17, 1979, shows a deed to the City of Chicago, possibly by court order, building code violations, unpaid taxes, who knows. That same year, the city transferred the property to Reverend Simmons, in his individual capacity, figures. February 15, 1983, Reverend Simmons transfers the property to a land trust with the Lincoln Financial Trust and Savings Bank, consistent with the Reverend's recollection. A mortgage on the property is recorded on May 2, 1983, by Lincoln Financial, amount unknown, so Lincoln Financial must have loaned some money to somebody for something at that time, and while it could have been for anything, the warehouse looks practically brand new, and construction financing had to come from somewhere, in all likelihood, Lincoln Financial. A notation, dated December 8, 1983, indicates that an O'Neil Electric, Inc. filed a mechanics lien against the property, which was followed by a notation that a Lis Pendens notice was recorded on December 15, 1983. Lis Pendens, Latin for "suit pending," filed when a plaintiff has filed a lawsuit involving the real estate and wants to fuck with the owner by putting a cloud, doubt, on the owner's title to the property. The notation in the book reads simply, "Lis Pendens, December 15, 1983, O'Neil Electric v. New Life Blessing Corp, 83 C 5378." There we go, there's something, Billy thought, a blessing, a lead, can't be sure, case file would show, but O'Neil probably did some electrical work on the warehouse rehab and didn't get paid. Then, the next entries, on April 2, 1984, show that the mechanics lien was released and the Lis Pendens stricken, lawsuit over, settlement, dismissal, unknown. Final entry is recorded on May 3, 1984, a deed from one land trust to another, no way of knowing who or what involved or why. And there you have it, nine entries taking up at most three inches of space in a thick book off a tall shelf purportedly showing everything that's happened to 2620 W. Jackson Boulevard over a sixty-year period of time, ultimately, revealing little. Except for that lawsuit, that case number, might be enough, so Billy wrote down the caption of the lawsuit and the case number on another torn pink piece of paper, put it in his pocket, returned the book to the counter, and left the County Building through the eastern revolving doors onto Clark Street, cars honking, pedestrians hustling, the Elevated rumbling a couple blocks away.

Across the street, the rusted steel jacket of the Daley Civic Center, thirty-one sleek stories of glass and courtrooms, hung over the wide plaza like a shroud, hiding the Picasso in its folds against the gray humid sky. Billy could see more action in ten minutes from where he stood outside the Clark Street doors than you would see in a whole year on Main Street in downtown Lone Rock, and the extent of it all wouldn't even be apparent to any of the players playing their parts at this particular time in the life of downtown Chicago, you wouldn't notice it, really, unless you were from Lone Rock, otherwise it's just life, every day, in the big city, and Billy stood, a little in wonder, surprised at how familiar it felt, the pulse, his life, too, the energy, to join the fray, set off running, and off you go and there's no turning back, and the road could lead nowhere, or into a wall, or into a corner office on the fiftieth floor with a view of the lake and a shitload of money, but one thing for sure it would be fast, you'd have to hang on, and shit was bound to happen, and either you rode that wave or you went over the falls, landing any one of a number of places you never thought possible, like a one room apartment over the Mad House Inn on Main Street in Lone Rock.

Billy stepped into the clearly marked cross walk that led over to the Daley Civic Center Plaza and almost got hit by a Marathon Yellow cab.

Lives have ended just that way. Little more careful this time, he crossed three lanes of traffic on Clark Street, and the one-lane ramp that came up onto the street from the underground parking garage where his father used to park the Eldorado, and stepped onto the Plaza, of polka dances at noon-time and protests and speeches and Santa every year with his folks under the gigantic Christmas tree. It was still morning, the parade of lawyers and briefcases attending motion calls in full force, back and forth through the revolving courthouse doors, spinning a little too fast, flinging guests into and out of the building.

Billy took his chances, spun through the doors, into the glass encased, high ceiling, first floor lobby, wrapped around six stone elevator banks, Billy looking for floors six through eight, because the 'C' in the notation of the case on which the Lis Pendens was based stood for Chancery, and the Chancery records of the Circuit Court of Cook County were housed on the eighth floor, to the left off the elevators. Upstairs, on the eighth floor, west side, plenty of light, floor to ceiling windows, one room, the length of a city block, counter almost as long, space to retrieve files, file documents, cashier, everything you wanted in one place to support the Chancery Division of the Circuit Court of Cook County. Chancery, the court of equity, black robed Solomons who wouldn't be there if they didn't know somebody, owe somebody, in charge of equity.

Same drill, cousins and in-laws shuffling back and forth behind the counter, with attitudes, resentful of young law students and clerks from private firms who were going somewhere, torn pieces of paper, no eye contact, grunts, another file, another day in paradise. Billy handed his torn pink piece of paper with the case number to a thin pockmarked man behind the counter, who looked askance at the paper, because it was pink, and they didn't use pink paper, so he made Billy write the case number on one of the Chancery Division's gray pieces of paper, and Billy gave that to the clerk, who disappeared into the shelves with a look of disgust, and returned with a not so very large file, that he threw on the counter.

"Put your name and date on the card inside," the man mumbled and turned away, no point in saying thank you, wouldn't mean anything.

Billy took the file over to the reading tables opposite the long counter and pulled out the documents, placing the sign-in card over to the side.

Okay, so the first thing is to start at the beginning, with the Complaint, filed by O'Neil Electric, back on December 15, 1983, and his assumption had been correct, looked like O'Neil had been retained as a subcontractor in June of 1983 to provide electrical equipment and services in connection with the warehouse reconstruction project at 2620 W. Jackson Boulevard, that O'Neil had performed all the work required in a satisfactory manner, of course O'Neil would say that, but was not paid the amount to which it was entitled pursuant to its contract, and, therefore, O'Neil was entitled to $43,457 in monetary damages, from the owner, the general contractor, the architect, the person who lived down the block, anybody with a deep pocket. The Complaint was entitled "Complaint to Foreclose on Mechanics Lien and Other Relief," and it is true that the first count of the complaint sought a foreclosure of the mechanics lien, but nobody ever really wanted to foreclose on the mechanics lien, that was too expensive and took too much time, all they wanted was their money, which is what O'Neil alleged in the second count, for monetary damages. The signature page disclosed that the law offices of Anthony V. Marzullo, 6 North Michigan Avenue, Chicago, filed the Complaint on behalf of the plaintiff.

So next comes the Answer filed by the owner, New Life Blessing Corporation, which, without bringing God into it, admits nothing, denies everything, affirmatively states that O'Neil did shitty work, or words to that effect, that O'Neil is not entitled to any relief, and that, in fact, O'Neil owes

New Life Blessing money. The Answer was filed on behalf of the New Life Blessing Corp. by a Sydney L. Black, Esquire.

Next came some discovery documents filed by the plaintiff, subpoenas, document requests, interrogatories, requesting from New Life Blessing Corp. and Lincoln Financial all sorts of documents and information about the warehouse project that New Life Blessing Corporation refused to provide, until a court order required it to do so, which must have proved a tipping point, because other than the court order dismissing the case there was only one other document in the court file, and that was an Amended Complaint that Tony Marzullo filed on March 13, 1984.

The Amended Complaint was identical to the original Complaint except in one critical respect. In the "Parties" section of the Amended Complaint, where all the plaintiffs and defendants are described and their involvement alleged, a new name had been added, that of Ronald T. Gusman, who, "on information, and belief," which in the business is another way of saying the plaintiff has no idea whether the allegation is true or not but it's helpful to say so for leverage purposes, "is the principal owner of the New Life Blessing Corporation, and real party in interest." The Amended Complaint was revised to include a claim for damages against Mr. Gusman, and the caption of the case, which appears on the first page of the Complaint, and identifies all the plaintiffs and defendants, was revised to include the name of Ronald T. Gusman. Gusman. Wow.

No wonder the case settled a little more than two weeks later. Someone must have fucked up, big time. No way the owners of New Life Blessing Corp. had to be disclosed in discovery, unless Marzullo's a hell of a lawyer, or the judge had it in for Gusman, and the likelihood that Sydney Black would have voluntarily given up the man behind the curtain of New Life Blessing Corp. is remote to non-existent. Somebody at the bank maybe, but then, after all, how Mr. Marzullo acquired his "information and belief" didn't really matter, all that mattered is that it worked, because the court's final order dismissing the case reflected that it was done "pursuant to confidential settlement agreement," confidential to be sure, because no defendant ever wants anyone to know how much it paid to resolve a "baseless" claim, but you can bet that O'Neil got most of what it wanted, given the speed with which the case was resolved, two weeks after Gusman surfaced in the dispute.

Wow, Billy thought, Gusman's involved, makes it a big deal, now Billy really was interested. Gusman was an asshole, but a powerful one, like his dad, the two not exactly getting along as much as staying out of each other's way, Billy thought, as he returned the pile of documents to the court file, about to return the file to the counter, when he noticed the sign-in card off to the side, picked it up, grabbed a pencil off the table, and began printing his name in the first empty row, when he stopped, dropped his pencil, and stared at the name clearly printed in the row just above, which read, "Daniel Hurley, May, 29, 1984." His father had been there, looked at the file, knew what was in it, Billy following his father's footsteps.

Ron Gusman came from nothing. Scrapped and fought for everything his whole life. Grew up on the west side with five adults and three kids squeezed into a one-bedroom apartment. His father, flimflam, racetrack bagman. His mother, alcoholic. The street gang Gusman joined at ten-years old was the Thirtieth Ward Democratic Organization, his ticket out, of that house, his folks, the hardscrabble. He would do anything, endless energy, strong constitution, good build, thick head of hair, square jaw, handsome, he worked hard, got ahead, and it helped that he was smart, street smart, calculating, and ruthless, and he never warmed up to anybody who hadn't something to offer.

Alderman Casimir Wiskowitz, Alderman of the Thirtieth Ward and ward committeeman for as long as anyone could remember, took Gusman under his wing, mentored the young man, liked his toughness, his grit, showed him the ropes, took him to City Hall, introduced him to everyone, the Old Man, Alderman Terry Flanagan and his wife Audrey and their nephew Dan Hurley, both of them, Gusman and Hurley, just kids, looking for a leg up. Gusman got straight A's and never lifted a finger, but school wasn't for him, too tame. He inherited from his father a nose for the grift, the angle, but unlike his father had the brains, skill, and patience, to pull it off, logistics, project management, get it done, and Alderman Wiskowitz, childless, came to rely on Ronnie, and Ronnie, no one dared call him that but Alderman Wiskowitz, became indispensable to the aging alderman, as the White ethnic majority in the "Fighting Thirtieth" started getting squeezed, by African Americans from the north, Hispanic Americans from the south, and Alderman Wiskowitz, from a different generation, caught in the middle, deferring to Ron Gusman, the neighborhood kid, who believed, to his credit, that when it came to politics there were no colors, just human beings, all of whom deserved to be represented, which was not something that came naturally to Alderman Wiskowitz, who preferred kielbasa fundraisers at the Polish American Congress. So it's fair to say that Gusman was in his ascendancy by the time Alderman Wiskowitz suffered a mild stroke in the summer before he was to run for reelection the next year, and as the alderman recovered, Gusman took the pulse of the community, African Americans, Hispanic Americans, and discovered they were just in need of jobs as the Whites who already had them, just needed to become voters, so he organized registration drives, all summer long, in precincts he'd worked for twenty years, knew every house, and by the time autumn rolled around, and the alderman was able to get around with only a slight limp, Ron Gusman decided to challenge his mentor to a winner take all grudge match in the Thirtieth Ward, which lasted into the winter, bitter like the cold. How could he, but those who felt that way were bitter, too, and old, and there weren't many of them left, at least that's what the results showed, in February, when Gusman's efforts in the community, convincing people of all stripes that he really cared, and he really did back then, paid off big time when he won a plurality of the vote, which avoided a run off, and served as an embarrassment and death sentence to Alderman Wiskowitz, who was buried less than one year later.

But all such bold moves come at a price. If you wanted to get ahead, you played it smart, from the inside, waited your turn, you didn't buck the system, make waves, let alone have the audacity to win. So Gusman's hubris was short-lived, couple weeks maybe, until the day he took office, polite knowing smiles, disguised smirks, good luck kid, you're gonna need it, frozen out of virtually anything meaningful, left to wander the desert, the trash heaps, couldn't get a streetlamp replaced, a garbage can emptied, waited two years to get a committee assignment, and then it was the Committee on Special Events and Cultural Affairs, which rarely met, and then only because he tried to toe the line at first, against his nature, be respectful, kiss ass, wear the hair cloth, but he did it for his ward, and took care of his people as best he could. Hired a staff of smart kids from the neighborhood, no relatives, no political background, unheard of, and when somebody called his office they got a call back that day, from him, he actually worked for them, they weren't just another pain in the ass for a powerful alderman who had better things to do, his constituents *were* his better thing to do, and they couldn't help but respect him for it, even if his colleagues didn't. The Old Man? Forget about it, never said a word to him after Wiskowitz died, and Hurley was instructed to do the same, even if he did respect what Gusman had done, was trying to do, and all the others in the Old Man's camp followed his instructions, what choice did they have, so it wasn't a surprise that Gusman, while raised in the machine, drifted toward the opposition, the handful not in the Old Man's pocket, and never would be, gadflies and grandstanders, four or five African Americans, one or two Hispanics, a lefty from Hyde Park, one from the far North Shore, all of whom ran against the machine and were forever locked out, powerless, left to rant and rave out in the cold, barred from entry to the promised land. But at least they had that in common, so Gusman, carefully, diplomatically, without stepping on sensitive toes, over time tried to herd the black sheep, organize, strategize, develop an agenda, a platform, block of disaffected, with one voice, which, in the short term, got them absolutely nowhere, but long term, as the Aldermen Wiskowitzes of the world slowly died off in neighborhoods that were changing color, the opposition began to grow, flex a little muscle.

The outsiders, not so much Gusman, thought they saw an opportunity when Tom McLean died, ramped up, bellicose, sow confusion, machine in disarray, beginning of the end, and they made quite a fuss, but they were way ahead of themselves. The Old Man didn't miss a beat, because he had Hurley, after all, who took over for McLean as Finance chair as if not a thing had changed, and it hadn't, because Hurley had been working hard, waiting his entire career, for just this chance, for just this job, the only job he ever really wanted, learned from his uncle, the Old Man, but best from McLean, and now it was his, and he took full advantage, tightened the ship, squelched opposition, tinkered, retooled, greased the zerks, and got that machine humming, churning out favors and projects and patronage and piles of chits for all those feeding at the trough.

Gusman knew better. Angry voices weren't going to change anything. He knew Hurley would step into the breach. And while McLean's passing may not have changed the guard, it did signal the end of an era, because the demographics were changing, the old White guys were dying out, and who would replace them was what mattered, up for grabs, if you had the energy, the industry, the desire. So Gusman opened for business, exported his strategy to West and South Side wards, and, while he lost a few, he never had those wards in the first place, but when his horse did win it was a solid pick up, slow changing of the guard, and the Old Man didn't seem to care, because he was getting old, but Hurley did, and worked, just as hard, to stem Gusman's tide, hold it in check, and they went head to head with proxies, Hurley holding the cards, the advantage, and at that rate it would take Gusman years, more years than he had left.

But he still enjoyed the game, took care of his ward, his people, now solidly African American, no reason to complain, because Gusman cared for them, and so while he and his staff stayed on top of ward business, Gusman turned to a side job, something he'd dabbled in at first, until it became too lucrative to ignore. Two-flat here, three-flat there, money where his mouth was, construction, drug house to condos, sprucing neighborhoods, African American, Hispanic, making a buck, a name for himself. Hired a property manager, bona fide business, one led to another, coffers started to fill, enough to spread around the ward, other wards, fledgling empire on the West Side, tentacles across the city, urban renewal with big payouts, spreading the wealth, collecting debtors.

By the time the Old Man died, shaking the Hall's foundations, Gusman had recruited or subsidized most if not all of the loyal opposition, a solid fifteen aldermen, even a woman or two, an unruly group of colorful unreliable characters whose common denominator was a credit line from Gusman. And they made some noise when the Old Man passed away, couldn't stop the hand-picked successor, the South Side Serb, from taking over, but they did have fun with his fumbling about, pouncing on each garbled word, wooden appearance, empty gesture, and the new mayor was full of them, full of it, really. If it wasn't for Hurley he'd have been run out of town, or at least out of the South Side neighborhood he'd spurned for the Gold Coast, and the opposition mocked him for that, too, and when the time came several years later for the deluded Serb to waltz into a four-year term, Gusman had other ideas.

No one thought it possible, but Gusman thought it worth a try, so he convinced his band of renegades to back Earl Williams, alderman of the Fifteenth, to run against the Serb in the primary, knowing that Earl could never win on his own. But Gusman had something up his sleeve: a large red-faced affable Irishman from the Northwest Side, more ambition than talent, dumb as a box of rocks, left on the altar numerous times by Hurley and his gang who did not back losers, resentful, vengeful, looking for payback and a way into the club. How about a deal with Gusman, throw your hat in the ring, run against the Serb, lose, of course, and we'll find you something, somewhere, Board of Tax Appeals maybe, what do you think, win by losing. And as dumb as the Irishman was he was smart enough not to look a gift horse in the mouth. So Gusman backed two horses in the same three-way race, spent good money, after some bad, and in the three-way primary, despite all of Hurley's efforts, something about a silk purse and a sow's ear, the Serb and the Irishman split the White vote, and Earl Williams, unexpectedly, with solid African American support and just enough lakefront liberals, eked out a win in the primary, and, since only those in straitjackets voted Republican, handily won the general, the first African American, upsetting more than one hundred years of City Hall machinery, making national news, and owing it all to Gusman.

Except that Hurley was no South Side Serb. He knew the lay of the land. He had the votes, and the Council Wars began. Gusman on one side, consigliere to Williams, Hurley and his gang of twenty-nine on the other, controlling the chamber, fighting it out on the Council floor, Hurley winning battles, budgets, appointments, but losing the war, the press, his reputation, his son.

For four years, according to the Chicago Defender, Hurley and his klansmen rode roughshod over the aspirations of the downtrodden in a changing landscape of demographics and public opinion, and over time, everyone, Hurley, Williams, Gusman, they all got tired of the constant bickering, blaming, harping, grousing, bad mouthing, back stabbing, and everybody knew that Hurley wasn't going to let Gusman get away with that cute trick of his a second time, not as long as he was around. So four years later Hurley and the twenty-nine and their White wards coalesced around milquetoast Joe Jablonksi from the North Side, who swept to victory, and ushered in four years of effective management and a vibrant economy, thanks to Hurley, and ungodly boredom and apathy, thanks to Jablonski.

In the meantime, Gusman, with more time on his hands, expanded his empire, becoming a lender of first and last resort, for skyscrapers and subdivisions, in and around Chicago, millions of dollars, compounding, at 10 percent. Bought a bank, took the top floor with a city view, where developers came, with hats in hand, and left, with money in pockets, so long as they paid top dollar, assumed all risk, pledged their first born, and played by his rules, insisted on, enforced, by Gusman, who, they came to know, through threats, intimidation and lawsuits, was nobody to fuck with. And over time, seemed like Gusman was everywhere, hand in everybody's pocket, piece of every deal, and all behind the scenes, limited partnerships, land trusts, covert operations, an undisclosed principal, impossible to trace, all part of the game.

By the time Jablonski's four years were coming to an end, even Hurley was tired of him, getting tired of a lot of things, saw the writing, the city was changing, and so was he, which is when he cut his deal with Gusman for peace among the factions, and the two of them decided, unbeknownst to Jimmy Jefferson, that Jimmy would be the next mayor. Safe bet, county exec, old machine pol, no Gusman renegade, steered clear of the wars, and in debt to Hurley, who continued to control a majority, and remained as Finance chair, with Gusman as floor leader, for Jefferson's first term. Uneasy, separate, ultimately unworkable peace, which they altered for Jefferson's second term, Hurley taking Budget, Gusman taking Finance, what he always wanted, and just as well for Hurley, because late in Jefferson's first term, Hurley's son ran away, and then his wife died, taking big pieces, it seemed, out of Hurley.

And then somebody rips a very large piece out of Hurley's chest, and here we are, thought Gusman, sitting behind Anton Cermak's desk, in Dan Hurley's old office, vicissitudes, and just after he tweaked us about that warehouse deal, just enough, just his way, just enough to let us know he knew all about it. Wonder if that's all he had in mind, what he would have done, not one to wear the white hat, had his share of the spoils, never know now, doesn't matter, thank God, sweet little deal. Strange timing though, you just never know, when somebody's gonna spring up from tall grass and rip your heart out. Probably had it coming, line around the block to pull the trigger. Anyway, worked out fine for us, nobody left without him sniffing around, just have to manage the situation now, see it through, where the hell *is* Black anyway?

Sydney Black, Esquire, toady, lackey, lawyer to Ron Gusman, was stuck in another of the interminable meetings attended by millions of bureaucrats in thousands of drab offices every day across the world, without agenda, timetable, or profit motive, public servants, with time on their hands and red tape on their sides, calling for meetings on the status of this, that, whatever, with no purpose other than to assure their bosses when asked that progress was being made, so their bosses could assure their bosses when asked that progress was being made, etcetera, etcetera. This particular meeting involved the status of a warehouse on the West Side, that the Director of the Illinois Department of Public Aid was anxious to move into, so that he could tell the governor that he was centralizing operations, a good government initiative, economizing, saving the taxpayers money, even though, in the long run, twenty years to be precise, the deal in all likelihood would *cost* the taxpayers money, but by then nobody would remember, know, or care, the Director would be in private practice somewhere making money from his state government connections, and the governor, if not in jail, would be facing indictment, hence, the short term horizon, the next election, beyond that, what they did today wouldn't matter.

The meeting did, however, have a sign-in sheet, a strict state meeting requirement, honored in the breach, which read: Bob Olson, Project Manager, Illinois Department of Central Management Services; Pete Vukovic, Assistant Director, Infrastructure, Illinois Department of Public Aid; Deirdre Cherry, Assistant Project Manager, Illinois Department of Central Management Services; Henry Vogt, Material Operations Manager, Illinois Department of Public Aid; Darnell Robinson, Deputy Commissioner, City of Chicago Department of Buildings; Deborah Larson, Deputy General Counsel, Illinois Department of Public Aid; Sydney Black, counsel, lessor attorney; and Mark Hamilton, Assistant Vice-President, Credit Financing, Lincoln Financial Trust and Savings Bank. The meeting had been called by Mr. Olson, charged with spearheading the warehouse project, ostensibly to receive a status report on the lease commencement date for the warehouse, which had been delayed due to a snag in the required rezoning; Mr. Olson's ulterior motive: a chance to travel with Ms. Cherry from Springfield to Chicago, which, while not disclosed, was obvious to Mr. Vogt and Ms. Larson, given Ms. Cherry's charming figure, onomatopoeia, and what they knew of Bob Olson.

Mr. Olson, dressed in wrinkled gray pants and a blue blazer, started out the meeting by saying he thought it a good idea to get together in light of the delay associated with the commencement date, that his boss, the Director, was not pleased, the warehouse was high priority, they needed some assurance, as to when the Illinois Department of Public Aid would be able to move into the warehouse, because Mr. Vogt, who was in charge of logistics for the move, needed to arrange for all the trucks and personnel, large undertaking, and, because of the zoning issue, they'd already been postponed once, and they didn't want it to happen again, Mr. Olson, putting his foot down, Mr. Vogt nodding his head, all looking at Mr. Black.

Mr. Black explained, with some confidence in light of what happened to Mr. Hurley, though that was not articulated to the group, that everything was a go for the next City Council meeting, there would be no more interruptions, the rezoning item was on the agenda, nothing could be done to delay it further, no one would be raising any more issues, and even if they did they had more than enough votes to pass. Mr. Robinson, on behalf of the city and his boss, nodding his agreement. And so, as he, Mr. Black, had said in his most recent letter, the next Council meeting will take place September 6, the rezoning will become effective immediately, all related transactions will be finalized by September 13, Mr. Hamilton nodding his encouragement, and the Department can start moving in on Friday, September 14, which will be the new commencement date, and he had taken the liberty, passing a one page document across the conference table to Ms. Larson, to prepare a draft lease amendment for the purpose of continuing the commencement date to September 14.

Ms. Larson, feeling a bit prickly, asked why the zoning item for the warehouse had been delayed, whether all the other zoning items on the agenda had been delayed as well, if not, why was this one singled out, what did it mean to defer and publish, why would anyone want to do that anyway, and why hadn't they been aware of the zoning issue from the get go, to which, unfortunately for Mr. Black, there were no good answers. So Mr. Black and Mr. Robinson proceeded to entertain the group with a song and dance involving circuitous drawn out and deflective responses which effectively ducked Ms. Larson's legitimate questions and so bored the group that after a while even Ms. Larson lost interest, because it wasn't her warehouse anyway, and besides, she had one kid home sick from school she was nervous about, and she needed to get home to relieve her mom who could only stay until noon. Mr. Hamilton then went on to explain, completely unnecessary, but he was dressed much better than the others and they deserved to hear what he had to say, that the lawyer retained by the bank to render the tax opinion had discovered, much to everyone's surprise, that sometime in the early seventies the property owner arranged to rezone the property in hopes that gentrification might someday increase its value, and that once that was discovered, the zoning had to be changed back to allow for the operation of a warehouse. Had her child not been sick at home, Ms. Larson would have acted on her instinct to ask why they needed a tax opinion, but, knowing how upset her mom would be, thought better of it.

Then, for God's sake, Mr. Vogt, who rarely attended meetings with higher ups, thought everyone needed to know the most minute details about the upcoming move, and went about mansplaining how IDPA, and he in particular, were going to move all of the Department's materials from five different locations into the new warehouse. During which time the three cups of coffee Mr. Vukovic drank that morning began to press against his bladder, and he began to squirm in discomfort, so that by the time Mr. Vogt had told everyone everything they didn't need to know, everyone in attendance couldn't wait to get the hell out of there, except for Ms. Cherry, who thought Mr. Hamilton looked kind of cute. It was just about at that point in the meeting when Alderman Gusman started wondering what was taking Mr. Black so long.

Mr. Olson, satisfied, wondering where he was going to take Ms. Cherry to lunch, then wrapped up the meeting, said he was pleased the meeting was so productive, said he knew a lot of work had been done over a long period of time by everyone involved, that he'd been out to see the warehouse and was very impressed with the workmanship, and that the entire project would prove to be a fine example of a public–private partnership and a win–win for the State and the lessor. And with that the meeting came to an end, Mr. Vukovic and Ms. Larson scurrying out of the room, Mr. Hamilton talking up Ms. Cherry.

Sydney Black walked out of the meeting not at all happy about having to go back to City Hall and face Alderman Gusman. Not that he had anything bad to tell him, the meeting had gone just fine. It was just the usual pang of anxiety that started gurgling any time he had to see Gusman these days, and it was getting worse with age, which he thought was just the opposite of what should be happening. He'd been around the block, knew a thing or two, should be more confident, stress resistant, resilient, but it didn't seem to be turning out that way. Maybe it wasn't so unusual, maybe it started happening to most everybody in their fifties, he didn't know, but it was a pain in the ass, because things were tough enough. He had a mortgage, two kids in private colleges, a young girl in high school who was not fond of either of her parents, and while he still loved his wife, it was unclear whether she felt the same way, the mirror every morning a reminder he had grown lumpier, rounder, never accused of good looks, but, on the plus side, he'd been a good provider, been to law school, paid the bills, nice house, kept the lid on, woke every morning, schlepped down to his not so very nice office every day, and did what he needed to do to get along in the world, which, although modestly successful, in truth, from an ethical standpoint, had been inconsistent, because life wasn't softball, and at his level of the profession you had to do things sometimes that later you might not be proud of, but at the time made sense to do, from a practical standpoint, and so he had, and some of them paid off rather well. But about ten years ago he got into a little scrape with the Attorney Registration and Disciplinary Commission which left him suspended for six months, and it was during that time he was introduced to Alderman Gusman, who happened to be looking for a lawyer, a lawyer, it turns out, just like Sydney Black. Someone who knew their way around, the law and judges, someone not afraid to look the other way, someone he could control, someone desperate enough to do anything he asked, someone who needed his money. So after his suspension Black started working for Gusman, and only for

Gusman, full time, real estate deals, business transactions, foreclosures, evictions, actions on notes and guarantees, threats of civil litigation, filing and defending lawsuits, all the while getting paid when Gusman saw fit, when the next deal closed, keeping Black on a short leash, just enough to stay on, but no more than he deserved, trapped, subservient, dependent, and it worked well, for Gusman, for ten years running, not as well for Black, forced to take on other matters, on the sly from Gusman. Like that other thing hanging over his head, that he thought was over and done with, but things like that have a way of lingering at the fringes, until they wake you bolt upright in the middle of the night, hoping it was just a dream, everything he had worked for in the balance, in another's hands, like that old joke his father used to tell, only two people need to know if you're cheating on your wife, and that's one too many. Cheating on his wife would be bad enough, this was worse. But he was dealing with that, too. Once this deal closed he could put that to bed, Black thought, as he crossed Randolph Street toward City Hall, no other option than exactly what he was doing, he thought, as he walked into City Hall in his brown suit with the light blue pinstripes, and up the marble steps, his stomach gurgling, to the second floor Office of the Chairman of the Finance Committee.

In the meantime, after grabbing a halibut on rye and a root beer at the Berghoff stand up, Billy walked down Adams Street to Michigan Avenue, and north up Michigan Avenue toward the Law Offices of Anthony V. Marzullo, at 6 North Michigan. Billy had placed a call to Mr. Marzullo's offices after looking at the court file on the off chance he could stop by and speak to Mr. Marzullo. Mr. Marzullo's secretary asked if he had an appointment, Billy said he did not, she then asked what his call was regarding, he said it was none of her business, she then asked who was calling, he said Billy Hurley. Duty bound, she put him on hold, and, to her surprise, Mr. Marzullo told her to ask if he was the Billy Hurley who was the son of Dan

Hurley, and when asked, Billy said yes, after which Mr. Marzullo agreed to meet with Billy at one o'clock that afternoon.

When built in 1898, Montgomery Ward's tower at Six North Michigan Avenue looked down upon all other buildings in the City of Chicago, part of the Park Row streetscape looking out on the expanse of open land that later was to become Grant Park. Billy walked into the lobby, which had clearly seen its day, asked for the office of Mr. Marzullo, and was directed to the furthest elevator on the left, which, to his surprise, went to one floor only, the penthouse office, an open square office perched atop the building, with three tall roman arched windows on each side, where Mr. Ward himself once ruled his empire.

Tony Marzullo, shiny black hair combed back, dark features, deep brown eyes, athletic, finishing a submarine sandwich behind an ornate wooden desk, his Hermès tie tucked into his crisp white shirt, silk suit jacket hanging off the back of his red leather chair.

"Come on in, sit down," he said, waving his arm.

Billy looked around the office, full-sized skeleton in the corner looking out over the park, red velvet day bed, moose head, antique globe, Art-Nouveau chairs, end tables, looked original.

"Some of these pieces Mr. Ward left behind," Mr. Marzullo said proudly, "Montgomery Ward, that is, welcome to a little Chicago history, here have a seat," he said, pointing to a chair in front of his desk.

"Thanks for seeing me."

"Wouldn't do this for just anybody."

"I'm nobody."

"Maybe, but your old man wasn't, sorry about all that by the way."

"Thanks."

"So what can I do for you?"

"Well, I just came from the Chancery Division clerk's office, where I looked at a file you might know something about."

"Yeah what case is that?"

"I believe you represented O'Neill Electric in a case against New Life Blessing Corporation."

"Yeah, that was a fun one, what about it?"

"Well, I saw that the case settled, and I know it was supposedly confidential, and I don't need to know the details of that, but what I'm interested in, is what was Gusman's involvement?"

Tony Marzullo eyed Billy suspiciously.

"Now why would you wanna know about that?"

"You know, that's a really good question, I'm not sure to be honest, it just so happens I've got a couple of days to kill and I didn't have anything else to do, and I was just curious about something my dad did the day before he died that was very unlike him, and I started looking at a few things which led me to the court file, which led me to you."

"And what was it your dad did?"

"Well, he put a hold on a zoning matter that was up for passage in a ward that wasn't his."

"Why is that so unusual?"

"It's a long story. Aldermanic prerogative. You just don't do that."

"Okay, so what's that have to do with me?"

"The zoning matter involved the warehouse at 2620 West Jackson Boulevard."

"Oh, I see," Tony Marzullo said, connecting the dots, as he looked out the windows at the waters of Lake Michigan, haunting and gray in the distance.

"So was your dad fucking with Gusman?"

"I don't know, I don't know what my dad was doing exactly."

"So what do you want from me?"

"The case settled within weeks of your adding Gusman as a defendant. I was just wondering what happened, how did that all come about?"

Tony Marzullo smiled.

"Yeah, that was a nice piece of work, really. I didn't have any idea Gusman was involved, I was just trying to hassle the owners as much as possible, make 'em take notice, make it costly, let 'em know I wasn't to be fucked with, that it was in their best interests to cut a deal, so I find out that Lincoln Financial had a mortgage on the property…"

"From the Recorder's office."

"Right, from the Recorder's office, so I serve a subpoena on Lincoln, get a call from some junior paralegal in their law department who's handling the subpoena, and, lo and behold, I get a shitload of documents back, without any objection, one of which is a personal guaranty from a guy named Ron Gusman, and there's only one of them in town far as I know. Paralegal fucked up. Found out after, paralegal no longer works there, sent me a resume."

"Yeah, so?"

"So it turns out Gusman personally guaranteed $500,000 in construction financing that was used to rebuild the warehouse. So I have no idea what Gusman's interest is in the property, but I know he's involved somehow, right?"

"Right."

"So I call Sydney Black, the defendant's lawyer, he's a real piece of work, know him?"

"No."

"So, I call up Black, tell him I'm going to amend the complaint and add Gusman, and I could just tell, just by the way Black hesitated, changed his tone, swore he'd seek sanctions, that I had them by the balls. So I amend the complaint, name Gusman, allege some bullshit about him, and two weeks later my client gets his money, sweet little piece of work, Gusman must have been super pissed."

"But Gusman must have had an ownership interest, right?"

"Well, I don't have any proof, if that's what you're asking, but absolutely, you don't give somebody a $500,000 guaranty without skin in the game."

"Could I get a copy of that guarantee?"

"Don't see why not."

Marzullo calls out for his secretary, asks her to bring in the client document file for the mechanics lien case.

"Okay, thanks," Billy said, wondering, if there was anything else to ask, and just before he was about to leave, he thought of something.

"One more thing, if you don't mind, what do you know about this guy Sydney Black, you said he was a piece of work, how so?"

"To be fair, I don't know him that well, just had that one case with him, know his license was suspended for six months a while back, not sure what for, found out later he's Gusman's guy, does all his work, seemed capable enough, and when it came down to working out the settlement agreement, he wasn't such a bad guy, anachronism, seems like he's out of the thirties, kind of rough and tumble, if you know what I mean."

"Yeah, I get it," Billy said, and got to his feet.

Marzullo's secretary came in with the documents. Marzullo looked through them, quickly found the guaranty, and asked her to make a copy.

"But there was something else," Marzullo offered, "scuttle butt I heard after the case settled, Black may have run into some trouble, seems his name came up in the feds' investigation of Cook County judges, wouldn't be surprised, seemed the type, but the judge who was going to take Black down with him up and died, and apparently, without the judge, there was nobody else to put the finger on Black, or so I heard, don't quote me on that, all third and fourth hand, stuff you hear around the courthouse."

"Gusman involved?"

"Not that I know of, too smart for that."

"Yeah, the smart ones never get caught."

"Yeah, like your old man."

"Yeah, like my old man."

"So, what are you gonna do now, what's next?" Tony Marzullo asked.

"Oh, God, I don't know, nothing probably, I'm just in town for a couple of days."

"Where you living now?"

"Wisconsin."

"What are you doing in town?"

"I've got this guardianship thing going on I have to show up for. Know anything about guardianships?"

"Only there's no money in it, so, no, I don't, and in this business, it's important to know what you don't know."

Marzullo's secretary came back into the office with a copy of the guaranty, handed it to Marzullo, who gave it to Billy.

"Here you go, kid."

"Yeah, thanks," Billy said, extending his hand across Tony's submarine sandwich, "thanks again, and good luck," shaking Tony's hand, "but from the look of all this," Billy said looking around Tony's office, taking in the view, "you might not need luck."

"Take as much of it as I can get."

"And thanks for this," Billy said, waving the guaranty.

Billy walked out onto Michigan Avenue, heavy damp air, felt like rain, and headed north, thinking about Gusman and Black, just as the two of them were finishing up their meeting a couple of blocks away.

"So everybody's all good, then?" Gusman asked.

"All good," said Black.

"No more zoning fuck ups?" Gusman couldn't resist, one more dig, his habit with Black, needling weakness, keep him on his toes.

"We're all good," ignoring the needle.

"You'll get a good chunk of change out of this."

"Finally," Black muttered as he got up to go.

"What?"

"Yeah, it'll be nice to finally get paid," Black said heading for the door.

"You wanna negotiate down from your 15 percent?" Gusman called out after him, "you should be so lucky," which was all Gusman had to say, as Black, shaking his head, walked out of the office, down the marble steps, and out the City Hall doors leading onto Randolph Street.

Billy walked west down Washington Street, cut through Marshall Field's, cosmetics, jewelry, came out on State Street, Chicago Theater marquee, and headed west down Randolph, past the Daley Civic Center, crossed Clark Street, west along the sidewalk next to the County Building and City Hall, when a man in a brown suit with light blue pinstripes came out of the City Hall doors, turned left, and started walking west down Randolph several steps ahead of Billy.

For some reason, Billy was struck by the haggard, bedraggled, look of this older man, carrying his accordion file briefcase, stomping flat footed ahead of Billy down the street, kind of felt sorry for him somehow, hunched shoulders, not at all happy, epitome of big city hustle grown old, what can happen in the ebb and flow, after so many years of schlepping here and there, to get by, the golden ring always out of reach, always in someone else's pocket, picking up scraps. God I hope, Billy thought, with acute empathy, that somewhere that poor man finds some happiness, as the first raindrops began to fall from the heavy sky. And maybe it was just the rain, or the bullshit he was knee-deep in all day, couldn't seem to avoid in this town, but it all seemed to come down upon him suddenly, a veil of incredible melancholy, an overwhelming sadness, for all the unhappy people in the world, and for his mother and his dad and his kids and his life and the city that was no longer his, the sky crying harder, on Sydney Black walking back to his office, on Billy to his motorcycle, waiting in the alley to take him away.

Sydney Black's coat was damp and his shoes wet when he reached his building's lobby, entered the elevator, close and warm, and joggled up to the eleventh floor, where he walked into the empty tight corridor, down the hall, turned the corner, and stopped, at the presence down the hall. And there he was, tall and lean, like a Texan, leaning up against the wainscoting, one leg crossed over the other at the knee, chewing on a toothpick.

Neither said a word as Sydney Black approached the glass door, his name printed across the wavy glass, inserted the key in the lock, opened the door, and led the tall Texan, who backed off the wall, into his office. They stepped through what some might call a reception area, back through stacks of mussy files and boxes, and into Black's cramped cheaply paneled office.

"Don't know what I'd think if I was a client," the Texan said, looking around, sitting down in one of Black's chairs.

"You'll never be a client. What're you doin' here? I told you never to come here."

"Just makin' sure we're cool."

"We're all good."

"Just makin' sure. Cuz it'd be a shame…"

"We're all good. Mid-September for sure."

"Quarter mil."

"Like I said."

"Okay, just makin' sure," the Texan said, and he unwrapped his long legs, got up out of his uncomfortable chair, and walked out of the Law Offices of Sydney Black, who leaned back in his wooden swivel chair, stunned, staring wide-eyed at the Texan's lean frame leaving his office, reaching for the ever present bottle of Tums at the far corner of his desk, behind a pile of papers where happiness did not exist.

CHAPTER SEVEN

The Tunnels

Billy had a bad sleep, thrashing about trying to find something in the doors and alleys and tunnels of his dreams, woke up anxious, out of sorts, not like him. He woke like he was trying all night to do something he couldn't get done, looking for something he couldn't find, just to wake and have to do it all over again the next day, searching, for what is lost, within reach, then gone, labyrinth, ball of string, elusive answers, frustration, fatigue, wondering, just for a second, if it was really worth it, why bother, why anything, addiction to apathy, but just for a second, that's all it was, because, fact was, there'd been a change, Billy had gone down the rabbit hole, saw things a little differently, couldn't stop thinking about that warehouse, for one thing, more interested in something other than his wife for the first time in a long time, not sure why, time on his hands, sure, but something about a good puzzle, a maze, with bloodlines, bad guys, doors, alleys, and tunnels.

Different now, more than just something to do, kind of psyched really, time to ask why, figure it out, his dad, Gusman, dig for bread crumbs left behind, follow the trail where the evidence leads, into the banging inner workings, rusty gears of the machine, clanking away, too loud for the faint of heart, most couldn't handle, but it took one to catch one, in the basement, under hot pipes, steam, the deep recess, where only strong women and men handle the pressure gauge deep in the red, about to blow, waiting for someone to sneak in and turn it all down, release the steam, turn the corner, the page, change the energy source, to solar and wind.

But he had few tools to do so. He'd run down the corporation, the deeds, the lawsuit, and, while a start, it wasn't close to the story, hidden behind land trusts and corporate veils, the most important question, the why, the reason, where's the money, and where does it go, that's what it's about, the inner logic, of every deal, every contract, who gets what, what's given up, what's the margin, makes the world go round, and he wasn't close to figuring that out. But there was that lease, in his father's file, how'd he get that, wait, didn't Dorothy say, maybe Dorothy would know.

"Dorothy? It's me, Billy."

"Why, Billy, what a surprise."

"You doin' okay?"

"Oh, Billy," she sighed heavily, "the sadness follows me like a shadow, don't know I'll ever be the same, I loved your father, Billy."

Wow, little strong right out of the box, hadn't expected that, Billy thought, not quite sure what that meant, really.

"Where're you at these days?"

"Working for Alderman Buchanan, the new Budget chairman, it's fine, he's nice enough, nothing like your dad."

Billy believed that, no one was.

"Dorothy, I had a question for you, has to do with that file you gave me in my dad's office that day."

Dorothy perked up.

"Really? Interested in your father's work, after all?"

"Well, yeah, I'm in town for a couple of days, and, well, I was lookin' at that stuff you gave me, and I got a little interested in why my dad would have D&P'd that zoning thing."

"Made absolutely no sense to me, Billy, I can tell you that."

"Yeah, well, I get that, makes no sense to me either, and I was just curious."

"That, is a very good thing," Dorothy said, little excited.

"Well, I'm not gonna make a big deal about it, but since I had a little time, I thought I'd take a look at a few things."

"Okay, how can I help?"

"Well, the file you gave me, it had a document in it, pretty long, that lease for the warehouse."

"The warehouse, yes, hey now, I heard you went to see Reverend Simmons?"

"I did."

"And what did you think?"

"Very impressed, liked him a lot, like what he's doin' out there."

"See, told you so, your father liked him a lot, too."

"Then we had one thing in common."

Dorothy smiled at her handiwork.

"I also heard you got married to that Mona girl."

"Yes, I most certainly did."

"Oh, my goodness! I am so happy for you, she's such a nice girl, how you ever managed that...."

"So I've been told."

"Anyway, congratulations, I pray the two of you will be forever blessed."

"Thank you, Dorothy, but about that lease."

"Yes, actually, I was the one who got that lease document, from the lease file at the State."

"Where at the State?"

"Wait, um, IDP..., wait no, is it CMS? I'm not good at acronyms, yes, it was CMS, Central Management Services, in the State of Illinois Building, your dad asked me to go over and see if there was a file, and, of course, I found it."

"Was there anything else in the file?"

"Yes, quite a bit, actually, but your dad just asked for the lease, so that's what I got for him. He said he might be going over to take a look himself, which was really odd, because he just didn't do that, probably would have too if he hadn't..."

"Can anybody look at it?"

"Sure, it's a state contract, public has a right to know what their government is doing."

"Since when, Dorothy."

"I know, I know, not the way we do things around here," Dorothy said with a laugh, "maybe they're a little more above board over there."

"Doubt that."

"Anyway, that's where you can find it."

"Great, I might go check it out."

"There's a lease number at the top of the document in that file I gave you, make sure you have that because that's how they look it up."

"Great, thanks."

"What're you going to do with what you find?"

"No idea, probably nothing, just curious is all, I'm heading back home on Friday, can't wait to get back."

"Where're you staying in town?"

"My dad's condo."

"That's nice, he'd like that."

"Doubt that, too."

"You have too many doubts, Billy, you've got to believe more."

"Yeah, well, that may be Dorothy, workin' on it though, thanks so much for your help, I hope that dark cloud goes away some day."

"Not any time soon, I suspect, but thank you, all the best to you and your new bride."

Billy hadn't been to the State of Illinois Building more than twice in his entire life, but he hopped on the Moto Guzzi for the second day in a row, rode down the Magnificent Mile in bright sunshine, across the Michigan Avenue Bridge to Wacker Drive, right on Wacker along the river to Wells Street, left on Wells, under the El tracks, and into the alley behind the State of Illinois Building. He took the elevator up to Central Management Services on the twelfth floor, no Bellow this time, down the hall to the records office, stepped up to the counter, gave them the number as Dorothy had instructed, and received in return two files stuffed with documents.

He took out the first document, the original March 1, 1983, Request for Proposal disseminated to the public, which set forth the basic requirements for the warehouse, and requested a response by April 1, 1983. The RFP emphasized the State's preference to contract with an MBE, minority business enterprise, for a warehouse to be located in a DBZ, disadvantaged business zone, for the purpose of providing economic opportunities to historically disadvantaged businesses in low income communities. Like Gusman, right. The RFP sought up to 200,000 square feet of space to be used by the Illinois Department of Public Aid, and potentially other state agencies, depending on available space and agency need. Then came the lease, dated April 2, 1983, just one month later, pretty quick work, like the hoodie said. New Life Blessing, the lucky winner, an Illinois corporation, lessor, of a 200,000 square foot warehouse at five dollars per square foot, nice price, over ten years, to be constructed at 2620 West Jackson Boulevard. After the lease came a real estate disclosure form which identified the shareholders of New Life Blessing as Mr. Davis and Ms. Jones, attached to which was a minority business enterprise certificate for New Life Blessing issued by the City of Chicago. There was a First Amendment to the lease, with additional improvements, building requirements, and specifications to guide the reconstruction, followed by a Second Amendment, dated January 13, 1984, which extended the lease term five years, making the lease a fifteen-year lease, and provided that, after acceptance of the warehouse, and occupancy upon the commencement date, the State would assume responsibility for all repairs and improvements on the property. The Recitals for the Second Amendment explained that one of the reasons for the extension was to incentivize a potential investment in the lease, whatever that meant. A Third Amendment, dated April 11, 1984, added another five years, making the lease a twenty-year lease, the Recitals reflecting that, what the taxpayers were getting in exchange for agreeing to another five-year extension, was a promise that the lessor would make certain additional unspecified improvements, when, in fact, unbeknownst to Billy, the only thing anyone from the State of Illinois got in exchange for adding another five years to the lease was the night of drinking and lap dances Bob Olson received courtesy of Sydney Black, on Gusman's dime. The Fourth Amendment, dated April 30, 1984, amended the lease to set a new commencement date, for June 8, 1984, two days after the scheduled City Council meeting for June 6, at which his father put the kibosh on the zoning change. Then, on May 3, 1984, a little more than a month before his dad dies, the short and happy life of the New Life Blessing Corp.'s interest in the lease mysteriously comes to an end, when, in the Fifth Amendment to the lease, all of New Life Blessing Corp.'s right, title, and interest in and to that certain lease dated April 2, 1983, is assigned to the New Life Blessing Limited Partnership, which, as the Recitals reflect, has become the owner of the property at 2620 West Jackson Boulevard, pursuant to a transfer of the property by deed to a land trust of which New Life Blessing Limited Partnership is the beneficial owner. Billy's head now spinning, which was the whole idea. The real estate disclosure form attached to the Fifth Amendment disclosed that the limited partners, i.e. owners, of the New Life Blessing Limited Partnership were West Side Development I, LLC, the agent of which was Virgil Davis, and West Side Development II, LLC, the agent of which was Viola Jones. The disclosure form on behalf of West Side Development I, LLC, was signed, on behalf of its president, by Sydney Black, as power of attorney. The disclosure form on behalf of West Side Development II, LLC, was signed by Viola Jones. No MBE certificate was attached. To make matters worse, the file also included a draft Sixth Amendment, which planned to assign all of New Life Blessing Limited Partnership's interest in the lease to the Lincoln Financial Management Company, a subsidiary of Lincoln Financial Trust and Savings Bank, on a date to coincide with the commencement date of the lease.

Well, if the intent of all the various documents in the file was to thoroughly confuse anyone trying to unravel what the hell was happening to this property, it was most certainly successful, at least as far as Billy was concerned. Bottom line, he knew Gusman was in there somewhere, and wherever Black surfaced, Gusman was right behind, which meant that, since Black signed one of the disclosure forms on behalf of one of the two new owners of the property, he must have been signing on behalf of Gusman, and the fact that he did not sign the other, meant that Gusman must have a partner, Viola Jones, or, more likely, someone behind her, someone Gusman didn't control, whether fifty/fifty, ninety/ten, impossible to say. Also fair to say his father did a number on this complicated enterprise when he deferred and published that zoning matter, no doubt requiring another lease amendment for another commencement date, putting everything at least two months behind schedule, and causing a great deal of heartburn, which, Billy was certain, made his father very proud. But what was up with that draft amendment, after doing all that work, over all that time, why would anyone want to just give it all up to the bank?

The answer to that question came in the last document in the file, a Letter Agreement, dated June 1, 1984, written by Mark Hamilton, Assistant Vice-President, Credit Financing, Lincoln Financial Trust and Savings Bank, no doubt ghost written by the bank's legal counsel, addressed to Bob Olson, with a carbon copy to DCMS' general counsel. In his letter, the second page of which bore the signatures of both parties, Mr. Hamilton seeks the State's approval, as discussed, of a plan for investment involving the lease, a credit tenant loan, whereby the American Patriot Insurance Company, of Atlanta, Georgia, will invest in the lease by purchasing the rental payments to be made by the State over the twenty-year term of the lease, at a purchase price equal to the present cash value of the rental stream, at an appropriate discount rate to ensure a reasonable rate of return on the insurance company's investment, the purchase price to be paid to the lessor, which will assign all of its interest in the lease to the Lincoln Financial Management Co., which will then become the owner and manager of the property.

Wait. What? What does that mean? What's a credit tenant loan, why would an insurance company want to do that, how much would it pay, who would get the payment, was Gusman getting bought out, what would he get out of it, what would his partner get, sounds like the only ones left would be the State, the bank, and the insurance company, were any minorities left, were there any really to begin with, how did it come to that, was that the plan all along, why so many questions, why did it have to be so complicated, who came up with this, why did Billy's brain hurt, did he really give a shit any more, wasn't it time to call off the dogs, pack it in, call it a day, didn't he have better things to do, wouldn't anything be better than this?

And that was the whole point. If anybody even knew to look at this mess, and cared enough to try and figure it out, they'd be so burned out by the time they got to the dead end in this miserable file that the last thing they wanted to do was have anything more to do with it, which is exactly how Billy felt, the room was warm, the air conditioning didn't seem to be working, it was a beautiful day, he couldn't begin to figure out what this deal was about, probably all legal anyway, so there didn't seem to be much of a point in wasting his time any longer, the water probably glistening off Oak Street Beach, hop on his bike, rev up his frustrations, ride off with a loud roar down LaSalle Street, and get the hell out of there and never come back.

Except that he didn't go home, he took LaSalle to North Avenue, then over to Lake Shore Drive, took the Drive north, at a clip, racing past North Avenue Beach, Lincoln Park, the Lincoln Park Zoo, swerving in and out of traffic, Diversey Harbor, the gun club, Belmont Harbor, boats bobbing at their moorings, in and out of high-rise shadows, up to Wilson Avenue, where he got off and turned around, and came back down the Drive, roaring back, faster, stripping away the godawful morning, the mire of details, racing ahead, into a bird's eye view, the big picture, of that goddamned warehouse, how they stole it from Reverend Simmons, who thought ten thousand was a lot of money, while the bankers and fat cats wallow in dough, at his expense, way of the world, and instead of letting it all wash away, like he thought he wanted to do, Billy was getting pissed, the faster he rode, into the canyons of town, the lake beckoning, would have to wait, he had one more idea, before he let it all go, so he got off at Oak Street, rode back to the condo building, and went upstairs to make one last call.

Marshall Chapman had been one of Billy's running mates at Latin, father a silk stocking lawyer, mother a pediatrician, Gold Coast milieu, never missed a party, early into drugs, and, unlike Billy, early out, Dartmouth, University of Chicago Law, now a bond lawyer at his father's firm, kind soul actually, always stayed in touch, sent Billy a nice note when his father passed, one of the few. Marshall was at his desk on the 70th floor of the Sears Tower when he got Billy's call.

"Hey, Chap, it's me, Billy."

"Billy Hurley!" he said, surprised, "nice to hear from you, man."

"So, you lookin' out over the lake?"

"No, no," he said, laughing, "got a view west, I can see Des Moines from here," he said, looking out at the flat expanse of grid blocks stretching to the horizon. "Maybe when I'm a partner. Hey, man, how are you, my condolences about your father, what a raw deal, to go out like that, he didn't deserve that shit, always liked your old man."

"Makes one of us."

"Yeah, well, be careful, like father like son, and all that rot."

"Applies to you, too."

"Yeah, dig that, but I got a plan," he said, whispering into the phone, "investment banking's where it's at, where I'm going, but nobody knows that around here, that's between you and me."

"Well, at least you've got a plan."

"What about you, man, what's your plan?"

"Doin' okay for now, Chap, I got married."

"Shotgun?"

"No, true love."

"Awesome, good for you, step in the right direction. You heading in the right direction?" Chap asked.

Billy knew what he meant.

"Been clean for a while now."

"Great, man, great news, happy for you, you'll do great if that shit's behind you."

"Yeah, took me a while, kind of fucked things up there, but at least I figured that out, not much else, but that shit's off my back."

"Hey, happy to hear that, man."

"Yeah, hey, Chap, I got a question for you."

"Shoot."

"Well, it's kind of a long story, but I'll try to keep it short. Let's just say, my dad left me some papers to look through, and in these papers an issue came up, and I'm having trouble trying to figure it out, has to do with something called a credit tenant loan, know anything about that?"

"Not a lot, we have somebody here who does that stuff, helped him out once my first year, I'm no expert, but I know something about it, what do you need to know?"

"Well, what the hell is it?"

"Well, it's an investment, really, a long-term investment, good for insurance companies, because they're in it for the long haul, looking for a safe long-term return, so what they'll do is, they'll work with an investment banker, who puts a deal together, where the insurance company will invest in a secure long term lease, like a government lease, and they'll pay X amount of money for the cash stream, the rental payments, and they get some kind of favorable tax treatment."

"Okay, not sure I get that. So the insurance company makes an investment, meaning they pay somebody money."

"Right."

"Who are they paying?

"Well, say it's a government lease, some governmental agency entered into a long-term lease."

"That's exactly my situation."

"Okay, in that case, the government has entered into a lease to rent-out property, say, for ten years. You know from the lease how much the government is required to pay over the ten years, and the rent is to be paid to the building owner who owns the space, the landlord, so the insurance company comes in, with the banker's help, and says I'll pay you mister building owner, landlord, 'X' dollars now, if you'll assign to me all your rights to the rent to be paid over the ten years of the lease."

"But why would they want to do that?"

"Well, the building owner gets a shitload of money up front, he doesn't have to wait ten years to get his money, and the insurance company gets a safe rate of return on its investment over ten years."

"Okay, but how much would the insurance company pay?"

"Depends, on the term of the lease, amount of space, rent, and then you do a present value calculation."

"I have no idea how to do that."

"It's not that hard, I could do it for you, but I'd need the lease. Do you have the lease?"

"Yeah."

"Okay, how many square feet?"

"200,000."

"What's the term of the lease?"

"Twenty years."

"How much a square foot?"

"Five bucks."

"Okay, from that I can figure out the total amount of the rental stream on the lease over the twenty years. Then I have to figure out what I would pay today, to get that amount over the next twenty years, and that all depends on the rate of return the insurance company would need to get on their investment. Let's assume, let's see, say, 6.5 percent return, hold on, let me do the math, it'll just take a second."

Billy was starting to get what was happening. Calculator clicks from the other end of the line.

"Okay, this isn't exact, but I think it might be reasonable for the insurance company to pay somewhere around, five, five and a half million dollars now, for the rental stream over twenty years on your lease."

"And that's all legal?"

"Of course, it's legal, why wouldn't it be?"

"What if the building owner paid bupkus for the property, and put, say, $500,000 into fixing it up, are you saying they could get five million dollars for doing nothing?"

"Well, however you look at it, it's not like they didn't do anything, they have a valuable asset, a piece of property, and, more importantly, a good reliable tenant, that's willing to pay a shitload of money over a long period of time to use the space. That has value."

"What if they lucked into the lease?"

"Then they got very lucky."

"What if after they get their money, they don't even own the property anymore, they deed it to the bank."

"That wouldn't be unusual, the insurance company would prefer that the bank manage the lease anyway, better to get guys they don't know out of the way of their investment, so the bank effectively becomes the land-lord, and, if it's done right, and the lease makes the government pay for all repairs, there's nothing much for the bank to do anyway."

"Wow."

"By the way, we never had this conversation, I don't know anything about this lease other than what you told me, I don't know who the parties are, one of 'em could be a client, we never talked about this, okay?"

"Sure, man, can't thank you enough. I always knew you'd turn out all right, Chap, I'm happy for you."

"Money can't buy me love, Billy, you've got a leg up on me there."

"Well, I hope you find someone like my Mona some day, Chap, and when you do, we'll throw a party."

"Not like we used to."

"Please, no, not like we used to."

Billy sat for quite a while, staring at the lease, out at the lake, back at the lease. Okay, so, if he had this right, Gusman, or some crony of his, gets an inside tip from somebody at the State about a warehouse deal, needs to get a minority involved, that's no big deal, he's able to track down a warehouse, pays $10,000 for it, gets the lease from the state, puts $500,000 into fixing up the building, gets Lincoln Financial involved, wheedles ten years' worth of extensions, shifts all repairs onto the State, and, a little more than a year later, he and his partner walk away with five million bucks. About a 900 percent return. Not bad. Five million bucks that could have gone to Reverend Simmons, if he had the right help. But inside jobs aren't meant to benefit the needy, because the needy are never on the inside, they're out on the street, looking into the windows of a brand new warehouse generating millions of dollars of which the community gets squat, made Billy sick, helpless, but what could he do about it, and if he couldn't do anything about it, what was the point, what would his father have done, had he known what Billy knew, what could he have done, other than stir up the pot, make things difficult, shine a light maybe.

So he decided to do just that, pick on the low hanging fruit, the naive, unsoiled, somebody not tainted by the inner workings, the inside job, somebody who thought it was all on the up and up, just doing his job, so he called Mark Hamilton, at the Lincoln Financial Trust and Savings Bank, just to let somebody know, that he knew, like his dad let somebody know. Maybe a little fear of God was all he could accomplish, let Hamilton spread it around, rattle the cage, all Billy could do, leaving day after tomorrow, after all, to his real life, far, far from here, thank God, Billy thought, as he picked up the telephone, and called the Lincoln Financial Trust and Savings Bank.

"Can I tell Mr. Hamilton what this is regarding?"

"No."

"Pardon me?"

"I said no, you cannot tell him what this is regarding, just tell him Billy Hurley wants to speak with him."

"Oh," she said, flustered, "okay then, please hold."

Muzak.

"He's in a meeting and can't be interrupted."

"Did you tell him who was calling?"

"Yes, as a matter of fact I did and he said he did not know a Billy Hurley," she said, with attitude.

"Tell him I'm the son of Dan Hurley, see if he knows me then."

"Well…"

"Just tell him."

Muzak.

"Hello, this is Mark Hamilton," haltering, tenuous.

"Thought you were in a meeting."

"Well, as a matter of fact…"

"Couldn't have been too, important."

"What do you want?"

"I just want you and your clients to know that I know what you're up to."

"What are you talking about?"

"The warehouse, on Jackson."

Silence.

"What about it?"

"The five million."

"How did you know…"

"So it is five mil."

"I can't speak to you about this; this is a confidential transaction."

"I'm sure it is, but before you hang up, I just want to know, who's Gusman's partner in this deal, who's Viola Jones, is it fifty/fifty, or something else?"

Mark Hamilton hung up the telephone, picked it back up. "Shit," he said aloud, as he dialed the number for Sydney Black.

"Hello?"

"Sydney?"

"Yes."

"It's me, Mark Hamilton."

"What's up?"

"We have a problem…"

Sydney Black hung up the telephone, reached for the bottle of Tums, popped two in his mouth, broke out in a cold sweat. He thought of calling Gusman, but he knew how that would go. Had another idea. Picked up the telephone.

"Hello?"

"We've got another problem."

Billy had been pacing up and down inside his dad's condo for about an hour wondering what he should do next when the telephone rang.

"Is this Billy Hurley?"

"Yeah."

"Heard you were interested in some information."

"Who's this?"

"I've got what you're lookin' for."

"What's that?"

"Names."

"Where?"

"City Hall, B-237, six o'clock. There's a phone on the table, call the number on the sheet of paper, and I'll be right down."

"But…"

Click.

Well, that didn't take long. Word travels fast when there's money on the line. Cryptic instructions, for sure. And why there? Interesting enough, but now, he had a decision to make, harmless curiosity just got real, maybe it was time to stop playing around, enough already, maybe he'd done what he set out to do, accomplished his goal, but what was that, shake things up, is that all it was, what his dad wanted, so now it was time to answer the question, that nagging question that dogged his life, whether to go, or leave well enough alone, that was the question. Everything he had done his entire life militated against it, keep your distance, aloof, withdrawn, don't get involved. He'd been toying around, tweaking these guys, killing time, but that was not a warm and fuzzy phone call, he got somebody's attention, somebody must be pissed, it could even be dangerous, he thought about that, thought about his dad, how he ended up, but that couldn't be, what were they going to do, shoot him with a bow and arrow in City Hall, that couldn't be it, four hours away, paranoia talking, still, the timing was odd, but that was ridiculous, Gusman wasn't that desperate, he and his dad might have been crooks in their own way, but they weren't violent, never needed that, million ways to take care of business, without resorting to that, no that didn't concern him as much, it was more just, just the same old question, summed up his life, never had a good answer, to why bother, why the effort, what would he get out of it, was that it, just like his father, what do I get out of whatever I do, never because it might be the right thing, never because it might make a difference, to someone else, what was it the hoodie said, "so, what, you just run away?" that's what he said, "don't suppose you're willing to stick around and fight for it," that's what Ms. Beecher said, well, what would Mona do, maybe it was time, maybe it was time to make the effort, time to bother, the only reason these fuckers keep getting their way is because nobody with any balls stands up to them, calls them out, enough's enough, yeah, he thought, maybe this was the time, time to be a little bold, show a little spine, stick around, fight for it, and accept the invitation, to meet this stranger at six o'clock in City Hall.

So Billy rode back downtown, against the current of after work traffic, parked his bike in the alley, and headed into City Hall, spinning through the doors, into the vaulted hallway, quiet and empty but for a few stragglers leaving work late, saying good night to the cop at the security desk. Billy thought it best to act like he knew what he was doing, waved to the cop, and walked directly to the stairs, taking them one flight down, into unknown territory. As many times as he had been in the Hall with his father he had never ventured below, had no idea what to expect, or where to go. When he reached the basement he roamed the narrow hallway, each marked door off the hall, B-110, B-120, B-130, took a right down an intersecting hall, B-180, B-190, then another hall, no B-237, no B-2 anything, there must be another floor. He looked for another stairway, and found one, at the far end of the last hall, behind an unmarked gray metal door. Dimly lit, metal stairs, down, into the unknown, each step, a dull clang, to another metal door, another hall, narrower, spare, industrial, inner mechanics, stoking fires, B-200, B-205, boiler room, into the belly, hot, close, intersecting hallway, rumbling, louder, B-210, B-215, door open at the end of the hall, B-220, B-225, B-237, open door, this is it.

Billy stepped up to the door, looked up and down the empty hall, peeked around the door frame into the open room, lit by a single bulb in the middle of the ceiling, metal walls, twelve by sixteen, door at far end, two long tables, one on each wall, telephone at the far end of one of the tables, pad of paper under the phone, all still, but for the steady rumble of machinery, the heart of the beast, Billy at the door, the portal he had finally chosen to enter, no turning back, no running away, trapped, one way or the other, in or out, he stepped in, carefully, thin ice, up to the table, picked up the phone, no ring tone, no cord, just a pad of paper, no number, handwriting, large letters, emphatic, warning, "Let It Go!," and the door suddenly slammed behind him, a switch, flipped, the light, off, leaving him in total darkness.

Billy thought of yelling, for a second, but knew that the only person who would hear was the one who slammed the door, and Billy was not about to give him, or her, the pleasure. He remained perfectly still, adjusting to the dark, focusing, concentrating, not a glimmer, no objects, no room, tables, phone, nothing, utter nothingness, pure blindness, the rumbling, the someone on the other side of the door, listening, faint steps walking away.

He walked softly over to where he thought the door was, tried it, locked. Remembered the other door, turned, walked into a table, felt his way along the table to the back of the room, felt for the door, the door knob, and, to his surprise, it opened, into a damp hole, emptiness. Billy stepped through the door into the space, edging one foot across the floor, into puddles, concrete, only the sense, of hemmed in, all sides, he stretched his arm out before him, into nothing, over his head, into concrete, crusty, falling, specks of dust, pebbles, on his face, ran his fingers along what was above, sloping down to his right, sloping down to his left, no wider than five inches beyond each of his outstretched arms, little more than one and a half feet over his head, narrow, horseshoe cavity, all he could figure, encased in concrete, leading off, into dank space, endless, or so it felt to Billy.

Billy edged back into the room, sliding his feet from side to side, reached, and sat down, on a table. Options: 1) Freak out. What he wanted to do. Reasonable under the circumstances, but, he knew, unproductive, so he stayed relatively calm, surprisingly clear headed, should have expected something like this, after that call. 2) Stay where he was. No way of knowing when anybody came down in that basement. Had to, somebody had to. Maintenance guys had to, but how often, every day, once a week. Whoever it was, physical injury was not the goal, if so, he'd already be dead, his body dumped in the sodden space behind that door, not to be found for years. No, this was something else, this was just a warning, "Let It Go!," okay got it, message received, but now what? If the mystery man didn't want him dead, at some point he'd see to it that the door was reopened, but how long would that take, hours, the next morning, he had his guardianship hearing the next morning. So does he wait and hope for the best? 3) Or venture into the deep hole, beyond that door. What was it, where did it go, nowhere, anywhere, he could lose his way, then what? But sitting, doing nothing? Billy may have shunned involvement most of his life, but he was not passive by nature, better on the move, on the road, even if to nowhere, better than standing still, so he got off the table, stepped through the back door, and began sliding one foot before the other into the dark hole, one arm stretched out before him, the other angled forward over his head, gliding back into the puddles, cold water seeping into his All Stars, slowly, carefully, about ten steps, when the flatness of the floor gave way. Billy reached down into the standing water to feel what his Chuck Taylors had found, an iron rail, parallel, about a foot apart, tracks recessed in the floor, tracks, for a small rail car, and it came to him, he knew where he was.

Stories as a boy his father would tell, of adventures and shipwrecks and treasures and islands and thunder and lightning and caves and mountains and jungles, and tunnels, a network of tunnels, below the streets downtown, underfoot, abandoned, forgotten, the sewers of Paris, full of mystery and death, phantoms, lost souls, ghosts who appear and disappear in the darkest night, saving the day or spreading fear, hope and despair, all mixed together, conspiring, scheming, in their underground world, alternate universe, alive while we sleep, haunting dreams, after late night stories, magical tunnels, lurking, waiting, beneath city streets. And it was all true, according to his father. The tunnels were real. Turn of the century, carved by hand, enterprise, transporting mail, freight, coal, cinders, packed away in little toy trains scooting back and forth beneath the city, under the river, the streets, until no one wanted them anymore, couldn't make a buck, better options, in daylight, so they left them there, abandoned in place, permanent holes, reminders, of no small plans gone bad, lurking out of sight, just waiting to be discovered, by unsuspecting excavators.

So at least Billy knew where he was. Didn't know for sure they existed, until he was in one, but now he knew, and knew they had to go somewhere, had to be other entries, exits, other basements, if he went the right way, and for now that was straight ahead, and what direction was that, played back his entry into the Hall, down the stairs, the hallways, the room, must be facing, east, he thought, made sense, away from the river, toward State Street, that great street, must be something over that way, and so he started out, stepping, deliberately, through pools of water and crud along the narrow tracks, rats scurrying away in the pitch-black, arms outstretched, developing a rhythm, cautious, to avoid collision with the unseen, but purposeful, for progress, and when he reached a fork in the tunnels, the sense of a bigger space, three prongs, one curving off to what he thought was south, the other north, he took the straight and narrow, east, hopefully, into nowhere, charcoal, slate, onward into nothing, the unknown, like everything else since the beginning of time, nothing else to do, no idea why, blind to what's ahead, just was, like everybody else, one step ahead of another, hoping it'll turn out all right, nothing else, nothing left of him, no outline, no silhouette, fading, disappearing, and in that total blackness, invisible to the world, a lost soul in the dark, Billy stepped headlong into pure clarity, somehow, here, for the first time, it all made sense, the careful steps, the motion, the flow, the effort, his children, his father, the reason to make his mark, the reason to step out from behind the curtain and say, fuck *you* guys, I'm not running away, you're not getting away with this, and with that he walked, with more determination than ever, straight away, chest out, smack into the steel mass of an abandoned rail car, hiding in the dark.

That, took the wind out of him. He reached out for it, felt the edge, just enough room to squeeze by, something still inside, dust, ash, back scraping against the curved wall, fragments falling against his neck, past the steel relic, bent down, hands on his knees, catching his breath. Tried to figure how far he'd come, slow going, but maybe, he estimated, under the Picasso, good guess, all the footsteps in the plaza of those above him, oblivious of the other world, him, forty feet below, guessed it had been about an hour, in a straight line, thank God, could always double back, but he had time, nothing but time in the dark, and he slogged on, arms at forty-five degree angles, very slowly, rats brushing up against his legs in the water, stopping, feeling, for openings in the walls, under Dearborn Street, subway rumble, another block, another hour, another subway train, muted metal scraping metal, State Street, about right, and as the muffled whoosh of the subway train faded into the black, in its wake, another sound, barely detectable, up ahead, broken bits of sound, as he approached, a radio, a sliver of light off to his left across the floor, a door.

Billy stepped up to the door, and listened, Gladys Knight and the Pips, singing *Midnight Train to Georgia*, he pounded his hand against the door and yelled out.

"Hey, I need help, anybody there? Hey!" pounding the door, to no answer, at first. Then the radio turned down.

"Hey, open the door, I'm trapped in here, help!"

Billy heard a slide bolt pushed back, a dead bolt turn, the door ajar, piercing light, and the door opening slowly.

Billy squinted into the broad face of a short heavyset shocked African American man in a blue maintenance uniform with the name Charles written in a white oval above the chest pocket.

"What the hell are you doin' in there?" Charles asked, bug eyed.

Billy rushed past him into the basement room, lunch box and thermos on a table next to the radio.

"Oh, man, thank you, thank you," Billy said, and tried to throw his arms around Charles, who stepped back from the apparition, dusted in coal ash, dipped in foul water.

"Whoa there now, whoa there," Charles said, spurning Billy's hug.

"Where am I?" Billy asked.

"You're in the subbasement at Marshall Field's," Charles replied. "How the hell you get in there?"

"Oh, man, some asshole locked me in."

"You're lucky you got out alive. Rats are ten feet long in there. You some kind of criminal or somethin'?"

"No, no, look, it doesn't matter, just, thank you, you have no idea, now how do I get out of here?"

"Take those stairs there," Charles said pointing, "they'll take you to some more stairs, and those'll take you into the store."

Billy stepped closer to give Charles a hug, but Charles backed off, shaking his head.

"Now go, get out of here, son, and please, don't you ever come back."

"Thank you, thank you," Billy said, ran over to the stairs, grabbed the rail, and leaped up, two stairs at a time.

Billy woke the next day, well, to say he woke is really not accurate, suggests he actually fell asleep, which he did not, more just got up, because he couldn't sleep, rats brushing against his legs all night, the rail car hiding in the dark, the harrowing darkness, couldn't wait for the first light off the Great Lake to come filtering through the blinds, and when it did he got up with a vengeance, adrenaline pumping, on edge, ready to go, because he had a plan, something he needed to do before the hearing at ten, a stop to make, and at nine o'clock that morning he walked into the lobby of Sydney Black's building, took the elevator up to the eleventh floor, stormed into Sydney Black's office, and began to violently, repeatedly slam the desk call bell, ringing its alarm, as Black, startled, rushed out of his office and appeared behind the cracked receptionist window, in a huff, indignant.

"What the hell do you want?" Black yelled through the window, as Billy continued to ring the bell.

"Do you know who I am?" Billy shouted.

"No, I don't know who you are, but unless you leave right now, I'm calling security."

"I'm Billy Hurley, and my dad was Dan Hurley, and we're going to fuck you *up!*" Billy shouted, pointing at Black behind the window.

Sydney Black turned white, taking a step back from the window.

"You tell Gusman for me," Billy shouted, Black aghast, "his goons don't scare me. Tell him I'm going to the papers, you tell him I'm gonna tell them all about his inside job on the West Side, I'm gonna kill that deal, you hear me, you tell him *and* you tell his partner, you got that?" Billy yelled, pointing through the glass, and he turned and stormed back out of the office, leaving Black shaken, cowering against the wall.

Sydney Black, dazed, walked back into his office, sat down at his desk. Confrontation, fighting it out in court, was one thing, physical violence another, his legs shaking, head in his hands. Gotta figure this out. It wasn't even so much about Gusman, or Gusman's partner, the hell with them, no, it was about Sydney Black, he needed that money, he needed that deal, how had it come to this, he knew too well, too late for that, was what it was, what could he do about it, that was the issue, think, if it weren't for that goddam Sweeney he'd just walk away from the whole goddam thing, from Gusman, this shitty practice, but Sweeney wasn't going anywhere, not till he got his money, and Black didn't have it, this deal was the only way, what the hell did Sweeney do to that guy anyway, Black thought, and reached for the phone.

"It's me, Black, what the hell did you do?" in a high-pitched voice.

"What are you talkin' about?"

"Billy Hurley just came into my office. I thought he was going to kill me."

Laughter on the other end of the line.

"Just gave him a warning."

"Warning? Well, your warning didn't work."

No more laughter.

"Whaddya mean?"

"I mean he's gonna blow the whole deal out of the water."

"How could he do that?"

"By going to the press. He said he's going to the press."

"So?"

"So? So what are you, stupid? He goes to the press this deal is done, you hear me, done, no money, for you, or for me."

"He's bluffing."

"Bluffing? I'm lucky he didn't break my door down and throttle me!"

"Yeah, well, you and I both know you got bigger problems than that," Sweeney said, in a low calm voice. "You remember the day you gave me that envelope for the judge? Did you think I was stupid then? I counted 'em all out, all ten thousand. Now, it's a shame the judge bought the farm, but I'm not goin' anywhere, and you know, I can't hold a tune, but I happen to know there're some folks down on Dearborn who'd love to hear me sing."

"Jesus Christ."

"He's not gonna help you."

"Jesus Christ."

"Give it time, it'll blow over."

"It's blowing *up*, you fool!"

"Well, we can't let that happen now, can we?"

"All rise."

Creaking wood. Judge Wozak breezes through the door from chambers, up the steps to his imposing perch, and without so much as looking at all those who have just reluctantly stood in his honor, growls at the clerk, "Call the cases," another good mood.

"Walsh v. Hurley, 84 P 1349."

"Ah, yes, I remember this one," said Judge Wozak.

"Petitioner," Mr. Hanneman called out with authority, stood up from one of the lawyers' tables, and walked up to the bench, accompanied by Ms. Topinka.

"Respondent," Billy called out, with authority, held the swinging gate open for Ms. Beecher, and the two of them walked up together, and stood next to Mr. Hanneman and Ms. Topinka, Ms. Beecher noticing something a little different about Billy, more upright, maybe.

"Good morning, Your Honor, William Hanneman and Mary Lou Topinka, on behalf of the petitioners."

"Good morning, Your Honor, Billy Hurley on behalf of Billy Hurley."

The judge smiled.

"Good morning, Your Honor, Harriet Beecher, Guardian *ad Litem*."

"Well, Mr. Hanneman, nice of you to join us, looking rather fit today," the judge said, looking down on Mr. Hanneman's rich dark tan.

"Yes, well…"

"Save it. Mr. Hurley, still no lawyer?"

"Like I said on Monday, Judge, he's up…"

"Yes, I remember. Isn't doing you much good today up in Wisconsin, is he, Mr. Hurley?"

Mr. Hanneman smiled.

"Please," the judge said looking down at Mr. Hanneman, "if you know what's good for you, you will not smile at anything I say this morning, do you understand, Mr. Hanneman?"

"Yes, Your Honor."

Ms. Topinka smiled; the judge smiled at Ms. Topinka.

"Good morning, Ms. Beecher."

"Good morning, Your Honor."

"Okay, this case is up this morning to set a final hearing date on the petition for guardianship, of course it also was up on Monday to set a final hearing date on the petition for guardianship, but while we were here trying to get some work done, in this courtroom without windows, Mr. Hanneman was working on his tan in the turquoise waters of the Caribbean Sea, so we weren't able to make much progress, although, to her credit, Ms. Topinka tried."

"Yes, I apologize…"

"We did agree on one day for the hearing though, did we not?"

"It might be a long day," said Mr. Hanneman.

"I have no problem putting in long days, do you, Mr. Hanneman?"

"No, Your Honor."

"Mr. Hurley?"

"No, Judge."

"Okay, so," he said looking at his red calendar book, "I'm looking at the first full week of September, I could do Tuesday, the 4th, which is the day after Labor Day, or Wednesday, the 5th, if that works for you."

Mr. Hanneman, looking at his calendar book, "Wednesday, the 5th, would be better for me, Judge."

"Mr. Hurley?"

"Whatever, Judge."

"Works for me," said Ms. Beecher.

"Okay, we'll set aside one day, September 5, at 10 a.m., for a final evidentiary hearing on the petition. This date will not be continued, for any reason," the judge said, looking at Mr. Hanneman.

"Understood," said Mr. Hanneman.

"I take it your position has not changed since Monday?" the judge asked Billy.

"Well, as a matter of fact, I was thinking about that."

"Were you? Well, this would be a good time to do that, it would also be a good time to let us know your intentions."

"I'm sorry, Your Honor, I wish I could let you know for sure one way or the other, I guess all I can say at the moment is that, well, I may be having second thoughts."

Ms. Beecher looked up at Billy.

"Second thoughts? About what?"

"About challenging the petition."

Ms. Beecher tried to suppress a smile.

Mr. Hanneman fluttered, looked at the judge with something to say, which the judge noticed, but ignored.

"I see, well, that certainly is your right," the judge said, considering the news. "Will that have any effect on the time set aside for the hearing?" he said to Mr. Hanneman.

"Well, it certainly could," Mr. Hanneman replied, "I mean, this is the first that any of us, certainly my clients, have heard that Mr. Hurley might care about his children at all, let alone consider taking responsibility for them, and frankly," his temper rising, "given everything, his past and all, the notion is nothing less than outrageous…"

"Well, if it's that clear cut, it shouldn't affect the presentation of your case," the judge said to Mr. Hanneman.

"Well, no, but if Mr. Hurley or his non-existent lawyer intend to present witnesses, we will need to cross examine them."

"Have you given any thought to that, Mr. Hurley, if you were to challenge the petition, do you intend to call any witnesses?"

Billy shrugged his shoulders,

"Not really, I guess I'd be the only one."

Mr. Hanneman shaking his head, exasperated.

"Yes, and I take it, you, in all likelihood, intend to call Mr. Hurley as an adverse witness anyway, Mr. Hanneman?"

"In all likelihood, Your Honor."

"Well, then, should Mr. Hurley make up his mind to act like an adult for the first time in this case, to have a say in nothing less than the future of his own children, it appears that may not have an appreciable effect on the time needed to present the evidence in this case, although, I must say, Mr. Hurley, your delay in doing so, your uncertainty all along, and your prior statements to this court on the matter have been duly noted."

"You look upset, Mr. Hanneman," the judge said, "do you believe you will need more time?"

"Well, Your Honor, we thought we needed two days as it was, and now this?"

"Do you want more time?"

Mr. Hanneman did not want more time, he wanted this case over with, he was a business litigator, he didn't do guardianships, he was only doing this case as a favor for Dick Walsh, whose company he'd represented for years, he thought this guardianship matter beneath him, this court, this judge, Dick Walsh had been a pain in the ass about this case from the beginning, like he was forced into it somehow, by his wife maybe, always harping about the fees, no, he had to get rid of this case.

"No, we do not want more time," Mr. Hanneman said affirmatively. "Mr. Hurley has no case, the idea that he could act responsibly for the first time in his life, as a father no less, to two five-year-old children he has endangered and criminally neglected is preposterous, and we could prove that in ten minutes time."

The judge looked down at Billy.

"Mr. Hurley, I must admonish you, this is not a game, this is a very serious matter."

"I understand that, Your Honor."

"Well then, we have a date, and that date will not be continued. Depending on how the trial goes, we can always add a day somewhere down the line if it looks like we may need to, but I don't see any reason to do that based on what I have heard today. Mr. Hanneman, prepare the order."

"Yes, Your Honor, thank you."

"Don't thank me. Next case."

Ms. Beecher walked with Billy through the swinging gate, out the door, and into the hallway outside the courtroom.

"What's got into you?" she asked him.

"I may have seen the light."

"How'd that happen?"

"You'd never believe it."

Billy couldn't make the trip back that afternoon. He was exhausted, after two nights of little to no sleep. He went back to the condo after the hearing, had no qualms about laying down on his father's bed, and slept until five o'clock that afternoon. Seriously dazed, he proceeded to settle, with conviction, into the bottle of Basil Haden his father had left in the liquor cabinet, on the rocks, cardinal sin, perhaps, but that's how he liked it, savored it, felt the clean crisp warmth nestle in his bones, the sleep, the bourbon, easing the hard edges, the world softening, would be his last night here on the twenty-third floor, forever, next day he'd be on his way home, to Mona, and he smiled, first time in four days, forget about all this, for a while anyway, until he had to decide, but not tonight, a reprieve in order, tonight, well deserved, a little let go, not the reckless abandon of old days, never again, but a measured alteration, good for the mind, a different state, a different view, see the same things, differently, throw it in the mix and see how it comes out, alongside the anger, and the hurtling drive, step back, slow down, savor, notice the sailboats along the horizon, the amblers, the lovers along the shore, revery, memories, his mother in this very chair, dying, thinking of him, as he now thought of her, working on the bottle, fading away, minute by minute, hour by hour, high-rise darkness creeping across the shore, the lake, the clouds, the gray light falling, city lights twinkling against brown stone, the constant flow of traffic around the Oak Street curve, and into the Magnificent Mile canyon.

When the light was gone, Billy in darkness, again, the bottle almost empty, Billy turned on the lamp that sat on the end table next to the love seat he had melted into, the light falling on the papers left there, the file from his father's desk, Tribune, Gold Coast News, Chicago Magazine. Billy picked up the file, flipped through the pages, came to the one page from the legal pad, with his dad's scribbling, the hieroglyphics, picked it up, the words fuzzy, his head swimming, made less sense than ever, "Grenade," his dad throwing a grenade, hilarious, "- Ald. Prerogative," Aldermanic Prerogative, not surprised his dad put that number one, makes the world, City Hall at least, go round, "Bench - Elected," no surprise there either, how they controlled the courts, he liked number nine, "- Committeemen, "first thing we do...," Committeemen always came first, and then came "D&P," well, he knew now what that was all about, didn't seem to belong on the list, though, didn't really want to think about it, made his head hurt, enough to know no one'll ever know what his dad had in mind, what he took it to his grave.

He returned the papers to the file, something lighter would do, saw the Gold Coast News, pure fluff, perfect, glossy photos, lawsuits over obstructed lake views, outcry over dog excrement, new art gallery opening, charitable galas, whole pages with photos of attendees, fur coats and diamonds and bright polished faces, CEOs and bimbos, cufflinks and plastic surgery, a gala at the Field Museum for muscular dystrophy, Com Ed's chairman and his lovely wife, Mayor Jefferson and his wife, smiling broadly before African elephants in the Great Hall, Ameritech's President and his wife, three fit laughing blondes from the organizing committee in sleeveless black dresses spilling drinks, and a number of lovely photos of the upper crust having just a wonderful evening raising money for a good cause, God bless them, every one of them, Billy smiling, about to turn the page, when, in the bottom left hand corner, he thought he saw someone he recognized, yes, it was, a photo of the Building Commissioner of the City of Chicago, none other than Johnny Jefferson, the mayor's son, Billy's old classmate, in a smart black tuxedo, with an attractive woman at his side, mugging for the camera, and Billy started laughing, thinking about his last meeting with Johnny in City Hall, thinking the photograph proof that Johnny really had arrived, and looking down at the caption, identifying the happy couple, as Building Commissioner Johnny Jefferson, and his wife, Viola Jones.

Wait. Viola Jones? *The* Viola Jones? Billy, stunned. Is she, no, is Johnny, Gusman's partner? But would Gusman do a deal with a Young Turk, a parvenu, like Johnny, there's no way, no, it must be, Billy looked up at the top of the page, at the photograph of the mayor and his wife, holy shit, Billy thought, it's the mayor, Gusman's partner is the goddam mayor, the trail from the warehouse leads to the mayor's door.

CHAPTER EIGHT

The Return

Time to go home, finally, Billy cleaning up, making the bed, scanning the rooms, removing all traces, crumbs, everything in place, except the file, he would take that, and the Gold Coast News, those he placed in his backpack, getting excited now, ready to go, when the telephone rang.

"This Billy?"

"Yeah," Billy replied, cautiously.

"Billy, this is Deputy Sheriff Walters, in Iowa County."

"Yeah?"

"Sorry to bother you, but the sheriff wanted me to give you a call."

"Okay."

"The sheriff was wondering if you were coming back any time soon, he's got something to show you."

"What is it?"

"Don't know exactly, but he found something, up at your property."

"I'm not a suspect again, am I?"

Laughter.

"No, nothing like that."

"Well, actually, I'm coming back today. Will it take long?"

"No, not at all, what time you getting back?"

"Should be up by three o'clock this afternoon. I could meet you there, before heading home, if that works for Walt."

"That'll be good, we'll see you up on top of the hill around three. Thanks."

Wonder what that's about, on the way, though, no big deal. Be good to get back on the hill, after this week, appropriate really, from here to there. How many times since he was a boy, his folks up front, he and Lola, his little Cockapoo, in the back seat, all packed up, leaving the big city for the big sky, the wide open, the tall hill and high grass, like a magnet, pulling them back to where they belonged. Soon as they got in the car, of one mind, single purpose, escape into their other selves, true selves, where even his father was bearable, different man, one and only place they got along, a family, from the time they got in the car, to the time they left the hill to come home, never the same, each time, the sun, the wind, the heat, the cold, the rain, the hail, the snow, the fog, the clouds, the stars, the storms, the moon, the rainbows, the mosquitoes, the river, the turkey, the deer, the goldenrod, the hawks, the coyotes, the fires, never the same, each time an adventure, and it was the setting off that was best, the exhilaration, expectation, knowing paradise was waiting at the end of the road, just miles away. Nothing like it, Billy thought, as he looked around his dad's condo one last time, the sun glistening on the lake, and had to admit, little bit of home actually, this time around, little solace, might even miss this place, but he was more than ready, ready to go, hop on his bike and take a long ride on a sunny day, into the country, to the arms of his bride, his new family, his home.

"Hello?"

"Hey, darlin."

"Your alive!"

"You have no idea."

"How've you been, when are you coming home?"

"On my way shortly, can't wait to get home."

"Oh, I have missed you so! Stay out of trouble?"

"Well, I got into some, to tell you the truth."

"Should I be scared?"

"No, no, it's okay, no big deal. Spent a couple of days lookin' into those papers Dorothy showed me that day in my dad's office, found some interesting stuff, pissed somebody off, had to go spelunking, but that's all over now, at least I think it is anyway, more importantly, I'm heading home."

"Spelunking, in Chicago?"

"City's full of surprises. I'll tell you all about it."

"Please be safe, and be careful in all that traffic."

"I will."

"What's your timing, so I'll know when to get worried?"

"No need for that, leaving now, should be up sometime around three, but I got a call from Walt's deputy. Walt wants to see me at the Property for something, so I'm gonna stop by there first, shouldn't take long, I'll be home right after that."

"What's that about?"

"Just something they want to show me, won't take long, I'll see you around three-thirty or four."

"Okay, are you really going to be in my bed tonight?"

"For better or worse."

"Better, much better, Billy, love you."

"Love you, too, see you soon."

Billy took one last look around, said goodbye to the memory of his mom and dad, and closed the door on the lovely view from the twenty-third floor for the very last time.

He took the elevator down to the basement, stepped into the garage, hopped on his bike and revved up the Moto Guzzi, loud bouncing echoes off cinder block walls. He shifted into first, steered up the garage ramp into the summer morning light, shifted into second, and roared away, Gold Coast brownstones, State Parkway to Division Street, where he turned left, away from the lake, heading west, through the empty after of Division Street bars in the morning, past Sandburg Village, La Salle Street, Cabrini Green, world unto itself, beehive of tall faceless brown slabs and open lots, scattered graffiti and gangs and families and lives lived and shots in the night, in shadows of sleek opulence blocks away. The sun bright, warm, perfect, blue sky, open, pointing the way to the interstate, concrete stilts, evacuation highway, on ramp to heaven, shifting into third up onto the roadway, five lanes of coursing blood, in one direction, five lanes the other, semis and taxis, Beemers and scrap metal pickup trucks, sharing random anonymous moments together, speeding off to different destinations. Shifting into fourth, the power, the merge, off and away to the north, the spires of Oz towering along the shore behind him, John Hancock, Amoco, Sears Tower, where Marshall Chapman sat looking out his seventieth floor window, City Hall, where Dorothy sat over her typewriter in sadness, the Rookery Building, where Ms. Beecher pored over a legal pad, the building on Randolph Street, where Sydney Black sat chewing his finger nails, the Daley Civic Center, where Judge Wozak scolded another counsellor, and all the doctors and lawyers and receptionists and traders in their funny coats and bankers and secretaries and investment advisers and bureaucrats and judges and business men and women all working away in their little spaces in tall buildings crowded together, rubbing shoulders, jostling, for a little piece of the sky, all the elevated lines circling the Loop, and rumbling subways, and commuter trains snaking in and out of Union Station, North Western Station, back and forth all day and night, all behind him now, as he sped away up the interstate, blending in, joining the flow of combustible engines, on the move, signs to Wisconsin, away from the great city on the Great Lake.

Heading up Interstate 94, past Morton Salt, the Budweiser sign, Billy looked down at the streets lining the Chicago River on its way downtown, Clybourn on the west, Kingsbury on the east, industrial, perfect, for the nameless clubs and bars, warehouse dance floors, cutting edge, young, privileged, elites, loud music, low lights, slithering numbing late night after hours hallucinating somnolence. Coke, 'ludes, anything you want, bathroom open for business, bizarre bazaar, right before the end, he and Jenny, first name basis, with everyone, if they could remember, from night to night, that was the challenge, kids somewhere, second thought, higher calling, riding the crest of a new wave, way high, drowning in collective cool, days only for nights, till the sun rose. Better he can't remember now, all just a daze of wasted nights, he thought, eons ago it seemed, behind him, everything changed, he thought, as he rode away, toward the parting of the sea, Kennedy to O'Hare or Edens north.

Traffic slowing, downshift, always congested, bumper to bumper, Billy's Moto Guzzi, dwarfed, exposed, among tractor trailers and mastodon buses. Billy hugged the left lane, slowed to a crawl, taking the fork to Interstate 90, toward O'Hare, bogged down in irrefutable proof of excess, when just three miles due east from where the great river of traffic split in two, his old neighborhood nestled, quiet, tree-lined, single family, Gardens they called it, hugging the North Branch of the Chicago River, languid, sluggish, flowing past Billy's backyard, the regal Georgian, wooden back deck at the edge of the water, where he learned to walk, fish, smoke cigarettes, get high, and squander life. Raised to be his father, which he never was, or would be, reserved, withdrawn, preferred shadows, perpetually embarrassed, of everything, Ward Nights, one heartache after another, too much information, too personal, depressing, ashamed to listen, the hard metal chair, all he could remember was the hard metal chair, and the Old Man's picture, could have been Stalin, watching over everything. He couldn't go to school at Waters, two blocks away, no, he had to go to Latin, seven miles away, and back, every day, where he didn't belong anyway, for twelve years, Latin, where all the rich kids went, what his father wanted him to be, what his father didn't see, political hack's son, what they thought, the parents, dismissive patronizing smiles, the distance, as did their kids, as they got older, learned the truth about life, castes, cliques, the inside, and out, the fringes, where Billy hung, with Black kids from Cabrini on scholarship, with Dexter, best friend all through grade school, inseparable, making fun of what they could never have, lots of money, someone he could tell how he really felt, about those godawful fundraisers, or that trip to City Hall with his dad in fourth grade. All dressed up in a suit and tie, mortified, show him around, this is my son, dad's debtors, everyone, fawning, tripping over themselves to shake his little hand, looking at the floor, tousled hair, hearty laughs, dad's footsteps eh?, big shoes to fill, ha, ha, ha, narrow little shoulders, crumbling, dying to melt in the floor, tears welling, and then up, to the fifth floor, the Old Man, into the abyss, the imposing desk, like you to meet the Old Man, no handshake left, just tears, the Old Man looking at his dad, puzzled, and his dad all quiet on the ride home, let down. All of which Dexter heard, but could not understand, shunning opportunity, notoriety, give me some of that, let me run with it, hanging with somebody famous, don't get much of that at Cabrini.

Don't get out your violins, Billy thought, traffic starting to move once they hit Bryn Mawr, pathetic really. Dexter was right, Billy had it made, house on the river, Latin School, loving mother, powerful dad. Billy didn't know why he didn't take to it, not so much rebellion, as status quo, it just wasn't in him, from the get go, just not a back slapper, go getter, never would be. He and his dad, night and day, dad didn't get it, never would, mother got it, hoped it would change, false hope, he thought, as he picked up speed, shifted into fifth, and sped up the Kennedy toward O'Hare, silver jumbo airplanes roaring overhead against the blue sky, one after another, back across the Great Lake to the east, floating down upon runways, taxiing forever to crowded gates.

At the O'Hare junction, Billy took the Interstate 90 ramp left as it swung around to the north under the Wisconsin sign, and he was officially away, the city giving way to suburbs, mostly the same but for the names. As Billy got older and his father more powerful, Billy started questioning, everything, why was it that way, why were people so poor when classmates lived in mansions, why were the people in power all White, and men, why was one neighborhood so different than another, in the same city, why did his school have brand new everything, when Englewood had nothing, why did judges take money, why were all the African Americans in jail, why did all the White men put them there, why did anybody who wanted to run for office have to kiss his dad's ring, why didn't anybody want to change anything, what did his dad stand for, what was it all about? He and Dexter used to talk about it a lot, Dexter the realist, that's the way it was, Billy the idealist, but why does it have to be, what could it be, back and forth on the back deck over the river. It was all about more, and less, Billy thought, hoarding chits, keeping it in the family, the neighborhood. The point was not to enlarge the pie, just a bigger slice, zero sum, winners and losers, life, who got what, all dinosaurs, the Fifties, Billy thought, inside the box, fixed, and anyone with an idea of different, change, reform, watch out, suspect, because you can't take the chance, of losing anything, you just never know what might happen, best to keep everything as it is, preserve the way of life, the machine, eat idealists for breakfast, not an inch, an opening, and everything will stay the same, if not better, for us, and them?, well, that's life.

Billy had a little more room to move, to breathe, as he rode into the no man's land of exurbia, real estate playground, what it looks like when you let real estate developers decide how people should live, which they did, homes and buildings, in shapes and sizes and laid out with one goal in mind, how to make a buck for people who would never live there, and those who did, means to the end of an entrepreneur's dream. Cornfields and farmland into shopping malls and parking lots, and endless rows of identical townhouses, and white garage doors, front and center, indistinguishable office complexes, built in phases, high-voltage power stations, no pedestrians anywhere, having moved from where they could walk or take the El anywhere to where they could get nowhere without a car, crossing four lane highways, sixteen to an intersection, strip malls with high-end restaurants next to laundromats, warmth, style, charm, comfort, the human condition, just not priorities. It was best to zoom by at sixty-five miles an hour on an interstate highway going somewhere else, to the Fox River, just ahead, rampart of the open fields beyond, gateway to the country, six lanes to four, few travelers left, heading northwest, highway to himself, aware of the sun, the sky, first time since leaving the garage, liberated, free, at home.

At this point of the trip, with his mom his dad and Lola, invariably, his mom would sigh, heavily, her trademark, lifting the weight of the world off her shoulders, in a deep breath, shedding her city skin, and Lola would sigh with her, the two girls, having crossed the mighty Fox, the Rubicon, the big city girl, subconsciously relieved at the bustle's passing, assuming her new role, a peace in herself she was surprised to have found, thanks to her husband, who had helped her find it. Billy's mom never got mad, just disappointed, and he had disappointed her, he knew, a lot, but she didn't dwell in the past, and wouldn't want him to, always held out hope, for him, and her husband, even at the end, the two of them, whom she dearly loved, together, and so far apart. But on these trips, mostly together, which is why she loved the journeys, the Property, their other world, why she sighed when she crossed the Fox, why she slept so soundly in the cabin, with her husband and son close by, wishing it were forever so, and knowing too well it was not, knowing it was her fault, her Catholic guilt, martyrdom, knowing her son would never be like his father, knowing he was too much like her, leave well enough alone, back seat, satisfied, needing little, striving less, accepting, not judging, honest to a fault, if there is such a thing, never seeking power, control, never wanting to dominate, never wanting more, never needing more, always you first. Yes, he was very much like her, without her virtues, Billy thought, as he sped through cornfields stretching to the horizon on either side of the highway, up toward and past Rockford, to Beloit, where, of all places, God's country began, leaving the interstate behind, for the country roads and long broken hypotenuse northwest.

The Council Wars were hard on Billy's mom because she knew they were hard on Billy. By the time he and his classmates reached their freshman year at Latin they were no longer children, they all knew too well who Billy's father was, read about him in the papers, at kitchen tables in lakefront liberal homes, pulling for Mayor Williams, vilifying the twenty-nine, racial politics, demon of our worst natures, polarizing, playing out on the ten o'clock news, pictures of Billy's father, White, smug, with his band of white-hooded aldermen in control, keeping the usurpers down, and Billy, son of the grand master, painted with the same brush, pariah, Dexter, best friend, turned his back, Billy didn't blame him, ashamed, sharing their disdain. The game for Billy's father was Billy's nightmare, and he never saw it, Billy thought, never cared enough to see it, all about him, and his fucking power trip, all press is good press, same old same old, quest for more, for him, and his White cronies. And so Billy drifted, to his mom's chagrin, toward the fringes, the outcasts, the tortured, the troubled, cigarettes and black leather jackets, on whom parents had given up, rebels without causes, the only ones left who'd have anything to do with him, and in their self-righteous banishment Billy found a belonging, an outlet, a way of life, an edge to explore, with drugs, and trips no one else was cool enough to understand, or so they thought. And his dad was so busy, so oblivious to what really was going on, that by the time he threw Billy's weed stash across the living room in Billy's junior year, Billy could only smile, his dad not knowing the half of it, dealing weed out of his locker at school, doing coke on weekends, getting blasted with friends, loving every minute of it, and caring less and less about anything else. Like school, which he didn't have time for, avoiding expulsion by his dad's intercessions, served him right, Billy thought, let him suffer for the harm he's done, let him deal with the cops after Bob the doorman snitched on Billy's New Year's Eve party at the condo his senior year, let him feel important that he could sweep it under the rug, do it for his son, when he did it for himself.

Billy took Highway 213 northwest out of Beloit, past young men slouching on picnic tables outside Dog World, clapboard houses in need of repair, pretty little gardens, the Mouse Tavern, the city limits, and beyond, where the country road opened, motorcycle dream, twisting and turning, rising and falling, over hills, through woods, long banks around farmer's fields, row after row of sturdy deep green corn stalks with golden tassels reaching for the sun, glowing down American Gothic across the heartland through which Billy passed, cleansing, therapeutic, north out of Orfordville, through little Magnolia, and up to the cozy homes of Evansville, about a half-hour south of Madison.

Billy's folks thought school in Madison would be a welcome change of pace, turn a leaf, wholesome, didn't know about the Days of Rage, but it was four, no five more years of the same, if not worse, school a distraction, a bother, the parties, a gas, and Billy didn't miss many. Billy had a great time in Madison, he just couldn't remember most of it. At various times, he lived at Witte, on Doty, Regent, Jennifer, Johnson, above the liquor store on State, Mifflin, Gorham, Bassett, Dayton, spent most of his time at the Plaza, 602 Club, Red Shed, Paul's Club, Flamingo, Stillwater, Cardinal Bar, concerts at the Orpheum, tended bar part time at the Church Key, then full time, where he met Jenny Walsh, the night she passed out on the bar. To say he had any kind of major overstates the case, more flopped around, majoring in classes frequented by large defensive linemen, cobbling together enough credits to graduate with a 2.1 grade point, honors in gaming the system. Winter breaks, spring breaks, hook ups with his old buddies at Latin, out late, sleeping all day, uppers to party, downers to sleep, way of life, back to school, and forth, then no back at all, summers in Madison, beers on the Terrace, parties at the Property, on the hill, bonfires and hell raising, the night he drove his car off the road into Parsons' field, the glorious May Day selling juiced Kool-Aid at the Mifflin Street Block Party, ruined by badges, God that must have been fun, if he could only remember.

What he did remember, only too well, was Jenny, Jenny Walsh. The night he helped her home, tall, willowy, angelic, with her cheek pressed hard against the bar, vulnerable, elegant train wreck, scattering pretty pieces of herself all over town, oblivious to those in her wake, gathering them up for her, returning them to her, pieces she no longer recognized, pieces she couldn't replace, kept in a little wooden box atop her dresser, overflowing lost mementos of her discarded life. Jenny, the shooting star, with satellites, an orbit, an aura, a magnet for the star struck, the It girl of State Street, darling of the homeless, the down and out, indiscriminate lover, of every moment, every day, every night, and anyone. But Billy had an upside, the Chicago connection, something she needed, of home, free drinks a plus, they were kindred souls, from the same place, going nowhere fast, and he was tall, and good looking, and a mess, just like she was, and if love can exist in a state of stupor, then they were lovers, without strings, limits, promises, or expectation. So that when Jenny Walsh got pregnant, a month before Billy finished school, she just looked at him, sitting on the edge of her bed, sad, far away, hopeless, Madison, her youth, her beauty, slipping away, and from somewhere deep inside, maybe his mother, his father, something somewhere he had learned, Billy knew what he had to do, knowing there were others, that he didn't know for sure, that she didn't know, but it didn't matter, he put his arm around her and said he'd take care of her, and she cried on his shoulder, because somewhere inside of her, her mother, her father, she knew she was going to have this baby, and become a mother, if she only could.

Billy and Jenny left their lives in Madison, but their lives in Madison never left them. After they moved into a one bedroom on Goethe Street in Old Town, his dad's dime, they both straightened up, for a while, for the baby's sake, Billy's mom, Jenny's mom, supportive, their dads, rolling eyes, disgusted. Billy and Jenny still drank, smoked cigarettes, got high, but no pills, warped cold turkey. Billy started driving a Marathon cab for the Yellow Cab Company, Jenny found a job around the corner behind a cash register at a Wells Street porn shop, and they existed, uneasily, bursting at the seams, craving the let go, let loose, holding on, to each other, hanging by threads, not much longer, the ultrasound, twins, double the reason, double the effort, the delivery, miraculous, healthy babies, blond boy, Sam, blonde girl, Kate, to tired, withered parents, leaving the hospital for Jenny's mom's house in Bridgeport, and, after three days, Jenny back on her feet, the kids safe, Billy and Jenny on a binge three days straight, surfacing after they ran out of money.

And it went on like that for two years, off and on, the precipice and back, Billy's mom, Jenny's mom, grandmas, back and forth, to and from Old Town, keeping an eye, always in touch, prayers at Sunday Mass, for their kids, grandkids, please God, give them the strength, show them the way, God wasn't listening. It was a cold February night when Billy and Jenny dropped Sam and Kate off at Jenny's mom's for a night of clubbing, regular circuit, Clybourn, Kingsbury, denizens of kaleidoscopic dark, throbbing, pounding, electronic music, everybody sniffling, flying, Oak Street beach for sunrise, proud parents return to Bridgeport, in Billy's cab, buzzing internal breakneck speed, crawling walls in the rooms of the bungalow on Lowe Street, picking up Sam, Kate, soft, beautiful, into the cab, little too high this time, even they know that, know what to do, need to settle, calm down, be responsible, Quaalude maybe, on the way to get diapers, just the thing, and kicking in, big time, as Billy pulled the cab into the Jewel parking lot.

The rest of the story, read all about it, first page, banner headlines, kids in the back seat, crying, Billy and Jenny passed out, titillating, dirty laundry, everybody loves a privileged kid gone bad story, what they deserved, in spades. Jenny, leaving the hospital, unsteady, straggly hair hanging over her face, Billy, the district station, smirking, at them, the cameras, the show, playing the role for them, derisive object, cut to size for ratings, mighty fallen, those are the best, the fourth estate, playing its own game, nothing's on the level, Dan and Nell futzing with the car seats, for shame, for shame, give the people what they want.

Jenny went to live with her mom for a week, then disappeared, Billy hung around long enough to plead guilty to a reduced child neglect charge, entered by a judge indebted to his dad, represented by a lawyer paid by his dad, all good, under the circumstances, except that little detail the lawyer didn't think Billy's dad needed to know about, Billy barred from contact, until further order of court, bad enough, painful enough as it was, details didn't matter, big picture clear enough, broadcast on the ten o'clock news, all just as well, whose son?, my son?, what son?

Billy took the back road from Evansville to Belleville, same route he'd taken when he ran away, for the only other place he'd known, Wyoming Township, Lone Rock, and the one room apartment above the bar at the Mad House Inn, his great escape, right on 92 outside Belleville, skirting Primrose, high atop the ridge with a view of Blue Mounds, blue whales floating on the green horizon in the distance, where Governor Dodge and his militia rested, hunting Black Hawk, and then down into the watershed, to Mount Vernon, west to 78, then north to 18, running west out of Madison to the Mississippi, getting close now, Lola would have started to whimper.

Called his mom a few times after, but even those calls stopped, and it was just as well, to be cut off, from everything, his parents, that life, drugs, never again, one good thing anyway, alone with his mess of a life, adrift, insular, underground, in a town time had forgotten, the new leaf his parents had hoped for, way too late. Got a job at Ray's. No surprise there. Billy had the perfect resume, no job history, no training, no experience, shitty grades, criminal record, no money, no hobbies, down and out, nowhere to go. Ray would have hired him even had Ray not known Billy's dad, Ray's kind of guy, heads up whenever Billy's dad came around, went on like that more than a year, until that one time, by mistake, the last knock-down drag-out.

Usually Billy's dad would call Ray to let him know he was coming, not this time. He drove the Eldorado into the parking lot after the long ride, walked into the bar, asked Ivy if Ray was around, told he'd be right back, ordered a drink, and went out on the back deck overlooking the river, weekday, early afternoon, no one else around, at the same time his bedraggled son dragged a canoe out of the water onto the beach. Didn't even recognize him at first, his hair longer, dirty jeans, looked like a bum. Recognized him. Was a bum. Sat down. Just watched him, hauling the canoe across the gravel, until Billy looked up, saw his dad, and froze.

"See you got yourself a good job," Dan Hurley yelled down the hill.

Billy didn't answer, kept dragging the canoe.

"Nice to know all that money I spent on your college education paid off," he shouted at his son.

"What do you want?"

"Nothing from you, I'm here to see Ray."

"Good."

But Dan Hurley couldn't help himself. He set down his drink and walked down the hill toward Billy and the canoe, Ivy now watching from the window.

"What the hell is wrong with you?"

Billy dropped the canoe, took one step back.

"I said, what the hell is wrong with you?" Dan Hurley hollered, coming down the hill.

"Seen your kids lately?"

Billy ignored it.

"Didn't even come to your mom's funeral."

"You told me not to."

"That's not what I told you. I told you the only one who wanted to see you was dead. And that was true."

"Same thing."

"No, it's not the same thing. She was your mother; you didn't even show your last respects."

"I did, my own way."

"What, sniffing coke up your nose?"

"I don't do that anymore."

Dan Hurley started laughing.

"Like that'll be the day."

"What do you want from me?"

"How about a little respect?" Dan Hurley yelled, pleaded.

How did it come to this, from the proud day the kid was born, to this, crushed with purple rage, and the hollow, stricken sadness of loss, his wife, the son he loved, despised, the cruelty of fate, leading to this, his whole life, what was left of it, in this place, of all places.

Billy just stared at his dad.

"I did everything I could for you," Dan Hurley said to his son.

"Oh, give me a break, you did it for *you*," Billy said with disgust. "It was always about you, mom and me, we were props, it was your show, your life, what's best for you, the Old Man, your cronies and fat cats, more for us, long live the machine, fuck everybody else, fuck anybody who wasn't like us, all that bullshit clout, greed, your pinky rings and backrooms, smoke and mirrors, it was all bullshit, it was all selfish bullshit."

"You don't know," Dan Hurley said, defensively.

"I know what I saw."

"It was about helping people."

"You helped yourselves."

"We got people jobs."

"So they would vote for you."

"Jesus, we ran one of the biggest cities in the world!"

"And who'd you do that for? At whose expense? It was all a game for you. Did you ever ask yourself why? Why did it mean so much to you? Who was it all about? Did you ever ask yourself that? Of course not. You never cared enough to ask why. Maybe you weren't smart enough. Maybe that was your problem."

"Not smart enough? You little shit. Not smart enough?"

"Ever think through that whole White supremacist thing? And how'd that work out for you? Ever give one thought to how that might have affected us? Ruined my life, your reputation, that's all. But you didn't give a shit, you were having too much fun playing your goddam games."

"Yeah, sure, if I were as smart as you, I'd be dressed like a bum living in a shit hole schlepping canoes for a living. If I were as smart as you, I'd do a bunch of drugs, and pass out with my kids crying and hungry in the back of a car. If I were more like you, I wouldn't go to my mother's funeral, I'd run away, and turn my back on my own kids."

Billy had nothing to say to that.

Dan Hurley turned to walk away, but this was his son, his only child, and after several steps up the hill, he turned back around.

"You know, it's easy to blame me for all of, this," he said waving his arm at Billy, his life. "I didn't have a father to blame. Maybe that was my fault, too. I did the best I could. I wasn't perfect. But I did, and still do," he said, his voice cracking, "love my son, and his kids, who need a father," he said, with tears in his eyes. "And I know your mom felt the same way."

Those were the last words Billy heard from his father. Shame they came too late, Billy thought, as he rode due west in the early afternoon sun, legions of cumulus cotton, white against deep blue, floating softly across the Great Plains, riding the wind from the infinite beyond, to the horizon, overhead, and away, behind him to the east, over the Great Lake. Billy had learned a few things about his father since then. Pieces that didn't fit one dimensional contempt, anger, and derision, everything more complicated, than it seems. Billy stared up the road into the wind riding west on

Highway 18, and saw, for the first time, something different about his father as he walked away up the hill that day, something a little less sturdy, older, vulnerable, unlike him. Maybe noticed at the time, but too angry to see, as he saw now on a clear summer day. Could it be, his dad was asking why, Billy thought. Could that have been it, what he saw as his father walked away, what his father was doing with Reverend Simmons, that warehouse. Maybe he was smart enough, finally asked why, and didn't like the answer, unlikely, but maybe, maybe he had a plan, maybe he wanted to throw a wrench into the works, maybe a …, maybe a *grenade*, Billy thought, as he approached his exit, downshifted, and rode the ramp up toward Barneveld, his gateway to the Driftless.

Billy followed Highway T out of Barneveld, down off the high ridge, into a narrow valley, and turned onto a gravel road leading into the empty county park nestled at the bottom of the hill. He pulled up next to the open-air pavilion, shut off the engine, grabbed his backpack, and sat down on one of the picnic tables outside in the sun, looking out over the baseball field, the shade trees, monkey bars, pond, outcroppings on the far side of the road. He pulled the file out of the backpack, stuffed and wrinkled, and took out one page, the one entitled *Grenade*. Maybe it was the long ride, what he'd been thinking, maybe it was the full sun on the white page, the texture of the paper, his dad's handwriting, but he saw something on the page he had not seen before, something he might have misread, what he thought were dashes were now something different, something he'd read about in a logic class he'd almost flunked out of, something called a *tilde*, which had a meaning, of negation.

So that when his dad wrote the first item on the list "~ Ald. Prerogative," aldermanic prerogative referring to the corruptible power of aldermen to nix anything in their ward, the tilde represented the *negation* of aldermanic prerogative. That was heresy. Why would his dad write that? When he wrote "Bench ~ Elected; Merit," did he mean judges should no longer be elected, appointed based on merit? The third item "~ Patronage…," referring to the time-honored patronage system by which aldermen traded jobs for lifetime servitude, the tilde represented the *negation* of patronage. Had his dad lost his mind? Using the tilde, the fourth item, "Electds, Emplees ~ Govt business," meant that elected officials and government employees could *not* engage in government business, i.e. no more warehouses for Gusman. The fifth item probably meant to reform the Assessor's office, the seventh to change how bond counsel were appointed, item nine, "~ Committeemen, "first thing we do…," meant *no* committeemen, "first thing we do is kill all the" committeemen. The rest of it then made more sense, each rank in the police department had to reflect the racial percentage of the city, percentages of government contracts had to go to minorities, the infamous "D&P," and finally, "Press," he wanted to take his traitorous putsch to the press. Jesus, was it possible? What got into him? Was it a goddam manifesto? Dorothy said he might be having second thoughts, but this? Beyond belief, Billy thought, as he looked out at the clouds, the wrinkled piece of paper, his dad's manifesto, shaking in his fingers.

Billy stuffed the page and file into his backpack, hopped on the bike, and roared off down the two lane road, as it twisted and turned in the valley carved millennia ago, by rain and snow, flowing down towering ridges on either side into the stream now called Trout Creek, that ran alongside the country road, into the deep Driftless, so familiar, but now entirely different, as if for the first time, terra non-firma, blacktop buckling, plates, tectonic, shifting, scraping, turning his world view, his father, upside down, the resentment, the blame, that protected, nourished, and sustained him, now shaken, confused, no longer so clear, so easy, the key in the lock, the cell door open, a beginning, ending, fifty miles an hour, maelstrom of thought, gale force questions, possibilities, disbelief, buffeting the bike, his brain, up and over small rises, the valley disappearing, woods lining the shoulders, blocking the sun, close, thick, around the bend, when, out from the woods, to his right, a deer, a doe, suddenly leaped from the woods, onto the roadway, sensed the danger, skidded in fright, and bounded across the road, Billy, hard brakes, swerving, missing her hind legs by inches, and coming to a stop, between the mother, and two fawns, trembling, on the opposite shoulder.

Billy, shaking. Deep breath, Billy, and the fawns. Mother standing, nervously, on one side, fawns twitching, on the other, staring in fear at the strange loud animal in the middle of the road. Wasting no time, they bolted across, past Billy's front tire, and disappeared in an instant, with their mother, into the deep woods, gone, certain death, gone, without a trace. Billy pulled the bike slowly around the bend, to a straight stretch of road where the woods gave way on one side, brought the bike to a stop, and took a deep breath. One vehicle approaching in the opposite direction, around the curve, at the wrong time? All over, an ending, to be sure. One minute roiled by *his* life, *his* father, the world, the sun, the universe, revolving around *his* importance, the next, nothingness, the world, the sun, the universe, perfectly fine without him, not missing a beat, carrying on as if he never existed, another grain of sand, no funeral lies to tell, just hard truths, of a wasted life, Billy thought, as he caught his breath, grateful for the do-over, second chance, to make amends, and for starters, slow down, on a motorcycle in thick woods. Maybe a little focus on the here and now, instead of a past he couldn't change, Billy thought, little more careful now, as he steered up and down and around to Lower Wyoming Road, Far Look, and finally, Bear Creek, up and over ridges, in and out of tight green glens, red-tail hawks circling over silver silos, Holsteins in the fields, turkey vultures banking in the wind, the Moto Guzzi, humming alongside muddy creeks slithering toward the Wisconsin River, close now, closer to the Property, home.

At the turn onto Hill Top Road, he let out a small whine, a plaintive cry, as Lola would have whined, as they all did, every time, feral roots just up the road, over the creek, up the disappearing valley, ridges closing in, hugging the edge on the right, shoulder dropping off on the left, oak and birch crowding the road, tunnels of overhanging branches, down to one lane, no more room, around the bend, clinging, steep, and there, on the right, opening through the trees, hidden from view, cattle gate, moss-orange, lock and key, standing guard, patiently waiting to be opened, to welcome, with bow and flourish, grand entrance, the sanctum, kingdom, peace.

First to arrive, Billy opened the gate, left it open, for Walt, and rolled up the grass farm road along the edge of the ridge on his right, ravine falling deeply off to his left, past the first Buddha, peeking above the overgrowth, smiling, glad you could make it, and on, straight up, the ravine a chasm, ancient oak and beech, sanctuary, too steep to tame, through a shaft of branches, vines, climbing to the hard turn, the second Buddha, perched above the hairpin, benevolent, calm, praying for safe passage, rising, rushing, up and hard to the right, the bike spitting dirt and gravel back upon the road, past the Ford-150 tucked in the woods, a last climb, the last turn, out of the woods, the third Buddha, orange solstice glow, contemplative, and into the field, wide meadow, big sky, straight run up the hill, to the cabin reigning above, Petroglyph Man, welcoming hand, congratulations, we've been waiting for you, to return, to where you belong.

Billy hadn't mowed since his father died, no paths, hip high grass, wild, uncivilized. His dad loved mowing those paths, around the cabin, top of the hill, veranda, down to the Duffy's barn, through his dad's trees, standing tall, spruce and pine, up and to the right above the cabin, uniting the woods on either side of the field, Billy's job now, to carve the garden, tend the memories. Billy unlocked the cabin, took out the bent willow chair, settled it on the front porch, and took a seat, looking out across crowns of trees in the deep coulee below, cattle grazing on the sloping green field on the far ridge. Billy sat, waiting for Walt, wondering what was up, what it could be, didn't look like anybody'd been up here, Billy thought, no bent grass on the road coming up, no evidence of footsteps around the cabin, better get here soon, wanted to get home, waited ten minutes, come on, show on the road, antsy, got up to walk through the four rows of spruce and pine his father had planted, tended, grew up with, children, walking past the reclining Bodhisattva, through the passage of mighty spruce, soft path of golden needles and mushrooms underfoot, through the trees to the top of the hill, pushing a spruce branch aside, and there, at the very top, in a clearing among eight towering evergreens, north and south, stood Ganesh, always at the ready, looking east, west, always, sunrise and sunset, perch for songbirds, two heads are better, one for grace, one for dignity, holding out hope, for woman and mankind, all fine and good, Billy thought, squinting into the sun, but where the hell are those guys.

The same light blinding Billy glistened off the river, shone through the windows at Ray's Resort, and flooded the bar, Friday afternoon, beautiful day, regulars assuming their positions, Deano on his stool, waiting for the Camo boys to get off work.

"Hey Ivy, grab me a cold one," Deano called out.

"Give me a second," Ivy said, "I've gotta get some change," stepping out from behind the bar, out to the front desk, Mona on duty, weekend campers, checking in.

"So when's your man getting back? Is he ever coming back?" Ivy asked, exchanging twenties for singles in the till.

"He's coming back. He'll always come back,"

"If he has half a brain."

"He should be here any time now. He's probably already back, he's meeting Walt at the Property. Said Walt wanted to show him something,"

Mona said, printing out paper work, address, credit card, make of car, license, check out time, campers, waiting, keep 'em moving.

"Walt?"

"Yeah."

"You sure about that?"

"That's what he said."

"I don't think so."

"What do you mean?"

"Walt's out of town. He's in Montana."

"Well, he can't be in Montana if he's meeting Billy today on the hill."

"That's what I'm saying," said Ivy.

Mona stopped, transaction halted, camper impatient.

"You sure about that?"

"Well, his deputy, Johnny Walters? He was in last night, braggin', sayin' he was the new sheriff in town, cuz Walt left for Montana the day before."

Mona stared at Ivy, not for a minute suspecting Billy.

Ivy stared at Mona, suspecting Billy.

"Miss?" the camper asked.

"Is Deano at the bar?" Mona asked.

"Yeah," Ivy said.

"Tell him to take over the bar. You handle this crowd, I don't feel good about this," Mona said, and hurried into the back office.

"Oh, come on," the camper said, frustrated, looking at his wife.

"You can just fucking relax," Ivy said to him, "or you can find another place this late on a Friday afternoon."

Mona grabbed the phone and called the sheriff's office.

"Trudy, this is Mona, at Ray's, I need to speak to the deputy."

"Deputy Walters isn't in, Mona; he's tending to an accident out on Highway 14."

"Okay," Mona hesitated, afraid of the answer, "can I speak to Walt?"

"Walt's in Montana, Mona; he won't be back 'til next week. Is there something I can do for you?"

"No, thanks."

Mona hung up the phone, warding off panic, figure this out.

Would Billy lie to her? Ivy thought so. No way. Trusted him.

Then what?

Somebody called him, said they were Deputy Walters, and set up a meeting at the Property. She looked at her watch: three-thirty. Maybe already there. What did he say over the phone? Got into some trouble, pissed somebody off, looking at those goddam papers, and the last one who looked at those papers…

Mona ran out to the front desk.

"Ivy something's wrong, I think Billy might be in trouble, I gotta go, let Deano know."

"Where you going?"

Mona rushing out the door.

"To the Property," and she was off. Thought of taking her motorcycle, but the fastest way to the Property was upriver, as the crow flies, in her new boat. Deano saw Mona run out the glass door onto the back deck, he stood up off his stool, saw her run down the grassy hill and hop into her flat-bottomed Jon boat, fourteen foot, forty horses, jet outboard, brand new, wedding gift, to herself. Mona started the engine and took off, full throttle, plenty of wake, hell with the tubers, into the main channel, broad sweeping turn around a sandbar, heading fast upriver.

Billy turned from the Ganesh at the top of the hill, flanked by his father's trees, and took in the long view to the west, the horizon, into the sun, invasion of endless bulbous clouds floating toward him, little bit of paradise, all in all, had to hand it to his dad, credit where credit due, he might have fucked up a lot down there, but not here, here he got it right, here he proved there was hope, in his trees, his paths, his Buddhas, hope to the very end, here, where he probably saw the light, Billy thought, must have been, looking out on these far off ridges, this same way, from his trees, into a different world, of constant change, never the same, never too late, he might have thought, for change, to leave a mark, turn his old world upside down, never know, Billy thought, such a shame, what could have been. Billy forgot about Walt, as he made his way down from the top of the hill into the field, throngs of goldenrod, Queen Anne's lace, abounding, hitting stride, golden-white, swaying in the meadow breeze, past the fire pit, just over there, hidden from view, echoes of voices singing with blazed faces, a young boy and his dog, running through tall grass, fireworks, softballs, kites flying, silenced now, in death and regret, and hope, hope for the living, that they may find in themselves the reason, to strive, to give, themselves, to love their children, my children, Billy thought, maybe he could do that much, maybe he owed it to them, to his mother, his father, to Mona, maybe it wasn't all about him, after all.

Billy walked down through where the baseball field would have been, down what would have been the path, to the grassy veranda where the sunsets fall, where his father fell, tall oak either side of the wide meadow, total silence but for the wind, random whoosh of wings overhead, passing of day, but then, a sound, a rustle, down the steep hill, lying low, crawling, louder, tips of grass, dancing, together, over there, a man, camouflage, pops up, from goldenrod, stiffens, takes aim, a turkey, hidden, startled, leaps from the grass, Billy, frightened, steps back, the man aims, fires, a feathered arrow rips through the air, hurtling, slow motion, arrowhead, sharpened blade, razors, twirling, rushing, toward him, Billy falls backward, the arrow, zings above his shoulder, misses its mark, pierces the slope of the hill over Billy's head, and Tex Sweeney is off and running.

Billy, in shock, looks down at his chest, see if he's been hit, can't even tell, shaking, "Jesus Christ," looks back, sees the arrow, snaps to, scrambles to his feet, watches a tall man, in camouflage, bow strapped on his back, bounding through high grass down the hill toward the river, shock then fury, "son of a bitch," Billy yells out after him, loud enough for him to hear, echoes in the ravines, coming after you, you son of a bitch, and Billy takes off after the hunter of men, running down the steep hill toward the woods, reaching the fence, spreading the barbed wire, falling through, scraping his cheek, bleeding, racing into the woods, down the steep ravine, tracking the hunter, into the ravine, Billy trips, falls into the stones at the base of the ravine, sees Sweeney up ahead, running through the ravine toward the pine forest, which leads to the field, that opens out onto County C and the river just beyond.

Mona brought the boat to shore at a landing she and Billy used on day trips to the Property, saw another boat tied to a tree forty yards away, scrambled up the bank, ran through a stretch of woods up to the road, across the road, across a field, into the pine forest at the edge of the deep hollow where the ravine emptied at the base of the Property's ridge, she darted through rows of pine, came around a bend, and, out of nowhere, ran headlong, into Tex Sweeney, running like a madman through the woods, Sweeney absorbed the blow, kept his balance, kept running, Mona flattened, wind knocked out of her, Billy rushing up, confused, at Mona in the woods, Sweeney getting away.

Billy bent down to Mona, a lump in soft pine needles.

"My God, did he hurt you?" Billy gasped, out of breath.

Mona looked up at her husband.

"Come on, let's get him," she said, reaching out an arm, Billy pulling her up, and they hightailed after Sweeney, dodging through pine trees, into the field, Sweeney, up ahead, racing across the road, leaping into the woods on the far side, Billy and Mona running, losing ground, through the field, Sweeney in his boat, and off, downriver, Billy and Mona across the road, into the woods, to the landing, into the boat, and the race was on.

Sweeney had a head start, and there were two of them and one of him, but Mona had a forty-horse outboard, and Sweeney a twenty-five, and Mona knew the river, knew to read the ripples, the main channel, stay out of the shallows, avoid the sandbars, but Sweeney was no fool, he knew the river, too, if he could get to Bakken's pond, slough morass, hidden channels, he could ditch the boat he stole, get to his truck, and get the hell out of there, and he could make it, he thought, measuring the distance, his lead, looking back over the engine, over the waking waves, at the prow of Mona's boat, they're gaining, but I can make it, Sweeney thought, as he aimed for deep water, swerved past canoes, swearing at him, steered through pilings of the Highway 23 bridge, and into a broad sweeping bend in the river, from the north to the west, a broad sandbar hugging the inside of the curve on the north bank, affording a long view upriver from the pine trees at the edge of the resort, where Deano now sat, watching, from his Tracker boat.

Deano tended bar only as long as he had to, and as soon as one of the Camo boys showed up, he'd sprinted to the shore. Ivy said the words, "trouble," the "Property," and "Billy," in the same sentence, he had seen Mona run and jump into her boat and take off at a clip, and he knew what he had suspected all along, so he jumped into his Tracker, started the engine and pulled out into the river, just in time to see two boats racing around the big bend upriver, Mona's boat, unmistakable in the distance, full bore, entering the bend, chasing another, full bore, scattering kayaks, about half way around the turn, racing toward him.

Mona gaining, Sweeney sweating, the two boats racing madly around the bend, engines whining, heading Deano's way, as he pulled his boat into the main channel and turned upriver, the large sandbar on his left, the main channel narrowing between shallows and a sheer sandstone wall on his right, has to go that way, Deano thought, turning toward the sandstone wall, Sweeney approaching, Deano could see his camouflage, his blackened face, the bow strapped around his chest, Mona fifty yards behind, closing, Sweeney recalibrating, Deano angling toward him, off at the pass, opening the throttle, heading straight at him, Sweeney sees Deano, what the fuck, shallows to Sweeney's right, only one way, hug the wall, closing in, narrows, collision course, ramming speed, Mona on his tail, three boats, full throttle, engines screaming, escape shrinking, one chance, hit the opening, Deano five yards, Mona forty, Deano braces, looks at Sweeney, look of panic, rams Sweeney broadside, full speed, Mona behind, Sweeney crashes into the sandstone wall, flies over the prow of his boat, slams his head into the sheer cliff, bounces off the wall, under his surging boat, a thud against the propeller, and disappears, into the dark water, the fast moving current, and the constant, unforgiving flow.

Leonard Tex Sweeney's mangled body was found three days later, seven miles downstream, washed ashore on a sandbar outside the town of Avoca. It took another week before his body could be identified. Front page news. Deano, a hero.

Even after Tex Sweeney's body was identified, no one, including Billy, had any idea why Sweeney would want the Hurleys killed. Well, there was one person: Sydney Black, and he wasn't talking, he was sitting pretty. The "one person too many" of his father's joke had just been rubbed out. He'd won the trifecta. The feds were off his back, his blackmailer was dead, and he no longer had to share any spoils on the warehouse deal. Whatever Sweeney did to piss off Billy Hurley, Black had nothing to do with that, just deny having anything to do with Sweeney, besides, he didn't know what Sweeney did to Billy Hurley, didn't know anything about what Sweeney did to Dan Hurley, either, although, now it was pretty clear. The more he thought about it, the more Black couldn't believe his good fortune. No one, especially Gusman, will ever find out, Black had swallowed the canary, thrown the bottle of Tums away, while all the coffee shops from Lone Rock to Chicago were asking: who the hell was Tex Sweeney?

The Chicago papers didn't come up with much. North sider, Lane Tech, Navy for six years, father a precinct captain, wrangled a job out of the service in the Cook County Circuit Court Clerk's Office, moved around, became a judge's clerk, several different judges, until he settled in with Judge Murphy, eight years, which at least was interesting, something maybe, Murphy indicted in the judiciary scandal, courthouse rumors about Sweeney, at the hip with Murphy, but no evidence, although anybody who knew Sweeney in the courthouse suspected the worst, because Sweeney, well, for as long as he'd worked there, no one really knew him, or liked him, he was quiet, in a guilty way, smug, like he knew something nobody else knew, hiding something, and better than you because of it, pompous, without apparent reason, little on the sleazy side, to tell the truth, if the truth were known, but mostly it wasn't, mostly dead ends on Sweeney, got a job in the City Clerk's office after Murphy got indicted, Chief Judge cleaning house, but then something did come up, the owner of an archery shop, in Hegewisch, blocks from Hammond, fifteen minutes of fame, stepped up to the microphone, to say that Sweeney happened to be the finest bowman he'd ever seen, trophies, awards, Montana elk, knew his way around a woods, and when Deano heard that he just smiled.

Everybody hailed Deano as a hero, except the Iowa County District Attorney. Didn't like the story, ramming the guy's boat like that, killed somebody, hero, vigilante, what would the evidence show, considering charges, until Walt paid him a visit, you know that election right around the corner, snowball's chance if you press charges, eye on the ball, don't piss up the rope, and besides, the DA's job was just a stepping stone, to a coveted black robe, so the DA announced, with some fanfare, that no charges would be filed, hailed Deano as a hero, and, at Walt's suggestion, attended the tribute Lee Anne threw for Deano at the Mad House Inn.

Place was packed. Lee Anne and Mona and Billy and Ben and Colleen and Dirk and Bonnie and Ivy and Mr. Wilcoxsin and all the Camo boys and drunk Joe Gilliam and Walt and Deputy Walters and Senator Fitzgibbons and State Representative Fletcher and Joey Larocca and Danny Redbird and Judy and Nick and half the town of Lone Rock, even Cecil Hampton, in the first tweed coat to grace the Mad House in twenty-five years. Shots poured, more shots poured, loud music, louder voices, hearty laughs, slaps on the back, for Deano, and Billy, and everyone in attendance, their little town, big time, the New York Times, and it was a good story, about fathers and sons and strong women and good friends and the river, and there were speeches, by State Representative Fletcher, not to be outdone by Senator Fitzgibbons. Walt got the biggest cheer saying he wasn't going to make a speech, the DA the same. Everybody wanted to hear from Deano, in his camo coat, thick long brown hair, round face, bushy beard, eyes shining, short and sturdy, not much for speeches, as they all knew, having watched and laughed when national reporters came to town, and couldn't get five words out of him. Deano, hero of the Mad House, raising his bottle of Pabst Blue Ribbon to the crowd, looking at the floor, shaking his head, and mumbling, "hell, thanks, everybody," and that was it, and everyone cheered, because they were all very proud of one of their own, who was just like all of them, plain folk, with few words, big hearts, and bigger deeds.

Billy told his story to Walt, about the warehouse, the documents, the tunnels, asked Walt to keep it close to the vest, which, knowing Walt, went without saying. Billy had other plans. He'd been holed up on Ben's front porch for a week, working on a strategy for the upcoming hearing. He'd made up his mind, on the hill, before death passed him by, he would challenge the petition, make the effort, for his kids, his father, his mother, himself. There was a lot to do. They called on Mr. Wilcoxsin for help, for wisdom, and his Illinois law license. Mr. Wilcoxsin filed an appearance in the guardianship proceeding, filed a motion *pro hac vice* for Ben, and Ben filed his appearance. Billy was lawyered up. His lawyers sent out subpoenas, served notice on Mr. Hanneman, who blew a gasket, when he saw subpoenas for Ms. Beecher's report, subpoenas to appear at trial on Dick Walsh, Mrs. Walsh, sure, but on Sydney Black, Ron Gusman, Mark Hamilton, Reverend Simmons, who the hell were these people, what did they have to do with a guardianship hearing, how the hell was this supposed to happen in one day, oh this goddam case, Mr. Hanneman moaned.

Mona, so proud, thrilled, knew, well, hoped, he'd come around, see the light. Never good to push things too strongly. Slap upside the head maybe in a rare moon, but gentle persuasion, subtlety, indirect suggestion of self-interest, that was the ticket, it helped he was smart, in the right place, his heart, just needed to find it, is all, all it took, one murder, one attempted murder, hopefully less, in the future.

Mona knew the odds were stacked against them, her husband's misdeeds, she understood that, but she also knew, convinced really, his kids were best with them, in Ray's house, the four of them, maybe five, plenty of room, a business, a family, my God, just a couple of months, must have done something right, some stars aligned, and even if it doesn't work out, not for lack of trying, just the right thing to do, fight for your kids, and if not now, then maybe someday, because, one way, or the other, Sam and Kate would be a part of their lives.

Labor Day got rained out, so hard the dam opened, the river rose, sandbars disappeared, reservations canceled. Mona busied herself getting ready for the trip to the big town. She bought a bag of Twizzlers and some Tootsie Roll Pops, couple Babar books, Jeremy Fisher, and Ferdinand, just in case. She pulled the tarp off Ray's antique car and pulled it out of the pole barn, the buff colored 1956 Cadillac Coupe de Ville convertible, thorough wash, gleaming, going in style. And the day after Labor Day, clear blue skies, Mona, Billy, and Ben piled into the front red leather seat of the old Cadillac, threw their bags and legal pads in the back, pulled the top down, put their sunglasses on, and drove off down Highway 14, across the green bridge over the Wisconsin River, toward Madison, Chicago, and the guardianship hearing the next day.

CHAPTER NINE

The Trial

IN THE CIRCUIT COURT OF COOK COUNTY, ILLINOIS, COUNTY DEPARTMENT, PROBATE DIVISION

RICHARD WALSH,	)
AND MARY ALICE WALSH,	)
	)
Petitioners,	) Case No. 84 P 1349
	)
v.	)
	)
WILLIAM HURLEY *et al.*,	)
	)
Respondents.	)

DATE: SEPTEMBER 5, 1984

BEFORE: HON. JOSEPH WOZAK

APPEARANCES: WILLIAM J. HANNEMAN
Stone, Doherty & Hanneman
On Behalf of Petitioners

BENJAMIN GOLD
On Behalf of Respondent Hurley

CONRAD E. WILCOXSIN
Law Offices of Conrad E. Wilcoxsin
On Behalf of Respondent Hurley

TRANSCRIPT OF PROCEEDINGS

Reported by Jennifer K. Bischoff, RPR
Official Court Reporter
(Convened at 10:00 a.m.)

THE COURT: Court will call the case of Walsh vs. Hurley, et al., 84 P 1349, Appearances, please.

MR. HANNEMAN: William Hanneman, on behalf of the petitioners, Richard and Mary Alice Walsh, who are in court this morning.

MR. GOLD: Benjamin Gold, on behalf of the respondent, William, Billy Hurley.

MR. WILCOXSIN: Conrad E. Wilcoxsin, also on behalf of respondent, Billy Hurley.

THE COURT: Well, Mr. Hurley, I see you have outdone yourself this morning on the lawyer front. Gentlemen, have you filed your appearances?

MR. WILCOXSIN: I have Your Honor, my name is Conrad Wilcoxsin...

THE COURT: You have already told me that counsel.

MR. WILCOXSIN: Yes, Your Honor, quite, as I was saying, I have filed my appearance in this cause, being licensed in Illinois, although my practice is in Spring Green, Wisconsin, and I also have taken the liberty of filing a Motion Pro Hac Vice, [Counsel handing a copy of the Motion up to the judge], to allow Mr. Gold to appear in this honorable court as the first chair attorney representing Mr. Hurley, with my assistance. As the Motion sets forth, I am well aware of Mr. Gold's integrity and professionalism and can vouch for his appearance in this court.

THE COURT: [Reading through the Motion]. Mr. Gold, have you ever tried a case before?

MR. GOLD: No, Your Honor.

THE COURT: Great...

MR. HANNEMAN: Your Honor...

THE COURT: I'm reading, Mr. Hanneman, as you
can see.

MR. HANNEMAN: Yes, Your Honor.

THE COURT: Mr. Hanneman, any objection to
the Motion?

MR. HANNEMAN: No objection to the Motion, Your
Honor, but...

THE COURT: Counsel's Motion Pro Hac Vice is
granted. Mr. Hanneman?

MR. HANNEMAN: Your Honor, as you know, this matter
was set for hearing today predicated on Mr. Hurley's unequivocal expres-
sion of total disinterest in the well-being of his children, as confirmed
several times in open court...

THE COURT: Except at the last status, when he told us
his position might change.

MR. HANNEMAN: Be that as it may, Your Honor, he has
now gone from totally abandoning his children, to what could best be
called equivocation, to this, [Counsel flourishing a number of documents
in his right hand], an ambush of subpoenas served on people who have
nothing whatsoever to do with this matter, with two separate lawyers, for
a one-day hearing...

THE COURT: What are these subpoenas about, Mr.
Wilcoxsin, Mr. Gold?

MR. GOLD: Your Honor, we believe that Mr. Hurley,
the father of the children involved in this case, has every right to partici-
pate in this hearing to the fullest extent possible to protect the interests of
his children...

MR. HANNEMAN: Protect the interests of his children? Is he kidding, Your Honor? Where was counsel when Mr. Hurley told us he didn't want anything to do with…

THE COURT: Mr. Hanneman, I will tell you this one time today, you are not to interrupt me or counsel in this courtroom, do you understand?

MR. HANNEMAN: Yes, Your Honor, but…

THE COURT: Mr. Gold, I didn't ask for your opening statement, I asked you about the subpoenas, what are these subpoenas about?

MR. GOLD: Your Honor, we have served subpoenas on the petitioners, Mr. and Mrs. Walsh, to ensure they would appear at the hearing, so we could call them as witnesses in the event Mr. Hanneman chose not to…

THE COURT: Well, I see they are in court this morning, so I take it that is not an issue, Mr. Hanneman?

MR. HANNEMAN: No, of course not, Your Honor, but…

THE COURT: What are the other subpoenas, Mr. Gold?

MR. GOLD: The other witnesses subpoenaed may not even be necessary, depending on how the testimony goes, and we expect that if the subpoenaed witnesses are called, their testimony will be quite short, but we wanted to make sure they would be available just in case.

THE COURT: Are they in court this morning?

[The judge examined the back benches, Mona and Dorothy sitting together in the first row, in front of the swinging gate, on the judge's right, directly behind the respondent's counsel table, four rows behind them, behind the swinging gate, unoccupied, as were the four back rows of benches behind petitioners' table, but in the first row, before the swinging gate, sat Ms. Beecher, to the judge's left behind petitioners' counsel table.]

MR. GOLD: No, Your Honor, we have reached out to each of them to let them know they didn't need to arrive until 2:00 p.m., after lunch, at which time we should have a better idea of whether their testimony will become necessary.

THE COURT: Who are these people?

MR. HANNEMAN: Well, one of them is Alderman Gusman, another is…

THE COURT: Gusman?

MR. HANNEMAN: Yes, Your Honor…

THE COURT: Mr. Gold?

MR. GOLD: Mr. Gusman; Reverend Simmons, of the Saving Grace West Side Community Center; Mr. Sydney Black, an attorney; and Mr. Mark Hamilton, of the Lincoln Financial Trust and Savings Bank.

THE COURT: And what do they have to do with your client's children?

MR. GOLD: They may be called to testify on the issue of my client's relationship with his father if that should come up.

THE COURT: Do you expect that might come up, Mr. Hanneman?

MR. HANNEMAN: Well, yes, Your Honor, I expect that may well become an issue, but…

THE COURT: Not at all clear how Alderman Gusman and Sydney Black, with whom I'm familiar, have anything to do with Mr.

Hurley's relationship with his father, but we don't need to jump the gun on that for now. Mr. Hanneman, I share your concern that this hearing not be prolonged unnecessarily, and I am not going to allow counsel [the judge staring at Mr. Gold] to make a circus out of the very serious matter that is the subject of this hearing today. But, at least for now, it appears the mere fact subpoenas were issued will not necessarily complicate what we have set out to accomplish today, and in any event, I am not now in a position to quash them, and I have not heard any motion to that effect, so let's proceed.

Counsel, in the interest of time, might I suggest you consider waiving opening statements and get right to the testimony.

MR. GOLD: I'm fine with that, Your Honor.

MR. HANNEMAN: Anything to move this along, Judge.

THE COURT: Then let's proceed. Mr. Hanneman, you may call your first witness.

MR. HANNEMAN: Your Honor, the petitioners call Richard Walsh.

[Richard Walsh stands from the petitioners' attorney table and walks up to the witness box, six-feet tall, broad shoulders, suit coat buttoned to conceal a protruding waistline, rectangular head, jowls, thinning hair slicked back, light gray pinstriped suit, white shirt, polka dot mauve tie with matching pocket square, tasseled black shoes, confident, a cut above.]

THE COURT: Sir, you may have a seat here in the witness box. Swear the witness.

COURT CLERK: Raise your right hand. Do you swear to tell the truth, the whole truth, and nothing but the truth so help you God?

MR. WALSH: [To the Clerk.] I do.

[Settles in the witness chair, turns to Mr. Hanneman, standing next to his attorney's table, legal pad in hand, reading glasses perched on his nose, six-feet three inches, patrician, dark blue pinstriped suit, light blue shirt, burgundy patterned tie, silk stockings, longish white hair curled behind his ears, rosacea, Roman nose, tapered jaw.]

MR. HANNEMAN: Will you please state your name and spell it for the record?

MR. WALSH: [Leaning forward to the microphone]. Richard Walsh, W-a-l-s-h, my friends call me Dick.

MR. HANNEMAN: Are you one of the petitioners in this case, Mr. Walsh?

MR. WALSH: I am proud to say I am.

MR. HANNEMAN: And where do you live, Mr. Walsh?

MR. WALSH: I live at 3220 S. Newberry Avenue, in Chicago.

MR. HANNEMAN: And what neighborhood is that, Mr. Walsh?

MR. WALSH: Beverly, the Beverly neighborhood, on the far South Side.

MR. HANNEMAN: Are you married?

MR. WALSH: I am, I'm married to Mary Alice Walsh [smiling at Mrs. Walsh, sitting at the petitioners' attorney table.]

MR. HANNEMAN: For how long?

MR. WALSH: Fifteen happy years.

MR. HANNEMAN: Where did you grow up?

MR. WALSH: Bridgeport.

MR. HANNEMAN: Please tell us about your academic background?

MR. WALSH: Well, I went to Brother Rice, and the University of Notre Dame, in South Bend.

MR. HANNEMAN: [Smiling.] I think we all know where Notre Dame is Dick. Play any sports in school?

MR. WALSH: Yes, I lettered in football at Brother Rice, and played four years of football at Notre Dame.

MR. HANNEMAN: Rockne years?

MR. WALSH: No, little bit after.

MR. HANNEMAN: Spend any time in the service?

MR. WALSH: Yes, when the war broke out, I enlisted as an officer and served in the Army, First Infantry Division.

MR. HANNEMAN: See any action?

MR. WALSH: D-Day, Omaha Beach.

MR. HANNEMAN: [Let that settle in a bit, stepped back to his counsel table, pretended to look at documents.] How long were you in the service?

MR. WALSH: Until 1945, when I received my honorable discharge, as a Captain.

MR. HANNEMAN: You mentioned your house earlier, could you please describe your home in Beverly for us?

MR. WALSH: Well, it's a five-bedroom, four-bath, brick Colonial, with a finished basement that's now a play area for the kids, a redone attic with its own bedroom and bath, a large backyard with a swing set, and a two-car garage with an office over the garage.

MR. HANNEMAN: Sounds nice.

MR. WALSH: [Laughing.] Yes, thank you, it is.

MR. HANNEMAN: The children who are the subject of this hearing, Sam and Kate Hurley, do they live with you now?

MR. WALSH: Yes, for several years now, since we became temporary guardians. They each have their own bedroom, and plenty of friends, kids live up and down the block.

MR. HANNEMAN: Do they attend school?

MR. WALSH: Pre-school, which is two blocks away. They walk there with our nanny.

MR. HANNEMAN: What about grade school, what grade school will they attend?

MR. WALSH: Sacred Heart, that's a whole three blocks away.

MR. HANNEMAN: That's a long commute. [Mr. Walsh and Mr. Hanneman, only ones laughing.] Are you parishioners at Sacred Heart?

MR. WALSH: I have been for fifteen years, where we were married, my wife for much longer.

MR. HANNEMAN: Do you hold any positions with the church?

MR. WALSH: I've been the chief usher for ten years now. Think they're getting a little tired of me. [More chuckling.]

MR. HANNEMAN: Do you hold a position in any other organizations?

MR. WALSH: Well, I'm a past President of the Beverly Country Club, and I currently serve on the Board of Directors of the local Rotary International branch.

MR. HANNEMAN: Are you employed, Mr. Walsh?

MR. WALSH: Yes, I own my own company, Walsh Equipment Leasing.

MR. HANNEMAN: Tell us a little about that.

MR. WALSH: Well, I started the business twenty-five years ago. We lease heavy equipment, front-end loaders, dump trucks, cherry pickers, forklifts, that type of thing, to various businesses and governments.

MR. HANNEMAN: Has your business been successful?

MR. WALSH: Yes, I believe we have, we're a multi-million-dollar company that's turned a profit each of our twenty-five years. I'm very proud of what we've accomplished.

MR. HANNEMAN: Sounds like you have a right to be.

MR. GOLD: Object to the commentary, Your Honor.

THE COURT: Sustained.

MR. HANNEMAN: Do you have any children, Dick?

MR. WALSH: Yes, I have one daughter from my previous marriage, Jennifer.

MR. HANNEMAN: And is Jennifer the mother of Sam and Kate?

MR. WALSH: Yes.

MR. HANNEMAN: Where is Jennifer today?

MR. WALSH: I'm heartbroken to say I don't know. I love her dearly, we did everything we could for her, but, like Mr. Hurley, she succumbed to drugs, and just couldn't get off them, I pray for her every day.

MR. GOLD: Move to strike the reference to
Mr. Hurley.

THE COURT: The reference to Mr. Hurley will
be stricken.

MR. HANNEMAN: You love your grandchildren, do you
not Dick?

MR. WALSH: With all my heart.

MR. HANNEMAN: You'd do anything for them?

MR. GOLD: Objection, leading.

THE COURT: Sustained.

MR. HANNEMAN: Please describe your relationship with
Sam and Kate for the court Dick.

MR. WALSH: [Voice cracking.] Well, I love them
very much. They're such beautiful kids, and they sure didn't deserve to
come into this world and have to live in the mess that he [sneering at Mr.
Hurley] made for them. Someone needs to care for them, be there for
them every day, make sure they're brought up right, they're my blood,
they've been a joy to have around the house, and I'm committed to doing
everything in my power to see that they're well cared for, happy, well-adjusted, and raised to be responsible members of our society.

MR. HANNEMAN: Thank you, Your Honor, that is all I
have of Mr. Walsh.

[Mr. Walsh starts to get up from the witness chair.]

THE COURT: Stay seated, Mr. Walsh, please. Mr.
Gold, do you have any questions of Mr. Walsh.

MR. GOLD: Yes, Your Honor. [Mr. Gold rises from
respondent's counsel table, tall, angular, fluid, jet black hair tied in a pony

tail hanging down to his shoulder blades, black corduroy pants, hush puppies, chocolate suede jacket, white shirt, narrow black tie, tawny-olive skin, dark brown eyes, nose of a bird of prey, approaches the witness box, without notes.]

Good morning, Mr. Walsh, my name is Ben Gold, and I am Mr. Hurley's attorney.

MR. WALSH: Good morning.

MR. GOLD: Your company has done work for the City of Chicago, has it not?

MR. WALSH: Yes.

MR. GOLD: It's true isn't it that over the twenty-five years your company has been in business a significant percentage of your company's business has come from the City of Chicago?

MR. WALSH: Well, I don't know that I'd say a significant percentage.

MR. GOLD: It's a fact isn't it, Mr. Walsh, that three years ago at a barbecue in your backyard, you bragged to my client, Mr. Hurley, that 95 percent of your company's business over the years came from the City?

MR. WALSH: I don't recall saying that.

MR. GOLD: That was the night you passed out and had to be helped to bed, do you recall that?

MR. WALSH: I definitely do not recall that.

MR. GOLD: I'm not surprised.

MR. HANNEMAN: Objection.

THE COURT: Sustained, watch it, Mr. Gold.

MR. GOLD: Well, as you sit here today, over the past twenty-five years [Mr. Gold stepped back to his attorney's table and picked up a document as if he were reading from it, which he wasn't], how much of your business would you say came from the City of Chicago, if it wasn't 95 percent, what was it, 90 percent, 85 percent?

MR. WALSH: [Looking at Mr. Gold looking at the document.] Oh, I don't know, maybe, 75, 80 percent.

MR. GOLD: 75, 80 percent, that sounds like a significant percentage to me, isn't that a significant percentage to you, Mr. Walsh?

MR. WALSH: Yes, I guess it is.

MR. GOLD: You were childhood friends of Mayor O'Brien, were you not?

MR. WALSH: Yes.

MR. GOLD: Attended Brother Rice together?

MR. WALSH: Yes.

MR. GOLD: In fact, you started your business the same year Mayor O'Brien was first elected.

MR. WALSH: Well, yes, I guess that's right, never looked at it that way.

[Judge Wozak looks over his glasses at Mr. Walsh.]

MR. GOLD: Have you received any contracts from the City of Chicago, since Mayor O'Brien passed away?

MR. WALSH: Of course we have.

MR. GOLD: How many?

MR. WALSH: Well, two.

MR. GOLD: How long ago.

MR. WALSH: Well, let's see [thinking], about eight years ago or so, I guess.

MR. GOLD: What were the terms, the duration, of those contracts?

MR. WALSH: Ten-year terms.

MR. GOLD: And when do those contracts expire?

MR. WALSH: Oh gee, I don't know, [Mr. Walsh looked at the judge, who was staring back at him], gee, I guess, maybe, in a year or so.

MR. GOLD: And after those contracts expire your company's twenty-five year run with the City of Chicago, at least 75 to 80 percent of your business, will have come to an end, isn't that right, Mr. Walsh?

MR. WALSH: We'll get more contracts.

MR. GOLD: From Mayor Jefferson?

MR. WALSH: Sure.

MR. GOLD: You didn't go to school with Mayor Jefferson, too, did you Mr. Walsh?

MR. HANNEMAN: Objection, Your Honor, badgering the witness.

THE COURT: Sustained.

MR. GOLD: That house you mentioned, that isn't paid for, is it?

MR. HANNEMAN: Objection, relevance.

THE COURT: You brought the house up, Mr. Hanneman, overruled.

MR. WALSH: No.

MR. GOLD: What's the appraised value?

MR. WALSH: How should I know?

MR. GOLD: There was a mortgage recorded on your
home one month ago, wasn't an appraisal done then?

MR. WALSH: How do you know about that?

[Mr. Gold looks at the judge. Mr. Hurley looks back at Dorothy,
smiles.]

THE COURT: Mr. Walsh, just answer the question.

MR. WALSH: Yeah, we had a home equity loan, house
was appraised at $375,000.

MR.GOLD: And what is the outstanding balance on
that loan at the present time?

MR. HANNEMAN: Objection, Your Honor, relevance,
beyond the scope.

THE COURT: Mr. Gold?

MR. GOLD: Your Honor, the issue in this case is
who is best equipped to care for the children. I assume Mr. Hanneman
had Mr. Walsh testify to the size of his home and the success of his company to prove that Mr. Walsh will be the better provider for the children.

THE COURT: Overruled. [To the witness.] Please,
answer the question.

MR. WALSH: [Reluctantly]. $150,000.

MR. GOLD: And is that a thirty-year mortgage?

MR. WALSH: [In a low voice.] Yes.

COURT REPORTER: I'm sorry, I couldn't hear the answer.

MR. WALSH: [Louder, annoyed.] I said yes.

MR. GOLD: And how old are you, Mr. Walsh?

MR. WALSH: Sixty-five, but it'll be paid off long before that.

MR. GOLD: I should hope so. Now, Mr. Walsh, you're aware of the terms of a trust fund that has been established by Daniel Hurley for his grandchildren, Sam and Kate?

MR. WALSH: The terms? No, I don't know all the terms of the trust.

MR. GOLD: You have been advised about some of those terms, have you not?

MR. WALSH: Well, I guess I've had some of them explained to me.

MR. GOLD: And you are aware, are you not, that the trust authorizes those persons who have legal custody of the children to make expenditures from trust funds for the benefit of the children?

MR. WALSH: As it should be, yes, I'm aware of that.

MR. GOLD: And that providing suitable housing for the children is one of the expenditures specifically allowed for under the trust?

MR. WALSH: [Looks at Mr. Hanneman, looks at his wife.]

MR. HANNEMAN: Objection…

THE COURT: Overruled.

MR. WALSH: [Muttering.] Yes.

COURT REPORTER: I'm sorry…

THE COURT: Mr. Walsh, please keep your voice up.

MR. WALSH: [Loud voice.] Yes.

MR. GOLD: And you intend to use some of the children's trust funds to pay down your home equity credit line isn't that true?

MR. WALSH: Why you little…

MR. HANNEMAN: Objection, Your Honor, this is outrageous…

THE COURT: Overruled. [Looking down sternly at the witness.]. Mr. Walsh, please, just answer the question.

MR. WALSH: Is that what you think this is all about, the money? Look, I don't know who you are or where you come from, but I don't need to take on this responsibility, at my age, to raise two five-year-olds, this isn't something I asked for, or expected, but I'm willing to step up to the plate and do what should be done, do whatever it takes to make sure these beautiful kids are well taken care of, and for their sake, make sure they stay as far away from him [pointing in the direction of Mr. Hurley] as possible, so yes, if the funds can be used for housing for the kids and I'm providing a beautiful home for these kids to grow up in, then yes, it makes sense that the money should be used to provide that beautiful house for them.

MR. GOLD: Thank you, Mr. Walsh. I understand you're a Sox fan.

MR. WALSH: What? [Looking at Mr. Hanneman.]

MR. GOLD: I said I understand you're a Sox fan.

MR. WALSH: [Shaking his head, rolling his eyes.] I suppose that disqualifies me from taking care of my grandkids.

MR. GOLD: Is Sam a baseball fan?

MR. WALSH: [Little flustered.] Well, yeah, of course he is.

MR. GOLD: Is he a Sox fan, too?

MR. WALSH: [Sitting back in his chair.] Any self-respecting Southsider is a Sox fan.

MR. GOLD: How about Kate?

MR. HANNEMAN: Your Honor…

THE COURT: Mr. Gold, where is this going?

MR. GOLD: I'll wrap this up quickly, Judge.

THE COURT: You better.

MR. WALSH: Don't know that Katie likes baseball.

MR. GOLD: Mr. Walsh, you spoke with Ms. Beecher, the Guardian ad Litem assigned by Judge Wozak in this case, when she came to your house and asked you some questions?

MR. WALSH: Yes, I spoke to her.

MR. GOLD: Are you aware she also spoke to the children?

MR. WALSH: [Leaning up in his chair.] Well, uh, I guess so. [Looking at his wife, uncertain.]

MR. GOLD: Would you be surprised to learn that Sam told Ms. Beecher he was a Cubs fan? Said he liked the teddy bear on their sleeves.

MR. WALSH: [Sputtering.] Well, I…

MR. GOLD: And that his favorite player is Ryne Sandberg?

MR. WALSH: Well…

MR. GOLD: And that, according to Ms. Beecher's report, Kate is a Sox fan?

MR. WALSH: [Embarrassed, looking down.] Uh, no, I was not aware.

MR. GOLD: Now, Mr. Walsh, as I understand it, you divorced your daughter's mother when Jenny was, what, ten, eleven years old?

MR. WALSH: I guess that's about right.

MR. GOLD: And that was your idea, the divorce, wasn't it?

MR. WALSH: Yes.

MR. GOLD: And after the divorce, Jenny lived with her mom, isn't that right?

MR. WALSH: Yeah, well, we had a joint custody agreement, but yes, she did live most of the time with her mom, but I was always in her life, and we saw Jenny as much as possible.

MR. GOLD: So what was that, every other weekend?

MR. WALSH: And holidays, and whenever we could help out.

MR. GOLD: How about when Jenny was in high school? Did she stay with you every other weekend?

MR. WALSH: Well, just about, but, Jenny had her friends, in Bridgeport, from school, and if something was going on with them, we didn't want to deprive her of that, so, not as much.

MR. GOLD: Mr. Walsh, in your direct examination, [Mr. Gold steps over to his counsel table and picks up a legal pad], you said that you loved Sam and Kate, and that you were committed to see that they were "well cared for, happy, well-adjusted, and raised to be responsible members of our society."

MR. WALSH: Okay.

MR. GOLD: You love your daughter too, don't you?

MR. WALSH: Of course.

MR. GOLD: Would you say your daughter, who
you helped raise, is "happy, well-adjusted," and a "responsible member of
our society?"

MR. WALSH: [Reddening, clenching fists.]. You son
of a bitch, what do you know about raising kids…

THE COURT: Mr. Walsh, you will control yourself and
watch your language in this courtroom.

MR. WALSH: We did everything we could…

THE COURT: That's enough, Mr. Gold, do you have
any more questions?

MR. GOLD: Not of this witness, Your Honor.

THE COURT: Any redirect?

MR. HANNEMAN: [Soft voice, dialing it down.] Dick,
is there anything else you'd like to say to the judge in support of
your petition?

MR. WALSH: [Collecting himself.] Your Honor [turn-
ing to the judge], I don't know if you have any kids, but, you know, you do
the best you can, you love them, you do anything for them, but there's no
playbook, there's no right way, each kid is different, we thought we were
doing the right things, we gave her everything she needed, maybe that
was our mistake, maybe it was our fault, maybe it wasn't, I don't know,
and I don't think anybody really does, all I know is that my wife and I
filed this petition because we love these kids, and we want to give them
the best shot at a good life, we wanted to make sure these beautiful kids
didn't end up crying and hungry in the back of a cab in a Jewel parking
lot again, so we'll do everything in our power to keep them out of his
hands, and give them the shot at life they truly deserve. Thank you.

THE COURT: Thank you, Mr. Walsh, you may
step down. [Waits for Mr. Walsh to take a seat.] Mr. Hanneman, your
next witness?

MR. HANNEMAN: The petitioners call Mary Alice Walsh.

[Mary Alice Walsh stands from the counsel table, medium height,
Chanel style suit, cream silk blouse finished at the neck in a loose bow,
honey blonde hair, teased, coiffed, and sprayed, walks up to the witness
box in pumps, holding her hands, not as confident as her husband after
his cross-examination, sits in the witness chair.]

COURT CLERK: Raise your right hand. Do you swear to
tell the truth, the whole truth, and nothing but the truth so help you God?

MRS. WALSH: I do.

MR. HANNEMAN: Please state your name for the record.

MRS. WALSH: Mary Alice Walsh.

MR. HANNEMAN: Are you a petitioner in this case?

MRS. WALSH: Yes, along with my husband, Dick.

MR. HANNEMAN: How long have you been married to
Dick Walsh?

MRS. WALSH: Fifteen years.

MR. HANNEMAN: Where did the two of you meet?

MRS WALSH: Well, actually, we first met when he was
at Notre Dame. He was a senior at the time, and I was a sophomore, at St.
Mary's College, and we met at a party. I guess you could say he made an
impression, because I married him thirty-two years later.

MR. HANNEMAN: Where did the two of you get married?

MRS. WALSH: Sacred Heart Catholic Church,
in Beverly.

MR. HANNEMAN: Are you a member of the church?

MRS. WALSH: Yes.

MR. HANNEMAN: For how long?

MRS. WALSH: Thirty-five years.

MR. HANNEMAN: Have you any children?

MRS. WALSH: Yes, from my first marriage. My son Mark, who's thirty-four, is a doctor at Northwestern, and my daughter Margaret is twenty-eight, and a grade-school teacher.

MR. HANNEMAN: Is your first husband still alive?

MRS. WALSH: No, he passed away twenty years ago.

MR. HANNEMAN: I'm sorry.

MRS. WALSH: Don't be, he wasn't a very nice man, and I then met Dick again, everything for a reason, God has a plan for all of us.

MR. HANNEMAN: Can you describe what life is like with two five-year-olds running around the house?

MRS. WALSH: Well, they are a handful, as you might expect, and I'm not as young as I used to be, so when we first got custody of Sam and Katie, I tried to find the most qualified nanny I could to help us out with the children, and I'm pleased to say we found the most wonderful woman in Ophelia Rodriguez, who's been with us almost since the time the kids came to stay with us. Ophelia is thirty years old, energetic, makes most of the meals, takes the kids to the park practically every day, the park is right down the block, walks them to pre-school, plays with them in the backyard, in our basement, I don't know what we'd do without her.

MR. HANNEMAN: I've seen that basement, Dorothy, don't know that I've seen so many plastic toys in my life. [Mr. Gold pushed back his chair to make an objection, Mr. Wilcoxsin put his hand on Mr. Gold's arm; Mr. Gold remained seated.]

MRS. WALSH: Yes, it's a little playground down there, we've spared no expense.

MR. HANNEMAN: Could you describe your involvement with the children?

MRS. WALSH: Well, we watch movies together, read books, I'm particularly involved in their Christian upbringing, the church has been a very important part of my life, so I make sure they go to church every Sunday, we read Bible stories together before they go to bed, and just make sure they grow up with the blessing of knowing that Jesus Christ is their Lord and Savior.

MR. HANNEMAN: Have you made plans for the children's education?

MRS. WALSH: Yes, they will be enrolled in Sacred Heart Grade School, where my children went to school. It's a fine school, with a fine religious footing.

MR. HANNEMAN: How did it come about that you and Dick decided to file this petition?

MRS. WALSH: Well, that awful, unforgivable thing happened with those two little darlings in that car, and all those drugs, and oh it was just so, well, disgusting is what it was, that something had to be done, and then his [referring to Mr. Hurley] mother, God bless her, and may she rest in peace, and Jenny's mother, pitched in for as long as they could, but neither one of them was in the best of health anyway, and the stress and everything took its toll on both of them if truth be told, and they just couldn't physically continue doing that, so Dick and I prayed over it, and decided we had to do what the good Lord would have wanted us to do, so we consulted a lawyer, and decided to file this petition, to give these beautiful children a chance at a decent life, which they so deserved, and which their parents cruelly denied them.

MR. HANNEMAN: Thank you, Mrs. Walsh, no further questions.

THE COURT: Mr. Gold?

MR. GOLD: Thank you, Your Honor. Good morning, Mrs. Walsh. [No response from Mrs. Walsh, holding her hands tightly in her lap.] Mrs. Walsh, I apologize in advance, but I have to ask, it is true, is it not, that you suffer from acute and chronic rheumatoid arthritis?

MRS. WALSH: [Looks at her husband, holding her hands in her lap.] Yes, that is correct.

MR. GOLD: For how long now?

MRS. WALSH: Around five years.

MR. GOLD: And it's fair to say that your condition limits what you can do with the children?

MRS. WALSH: To a certain extent, yes.

MR. GOLD: How so?

MRS. WALSH: Well, now that they're a bit older, I find it difficult to pick them up anymore, or give them a bath, sometimes getting them dressed is an issue, that's why we hired Ophelia, who can do all of those things, under my supervision.

MR. GOLD: Under your supervision. What hours does Ophelia work?

MRS. WALSH: She works Monday through Friday, from eight to six, and sometimes, if we need her, on weekends.

MR. GOLD: Does she have her own children?

MRS. WALSH: Yes.

MR. GOLD: What ages?

MRS. WALSH: Five and seven, sometimes they come over and play with the twins.

MR. GOLD: So her children are young then.

MRS. WALSH: Yes, I would say so.

MR. GOLD: Who takes care of Sam and Kate on the weekends?

MRS. WALSH: We do the best we can, sometimes my daughter Margaret stops by, with her children.

MR. GOLD: Where does Ophelia live?

MRS. WALSH: What's it called [looking at her husband], I think, Pilsen? Isn't that a neighborhood in town? Yes, I think she lives in Pilsen.

MR. GOLD: That's quite aways from Beverly, isn't it, Mrs. Walsh?

MRS. WALSH: I, I'm sorry, I really don't know.

MR. GOLD: Who gets them dressed in the morning?

MRS. WALSH: Ophelia.

MR. GOLD: Who walks the kids to preschool?

MRS. WALSH: Ophelia.

MR. GOLD: Who takes them to the park?

MRS. WALSH: Ophelia.

MR. GOLD: Who makes their meals during
the week?

MRS. WALSH: Ophelia.

MR. GOLD: Who makes their meals on weekends?

MRS. WALSH: Well, Dick gets breakfast together,
cereal you know, sandwiches for lunch, we usually get carry out or go out
for dinner.

MR. GOLD: Are you able to cook with
your arthritis?

MRS. WALSH: It's very difficult.

MR. GOLD: Mrs. Walsh, I believe you said in
your direct examination that you don't know what you would do without Ophelia?

MRS. WALSH: Yes, I said that, and I meant it.

MR. GOLD: What would you do without Ophelia?

MRS. WALSH: We would have to find another nanny.

MR. GOLD: You just couldn't do it yourself, could
you, Mrs. Walsh?

MRS. WALSH: [Looking into her lap.] No, I couldn't.

MR. GOLD: To your knowledge, is Mrs. Rodriguez
paid out of the children's trust fund?

MRS. WALSH: I don't know for sure, but I believe now
she is.

MR. GOLD: I also believe you testified, in connection with the kids' toys, that you and your husband have spared
no expense?

MRS. WALSH: That is correct.

MR. GOLD: Is it your understanding some of those expenditures have come from the trust fund as well?

MRS. WALSH: There's nothing wrong with that, is there, [looking at her husband], they're for the kids, after all.

MR. GOLD: I also believe you testified that the children were cruelly denied a decent life.

MRS. WALSH: Yes, I believe that's true.

MR. GOLD: By whom were they denied a decent life?

MRS. WALSH: Well, by your client, of course.

MR. GOLD: And your husband's daughter?

MRS. WALSH: [Hesitating.] Yes, that would be true as well.

MR. GOLD: And it's your understanding drugs had something to do with it?

MRS. WALSH: Absolutely.

MR. GOLD: The parents' addiction to drugs.

MRS. WALSH: Yes.

MR. GOLD: Now, Mrs. Walsh, please don't take offense, but you have personal experience with addiction, do you not?

MRS. WALSH: [Looking down at her hands, at her husband, her hands, not answering.]

THE COURT: Did you hear the question, ma'am?

MRS. WALSH: Yes, the answer is yes.

MR. GOLD: Could you please describe that for us?

MRS. WALSH: I was an alcoholic, well, I suppose I should say, I am an alcoholic, although I haven't touched a drop in twenty-four years.

MR. GOLD: Have you ever received a citation for driving under the influence?

MRS. WALSH: [Hesitating, with difficulty.] Uh, yes, twenty-four years ago.

MR. GOLD: And your children were in the car at the time, were they not?

MRS. WALSH: [Faltering, embarrassed, low voice]. Yes, I am terribly ashamed of that, a low point in my life, but the shame helped me overcome my addiction, all part of God's plan.

MR. GOLD: But your own experience proves that a person can overcome their addiction and reform their lives, isn't that true, Mrs. Walsh?

MRS. WALSH: Yes, that is true, in some cases, like mine, not in others, like his [pointing at Mr. Hurley].

MR. GOLD: [Turns, walks away from the witness, stops, turns around.] One last question, Mrs. Walsh, you said several times this morning that what happens in life is all part of God's plan.

MRS. WALSH: Yes, I firmly believe that's true.

MR. GOLD: So I guess it was all part of God's plan that Jenny Walsh got addicted to drugs and abandoned her children, or that you became an alcoholic, or that some poor kid'll get killed today on the West Side by a drive-by shooter...

MR. HANNEMAN: Objection, Your Honor...!

MR. GOLD: ...and it must have been God's plan for Billy and Jenny to take a Quaalude on the way to buying diapers with their kids in the back seat of a Marathon cab?

MR. HANNEMAN: Objection!

THE COURT: [Forcefully.] Sustained, that's enough, Mr. Gold. [Mr. Gold walks back to his counsel table, shaking his head, takes a seat.] Any redirect, Mr. Hanneman?

MR. HANNEMAN: No, Your Honor.

THE COURT: Who's your next witness?

MR. HANNEMAN: Mr. Hurley, Your Honor.

THE COURT: Okay, then let's take a fifteen-minute break, and we'll start back up with Mr. Hurley.

(Recessed at 11:15 a.m.)

(Reconvened at 11:33 a.m.)

THE CLERK: All rise.

THE COURT: All right, let's resume, Mr. Hanneman, please call your next witness.

MR. HANNEMAN: Your Honor, the petitioners call Billy Hurley.

THE COURT: Please take a seat here in the witness box, Mr. Hurley.

[Mr. Hurley rises from his chair at the respondent's counsel table, six-feet tall, lean, black Italian wedding suit, white shirt buttoned at the

top button, no tie, steps across the courtroom to the witness box, long
thick brown hair parted in the middle, pulled back behind his ears, look
of Jesus about him, without the sanctity.]

COURT CLERK: Raise your right hand. Do you swear to
tell the truth, the whole truth, and nothing but the truth so help you God?

MR. HURLEY: I do.

MR. HANNEMAN: Your Honor, request leave to examine
Mr. Hurley as a hostile witness.

MR. HURLEY: I'm not hostile…

THE COURT: Mr. Gold?

MR. GOLD: No Objection.

THE COURT: Proceed Mr. Hanneman.

MR. HANNEMAN: Mr. Hurley, are you the same Mr.
Hurley who fell asleep high on drugs at the wheel of a car while your kids
were crying for an hour in the back seat?

MR. HURLEY: Yes.

MR. HANNEMAN: And that was about two and a half years
ago correct?

MR. HURLEY: That' s correct.

MR. HANNEMAN: And how many times have you seen
your kids since that time?

MR. HURLEY: Once.

MR. HANNEMAN: And when was that?

MR. HURLEY: My dad's funeral.

MR. HANNEMAN: Had you planned on seeing them there?

MR. HURLEY: No.

MR. HANNEMAN: And during that time, you never called my clients to see how your kids were doing, did you?

MR. HURLEY: No, I did not.

MR. HANNEMAN: You never offered any finan-cial assistance.

MR. HURLEY: I did not.

MR. HANNEMAN: You never called your father to see how your kids were doing.

MR. HURLEY: That is correct.

MR. HANNEMAN: Do you recall being present in this courtroom earlier this summer, on June 16, 1984?

MR. HURLEY: Well, I've been here several times now.

MR. HANNEMAN: The first time, the first time you both-ered to show up in court, do you remember that?

MR. HURLEY: I guess.

MR. HANNEMAN: At that time, which was June 16 of this year, you said in open court, at a status hearing in this matter, which was held to determine nothing less than the custody of your own children, you said, and I quote, "I don't want my kids."

MR. HURLEY: That's not what I meant to say.

MR. HANNEMAN: God forbid, we should find out what you meant to say, Mr. Hurley, just answer the question, you said, on that day, you said "I don't want my kids," didn't you?

MR. HURLEY: Yes.

MR. HANNEMAN: By the way, Mr. Hurley, if at any time during my examination you for any reason have difficulty remembering anything, please just let us know, because under the circumstances, I'm sure we'd all understand.

MR. GOLD: Objection, badgering.

THE COURT: Sustained.

MR. HANNEMAN: Which reminds me, Mr. Hurley, are you on any drugs or medication today which might prevent you from recalling events or providing accurate testimony?

MR. HURLEY: No.

MR. HANNEMAN: Are you sure?

MR. GOLD: Objection.

MR. HURLEY: Yes, I'm sure.

MR. HANNEMAN: Several years ago, my clients filed a petition for temporary guardianship for the purpose of taking custody of your children, were you aware of that?

MR. HURLEY: Yes.

MR. HANNEMAN: You received a summons to appear in that proceeding did you not?

MR. HURLEY: Yes.

MR. HANNEMAN: And even though you received a summons, regarding a matter that involved nothing less than who was going to take care of your kids, you never bothered to respond to the summons, did you?

MR. HURLEY: That is correct.

MR. HANNEMAN: Never asked anyone about it.

MR. HURLEY: That is correct.

MR. HANNEMAN: Never even asked what happened.

MR. HURLEY: That's true.

MR. HANNEMAN: By the way, you do remember your kids' names, don't you?

MR. HURLEY: Of course.

MR. HANNEMAN: Sam and Kate, in case you've forgotten.

MR. GOLD: Is that a question?

MR. HANNEMAN: Withdrawn. Mr. Hurley, growing up, you never felt abused or neglected by your parents, did you?

MR. HURLEY: No.

MR. HANNEMAN: They sent you to one of the finest schools in town, didn't they?

MR. HURLEY: I guess.

MR. HANNEMAN: And you repaid them by almost flunking out, isn't that right?

MR. HURLEY: I wouldn't say that.

MR. HANNEMAN: 2.0 GPA at Latin, isn't that right?

MR. HURLEY: Something like that.

MR. HANNEMAN: Never really applied yourself at Latin, did you, Mr. Hurley?

MR. HURLEY: That's fair to say.

MR. HANNEMAN: Doing drugs even back then, isn't that true?

MR. HURLEY: Some of the time, yes.

MR. HANNEMAN: And at the University of Wisconsin, took you five years to graduate, didn't it?

MR. HURLEY: Yeah.

MR. HANNEMAN: Parents paid for everything, didn't they?

MR. HURLEY: Yeah.

MR. HANNEMAN: 2.1 GPA at Madison.

MR. HURLEY: Yeah.

MR. HANNEMAN: You must have made your parents
so proud.

MR. GOLD: Objection.

THE COURT: Sustained.

MR. HANNEMAN: Doing drugs all five years in Madison
too, isn't that right?

MR. HURLEY: Yeah.

MR. HANNEMAN: After you got Jenny Walsh pregnant, the
two of you moved back to Chicago, didn't you?

MR. HURLEY: Yes.

MR. HANNEMAN: Never asked her to marry you, did you?

MR. HURLEY: No.

MR. HANNEMAN: Lived in an apartment your dad
paid for.

MR. HURLEY: Yes.

MR. HANNEMAN: And you and Jenny continued to party.

MR. HURLEY: Yeah.

MR. HANNEMAN: Like there was no tomorrow.

MR. HURLEY: I wouldn't say that.

MR. HANNEMAN: And after the kids were born, three days
after in fact, you and Jenny went out partying and didn't come back for
three days, isn't that right?

MR. HURLEY: That's right.

MR. HANNEMAN: You remember, good for you. And then you continued to do drugs and go to clubs up until the Jewel parking lot incident?

MR. HURLEY: Not all the time.

MR. HANNEMAN: Well, you didn't give up doing drugs that whole time, did you?

MR. HURLEY: No.

MR. HANNEMAN: Now on the night of February 18, 1982, you dropped Sam and Kate off at Jenny's mom's house in Bridgeport at eight-thirty in the evening, isn't that right?

MR. HURLEY: If that was the date, yes.

MR. HANNEMAN: And you told Jenny's mom you'd be back by one.

MR. HURLEY: I don't remember that.

MR. HANNEMAN: Not surprised. In fact, you didn't get back until nine o'clock the next morning, isn't that true?

MR. HURLEY: I guess.

MR. HANNEMAN: You guess. That night you did cocaine and drank alcohol.

MR. HURLEY: Yes.

MR. HANNEMAN: And the next morning, after picking up your kids in the Marathon cab, by the way you weren't supposed to be driving your family around in a Yellow cab, were you?

MR. HURLEY: No, I wasn't.

MR. HANNEMAN: So the next morning, you pick up the kids, and on the way home you stop to pick up some diapers at the Jewel.

MR. HURLEY: Yes.

MR. HANNEMAN: You and Jenny are on coke, alcohol, and Quaaludes at the time.

MR. HURLEY: That is correct.

MR, HANNEMAN: You get the diapers, come back to the car, Jenny is asleep in the passenger seat, the kids are in the back, and you decide it's a good idea to take a nap.

MR. HURLEY: I didn't decide anything. I fell asleep.

MR. HANNEMAN: The upshot is that you were charged with criminal neglect of your children as a result of that incident, were you not?

MR. HURLEY: That's correct.

MR. HANNEMAN: And pleaded guilty to child neglect.

MR. HURLEY: That's right.

MR. HANNEMAN: Neglect of the same children who are the subject of this hearing.

MR. HURLEY: That is correct.

MR. HANNEMAN: Let's talk a little bit about what you've done since then. After pleading guilty you ran away to Lone Rock, Wisconsin, population 950, and began living in a one-room apartment over a bar called the Mad House Inn.

MR. HURLEY: That's true.

MR. HANNEMAN: And you still live there today.

MR. HURLEY: Well, not exactly, I now live with my wife in a house…

MR. HANNEMAN: You're still renting out the one-room apartment, are you not?

MR. HURLEY: Well, yeah, because I didn't want to stiff
Lee Anne...

MR. HANNEMAN: And since moving up to Lone Rock,
you've been employed at a place that rents canoes.

MR. HURLEY: Well, it does more than that.

MR. HANNEMAN: But your primary job was loading and
unloading canoes.

MR. HURLEY: And driving people up and down the
river and outfitting them and...

MR. HANNEMAN: Oh, I'm sure this high powered job had
many other important responsibilities, but that was just in the summer,
in the winter you just did odd jobs around this so-called resort, isn't
that true.

MR. HURLEY: There's no use in arguing with you.

MR. HANNEMAN: I'm not arguing with you, Mr. Hurley,
I'm just trying to paint an accurate picture of what you've done with your
life for the past two and a half years. And for that work you were paid
what, the minimum wage, three dollars thirty-five cents an hour?

MR. HURLEY: Yes, with some bumps after that but not
much more.

MR. HANNEMAN: Mr. Hurley, do you have any
bank accounts?

MR. HURLEY: Yes, a savings account.

MR. HANNEMAN: What is the current balance in your
savings account?

MR. HURLEY: Around three hundred dollars.

MR. HANNEMAN: Do you own any other assets?

MR. HURLEY: Well, I have a Moto Guzzi motorcycle, and once my father's estate is finalized, I will be the owner of fifty-two acres of land in Wyoming Township, Iowa County, Wisconsin.

MR. HANNEMAN: Is that all?

MR. HURLEY: Yeah, I guess that's it.

MR. HANNEMAN: So your father is still giving you things, even after his death?

MR. HURLEY: Yes.

MR. HANNEMAN: You didn't like your father, did you, Mr. Hurley?

MR. HURLEY: No.

MR. HANNEMAN: Didn't like his politics.

MR. HURLEY: What I knew of his politics, no.

MR. HANNEMAN: Didn't maintain any semblance of a relationship with him, did you?

MR. HURLEY: No.

MR. HANNEMAN: From the time you ran away to Lone Rock to now, did you ever speak to your father?

MR. HURLEY: Yes, twice.

MR. HANNEMAN: And how did that go?

MR. HURLEY: Not well.

MR. HANNEMAN: Your father was the alderman of the Forty-Seventh Ward for over thirty-three years, City Council Finance chairman for twenty-five years, Chicago Catholic Archdiocese Man of the Year recipient, former Chairman of the Board of the Chicago Children's Hospital, DePaul College of Law Man of the Year recipient, and recipient

of numerous other awards and designations as a result of the work he
performed for the people of the City of Chicago, isn't that right?

MR. HURLEY: Yes.

MR. HANNEMAN: And what have you done for the City
of Chicago?

MR. HURLEY: Nothing.

MR. HANNEMAN: And what did you do for your father,
what did you do to repay the man who paid for all your education and
tried to give you everything in life?

MR. HURLEY: Not much.

MR. HANNEMAN: What have you done for anyone other
than yourself?

MR. HURLEY: Not much.

MR. HANNEMAN: That's right, not much. Your mother,
you didn't even bother to attend your mother's funeral, did you,
Mr. Hurley?

MR. HURLEY: I did not attend my mother's funeral.

MR. HANNEMAN: But you did attend your father's funeral.

MR. HURLEY: Yes.

MR. HANNEMAN: In high black Converse sneakers.

MR. HURLEY: Yes.

MR. HANNEMAN: And then walked out in the middle of
the cardinal's eulogy.

MR. HURLEY: Yes.

MR. HANNEMAN: And howled like a coyote at the back of
the church.

MR. HURLEY: Yes.

MR. HANNEMAN: And effectively killed the cardinal of the Archdiocese of Chicago.

MR. GOLD: Objection!

THE COURT: Overruled.

MR. HURLEY: Oh, please.

MR. HANNEMAN: So you thought the best way to honor your father's life work and his immense contribution to the City of Chicago and the State of Illinois was to make a mockery of his life and death?

MR. HURLEY: Under the circumstances, I did what I thought needed to be done.

MR. HANNEMAN: The fact of the matter is, Mr. Hurley, you haven't taken responsibility for anything in your entire life, isn't that true?

MR. HURLEY: I'm afraid that's mostly true.

MR. HANNEMAN: And you're now coming into this courtroom asking this judge to let you be responsible for the well-being of two beautiful five-year-old children?

MR. HURLEY: That is correct.

MR. HANNEMAN: That's all I have of this witness, Your Honor.

THE COURT: Do you have any other witnesses, Mr. Hanneman?

MR. HANNEMAN: The petitioners rest, Your Honor.

THE COURT: Mr. Gold, we have another half-hour before we'll break for lunch, does it make sense to proceed?

MR. GOLD: I think so, Your Honor, but I'd like to
reserve my examination of Mr. Hurley, and start with him after lunch, if
that's okay, and in the time left, I do have another witness who should not
take long.

THE COURT: Then proceed.

MR. GOLD: Respondent calls Ms. Mona Goodland.

[Ms. Goodland, five-feet-six inches, sleeveless black sheath, no
stockings, curvaceous, light brown skin, glowing, thick black hair pulled
back in a French twist, full red lips, high cheek bones, almond eyes,
sways, respectfully, in high heels across the courtroom, steps into the
witness box, smiles at the judge, and takes a seat.]

COURT CLERK: Raise your right hand. Do you swear to
tell the truth, the whole truth, and nothing but the truth so help you God?

MS. GOODLAND: I do.

MR. GOLD: Good morning, Ms. Goodland, Mona.

MS. GOODLAND: Good afternoon. [Smiling.]

MR. GOLD: Yes, already, so, please state your name
and spell it for the record.

MS. GOODLAND: Mona Goodland, M-o-n-a,
G-o-o-d-l-a-n-d.

MR. GOLD: Where do you reside, Ms. Goodland.

MS. GOODLAND: 12480 West Long Lake Road in Lone
Rock, Wisconsin.

MR. GOLD: Are you married?

MS. GOODLAND: Yes, to Billy Hurley.

MR. GOLD: Mona, you heard Billy's testimony just
now, about his financial situation, did you not?

MS. WOODLAND: Yes.

MR. GOLD: As Billy's wife, is it your understanding that his testimony was entirely accurate?

MS. WOODLAND: I think he was being too modest.

MR. GOLD: Please explain.

MS. WOODLAND: Billy and I were married on July 16th of this year. Just before we got married, about a month earlier actually, it so happened that my boss, Ray Devers, who owned Ray's Resort on the Wisconsin River in Spring Green, Wisconsin, well, Ray passed away, and much to my surprise, shock, really, Ray left all of his assets, including the resort, to me. One of the first things I did was to retain Mr. Wilcoxsin as my lawyer, who has assisted me with the financial issues involving the business, and Ray's assets. I am advised by Mr. Wilcoxsin…

MR. HANNEMAN: Objection, hearsay.

THE COURT: Well, Mr. Wilcoxsin's in court if you wish to examine him, Mr. Hanneman, and we don't have a jury in the box, so I'll overrule your objection. Go ahead, Ms. Goodland.

MS. GOODLAND: As I was saying, I've been advised by Mr. Wilcoxsin that by virtue of our marriage, Billy will become the owner of one-half of everything I own, which is the whole of the resort and all of Ray's assets, which includes the house we now live in on Long Lake in Lone Rock. So while Billy may only have three hundred dollars in his bank account, in fact he owns a considerable amount more than that, including the house we live in. But as far as I'm concerned, it doesn't matter what the law says, because he's my husband, and anything I own he owns.

[Mr. Wilcoxsin nodding his head in agreement.]

MR. GOLD: Tell us a little about what you inherited from Ray.

MS. GOODLAND: Well, Ray purchased the resort on the north bank of the river just outside Spring Green about thirty years ago, and ran it till he died a few months ago. The resort has cabins for let, an RV campground, swimming pool, main building with a bar serving drinks and bar food, and we rent out canoes and inner tubes, and provide transport for trips up and down the Wisconsin River. We've tried to give it a facelift over the years, and I've got plans for remodeling the main building, expanding the bar and food options, among a number of other improvements.

MR. GOLD: Is the business successful?

MS. GOODLAND: Well, before I got there, it was doing okay, from what Ray told me, breaking even, but we made some changes in the years before Ray passed, and it's made good money the past several years, enough to consider making some pretty substantial improvements over the next year or so.

[Mr. Wilcoxsin nodding his head.]

MR. GOLD: What about the house you live in now?

MS. GOODLAND: The house is a four-bedroom split level, with a three-car garage, on an acre of wooded property, floor to ceiling windows looking out through pine trees on a small hill that slopes down to the lake, and we have a pier, boats, that type of thing. Both of us just moved in, but that's where we live now. We're hiring a contractor to redo the kitchen. Ray was a bachelor, so it could use some updating.

MR. GOLD: If Billy gets custody of his children, where will they live?

MS. GOODLAND: With us, in our house, on the lake, each will have their own bedroom, plenty of room outside to explore.

MR. GOLD: And who will take care of them?

MS. GOODLAND: We will, of course.

MR. GOLD: Are you up for that?

MS. GOODLAND: Nothing would make me happier.

MR. GOLD: Will you need any help to do that?

MS. GOODLAND: What do you mean?

MR. GOLD: Well, like a nanny or anything.

MS. GOODLAND: Heavens no, why would we do that?

MR. GOLD: Where would the kids go to school?

MS. GOODLAND: St. John's Catholic Grade School in Spring Green.

MR. GOLD: Are you Catholic?

MS. GOODLAND: No, but it's a good school.

MR. GOLD: Are you supportive of your husband's effort to obtain custody of his children?

MS. GOODLAND: One hundred and ten percent. You see, I didn't know my parents, I don't know if I have any brothers and sisters, and I've never had a real family. I couldn't be more excited to help care for Billy's children, and hopefully [looking at Mr. Hurley], have some of our own.

MR. GOLD: Thank you, those are all the questions I have of this witness.

THE COURT: Mr. Hanneman?

MR. HANNEMAN: Yes, thank you, Your Honor. Ms. Goodland, what did you have to do to become the beneficiary of all of Mr. Devers's estate?

MS. GOODLAND: What do you mean?

MR. HANNEMAN: Well, you must have been pretty close to Mr. Devers.

MS. GOODLAND: Ray was like a father to me.

MR. HANNEMAN: Yes, I'm sure. When did you first meet Mr. Devers?

MS. GOODLAND: Well, I was with some friends one Labor Day weekend about five years ago and we came up to go canoeing down the river, and it happened that as we were pulling our canoe onto the beach, I saw a young girl slip out of an inner tube into the river and she was thrashing around, not able to swim, and I was the first to see it all happen, so I ran over and was able to drag her out, scared me half to death. After that Ray was super grateful, and from that we got to know each other and he then offered me a job. I've been there ever since.

MR. HANNEMAN: But what was the extent of your relationship with Mr. Devers?

MS. GOOLDAND: Look, I know what you're after, you're not the first one to think so, especially after Ray left me everything, but it was never like that, Ray had his share of lovers, but I wasn't one of them.

MR. HANNEMAN: And yet he left everything to you. How do you explain that?

MS. GOODLAND: Well, I don't know for sure, he never talked to me about it. First I heard of it was when Mr. Wilcoxsin told me, the day we had a memorial service for Ray, just a couple of months ago, the day after Mr. Hurley was killed it turns out. I was in shock then and

still am today. But I must say, I helped Ray out a lot, helped him make a
lot of changes for the better around the resort, it was going to seed you
might say, needed a new look, a different touch, and I helped with that,
and then he had me look at the books, and we made changes on the
financial side, too, and the past two years Ray made more money than he
had the previous five, and he appreciated that. I think…

MR. HANNEMAN: All right, Ms. Goodland…

THE COURT: You asked the question, Mr. Hanneman,
let her answer.

MS. GOODLAND: Well, as I was saying, I think Ray knew
that I would do a good job. He didn't have any kids, no relatives he knew
of, and he loved his resort, and he loved his community, and the community loved him, and the more I've had a chance to think about it, the more
I think he might have thought it'd be best for the resort and the community, and for me, to turn it over to me and make sure I would stick around
and preserve his legacy.

MR. HANNEMAN: Ms. Goodland, I'd like to change the
subject for a moment, because I'm kind of interested in the timing of your
husband's newfound interest in his children. The way I see it, first, my
clients file this petition, then Mr. Hurley's father dies, then you inherit
all of Mr. Devers's assets, then Mr. Hurley decides to marry you, then he
finds out his father left all his money to his children, and then he decides
to try and get his children back. I find that all a little suspicious, don't you,
Ms. Goodland?

MS. GOODLAND: You've got it all wrong.

MR. HANNEMAN: Really, seems straightforward to me.

MS. GOODLAND: Billy didn't decide to marry me, I
asked him.

MR. HANNEMAN: Asked him what?

MS. GOODLAND: It wasn't his idea to get married. It was my idea. I wanted to marry him, and I knew he loved me, but I was afraid he'd never get around to it, so I asked him if he would marry me, not the other way around. And as far as his father's estate is concerned, we don't need any of that money, we won't use it for a nanny or toys or anything, it's the kids' money, we'll take care of the kids out of our own pockets. Their money is theirs; it should be saved for them.

MR. HANNEMAN: [Pretends to look at his notes, awkward silence.]

THE COURT: Do you have any other questions for this witness, Mr. Hanneman?

MR. HANNEMAN: Uh, no, Your Honor, that will be all.

THE COURT: Any redirect, Mr. Gold?

MR. GOLD: No, Your Honor.

THE COURT: Then, we'll break for lunch. See you all back here at two.

(Recessed at 1:05 p.m.)

(Reconvened at 2:10 p.m.)

THE COURT: Good afternoon, are we ready to proceed?

[Judge looks out at the courtroom, notices more people in the back benches, Alderman Gusman among them.]

MR. HANNEMAN: Yes, Your Honor.

MR. GOLD: Yes, Your Honor.

UNIDENTIFIED VOICE: Your Honor, may I approach?

UNIDENTIFIED VOICE: Good afternoon, Your Honor,
Sydney Black, on behalf of myself and other subpoenaed parties.

THE COURT: What can I do for you, Mr. Black?

MR. BLACK: Your Honor, the respondent's counsel has issued subpoenas for appearance at trial on Alderman Ronald
Gusman, Mr. Mark Hamilton, and myself. We understand that the matter
before the court for which the subpoenas were issued involves a guardianship hearing to determine guardianship for the children of respondent.
Your Honor, I can say unequivocally on behalf of the subpoenaed parties
that we have nothing whatsoever to do with the issues involved in this
case, nor do we care. We all have much better things to do with our time,
especially Alderman Gusman, and it's nothing less than pure harassment
to require our presence here this afternoon. As a result, I would like to
make an oral motion to quash these subpoenas.

THE COURT: Well, we discussed this earlier this
morning, Mr. Black, and respondent's counsel believes that each of you
may have some relationship to an issue that already has come up in this
hearing, which is respondent's relationship with his father.

UNIDENTIFIED VOICE   [Approaching the bench from
the back benches.] Your Honor, this is ridiculous, I could care less about
his relationship with his father...

THE COURT: Let the record reflect that one of the
subpoenaed parties, Alderman Gusman, has addressed the Court and
approached the bench.

THE COURT: Mr. Gusman, according to Mr. Black, you are represented by counsel, so I ask that you please take your seat…

MR. GUSMAN: Really, Judge? You're gonna pull the high hat? On me?

THE COURT: Mr. Gusman, be seated, now.

MR. GUSMAN: [Returning to his seat, waving his arms.] This is ridiculous…

THE COURT: As I was saying, respondent's counsel has advised that the subpoenaed witnesses may have testimony relevant to this matter, and while I am skeptical of what that might be, I do not have a sufficient basis to quash the subpoenas at this time. If it should turn out that the witnesses are not called and there was no reasonable basis for them being here, you, Mr. Black, may pursue an appropriate sanctions remedy. In the meantime, the most efficient thing to do is proceed. So please take a seat.

MR. GUSMAN: [From the back benches.] Oh for God's sake…

THE COURT: And there will be no more outbursts. [Looking at Alderman Gusman.] Anyone interrupting these proceedings is subject to contempt of court.

Is there a motion to exclude witnesses?

MR. GOLD: No, Your Honor, we would prefer the witnesses hear the testimony.

THE COURT: Mr. Hanneman?

MR. HANNEMAN: They're all irrelevant, so it doesn't matter to me, Judge.

THE COURT: Okay then, Mr. Gold, call your next witness.

MR. GOLD: Respondent calls Billy Hurley.

[While Mr. Hurley takes the stand, the judge scans the back benches. Ms. Goodland and Dorothy are seated where they were in the morning session, in the first row behind respondent's counsel table, two rows behind them sits Reverend Simmons, and a companion, in the last row sits Alderman Gusman, on the aisle, ready to make his getaway. Across the aisle behind the petitioners' table, in the first row, sits Ms. Beecher, two rows behind her, Sydney Black, next to Sydney Black in the same row, Mark Hamilton.]

THE COURT: Mr. Hurley, you understand you're still under oath?

MR. HURLEY: Yes, Your Honor.

THE COURT: Go ahead, Mr. Gold.

MR. GOLD: Mr. Hurley, when was the last time you used illegal drugs.

MR. HURLEY: Two and a half years ago. I didn't remember the date until Mr. Hanneman used it in his questioning, but if he was right that we dropped the kids off on February 18, 1982, then the last time I ever took illegal drugs was February 19, 1982.

MR. GOLD: And what was the reason you stopped?

MR. HURLEY: Sounds like the same reason Mrs. Walsh stopped. It wasn't the getting busted part, or the charges, or the bad press, or whatever anybody thought of me, I didn't really care about that as much, it was much worse than any of that really, it was about what I thought of myself, it was like, waking up and realizing, that I actually could have done something like that, to two innocent kids, who were totally dependent on me, and that I was so messed up I thought getting high was more important. It was really pretty devastating, less than zero self-respect, just pure guilt, when I look back on it, knowing how low I could get, and I kind of felt, not just worthless, but irredeemable, total loser, bottom of the barrel, and those were understatements, knowing that everything I had done up to that point in my life didn't amount to squat, but it was worse than that, because I now was endangering other people, my own kids for God's sake, so I figured the best thing I could do, especially for my kids, was to get away. I didn't deserve to be around anybody, and the only good thing that came of it, was the possibility that drugs might have had something to do with it, hoping to God drugs had something to do with it, that otherwise maybe I didn't have that in me, and maybe if I got off that stuff I might some day be able to salvage something, that there had to be something better, I just couldn't go on like that, cuz if I did it wouldn't be worth it to go on at all. So the one positive thing I did as a result of all that was to stop partying, stop the drugs, cut back on liquor.

MR. GOLD: Did you stop drinking alcohol all together?

MR. HURLEY: No, I drink beer, a bourbon now and then, not a lot.

MR. GOLD: According to your testimony, after you left, you never tried to contact your kids, why was that?

MR. HURLEY: Well, I couldn't. The court order I agreed to specifically said I was barred from contacting my kids until further order of court.

MR. GOLD: [Turns to respondent's counsel table and takes three documents handed to him by Mr. Wilcoxsin, tenders one of the documents to Mr. Hanneman, and another to the judge.] Your Honor, may I approach the witness?

THE COURT: You may.

MR. GOLD: Mr. Hurley, I'm now showing you a document we've marked as Respondent's Exhibit No. 1 for identification, and ask if you recognize it.

MR. HURLEY: [Examining the document.] Yes, this is the court order that was entered on my child neglect charge.

MR. GOLD: And to the best of your recollection is Respondent's Exhibit No. 1 for identification a true and correct copy of the court order concluding your child neglect charge?

MR. HURLEY: Yes.

MR. GOLD: And does the language barring you from contacting your children until further order of court appear in that document?

MR. HURLEY: Yes, in handwriting at the bottom, before the judge's signature.

MR. GOLD: Your Honor, I now wish to introduce Respondent's Exhibit No. 1 into evidence.

THE COURT: Mr. Hanneman?

MR. HANNEMAN: [Look of displeasure.] Your Honor…

THE COURT: Mr. Hanneman, I can take judicial notice of a court order…

MR. HANNEMAN: No objection.

THE COURT: Respondent's Exhibit No. 1 is allowed.

MR. GOLD: What was your understanding of this order?

MR. HURLEY: What it says, that I couldn't contact or make any effort to contact my kids.

MR. GOLD: Mr. Hurley, in your direct examination you testified that you never asked about your children, can you explain that?

MR. HURLEY: Well, I couldn't talk to my dad about it, he didn't want to talk to me about anything, and my mom was sick with cancer, and the few times I talked to her I didn't want to inject that into it, probably should have, but I don't know, for some reason I thought I shouldn't, shouldn't make it worse than it already was, and bottom line is, I knew the Walshes would take good care of them, I know Mr. Walsh loves his grandkids, and that Mrs. Walsh was a good woman, and I guess I just figured if anything bad happened I would find out about it. Nothing good would come out of asking about them. Nothing I could have done about it anyway. I just felt it was best I should stay away, like the order said, stay out of their lives, best for them, for sure.

MR. GOLD: You mentioned your mother, you testified in your direct examination that you didn't attend your mother's funeral. How did that happen?

MR. HURLEY: Well, you have to know how bad things were between my dad and me at the time. He blamed me, what I did, for making my mom sick. He loved her a great deal, and he thought I was responsible for her death. So when he called to tell me about it, it was a tough telephone call, and I asked about the service, and he told me the only person who wanted to see me was dead, so I figured that was his way of saying I shouldn't come, so I didn't.

MR. GOLD: Did you love your mother?

MR. HURLEY: Of course, I loved my mother.

MR. GOLD: During your direct examination, Mr. Hanneman quoted you as saying that you didn't want your kids, and you said that wasn't what you meant to say. What did you mean to say?

MR. HURLEY: All I was trying to say was that I didn't intend to contest custody.

MR. GOLD: You also said in your direct examination that you didn't respond to the summons that was served on you for the Walshes' temporary guardianship petition?

MR. HURLEY: Didn't see why that would make any sense. I wasn't in a position to do anything about it at the time, and back then, the best thing for them was to stay with the Walshes.

MR. GOLD: You're recently married, are you not?

MR. HURLEY: That is correct.

MR. GOLD: Was that your idea, to get married?

MR. HURLEY: Well, it should have been, but to be honest, the idea hadn't crossed my mind, I mean I was totally into her, but I guess I still thought I was such a loser I didn't think it possible anybody, especially someone like her, would want to take the risk. But she did, and so we did.

MR. GOLD: So she proposed to you?

MR. HURLEY: Yeah, that's how it worked.

MR. GOLD: Where did that happen?

MR. HURLEY: Under a viaduct in the rain on Interstate 90 outside of Chicago.

MR. GOLD: Not very romantic.

MR. HURLEY: Probably doesn't sound like much, but I thought it was, still do, she's pretty cool.

[A door opens in the back of the courtroom and a man of medium height, harried, dyed black hair, atrocious brown plaid sport coat, walks into the courtroom, a notebook, spiraled at the top, in his hand, opens the swinging gate, sits on the far side of Ms. Beecher in the first row behind petitioners' table, flips open the notebook and removes a pen from his shirt pocket, poised to write. Alderman Gusman thinks he recognizes him, the judge does recognize him, Trib beat reporter for the courthouse, the judge wondering what took him so long. The reporter is followed into the courtroom by two court watchers, retirees, who tend to follow the reporter around to cases of interest in the courthouse. The court watchers take a seat in the last row on petitioners' side of the courtroom.]

MR. GOLD: From the sounds of your wife's testimony, you are now the co-owner of the resort?

MR. HURLEY: Well, to be honest, I didn't know anything about it until we started preparing for this hearing, didn't really care either, I've never spoken to Conrad, Mr. Wilcoxsin, about that, and anyway, to me it doesn't really matter, she can own it all as far as I'm concerned, but she's just not like that, I'm not either, we're not in it to make a bunch of money, or count up what we own, I'm just honored to share stuff with her, share a life with her. But it's fair to say, as you lawyers say, that the whole thing with Ray did change things a lot as far as this whole situation is concerned.

MR. GOLD: What do you mean by that, what whole thing, what situation?

MR. HURLEY: Well, we're both in a much better position to take care of my kids now. We didn't ask Ray to give Mona all his stuff, it just happened, but what it means is that we can afford to take good care of them, provide for them, give them a life, a pretty decent life actually, much more so than a few months ago.

MR. GOLD: And now, after the resort changing hands, and your marriage, will that change the nature of your work at all?

MR. HURLEY: Well, it probably will. If I'm a co-owner I'll have to act like it, I guess, take a little ownership, help out in any way I can, at the resort, in the community. A big part of what Ray did, the reason the resort was such a special place, is what Ray did around town, for everybody, and I think both of us will want to carry that on. We haven't really talked about it all that much, it's all pretty new for us, but I'll do whatever I can, Mona's really good at this stuff, she's got good ideas, she's a good businesswoman [Mr. Wilcoxsin nodding in agreement], so I plan on staying out of her way, and doing what she thinks is best.

[The door to the courtroom opens again, and Bob Olson, Illinois Department of Central Management Services, and Pete Vuckovic, Illinois Department of Public Aid, walk into the courtroom, no idea why they're there or what it's about, but they both got a phone call that made them nervous, so they decided to find out what was going on, and took a seat in the row behind Sydney Black and Mark Hamilton.]

MR. GOLD: Billy, in your direct examination, Mr. Hanneman asked you about your relationship with your father.

MR. HURLEY: Yes.

MR. GOLD: You attended your father's funeral.

MR. HURLEY: Yes.

MR. GOLD: I take it that didn't go as you had planned.

MR. HURLEY: Well, I didn't really have a plan. Wasn't even sure it was the right thing to do, but Mona thought I should go, and so we did. You see, my father and I just didn't get along, he didn't like me, and I didn't like him, and I thought my going might have caused trouble, and I was right about that, but I think in the end she was right, that it was the right thing to do.

MR. GOLD: Even though you walked out?

MR. HURLEY: I didn't plan on doing that. But here we were in this church, the heart of the Catholic church in all Chicago, and the cardinal, the highest priest, is on the altar, and he's telling lies about my father, in front of all those people, and lies about our relationship, and everybody there [Mr. Hurley looks at the judge] knew they were lies, and I don't care who he was, he didn't have the right to tell lies about us...

MR. GOLD: You're referring to the cardinal?

MR. HURLEY: Yeah, he was lying in his own church, before his God, I thought it was disgusting, and didn't want to be a part of his charade, used like that, so I walked out.

[The Trib reporter in the first row writing furiously. Alderman Gusman eyeing the reporter suspiciously, what the hell is going on.]

MR. GOLD: And the howl?

MR. HURLEY: Yeah, everybody thought that was so disrespectful, but my dad actually would have appreciated that, maybe not in church, but I think he would have understood, because it was an old family thing we did, something we'd always do at our property in Wisconsin, as we went to bed in our little cabin side by side on our cots we'd hear coyotes in the distance, and before we'd go to sleep, my dad would always let out a big howl, as would my mom, and then me, even our dog would chime in. It was our way of saying good night to each other, and to the coyotes, and so it really was a tribute to him, that was my way of saying goodbye, even though nobody got it, especially the cardinal, and I am sorry that happened, but he was telling lies on the altar.

MR. GOLD: So, did you ever reconcile with your father?

MR. HURLEY: Not while he was alive.

MR. GOLD: What do you mean by that?

MR. HURLEY: Well, I think I might be reconciling with him now.

MR. GOLD: Now, you mean now in this courtroom?

MR. HURLEY: Yes, now, in this courtroom, and in the past several weeks. To my surprise, I've come to learn something about my father that I never knew before, a totally different side of him I didn't know existed, but I'm pretty sure about it now.

[The door to the courtroom opens again, Alderman Gusman looks up, surprised, to see Johnny Jefferson, Commissioner of the City of Chicago Department of Buildings, son of the mayor, step into the courtroom. Commissioner Jefferson also is surprised, not pleasantly, to see Alderman Gusman, Sydney Black, and Mark Hamilton, all of whom are surprised to see each other. Commissioner Jefferson steps into the back row and slides by Alderman Gusman to take a seat next to him. "What the fuck," he whispers to Alderman Gusman, who shrugs his shoulders, increasingly uncomfortable, Sydney Black melting into his bench seat.]

MR. GOLD: How so?

MR. HURLEY: Well, a big part of the problem between my dad and me was his politics. He was a political animal and I wasn't, but it was more than that, because it also was his brand of politics, all the clout, and back slapping and control and power trips, really turned me off, and then that whole Council Wars thing sent me over the edge, I thought it was racist, and everybody thought I was the same way because of what my father did, and I didn't appreciate that, and he never tried to see it from my point of view.

MR. HANNEMAN: Objection, Your Honor, we're getting pretty far afield here.

THE COURT: [The judge, all too aware of the back benches filling, the Trib reporter scribbling, Alderman Gusman, Johnny Jefferson, getting interested.] Well, I might agree with you Mr. Hanneman, except that, let's see [the judge flipping pages in a legal pad], according to my notes, Mr. Hanneman, you specifically asked him whether he agreed with his father's politics, and whether he had any semblance of a relationship with his father, so I believe you were the one who opened the door. Your objection is overruled. Go ahead, Mr. Gold.

MR. GOLD: So what if anything has changed about your view of your father's politics?

MR. HURLEY: Well, it all began with a procedural maneuver my father pulled at a City Council meeting the day before he died.

[Alderman Gusman, Commissioner Jefferson, and Messrs. Black and Hamilton, squirming. Dorothy beaming.]

My father did something that day I know he'd never done before, something nobody might have done in a hundred years in the Council chamber. He deferred and published a rezoning matter in a ward that wasn't his.

MR. GOLD: Why is that so unusual?

MR. HURLEY: Because of a thing called aldermanic prerogative, which makes the alderman of each ward king of his castle, and nobody wants to mess with what an alderman is doing in his or her ward, because well, it's just not done, but, more importantly, if you do, then somebody might come after what you're doing in your ward, and nobody wants that to happen.

MR. GOLD: So what was different about this particular zoning matter?

MR. HANNEMAN: Your Honor, zoning matters? Really? This guardianship hearing is now caught up in zoning matters?

THE COURT: Do you have an objection, Mr. Hanneman?

MR. HANNEMAN: Yes, Your Honor I have…

THE COURT: Overruled.

MR. HURLEY: Well, this rezoning matter involved a warehouse located at 2620 West Jackson Boulevard, which is next door to Reverend Simmons's Saving Grace West Side Community Center. [The Reverend nodding his head.] The item up for passage was to rezone the property for a warehouse operation. And when the matter came up, my father took advantage of a procedural rule which allows any two aldermen to defer a matter to the next meeting, which is what my father did, and it so happened he did so at the last meeting before the Council's summer break, which meant the matter couldn't come up again until the fall, which would be the City Council meeting scheduled for this Friday.

MR. GOLD: So, what does this have to do with you and your father?

MR. HANNEMAN: Good question, I would like the record to reflect a continuing objection to this entire line of questioning.

THE COURT: So noted. Mr. Hurley, you may answer the question.

MR. HURLEY: Well, Your Honor, you might recall there were some delays before the last two statuses in this case, delays which required that I spend some time in town, and I didn't have anything else to do really, so I decided to look into what my father was up to, and in the course of doing that, I discovered that my father was having serious second thoughts about his own politics, and what his legacy might be, in such a way that it changed how I thought about him, helped us come together actually, helped me form some semblance of a relationship with him, in Mr. Hanneman's words, and the weird and sad part is that it only happened after he died. Oh, and, also, in the course of doing that, I found out why he was murdered.

[Low hum in the courtroom, shifting on wooden seats, some uncomfortably, some straining to hear, the reporter frantically writing.]

MR. GOLD: [Let that settle in.] What was it that you discovered which led to that realization?

MR. HURLEY: Well, the Illinois Department of Public Aid wanted to consolidate all of its warehouse operations around the city, and decided to look for a large warehouse to rent, near transportation, in a low income area, from a minority businessman or woman, some kind of win-win, for the State, the community, that kind of thing, [Mr. Olson and Mr. Vuckovic exchange a look], but before they went public with a Request for Proposal, somebody at the State leaked the information to Alderman Gusman.

[Alderman Gusman looks furiously at Sydney Black.]

MR. HANNEMAN: Objection, foundation, hearsay.

MR. GUSMAN: [Across the aisle to Mr. Black.] Don't just sit there, say something!

MR. BLACK: [Jumps to his feet from the back benches.] Objection, Your Honor, this is slander!

THE COURT: [Calmly.] That is not an objection, Mr. Black. Mr. Gold please provide a foundation.

MR. GOLD: Mr. Hurley, how did you come by this information?

MR. HURLEY: My dad's secretary, Dorothy [nodding to Dorothy], was cleaning out my dad's desk after he died, and she found a file my dad kept under lock and key in a desk drawer that she didn't know what to do with, thought she had to show it to somebody, and figured that should be me. In that file, my dad had a copy of the original warehouse lease entered into by the State, and another document we can get to later, but the lease had the address for the property, which was 2620 W. Jackson, which matched the address for the zoning matter my dad deferred and published. Dorothy knew about the property because she knows Reverend Simmons, and knew it was right next door to his church. So I went out to see Reverend Simmons, to ask him some questions about the warehouse, looked at the warehouse, found out my dad had done the same thing, [Reverend Simmons nodding], and somebody from the church, who worked at IDPA, found out I was asking questions, and this guy says he wants to meet with me, so we met in the Art Institute gardens, he never told me his name, I'm sure you could find out who he is, but he said he'd been working on the warehouse deal long before it went public, and he told me there was no way the winning bidder ever could have responded as fast as they did with the exact information required without getting an inside tip.

MR. HANNEMAN: Obviously hearsay, Your Honor.

MR. GOLD: Your Honor, the information is being provided not for the truth of the matter asserted but for the purpose of showing that my client relied on the information to conduct his own investigation.

THE COURT: [Hesitating.] The testimony concerning the conversation with the anonymous IDPA employee will not be allowed for the truth of the statement, but you may proceed, Mr. Gold.

MR. GOLD: Then what did you do Mr. Hurley?

MR. HURLEY: Well, then I got married.

MR. GOLD: What did you do next, after you got married, in connection with your investigation?

MR. HURLEY: After I got married, I was back in town for another status that got delayed, and I went to the Recorder's Office to look up the 2620 W. Jackson address, and found it'd been sold by Reverend Simmons just a couple of months before the lease was entered into, for $10,000, according to the Reverend. I also found that some electrical company had filed a lawsuit against the property, so I went to the Chancery Division Clerk's office, looked at the court file for the lawsuit, and discovered that Alderman Gusman had been added to the lawsuit as some kind of an owner of the property because he'd signed a $500,000 guaranty for the warehouse construction financing, and that a couple of weeks after that was discovered, and made part of the public record, the case settled. I also saw on the checkout sheet for the court file that my dad had looked at that same file, one week before the June City Council meeting, so he must have known Alderman Gusman was connected to the property.

[The judge tried to suppress a smile. Alderman Gusman glowering across the aisle at Sydney Black, looking over his shoulder at Alderman Gusman, and checking his pockets for loose Tums.]

MR. BLACK: [Standing.] Objection, Your Honor, foundation, there's no proof of any such guaranty.

MR. GOLD: Your Honor, we're not trying to prove any such guaranty, Mr. Hurley is simply trying to explain how he's reconciled with his father...

THE COURT: Well, it's taking him a while.

MR. GOLD: …and in any event, Your Honor, we do
have a copy of the guaranty [Mr. Gold stepping over to his counsel table,
Mr. Wilcoxsin handing him several documents, Mr. Gold walking back
to the benches, handing one of the documents to Mr. Black, one to Mr.
Hanneman, and another to the Trib reporter. Mr. Black reaches over the
bench to take the document out of the reporter's hand, but the reporter
brushes him away.] I don't think it necessary for our purposes, but if
Your Honor should require that we do so we can always call Alderman
Gusman to authenticate the document and his signature.

   THE COURT: That will not be necessary.

   MR. HANNEMAN: Continuing objection, Your Honor.

   THE COURT: Understood, Mr. Hanneman. Proceed,
Mr. Gold.

   MR. GOLD: Please continue, Billy.

   MR. HURLEY: From the guaranty, the court file, the
property documents, and some info on the landlord in the Secretary of
State's office, I knew that Alderman Gusman was involved in the warehouse deal, and that Sydney Black was his lawyer, registered agent, and
all around straw man, and then things started to get really interesting,
because the next day I went to the State of Illinois Building and looked
up the file on the State's lease of the warehouse, and looked at a bunch
of documents, and the bottom line is that this lease is all caught up in
something called a credit tenant loan, which Mr. Hamilton, of Lincoln
Financial, one of our subpoenaed witnesses, who is in court today, [Mr.
Hamilton, looking for a place to hide], can tell us about if necessary, but
in a nutshell, it works like this: Mr. Hamilton lines up an insurance company, in this case, American Patriot Insurance Company out of Atlanta,
that's looking for a safe long-term investment, and the insurance company
is willing to pay a certain discounted amount now for the right to receive

all the rental payments the State is going to pay over the twenty years of this warehouse lease, which, best I can tell, given the terms of the deal, works out to be around five million dollars, that the insurance company pays the landlord. Mr. Hamilton can correct me if I have any of this wrong.

[Mr. Hamilton, mortified, holding his head in his hands, Messrs. Olson and Vuckovic holding their heads in their hands as well. Mr. Black melting into his seat.]

MR. GOLD: And to whom does that get paid?

[Alderman Gusman and Commissioner Jefferson, sweating, profusely.]

MR. HURLEY: To the landlord, the owner of the property at 2620 W. Jackson Boulevard, which turns out at least in part to be a company controlled by Alderman Gusman.

[Alderman Gusman and Commissioner Jefferson, watching five million dollars swirling down the drain. The Trib reporter can't write fast enough.]

MR. GOLD: Did you determine who else may have had an ownership interest in the property?

MR. HURLEY: Yes.

[Alderman Gusman and Commissioner Jefferson, realizing at the exact same moment there's much more involved than just the money.]

MR. HURLEY: According to the lease documents and the property ownership documents, another one of the owners, a 50% owner along with Alderman Gusman as far as I can tell, is a person by the name of Viola Jones [Commissioner Jefferson hangs his head], and Viola Jones happens to be the wife of Johnny Jefferson, the Commissioner of the City of Chicago Department of Buildings, who also happens to be the son of the mayor of the City of Chicago. Commissioner Jefferson can correct me if I'm wrong as well, because I see he's in court today, too.

MR. GOLD:　　　　　　　Okay, so, that was a lot to digest, could you summarize all of that for us, Mr. Hurley?

MR. HURLEY:　　　　　　Sure, my investigation determined that the owners of the property at 2620 W. Jackson Boulevard, who include at a minimum Alderman Gusman and the daughter-in-law of the mayor of the City of Chicago, took a very valuable piece of property from Reverend Simmons for $10,000, invested about $500,000 into rehabbing the building, and were about to walk away, next week, with around $5 million, for a return of around 900%, on a deal that was supposed to benefit a low-income community and its minority members, who happen to be the mayor's constituents.

MR. GOLD:　　　　　　Is that all?

MR. HURLEY:　　　　　No, most importantly, it turns out, my dad was killed because of this deal.

[Collective, "What did he say?"]

MR. GOLD:　　　　　　Go on.

MR. HURLEY:　　　　　Mr. Hamilton can confirm, that once I put all this together, I called him to let him know that I was on to them. Within two hours of my call to Mr. Hamilton, I got a call from someone who said they wanted to meet me in City Hall to give me some information about the deal, and like an idiot I go down there, and whoever it was who called me lured me into a room, where I was told to "Let It Go," which I took to mean my looking into the warehouse deal, and I got locked in a room, where the only way out was into the old transport tunnels beneath the city. I escaped the room through the tunnels and out through the subbasement at Marshall Field's, confronted Sydney Black the next morning, and attended the last status before Your Honor [looking at the judge]. The next morning, before I left to go back home, I got a call from who I thought was the deputy sheriff up in Iowa County, Wisconsin, who said they had something they wanted to show me at my dad's property having to do with my dad's death, so after I rode my motorcycle back to Wisconsin, I stopped off at my dad's property at the time we'd agreed on, and when I got there, I walked over to the same spot where my dad was killed, and someone fired an arrow at me in the exact same way my father got killed, but he missed, and I chased him through the woods, and with my wife's help chased him in a boat down the river, until he slammed into a sandstone wall, fell into the river, and drowned. Turns out, that man's name was Leonard Sweeney. Sweeney used to work for Judge Murphy of the Cook County Circuit Court, who was indicted for taking bribes. Up until he died, Sweeney worked in the City Clerk's office in City Hall, and, on information and belief, [Mr. Hurley smiled], I understand that Sweeney was a known associate of Mr. Sydney Black. [Mr. Hamilton slid a distance away from Mr. Black on the bench seat.] Mr. Black is one of our subpoenaed witnesses and I believe he can testify about his connection with Sweeney and Sweeney's connection with the warehouse if Your Honor should want to hear about that.

[Mouths open. Dead silence in the courtroom, but for the furious scratching of the reporter's pen in his spiral note book. Alderman Gusman and Commissioner Jefferson, horrified. Sydney Black, about to faint. And then, the silence was shattered.]

MR. GUSMAN: [Jumping to his feet, shouting.] Your Honor, I want the record to reflect that I don't know anything about this Sweeney guy, and I have no idea how he could have been connected to our deal!

UNIDENTIFIED VOICE: [Mr. Jefferson jumps to his feet, equally loud.] That goes for me too, Your Honor, and my wife, and my father!

[Alderman Gusman, frantic, helpless, looks around, desperate, he lunges across the aisle toward Mr. Black, reaches for his neck, and starts strangling him in open court, Mr. Black gasping for air, Mr. Hamilton, sliding back against the wall.]

THE COURT: [Slamming gavel.] Order! Order! Bailiff!

[Commissioner Jefferson slips out of the courtroom. Mr. Gold and Mr. Wilcoxsin run to the aid of Mr. Black, Mr. Gold wedges in between the two men, Mr. Wilcoxsin grabs Alderman Gusman from behind.]

THE COURT: [Shouting.] Mr. Gold, please tell me Alderman Gusman is free to go!

MR. GOLD: [Bent down between Mr. Black and Alderman Gusman.] Absolutely, Your Honor!

THE COURT: Alderman Gusman please remove yourself from this courtroom at once!

[Alderman Gusman, huffing, confused, looks at Sydney Black's purple face, takes his hands off his neck, looks around the courtroom, at the judge, turns, retreats, and rushes out the courtroom door.]

THE COURT: We're taking a fifteen-minute break for everyone to cool down! [Slamming his gavel.]

(Court Recessed at 3:20 p.m.)

(Reconvened at 3:45 p.m.)

THE COURT: Mr. Gold, are you close to completing your examination?

MR. GOLD: Almost, Your Honor, just a few other things. Mr. Hurley, you mentioned earlier in your examination that you were reconciling with your father in part because of what you discovered about a change in his politics, could you tell us about that?

MR. HURLEY: Yeah, the other document in that file he had locked in his desk was a one-page handwritten document, with the word "Grenade," written at the top. From what I can tell, it was the grenade he planned on throwing into the political machine he'd served his whole life. The document has a list of bullet points on it, reform ideas he planned on announcing at a press conference. One of them was the defer and publish rezoning item that we've already talked about. He saw that as one of his reforms.

MR. GOLD: [Mr. Gold turns back to his counsel table and Mr. Wilcoxsin hands to him several pages of documents. Mr. Gold hands one of the pages to the Trib reporter, one to Mr. Hanneman, and one to the judge.] May I approach, Your Honor?

THE COURT: You may.

MR. GOLD: Mr. Hurley, I'm now showing you a document we've marked as Respondent's Exhibit No. 2 for identification, and I ask you if you recognize it.

MR. HURLEY: I do. This is the one-page document that was in my dad's file that I just testified about.

MR. GOLD: Do you recognize the handwriting on this document?

MR. HURLEY: Yes, it's my dad's handwriting. [Dorothy nodding.]

MR. GOLD: Your Honor, I move Respondent's Exhibit 2 into evidence.

MR. HANNEMAN: [Recovering from the shock of Mr. Hurley's prior testimony.] Objection, relevance.

THE COURT: Yes, I'm not exactly sure about the relevance of this document, Mr. Gold, although it does relate to Dan Hurley's politics, which was one of the subjects of Mr. Hanneman's questions. I'll reserve ruling on admission of the document, but you can go ahead, and we'll see where this goes.

MR. GOLD: Billy, what is your understanding of the bullet points on this document?

MR. HURLEY: Well, as far as I can tell, this document is nothing less than a manifesto, a wrench my dad wanted to throw in the works. [The judge, Mr. Hanneman, and the Trib reporter, all carefully examining the bullet points on the document.] If you look closely, the dashes aren't dashes, they're what's called a tilde, a mark my dad used as an abbreviation, which in logic means a negative, so you can see from this document that my father wanted to do away with aldermanic prerogative, appoint judges based on merit, do away with patronage, prohibit anyone in government from doing business with government, reform the assessor's office, make each rank of police reflect the city's racial percentage, reform the way bond counsel are appointed and charge for their work, set percentage goals for minority participation in government contracts, and do away with the committeemen system. You can see the tenth item is the defer and publish matter, and the final item refers to announcing all of these things at a press conference, which he planned on doing before he was killed. Seems to me that by this he's trying to gut the machine.

MR. HANNEMAN: Objection, Your Honor, it is not at all clear from this document that it says what Mr. Hurley says it says.

THE COURT: I'm having a little difficulty with that as well, but it certainly appears to be a reasonable interpretation.

THE COURT: [To the court reporter.] Madam court reporter, let's go off the record for a moment.

[Off the record. The judge: [To the Trib reporter], "Mr. Ritchey, do you have a copy of this document?" Mr. Ritchey: "I do, Judge." The judge: "Did you get all that down?" Mr. Ritchey: "Yes sir!"]

THE COURT: [To the court reporter. "Then let's go back on the record."]

THE COURT: I'm going to sustain Mr. Hanneman's objection and disallow Respondent's Exhibit No. 2. Anything further, Mr. Gold?

MR. GOLD: Yes, Your Honor, we're just about to wrap it up. Mr. Hurley, much of the testimony you have provided this afternoon has to do with your father, could you explain the reason you thought that information was important with regard to your children.

MR. HURLEY: Well, I spent most of my life at war with my father, I really didn't have much of a relationship with him, and I know he was really disappointed in me, and he had good reason for that, he was mad at me and I was mad at him, and in the last conversation we ever had together we really ripped into each other, but even then, even after all that, his last words, the last words he ever said to me, was that he loved me, and loved my kids, and that they needed a father. And for the first time in my life, over these past few months, I think I finally understand him, I know he loved me, and like him, I love my kids, and I know that if he had a dying wish, it would be for me to take responsibility for my children, and be a father, the kind of father he wished he could have been for me.

MR. GOLD: Those are all the questions I have, Your Honor. The respondent rests.

THE COURT: Mr. Hanneman, any further examination of Mr. Hurley.

MR. HANNEMAN: [Looks at his clients, exhausted, numb, shaking their heads.] No further questions, Your Honor.

THE COURT: All right then, before we close, I have a couple of questions of one of the witnesses. Any problem with that counsel?

MR. GOLD: No, Your Honor.

MR. HANNEMAN: No, Your Honor.

THE COURT: Ms. Goodland?

MS. GOODLAND: [Stands from her bench seat.] Yes, Your Honor?

THE COURT: Ms. Goodland, how long have you been acquainted with Mr. Hurley?

MS. GOODLAND: Oh, let's see, it's been about two and a half years now.

THE COURT: And during that time, have you seen Mr. Hurley on a regular basis?

MS. GOODLAND: Yes, Your Honor, we worked together for about a year before we actually started seeing each other, if you know what I mean, but sure I'd say I was pretty familiar with him that entire time.

THE COURT: Now, I want to remind you, Ms. Goodland, that you are still under oath.

MS. GOODLAND: You don't have to do that Your Honor. I wouldn't lie to you.

THE COURT: Yes, from what I've seen I think that's probably true. My question, Ms. Goodland, is whether, during that entire time, you ever saw Mr. Hurley take illegal drugs?

MS. GOODLAND: No, Your Honor.

THE COURT: Or drugs of any kind?

MS. GOODLAND: No, Your Honor.

THE COURT: During that entire time, did you ever hear from others that Mr. Hurley had taken illegal drugs?

MS. GOODLAND: No, Your Honor.

THE COURT: Or drugs of any kind?

MS. GOODLAND: No, Your Honor.

THE COURT: Thank you, Ms. Goodland, you may be seated.

Counsel, do you wish to take a short recess before closing arguments?

MR. HANNEMAN: [Consulting with his clients.] Your Honor, I don't know about Mr. Gold, but after everything we've heard, I really don't know that a lengthy closing argument will shed much more light on these matters, or give you anything more than what you've already heard.

THE COURT: Frankly, I agree with that Mr. Hanneman. Mr. Gold?

MR. GOLD: [Consulting with Mr. Hurley, Mr. Wilcoxsin.] We agree with Mr. Hanneman, Your Honor.

THE COURT: Then Mr. Hanneman, do you have anything else?

MR. HANNEMAN: Only that the petitioners have proven
that Mr. Hurley has been an inveterate drug user, that he has criminally
neglected his children, that he has pled guilty to doing so, that he has
been and is currently barred from any further contact with his children,
he has had no gainful employment, and no prospects whatsoever until
perhaps the past few months, and we firmly believe that he poses a substantial risk to the children's well-being in the future. We have heard the
testimony that Mr. Hurley may no longer be on drugs, but nothing less
than the fate of these children is at stake here, Your Honor, and my clients
do not believe it worth taking the chance, rolling the dice, that a former
drug user has changed his ways, the potential downside is simply far too
great. My clients have done an admirable and commendable job caring
for these children over the past two and a half years, my clients love these
children as if they were their own, and taking these children from my
clients at this time would cause a substantial and unnecessary disruption
in the children's lives. For all these reasons, the petitioners respectfully
request that this Court grant petitioners' petition, and grant full legal
custody of Sam and Kate Hurley to the petitioners. Thank you.

THE COURT: Mr. Gold?

MR. GOLD: Your Honor, we wish to express Mr.
Hurley's sincere gratitude to Mr. and Mrs. Walsh for all of their efforts
over these past two and a half years caring for Mr. Hurley's children. We
know it has not been easy, and appreciate that they stood up at a very
difficult time and did the right thing when Mr. Hurley was incapable of
doing so. But we also believe the evidence has shown that Mr. Hurley is
now fully capable of providing for his children, and acting as a responsible father, and it is important to emphasize the obvious, that Sam and

Kate are his children, and if he has proven to you that his drug use is behind him, then, as the father of Sam and Kate, he should have the right to raise his own children, regardless of all the love and care the Walshes have provided over these past two and a half years. We have proven that, by virtue of the work Mr. Hurley has undertaken, at great risk to his life, to uncover public corruption, solve his father's murder, and reform politics in the City of Chicago, he has entered a new chapter in his life, where he has learned the importance of making an effort, a contribution, and a difference. Finally, and most importantly, we have proven that Sam and Kate will be brought up by two young, responsible, caring, and loving individuals, who have the resources to do so, and who will do nothing less than their very best to provide a healthy and happy home for their young family. Therefore, respondent requests that Your Honor deny the petition, amend the prior court order prohibiting my client from contact with his children, and grant permanent custody of Sam and Kate Hurley to their father, William Hurley. Thank you.

THE COURT: Is there anything else before we take a short recess?

MR. BLACK: [Plaintively.] Can we go now?

THE COURT: I see no reason why they need to stay any longer, do you, Mr. Gold?

MR. GOLD: [Consulting with Mr. Hurley and Mr. Wilcoxsin.] Your Honor, if Mr. Hamilton and Reverend Simmons would just stick around for a couple of minutes, we would like to speak with them about something during our break. We're done with Mr. Black.

THE COURT: Do you have a problem with that Mr. Hamilton, Reverend Simmons?

UNIDENTIFIED VOICE: [Mr. Hamilton.] I guess not, Your Honor.

UNIDENTIFIED VOICE: [Reverend Simmons.] No, Judge.

THE COURT: Mr. Black, you are excused. Ms. Beecher, I would like to see you in Chambers. The Court will recess, and when I return, I'll give you my order.

(Court Recessed at 4:20 p.m.)

(Reconvened at 5:00 p.m.)

THE COURT: Please be seated. [The judge looking out at the petitioners and the respondent.] These are difficult cases. They are unlike most of the cases filed in this courthouse. Most of our cases deal with money, who owes whom and how much, or who is entitled to what property, and of course it's of no significance to the money, the subject matter of those cases, whose pocket it ends up in. These cases, obviously, are very different. In these cases, the interests of the two parties are secondary to the interests of what they are fighting over, in this case, two five-year-old children. So my focus in deciding these cases is not on what either of the two parties might want to happen, or what might be fair as between the two of them, but rather what I believe would be best for Sam and Kate Hurley. That is my objective, and the principle that guides my ruling.

In that regard, I have to say, I am deeply troubled by Mr. Hurley's conduct, for from what I can tell is most of his life, or at least most of his adult life. The facts have established he's been a user of illegal drugs for more than five years, which is just about a quarter of his life, and while it appears he may have been clean these past two and a half years, I have to seriously consider, which is very real with any kind of addiction, that he may return to his bad habits. In particular, respondent has proven by his past conduct that his drug use poses a substantial risk to the children at issue in this case, because he already has placed them in jeopardy, and has pled guilty to criminally neglecting them in that unfortunate and frankly despicable incident which has been proven in this case.

I also am very concerned that his desire to take responsibility for his children appears to be something he has discovered just recently. I cannot help but take note of what at best could be called his indifference to this petition and the fate of his children's custody in earlier proceedings in this case, which casts suspicion on his newfound interest in his paternal responsibilities. I appreciate that he was barred from any contact with his children by order of court, but in the two and a half years since the order was entered, it does not appear he has made any effort to keep abreast of his children's upbringing, and certainly has made no effort over that period of time to petition for a modification of the order, to at a minimum visit with his children to maintain some sort of relationship. I understand the situation between respondent and his father was a difficult one, and with his mother during her sickness for that matter, nevertheless, his failure to show any interest in his children in two and a half years undercuts the efforts he is making today.

On the other hand, the actions of the petitioners in this case have been nothing but admirable. At a time in their lives when most people are scaling back, they've given of themselves, and devoted their time to provide a nurturing and loving home for Sam and Kate, and I find they have proven themselves capable of continuing to do so in the foreseeable future. But I also must take into account that it will become increasingly difficult for them to do so, particularly given Mrs. Walsh's medical condition, and while they have retained what appears to be a responsible person to assist in the care for the children, without that person, who has her own family and her own obligations, it would be next to impossible for the Walshes to care for the children on their own.

I also believe that, were it not for Mr. Hurley's drug use and dissolute past, it appears from the evidence that Mr. Hurley and his wife, Ms. Goodland, possess the resources and abilities necessary to provide for the well-being of the children, in an albeit very different, but I have no reason to believe any less of a formative environment. In particular, I find the testimony of Ms. Goodland credible, and believe she is committed to caring for the children and seeing to their proper upbringing.

So the wild card here is the respondent. Typically, the presumption in such a case is in favor of the biological parent. They are *his* children, as Mr. Gold pointed out, and the biological parent's right is paramount, except where the evidence shows that the parent is incapable of acting responsibly, and in particular where that parent may pose a danger to the children.

To me, this case comes down to weighing the probability that respondent may revert to his past conduct against his rights as the biological parent to raise his children. Mr. Hanneman is correct when he points out the serious risks associated with returning the children to their father, and this Court is not in the business of rolling dice over the fate of children. On the other hand, the Court must assess the possibility that respondent has indeed put his past behind him. Mrs. Walsh herself is proof that addiction can be overcome, and for me the difficulty here is in assessing the likelihood that respondent has done the same.

As to that issue, the Court finds credible the respondent's testimony, as corroborated by Ms. Goodland, that respondent has not used illegal drugs in the past two and a half years, which, while significant, is not dispositive, because that finding of course does not foreclose the possibility of a relapse. However, on that score, the Court finds that the likelihood respondent will do so is diminished by the presence in his life of Ms. Goodland, his wife, who I believe will have some influence, perhaps a great deal of influence, on how respondent conducts himself in the future.

Now, in light of the fact the Court cannot dictate the future and guarantee such an outcome, one reasonable conclusion to this hearing may be to recognize respondent's rehabilitation, but require an additional period of time for further proof that he will not backslide. However, it is impossible to determine with any certainty what that time period should be, recognizing that two and a half years is not an insubstantial amount of time, and the Court will be in no better position in the future to guarantee respondent's improved character than it is at the present. Furthermore, the Court is mindful of the substantial disruption in the children's lives should an order be entered granting custody to respondent, but if respondent should continue along the path he has chosen for the past two and a half years, which I believe will be the case, it is likely that some day he may be reunited with his children, and any delay in doing so now may just make the ultimate reconciliation that much more difficult in the future.

I recognize it may be argued that respondent's drug use was not the proximate cause, if you will, of his dissolute and irresponsible life, but rather a symptom of a more deep-rooted lack of character and responsibleness, but based on the testimony I have heard, I do not believe that to be the case. I believe that the evidence of the efforts respondent has made over the past two months, and weeks in particular, and his testimony about what he may have learned as a result of those efforts, about his father, himself, and his children, is credible, and suggests to me he may be in the midst of a turning point in his life, which may yet reflect the strength and character of the parents who tried their best to raise him. I agree with Mr. Walsh, raising children is not an easy thing to do, there is no roadmap, but I knew Mr. Hurley's father, and respected him greatly, and while I grant you there is not much now to go on, I cannot help but believe that Mr. Hurley may have some of his father and mother in him, and if that is the case, that bodes well for his future and the future of his family.

I also wish to make it clear for the record that my ruling is not based on the purported truth of the rather sensational testimony Mr. Hurley provided about the zoning matter, the warehouse transaction, or the murder of his father. For the purposes of this ruling, the relevance of that information is limited to the fact that Mr. Hurley cared enough to make the effort and showed a diligence and purpose that otherwise has been absent for most of his life, and which he will need to call upon as he embarks upon a new life of greater responsibility.

I also wish to express my gratitude for the efforts and report submitted by Ms. Harriet Beecher, who was appointed by the Court to assist in this matter. I have relied on the observations and conclusions in Ms. Beecher's report and, as always, have found them insightful and extremely helpful. I also have consulted with Ms. Beecher about my decision in this case, and she has expressed her agreement with my conclusions, as set forth herein. Having now heard my findings and conclusions, is that a correct statement Ms. Beecher?

MS. BEECHER: That is correct, Your Honor.

THE COURT: Thank you, and now, for all the reasons stated in court today, it is hereby ordered that: 1) the petitioners' petition is denied [Mrs. Walsh takes her husband's hand and starts to cry], 2) the previous order barring respondent from coming into contact with his children is amended to strike that restriction in its entirety, 3) custody of Sam and Kate Hurley is granted to respondent William Hurley and his wife Mona Goodland, effective immediately, [Dorothy takes Mona's hand and the two of them start to cry], and 4) the parties are to cooperate to arrange for a mutually agreeable exchange of the children to respondent's custody. Mr. Gold, please prepare the order.

Will there be anything else, counsel?

MR. HANNEMAN: [Dejected.] Yes, Your Honor, you said your order takes effect immediately, under the circumstances, I don't quite know what that means, it is late in the day, are we talking today, tomorrow, next week, next month...

THE COURT: There is no good time, Mr. Hanneman, I realize that. I think it might be best if the Walshes spend one last night with the children and that the transfer takes place tomorrow morning.

MR. GOLD: That works for us, Your Honor.

MR. HANNEMAN: [Turns back and consults with his distraught clients. Mrs. Walsh sobbing. Turns back to the Court.] We will make the necessary arrangements, Your Honor. I think it might be best for the parties to work that out between counsel?

MR. GOLD: That will be fine, Your Honor. Mr. Hanneman and Mr. Wilcoxsin can work out the details.

[Ms. Goodland stands and steps up and whispers to Mr. Hurley and Mr. Wilcoxsin.]

MR. WILCOXSIN: May we have a moment, Your Honor?

THE COURT: Certainly.

[Mr. Gold, Mr. Wilcoxsin, and Mr. Hurley huddle around a whispering Ms. Goodland. Mr. Hurley nods his head, as does Mr. Gold, and Mr. Wilcoxsin, and Mr. Gold steps up to the judge's bench.]

MR. GOLD: Your Honor, the respondent would like to know if it might be appropriate to include in the order some provision which grants petitioners some rights of visitation.

THE COURT: Mr. Hanneman, any objection?

MR. HANNEMAN: [Whispering to his clients, looking at Ms. Goodland.] Your Honor, petitioners appreciate the offer, and perhaps it might be appropriate to include in the order some language to the effect that the parties will make good faith efforts to work out suitable arrangements for grandparents' visitation.

MR. GOLD: We can work on that language, Your Honor.

THE COURT: Then our work is done for the day. Counsel, you both did a fine job. The court is in recess.

(Court Recessed at 5:33 p.m.)

* * *

Dick and Mary Alice Walsh, state of shock, Mrs. Walsh trying to compose herself, gather their things, consult with Mr. Hanneman, shake hands with him. Mr. Walsh, arm around his wife, heads down, slumped shoulders, no eye contact, leave the courtroom, Mr. Wilcoxsin holds open the swinging gate for them. Mona crying. Dorothy crying. Mr. Walsh opens the courtroom door for his wife, who steps into the hall, Mr. Walsh hesitates, turns, looks at Billy.

"This better not be some kind of act on your part, because so help me if anything happens to those kids…"

"You'd have to get in line," Billy said, nodding toward Mona.

"Thank you," Dick Walsh said, to Mona, and left the courtroom, saddened, but truth be told, as would become increasingly apparent to him and his wife as time went on, a sense of relief, confirming the wisdom of the judge's order.

The court reporter packed up her equipment and left the courtroom. Dorothy gave hugs around, quite proud of herself, and left the courtroom, happy for the first time since her boss died. Ben and Mr. Hanneman huddled together at respondent's counsel table, worked out the terms of an agreeable order, handed the proposed order to the clerk, who took it back into chambers, had it signed by the judge, and returned with copies, one each for respondent and petitioners.

Mr. Hanneman packed his briefcase, shook hands with Ben and Mr. Wilcoxsin, nodded to Mona and Billy, and left the courtroom, Billy, Mona, Ben, and Mr. Wilcoxsin remaining.

Upon Mr. Hanneman's leaving, in the midst of a respondent group hug, the clerk came back into the courtroom, and addressed the group.

"The judge was wondering if you would like to step back into chambers for a moment."

"I think we would like that very much," said Mr. Wilcoxsin.

Mona entered chambers first, followed by Billy, Ben, and then Mr. Wilcoxsin, Mona and Billy sitting in the two chairs before the desk, Ben and Mr. Wilcoxsin on the sofa against the wall. Judge Wozak, leaning back in a stuffed red leather chair, feet on his desk, hole in one shoe, black robe unzipped half way, cigar in hand, unlit, reading a newspaper, throws it on his desk, sits up.

"I suspect you might make headlines tomorrow."

"Don't ever want to be in another newspaper again," said Billy.

"Can't blame you," the judge said. "But that was some story you told in there today."

"Have a hard time believing it myself," said Billy.

"Do you really think your dad believed what he wrote on that piece of paper?"

"I know, but yeah, I think I do, pretty sure of it actually, kind of set it all in motion with that D&P."

"I thought I knew your dad pretty well. Never knew anybody who knew how to pull the strings like your dad. He should have been the mayor of this town. Sorry you two never got along, but glad you see him a little differently now."

"Yeah, other than getting my kids back that may be the best part of all this."

"I think he might actually have been pretty proud of what you did today," the judge said.

"Well, then that would have been a first," said Billy.

"You know, I wish you the best of luck, it's not easy to beat addiction. I have a daughter who was on that stuff for years, she's better now, thank God, but it was hard, she had a baby last year, that's my grandchild there," he said pointing to a picture of a newborn on the credenza, "life throws a lot of shit at you, but then you end up with something like him," he said shaking his head. "How the hell'd you ever end up with her?" the judge asked, motioning to Mona.

"Believe me I know."

"Maybe I'll take that little guy canoeing someday up by you," the judge said pointing to his grandchild.

"We would be honored, Your Honor," Mona said.

"So I can't wait to see what happens with Gusman and the mayor after all this," the judge said.

"I'm not going to stick around to find out," said Billy, "but it's kinda nice to know that my dad'll have a say about what goes on in this town even after he's gone."

"Would be just like him," said Judge Wozak. "And what about that warehouse? Lot of work for nothing."

"Not so sure," said Billy. "I introduced the banker guy to Reverend Simmons while you were working on your order, and got the IDPA and DCMS guys into the conversation, suggested they all get together, resurrect the deal, no reason it can't happen, the State still needs the warehouse, Gusman and the mayor can't do the deal any more, get the property back to the Reverend, let him reap the rewards."

"Well, maybe I made the right decision after all."

"You did," said Mona, smiling.

"Yes, this time I think I might have," said the judge, rising to his feet, "Look, I wish you all the best, it's been a pleasure meeting you all."

Everybody shook hands with the judge, walked out of chambers, gathered their things, said good night to the clerk, and walked out of the courtroom, satisfied, of a job well done.

* * *

By two o'clock the next afternoon, the Cadillac had pulled off Interstate 90, and was cruising up and over and around the hills and curves of a two-lane country road, bright sun, top down, blue sky, warm breeze, golden fields, Mona at the wheel, Ben asleep in the passenger seat. Mona looking in the rearview mirror, Billy in the middle of the back seat, Sam under one arm, Kate under the other, Billy and Kate fast asleep, Sam looking out at the tall corn, racing by, Mona gazing at her new family, the unmistakable resemblance, happier than she'd ever been, Sam, catching her eye, exchanging smiles, her full red lips flushed, framed in the rearview mirror, as she steered that big Caddy into their new lives, and the great wide open of a brand new world.

EPILOGUE

Dan Hurley's three wishes came true. His son got his kids, Reverend Simmons got a warehouse, and obsolescence seeped into the machine. Candidates fell over each other espousing Hurley's principles of good government. A litmus test developed, applied to every city, county, and state candidate: you in it for yourself or us? Started local, then statewide, maybe national. Simple, effective. If not us, fugetaboutit.

The headline in the Tribune the day after the trial read, "Hurley Exposes Mayoral Rip Off," and went on to tell the story Billy told in court the day before, with special emphasis on Mayor Jefferson's venal scheme to deprive a popular West Side minister of the church of his dreams. The mayor never recovered, monolithic African American support disappeared, leading to defeat in the next election to an African American woman from the South Side, a graduate of the University of Illinois Law School. Two times he ran for alderman in his ward, lost both times. Reverted to the world of business, started a school bus company, used his political connections, did alright. Johnny Jefferson and his wife, Viola Jones, started their own real estate brokerage business on the South Side, stayed away from warehouses.

Ronald Gusman came awfully close to losing his next aldermanic election, but Gusman was a fighter, publicly apologized for his greed, looked into the camera on public access television and said he'd fucked up, literally said, "I fucked up," into the camera, regained some respect. He ran as a reformer, co-opted Dan Hurley's fourth principle of good government, authored, and passed an ordinance prohibiting any government official or employee from engaging in business with any state or local government, went to Springfield, had the General Assembly pass a similar state statute, making it a crime for any public official to disclose inside information. He went back to the basics, rediscovered why he got into politics, started answering phone calls from constituents again, knocked on every door in his ward, and remained an alderman until he died twenty years later.

Sydney Black would never work for Alderman Gusman again, that was for sure. All in all, given he'd almost died in court that day, things turned out okay. Sure he lost a lot of money, but with Sweeney dead, no one knew or could know his connection to Sweeney, or Sweeney's connection to the deal. He transitioned his practice into real estate closings, got more involved in his synagogue, even improved his marriage. He still works out of his shitty office downtown.

Mark Hamilton saw the light that day in the courtroom, serving as Reverend Simmons's financial advisor the rest of his career. They had no difficulty getting the property back from the mayor and Gusman, good riddance, the rezoning passed, closed the deal with the State, took the insurance company's money, built a new church, functional, no waste, and used the remaining funds as seed money for a not-for-profit developing low income housing on the South and West Sides, which, over time, became quite successful, and a model for urban redevelopment taught in class-rooms at the University of Chicago business school.

The hoodie from IDPA, whistleblower, protected, promoted to the job he'd applied and qualified for ten years running.

Toby tried what he learned from Demetrius on his wife. Doreen got the passion she'd always wanted, and a house on a lake in the north woods.

Deano opened a taxidermy shop, full time, bugged Walt with unsolicited advice, part time.

Cecil Hampton returned each summer to live with Lee Anne, opening an acting school for young women.

Joey, Danny, Judy, Nick, Davey, and Rose spent the rest of their lives looking for another party like Billy and Mona's wedding, in vain, so they partied most nights like there was no tomorrow.

Conrad Wilcoxsin developed a fondness for Chicago, Harriet Beecher, the country.

After several years, Ivy accepted an ownership interest in the resort. Patti Smith, Bowie, a nose ring, and a good howl whenever she closed. Meredith became a principal player in the theater company, and Ivy's life.

Sam and Kate took to the river and woods like young Saukies, led by Dirk, Bonnie, and Ivy's girls, a tribe unto themselves.

The Golds lived in their Wyoming Township farmhouse ten more years, when they moved back to the East Side of Milwaukee, but that's another story.

One year later, on the anniversary of Dan Hurley's death, Billy, Mona, Sam, Kate, and Sylvie, a one-month old beautiful baby girl, hopped in the Cadillac and drove up to the top of the hill to commemorate the occasion. The cool north wind drove the mosquitoes away, the evening sun lit up the clouds. Billy threw a large quilt on the grassy veranda, where the

Hurley–Goodland family sat, surrounded by lush tall grass, munching on cucumber sandwiches, grapes, cheese, little cakes. Billy helped Kate and Sam launch kites in the air, flying over the hill, high over the spot Dan Hurley last saw clouds in the sky, where Billy, spade in hand, dug a shallow rectangle in the soft turf, into which he settled a flat red granite stone, brushed off the dirt, granite gleaming in the sun, with an inscription, that read *In Nomine Patris.*

NOTES

1 *Dubliners*, James Joyce, *The Dead*, First Modern Library Edition, 1969, ps. 223, 224.

2 *Why I Love Wisconsin*, The Wisconsin Magazine, 1932; "Why I Love Wisconsin" @ /66S, The Frank Lloyd Wright Foundation.

3 *The Wisconsin, River of a Thousand Isles*, August Derleth, The University of Wisconsin Press, 1985.

4 *These Truths, A History of the United States*, Jill Lepore, W. W. Norton & Co., 2018, ps. 20-21.

5 *These Truths, A History of the United States*, Jill Lepore, W. W. Norton & Co., 2018, p. 54.

6 *The Story of My Boyhood and Youth*, John Muir, Houghton Mifflin Company, 1913, Dodo Press, p. 91.

7 *Travels Through the Interior Parts of North America in the years 1766, 1767, and 1768* (by J. Carver, Esq. Captain of a Company of Provincial Troops During the Late War with France. Illustrated with Copper Plates, Colored, 1778).

8 *The Wisconsin, River of a Thousand Isles*, August Derleth, The University of Wisconsin Press, 1985, p. 75; Black Hawk, The Battle for the Heart of America, Kerry A. Trask, Holt Paperbacks, 2007, p. 72.

9 *The Wisconsin, River of a Thousand Isles*, August Derleth, The University of Wisconsin Press, 1985, ps. 85–86.

10 *The Wisconsin River, An Odyssey Through Time and Space*, Richard D. Durbin, Spring Freshet Press, 1997, p. 20.

11 *The Wisconsin, River of a Thousand Isles*, August Derleth, The University of Wisconsin Press, 1985, ps, 196, 205.

12 *The Wisconsin River, An Odyssey Through Time and Space*, Richard D. Durbin, Spring Freshet Press, 1997, p. 65.

13 *The Story of My Boyhood and Youth*, John Muir, Houghton Mifflin Company, 1913, Dodo Press, p. 26.

BIBLIOGRAPHY

Black Hawk, An Autobiography, edited by Jackson, Donald, University of Illinois Press, 1955.

Calloway, Colin G., *The Indian World of George Washington, The First President, the First Americans, and the Birth of the Nation*, Oxford University Press, 2018.

Derleth, August, *The Wisconsin, River of a Thousand Isles*, The University of Wisconsin Press, 1985.

Dexter, Freeland, *The News from Lone Rock, Observations and Witticisms of a Small-Town Newsman*, Wisconsin Historical Press, 2016.

Durbin, Richard D., *The Wisconsin River, An Odyssey Through Time and Space*, Spring Freshet Press, 1997.

Leopold, Aldo, *A Sand County Almanac, And Sketches of Here and There*, Oxford University Press, 1949.

Lepore, Jill, *These Truths, A History of the United States*, W. W. Norton & Co., 2018.

Loew, Patty, *Indian Nations of Wisconsin*, Wisconsin Historical Society Press, 2001.

Meine, Curt, and Kelley, Keefe, *The Driftless Reader*, The University of Wisconsin Press, 2017.

Muir, John, *The Story of My Boyhood and Youth*, Houghton Mifflin Company, 1913.

Oestreich Lurie, Nancy, *Wisconsin Indians*, Wisconsin Historical Society Press, 1969.

Shannon, Timothy, *Iroquois Diplomacy on the Early American Frontier*, The Penguin Library of American Indian History, Viking Penguin, 2008.

Theler, James L., and Boszhardt, Robert F., *Twelve Millenia, Archaeology of the Upper Mississippi River Valley*, University of Iowa Press, 2003.

Thwaites, Reuben Gold, *Historic Waterways, Six Hundred Miles of Canoeing Down the Rock, Fox, and Wisconsin Rivers*, A. C. McClurg and Company, 1888.

Trask, Kerry A., *Black Hawk, The Battle for the Heart of America*, Holt Paperbacks, 2007.

Turner, Frederick Jackson, *The Character and Influence of the Indian Trade in Wisconsin, A Study of the Trading Post as an Institution*, The Johns Hopkins Press, 1891.